E.F Benson

The Capsina

E.F Benson

The Capsina

1st Edition | ISBN: 978-3-75234-552-0

Place of Publication: Frankfurt am Main, Germany

Year of Publication: 2020

Outlook Verlag GmbH, Germany.

Reproduction of the original.

THE CAPSINA
By
E. F. Benson

"HE RAISED THE MUSKET TO HIS SHOULDER"

CHAPTER I

The little town of Hydra, white-walled and trailing its skirts in the Ægean, climbs steeply up the northeastern side of the island from which it is named, and looks towards the hills of Argolis on the mainland and the setting of the sun. Its harbor sheltered from the northern and southern winds, and only open towards the west, where the sea is too narrow ever to be lashed into fury by gales of that quarter, was defended in the year 1819 by a very creditable pier and a good deal of swift and rakish shipping. The inhabitants lived a life somewhat sequestered from their oppressed and down-trodden countrymen, supporting themselves by enterprises of fishing and the humble sort of commerce, and the hand of the Turk, then as now lustful, cruel, and intolerable, lay but lightly on them, for the chief products of the island itself were only stones and cold water, untaxable goods. But something of the spirit of stones and cold water, something of the spirit, too, of that quickly roused sea, soon made furious, soon appeased, but always alive, had gone to the making of the men of Hydra; and they were people frugal and hardy, resourceful and industrious, men of the wave and the mountain. Of its various clans—and its regime was highly feudal—that of Capsas was the wealthiest and most influential; but just now, a tragic prologue to this tale, a blow so direful had fallen on those much-esteemed men, and in particular on Christos Capsas, a youth of about two and twenty, that the clan generally, and Christos in particular, were in a state of paralyzed inaction strange to such busy folk. It had happened thus:

The head of the clan, Nicholas Capsas, had died some nine months before, leaving an only daughter, Sophia, henceforth officially called the Capsina, just nineteen years of age. The clan all remembered that they had warned each other that trouble would come on account of the Capsina, and they found to their unspeakable dismay, and without a grain of pleasure in the fulfilment of their prophecy, that their gloomy forebodings were completely accomplished. Sophia was a girl of much greater force of will than it was at all usual to look for in a woman, for the most refractory women, so the clan believed, chattered and scolded, but obeyed. The Capsina had struck out a new and eminently disconcerting line in following her own desires in silence, deaf to remonstrance. The beginning of trouble had been a very stormy scene between her and her father when, following the invariable law of clan etiquette, she had been betrothed on her eighteenth birthday to her cousin Christos, on whom now so paralyzing a consternation had fallen. She had submitted to the ordeal of formal betrothal only on condition that she should marry Christos when she thought fit, and at no other time. Such an irregularity was wholly unprecedented, but Sophia declared herself not only ready, but even wishful to throw the betrothal wreaths into the fire sooner than marry Christos at any time not fixed by herself, and the ceremony took place only on this understanding. Three months later her father had died suddenly, and when Christos on this morning, one tremble of timorousness, but conscious of the support of the entire clan, went to the Capsina, offering his hand and heart, to be taken by her with the greatest expedition that mourning allowed, she looked him over slowly from head to heel and back again, and said, very distinctly, "Look in the glass." This her betrothed had rightly interpreted as a sign of dismissal.

Sophia, after hurling this defiance at her family, gave Christos time to retreat, and then went about her daily business. Her mother had died some years before, and since her father's death she had had sole management of the house and of all his business, which was ship-building. But she had been accustomed from the time she could walk to be in and out of the building-yards with him, and the outraged clan, even in the unequalled bitterness of this moment, would have confessed that she was quite capable of managing anything. She was tall and finely made, and the sun had joined hands with the winds of the sea to mould her face with the lines of beauty and serene health. Her eyes and hair were of the South, her brow and nose of her untainted race, her mouth firm and fine. She watched Christos out of the gate with all the complete indifference her great black eyes could hold, and then set off down to the ship-yard where a new brig was to be launched that day.

There she stood all morning among the workmen, bareheaded to the sun and wind, directing, and often helping with her own strong hands, and though it would have seemed that she had her eyes and all her mind at the work, she yet found time to glance through the open gate on to the pier, where she could see a talking knot of her clan gathered round the rejected Christos; and, in fact, her mind was more given over to the difficult question of what step she should next take with regard to the question of marriage than to the work on hand. For, indeed, she had no intention of marrying Christos at all. Since her father's death her work and position had become more and more absorbingly dear, and she did not propose to resign her place to a somewhat slow-minded cousin, whom, as she had candidly declared on her betrothal, she loved only as much as is usual among cousins. The question was how to make this indubitably evident.

The ship was to be launched about mid-day, and, as the time drew near, Sophia began to wonder to herself, not without a spice of amusement, whether the clan would think it consistent with the correct attitude of disapproval to attend the launching to which they were as a matter of course invited. After the barrel of wine, in which the success of the new ship would be drunk, had been hoisted on deck, she even delayed the event a few minutes to give them time if they wished still to come. But it was evident that she had offended beyond forgiveness, and she stood alone on the ship when she hissed stern foremost, true to an inch, into the frothed water. Sophia, ever candid, was not at heart ill-pleased at the absence of the clan, for as she was godmother so also she was peculiarly mother to the new ship, departing therein from certain formulated rules as to the line of the bows and the depth of the keel, which, so she thought, if made deeper would enable her to sail closer to the wind, and she loved her great child more than she loved her betrothed. She had even, which was unusual with her, spent several intent and sleepless hours in bed at night when the ship was yet on the stocks, her mind busy at the innovations. Surely the ships that others built were too high in the water, especially forward; a sudden squall always made them sheer off into the wind, losing way without need. A less surface in the bows was possible. Again, a longer depth of keel would give more grip on the water and greater stability, and it was with much tremulous hope and frequent misgivings lest this new departure should involve some vital and unforeseen error that she had laid down the lines of the ship in a manner perfectly new to the shipwrights of the island.

And as the building progressed and the timbers of the hull rose to their swifter shape, her hopes triumphed over misgiving, and she felt that this new ship was peculiarly hers—hers by the irresistible right of creation, not shared with any.

She stayed on board till a late hour that evening, seeing to the hoisting of the tackle by which the masts should be raised the next day, absorbed in the work, and dwelling with a loving care on the further details, and it was nearly dark, and the workmen had gone ashore an hour already when she rowed herself back to the yard. Not till then did her mind return to the less enticing topic of Christos, which she had left undetermined, and she walked home slowly, revolving the possibilities. Her great, stately watch-dog, a terror to strangers, and not more than doubtfully neutral to friends, received her with the silent greeting of a wet nose pushed into her hand, and when she had eaten her supper, the two went out on to the veranda. That was the companionship she liked best, silent, unobtrusive, but sensitive, and she took the great brute's fore-paws and laid them on her lap, and talked to him as a child talks to its doll.

"Oh, Michael," she said—the adoption of a saint's name to an animal so profane had greatly shocked the clan, but the Capsina remarked that he was a better Christian than some she knew—"oh, Michael, it is an impossible thing they would have me do. Am I to cook the dinner for Christos, and every evening see his face grow all red and shiny with wine, while he bids me fetch more? Am I to talk with the other women as sparrows twitter together in a bush? Am I to say I love him? Oh, Michael, I would sooner stroke your hair than his. Then what of the cousins? They will call me an old maid, for many cousins younger than I are married. But this I promise you, great dog, that unless I love I will not marry, and what love is, God knows, for I do not. And if ever I love, Michael—yes, they say I am fierce, and of no maiden mind. So be it; we will sail together in the brig *Sophia*, for so will I name her—you and I and she. And if some one, I know not who, comes from the sea, all sea and sun, some one not familiar, but strange to me and stronger than I, you shall be his, and the ship shall be his, and I shall be his, all of us, all of us; and we all, he and I and you and the ship, will go straight up to heaven."

She laughed softly at herself, and buried her face in the dog's shaggy ruff. "Oh, Michael," she whispered, "the cousins are all saying how queer a girl I am. So perhaps am I, but not as they think. I should be the queerer if I married Christos, and yet to their minds my queerness is that I do not. Why did you not bite him when he came here this morning? for so he would have run away, and this thinking would have been saved. Yet you were right, he is a familiar thing, and we do not bite what is familiar. Perhaps, when the strange man comes, I shall hate him, although I do nothing else but love him. Yet, oh, I am proud, for we are prouder, as the proverb says, than the Mavromichales of Maina. But, Christos, he is slower than a tortoise, and less amusing than a mule; oh, well enough no doubt for some, but not for me. Perhaps I shall marry none; that is very likely, for the men I see here, for instance, are not fit things to marry, and so, I make no doubt, they think me. And there is always the ship-building. Oh, we will get very wise, Michael, and sail our ship ourselves, and see strange countries and over-sea people. There must be some one in this big world as well as I, and yet I have not seen him, but we will do nothing without thinking, Michael, unless it so happens that some day we no longer want or are able to think. Perhaps that—there, get down, you are heavy."

She pushed the dog's paws off her lap, and, rising from her chair, went to the end of the veranda to look out upon the night. The full moon swung high and white among the company of stars, and the sea was all a shimmer of pearly light. A swell was rolling in soft and huge from the south, and the end of the pier was now and again outlined with broken foam. Beneath the moonlight the massive seas looked only a succession of waving light and shadow, and the rattle of the pebbles on the shingly beach outside the pier in the drag of the swell came rhythmical and muffled. The Capsina, in the unrest and ferment of her thoughts, was unwittingly drawn towards that vastness of eternal and majestic movement, and slipping her embroidered Rhodian hood over her head, she whistled softly to Michael, and went down through the strip of garden towards the shore.

She passed along the quay and out beyond the harbor; all the wandering scents of a night in early summer were in the air, and the rough strip of untrained moorland which lay beyond the town was covered with flowering thyme and aromatic herbs, rooty and fragrant to the nostrils. She walked quickly across this and came down to the shingly beach which fringed the promontory. All along its edge the swell was breaking in crash and flying foam, for the south wind of the day before had raised a storm out to sea, and several ships had that day put in for shelter. Far out she could see a pillar of spray rise high and disappear again over a reef of rock, gleaming for a moment with incredible whiteness in the moonlight. Michael snuffed about in rapturous pursuit of interesting smells among the edge of rough herbs that fringed the beach, making sudden excursions and flank movements inland, and grubbing ecstatically among the tussocks of cistus and white heath after wholly imaginary hares. By degrees Sophia walked more slowly, and, coming to the end of the promontory, stopped for a moment before she began to retrace her steps. No, she could not marry Christos; she could not cut herself off from the thrill that her large independence gave her, from working for herself, from the headship of the clan. For her she thought was a wider life than that of the women of her race. How could she limit herself, with her young, strong body, and the will which moved it, to the distaff and the spinning-wheel? Christos! He was afraid of Michael, he was afraid of the sea, he was afraid of her. But how to make this clear to demonstration to the clan was beyond her. Moreover—and the thought was like a stinging insect—there lay at home the deed of her betrothal to her cousin.

She whistled to Michael and turned back into the town. Several groups of men were scattered along the length of the quay, and the Capsina, walking swiftly by, saw that Christos was among them. She hung on her step a moment, and then, with a sudden idea, turned round and called to him.

"Christos Capsas," she said, "I would speak to you a moment. Yes, it is I, Sophia."

Christos disengaged himself from the group a little reluctantly and followed her. He was a somewhat handsome-looking fellow, but rather heavily made, and slow and slouching in his movements. The Capsina, seeming by his side doubly alert, walked on with him in silence for a space, and then stopped again.

"See, Christos," she said, "I have no wish to offend you or any. If what I said this morning was an offence to you, please know that to me now my words were an offence. Yet I will not marry you," and on the word she suddenly flared out—"oh! be very sure of that! And I have something to say to the clan. Be good enough to tell them that I expect all the men to dinner with me to-morrow, when I will speak to them. You will come yourself. Yes? Let me know how many will be there to-morrow early. Good-night, my cousin. Michael, be quiet, and come with me."

The clan signified their intention of accepting the Capsina's invitation in large numbers, for they too felt that their family affairs must come to a crisis, and that something explicit was needed. The Capsina, they were sure, would supply this need. As the day was warm, she gave orders that the dinner should be served in the veranda, and that the barrel of wine which had been put on board the brig should be brought back, for it was her best. All morning she attended to the things for their entertainment, first going to the market to buy the best of the freshly caught mullet and a lump of caviare, wrapped up in vine leaves, and choosing with care a lamb to be roasted whole over the great open fireplace; then, returning to see that the *pilaff* of chicken was properly seasoned, that the olives were dried and put in fresh oil, and herself mixing the salad, flavoring it with mint and a sprinkling of cheese and garlic. After that the rose-leaf jam had to be whipped up with cream and raw eggs for the sweets, and another pot to be opened to be offered to the guests, with glasses of cognac as an appetizer; cheese had to be fetched from the cellar, and dried figs and oranges from the store cupboard. Then Michael, to whom the hot smells were a tremulous joy, must be chained up, and in the midst of these things there arrived a notary from the town, who, at Sophia's dictation, for she had but little skill at writing herself, drew up a deed and explained to her where the witnesses should sign or make their mark. By this time it was within an hour of dinner, and she went to her room to dress, and think over what she was going to say.

Sophia had an inbred instinct for completeness, and she determined on this occasion to make herself magnificent. She took from their paper-wrappings her three *fête* dresses, one of which had never been worn, and looked them over carefully before deciding between them. Eventually she fixed on the new one. This consisted of three garments, a body, a skirt, and a long sleeveless jacket reaching to the knees. The body was made of fine home-spun wool buttoning down the side, but the whole of the front was a piece of silk Rhodian embroidery in red, green, and gold, and a narrow strip of the same went round the wrists. The skirt was of the same material, but there was stitched over it a covering of thin Greek silk, creamy-white in color, and round the bottom of the skirt ran a trimming of the same Rhodian stuff. Before putting the jacket on she opened a box that stood by her bed, and took from it four necklaces of Venetian gold sequins, one short and coming round the neck like a collar, and the other three of increasing size, the largest hanging down almost as far as her waist. Then she put on the jacket, which, like the other garments, was bordered with embroidery, and draping her hair in an orange-colored scarf of Greek silk, she fastened it with another band of Venetian gold coins, which passed twice round her head. Then, hesitating a moment, she went back to the box where her gold ornaments were kept, and drew out the great heirloom of her clan, and held it in her hand a moment. It was a belt of antique gold chain, more than an inch in width, each link being set with two pearls. The clasp was of two gold circles, with a hook behind, and on each of them was chased the lion of Venice. Scroll-work of leaves and branches, on which sat curious archaic eagles, ran round it, and eight large emeralds were set in each rim. Sophia looked at it doubtfully for a moment or two, and then fastened it round her waist, inside her jacket, so as to hide the joining of the body and skirt.

Her guests soon began to arrive, the first of them being Christos, the father of her betrothed, with his son. The old man had determined to be exceedingly dignified and cold to Sophia, and as a mark of his disapproval had not put on his *festa* clothes. But the sight of that glorious figure, all color, walking out from the shade of the veranda into the brilliant sunlight to meet them, took, as he said afterwards, "all the pith" out of him.

Sophia received him with a sort of regal dignity as befitted the head of the clan: "You are most welcome, Uncle Christos," she said, "and you also, cousin. I was sorry that your business prevented your being able to come to the launching of the new boat, but perhaps you will like to see her after dinner."

Uncle Christos shifted uneasily from one foot to the other.

"I had no idea you would be so grand, Sophia," he said, "and I have come in my old clothes. Christos, too, you slovenly fellow, your shirt is no fresh thing."

The younger Christos's *fustanella* was as a matter of fact quite clean, but he smoothed it down as if ashamed of it.

9

"But, Sophia," went on the old man, "they will not be all here yet. I will run to my house and be back in a moment," and he fairly bolted out of the garden.

Christos and Sophia were thus left alone, but Sophia was quite equal to the occasion, and spoke resolutely of indifferent things until the others arrived. By degrees they all came, the elder Christos the last, but in the magnificence of all his best clothes, and they sat down to dinner. And when they had finished eating and the pipes were produced, Sophia rose from her place at the head of the table and spoke to them that which she had in her mind.

"It is not my wish," she said, "to hurt the feelings of any one, but I will not violate my own. As you perhaps have heard"—and the slightest shadow of a smile passed over her face, for she knew that nothing else had been spoken of for the last four-and-twenty hours—"my cousin Christos has asked me to fulfil my betrothal to him, and I wish to make my answer known to you all. You understand me, then: I will not marry my cousin, either now or at any other time. I have here"—and she took up from the table the deed of the betrothal—"I have here that which is witness of my betrothal to Christos Capsas. With the approval of my family and clan I will tear it up and burn it. If there is any one here who objects to this, let him say so, and I will tell you what I shall then do. Without his approval, and without the approval of any one else, I shall send to the town for the notary, procure witnesses, and sign my name to this other deed. I am no hand with the pen, but so much I can write. In it I bequeath all my property, to which I am sole heiress—for my father, as you know, died without a will, suddenly—not to my clan, nor to any one of my clan, but to the priests."

A subdued murmur of consternation ran round the table, and the elder Christos called gently on the names of five or six saints, for the clan were not on good terms with the church, and the Capsina herself had threatened to loose Michael on the first priest who set foot uninvited in her house. A paralyzed silence succeeded, and Sophia continued her speech.

"See," she said, "I am perfectly in earnest. We are prouder, as our proverb says, than they of Maina, and, being proud, I for one do not threaten things which I am unable or unwilling to perform. Perhaps marriage seems to me a different thing from what it seems to you. But that is no reason that I am wrong or that you are right. My betrothed I believe to be an admirable man, but I am so made that I do not choose to marry him, nor, at present, any other man. And now the choice is with you. I destroy in your presence and with your consent both these papers, or I will sign in your presence and without your consent that which only needs my signature. I will leave you here for half an hour, and when I return, Christos Capsas, the father of Christos, my betrothed, will tell me what you have decided. Uncle Christos, you will please take my place here and tell the servants to bring you more wine when you want it. You will find the white wine also very good, I think."

And with these paralyzing words the Capsina dropped her eyes, bowed with a wonderful dignity and grace to the clan, who rose to their feet despite themselves at the beauty of the girl, and marched into the house.

At the end of half an hour she returned, and standing a moment in her place turned to the elder Christos.

"You have decided," she said, and taking up the two deeds in answer to a nod from her uncle, she tore them across and across. Then she gave the pieces to a servant.

"Burn them," she said, "there, out in the garden, where we can all see."

Certainly the Capsina had a sense for the dramatic moment, for she stood quite still where she was in dead silence until a puff of wind dispersed the feathers of the ash. Then she turned briskly and filled her glass.

"I drink prosperity to him who was betrothed to me," she said, "and wish him with all my heart a better wife than I should ever have made him. And here," she cried, unbuckling the great gold belt, "take your wife to-morrow, if you will, or when you will, and here is my gift to the bride."

And she handed the gorgeous thing across to her cousin, clinked glasses with him, and, draining her own, flung it to the ground, so that none other should drink from it.

Then sitting down again:

"This is a fortunate day for you, Christos, if only you knew it, and for you all. For here am I, a free woman, who knows her trade, and will give all her time and energy to it, and indeed I am not lazy, and so double the riches of the house, instead of sitting at the distaff and picking up the olives. For, in truth, I do not think that I am of the stuff that wives are made of. You have often told me, uncle, that I should have been a man, and, before God, I think you were right. And you, dear Christos, some day I should have tried your patience beyond all bearing, and you would have raised your hand to strike me, and then, perhaps, you would have felt my fists rattling about your face, or maybe, if I really was angry, for I do not think I could take a blow from any man, I should have set Michael at you. And then, if you were wise, you would have run away, for I think Michael would kill whomever I told him to kill, for he is greatly obedient, and a fine thing it would have been for the folk to see the head of the clan running from a four-legged dog, while his wife hished the beast on from the threshold."

A roar of laughter greeted this, and Sophia looked up, smiling herself. "So we are friends again, are we not?" she said; "and we will never again give others cause to say that they of the clan are of two minds among themselves. And now, cousins, if you have smoked and drunk what you will, let us go down and see the new brig, for indeed I think she will have no luck unless you all come. To-morrow the masts are hoisted; this morning I have had no time to attend to my business."

The brig was duly inspected, and though some of the elder men shook their heads over this new-fangled keel, and the somewhat egoish name of *Sophia* for the Capsina's ship, the general verdict was satisfactory. To celebrate this day of her emancipation she let all the workmen go home, giving them half a day off work, and returned alone to her house towards evening. She went at once to loose Michael from his unaccustomed confinement, and stood for a moment with her hand on the dog's neck.

"Michael," she whispered, "does it not seem to you that Christos desired the money more than he desired me? Yet, perhaps, it was the others who urged him, for, in truth, he looked a little downcast. But that a man should consent to that! Well, I am too happy to-day to find fault with any one."

For that year and the next Sophia worked with unintermittent energy in her ship-yard. Sometimes it seemed to herself that a kind of frenzy for ships and the sea had possession of her, and, busy with open-air thought, she never even noticed the glances which men cast on her. Her fame, the stories of her wonderful knowledge of ships, her fiery beauty, her utter unconsciousness of men, had passed beyond the island, and sailors who had put in at Hydra would wait about on the quay to catch a glimpse of her, or speak to her, for she would always have a word for sailors. She was not content to know that her ships were truly built and seaworthy, but she cruised about, mastering the individuality of each; for, as she said, a ship, like a horse, would obey one master when it would not obey another, and her own brig, the *Sophia*, turned out a miracle of speed, and could sail, it seemed as by magic, into the teeth of a gale. She commanded it herself, directing its course with an apparent recklessness, really the result of knowledge, through the narrow channels and swirling currents of the close-sown islands, through passages where rocks were ranged like a shark's teeth, row on hungry row, and the green water poured over them with the speed of an autumn gale, or beating about, close-hauled, past the reef of wolves which lie waiting off Methana. Sometimes she would charter herself to a merchant, and carry trading produce as far as the Asiatic coast, or to Alexandria; but for the most part she seemed possessed merely by the desire for the sea, an instinct of her race, but coming to flavor in her, for the fierce battling of skill calculated against the brute force of the incalculable elements, for the hundred tactics which nothing but practical intimacy can teach. To her clan she became a sort of cult, the more so as she had left all her property, if she died unmarried, to Christos, who, in point of fact, took to himself a wife within six months of the final rejection.

In 1821, when she was now near the end of her twenty-first year—alert for adventure—came the stinging news of the outbreak of the revolution.

To Hydra, that small and frugal island, tales of Turkish cruelty, greed, and lust, and the inchoate schemes of vengeance, had come only as echoes vague and remote, and the news of the outbreak was like the bolt out of the clear sky. For the Turks had formed a sufficiently accurate conception of the character of those dour islanders, and while there were women, and to spare, in the other places, and it seemed that on the mainland, peopled, so they considered, with richer and softer folk, taxation might be indefinitely increased, it was not for a fattened pasha to procure with trouble and fighting what an indolent order given over his pipe could bring him. Sophia, on the eve of her return from a prolonged and prosperous cruise, interviewed the captain of a caique who had put in with the news of the taking of Kalamata, and heard a tale to make the blood bubble and boil—how the rising had run like fire through summer-dry stubble from north to south and east to west, how that Greece was to be free, and pull no longer under an infidel yoke. Tale followed tale; the man had seen with his own eyes free-born Greeks, man, woman, and child, treated as an unmerciful master will not treat his beast; he had tales of torture, followed at the last by death, lingering and painful, but welcome as the end of pain—of things unnatural and bestial beyond word or belief. There had been a cousin of his living near Nauplia. He had come back from the fields one day to find his wife dead and abominably mutilated on the threshold; his two daughters had been carried off—with them his two younger sons; the elder lay stifled by his mother. They had—And Kanaris stopped, for the thing could not be told. It was on the quay, within half an hour of her landing, that the Capsina heard the first news, and in her brusque way she whisked the man up to her house and gave him wine and tobacco, and listened while he talked. Others of the clan were there to welcome her, and stayed to hear, old Christos among them, and the tales were stopped and pointed with exclamations of fierce horror and curses on the Turk. Sophia sat in dead silence, but her eyes were black flames, and more than once her lip trembled at some story of hideous outrage on women and children. She only asked one question—"They are Greeks, to whom the devils do such things?" And on the answer, "And we too are Greeks," she said, and her hand clinched.

Her foreman had been waiting for orders as to the unloading of the brig, and when the tales were over, she sent for him.

"Begin the unloading now, at once," she said, "and let the work go on all night. Oh, man, are you a stuffed bird, that you stare so at me? Do you not understand the tongue of your fathers, or shall I speak Turkish? I will be down there in an hour. Unload at once." Then turning to the captain of the caique, "You will sup with me," she said, "and you too, Christos. By-the-way, what is your name?"

"Constantine Kanaris."

"That is a good sea-name. Do you hate the Turk, and can you handle a boat?"

"The one as thoroughly as the other."

"I offer you a birth in the *Sophia*, directly under me. I command my own ship."

"And I, too," said Kanaris, "as my father and grandfather have done before me."

"You accept the post?"

Kanaris looked rather bewildered.

"Capsina," he said, "you are one of few words, and so am I when work is to be done. I have told you of Nicholas Vidalis, who is among the first movers of this revolution. Him I have promised to serve, in the cause of the war. I cannot go back from that."

The Capsina frowned, and struck the table impatiently.

"Do you not understand?" she said—"that his work is my work? Oh, Uncle Christos! what is the matter with you? Has the sky fallen, or do you hear the trumpet of the archangel? God in heaven! for the present there is no more trading for me. Do you not see that there must be a fleet, or these devils will keep on sending more arms and armies into the country? Are you a Greek, man—are you anything but a fiend from the pit, that you can wonder at me, when you hear how they treat other clans, free-born and scornful as ourselves, like slaves and beasts? That I should be busy like a mule carrying silk stuff, when such things are going on! There must be a fleet, I tell you, and the *Sophia* is the first ship of that fleet. By God! but I have found my work at last! It was not for nothing that I have built ships, and learned how to sail them, and take them where the devil himself would be afraid to trust to his luck. Now quick," she said to Kanaris—"do you take this berth or not? I want a man something like you, who hates and works and is silent. You will suit me, I think."

"Our purpose is war on the Turk and no other purpose?" asked Kanaris.

"That is better," said the Capsina—"we are getting to business. Yes, only war

14

on the Turk. War? Extermination, rather, for that is the only business of Christians with regard to them. And you shall be no loser, if we prosper; and if we do not prosper, I pay you still the wage of the captain of a brig."

Kanaris flushed.

"Why do you say that?" he asked. "Is it for that that Nicholas—God be thanked for him!—and those like him serve?"

"I was wrong," said Sophia, "but you were a stranger to me till this moment, but you are no stranger now. You will come?"

"I will come," he said.

With that they fell to supper, and when supper was over Sophia and Kanaris went down to the harbor. The brig was lying close in unlading, and returning boats were passing to and fro from it to the shore. Two great resin flares on the deck showed them a crowd of men working at the crane by which the freight was conveyed from the hold and swung over the side to the barges that received it. The cargo was of silk from the Syrian coast and was for Athens and Salonica; but the foreman, in blind obedience to Sophia's instructions, was unloading it and storing it in her shed on the quay. They found him there when they got down, and she nodded approvingly when she saw what progress the work had made.

"Have we another ship in?" she asked.

"Yes, the *Hydra*, but she is due to sail to-morrow to Syria," said he.

The Capsina stood for a moment thinking.

"May the Virgin look to Syria!" she said. Then, "What is your caique doing?" she asked Kanaris.

"Picking up chance jobs."

"Here is one then, and Syria is all right. Will you undertake to deliver the silk to Athens and Salonica?"

"Before what date?"

"This day three weeks. My men shall do the freighting for you, and you can sail to-morrow night. You will carry it easily; it is only a quarter of the *Sophia's* cargo, for we have discharged at Crete and Melos. Also it is the season of south winds."

The matter was soon arranged, and the two went on board the *Sophia*, that Kanaris might see the ship. To him, as to the Hydriots, the build of the vessel was new, but she had acquitted herself too well on her previous cruises to allow of any doubt as to the success of what had been an experiment, and

Kanaris, who had more than once been on board English and French cruisers and men-of-war, talked with Sophia as to the guns she should carry. They could obtain these, he told her, at Spetzas, where the revolutionists had formed a secret arsenal. It would be better, he suggested, to delay any alteration in the bulwarks and disposition of the ship till they saw what guns were to be got.

At the end of an hour or so they went on shore again, Kanaris to his caique, Sophia back to her house. The night was still and windless, and from her room she could see the flares on the *Sophia* burning upright and steady in the calm air, and the rattle of the gear of the crane was audible. She felt as if her life had suddenly burst into blossom, and the blossom thereof was red.

Chapter II

Next day came news that Spetzas had openly joined the insurrection, and two proselytizing brigs put into Hydra, to try to raise, if not more ships, at any rate recruits. They both carried the new Greek ensign, white and blue, and bearing the cross of Greece risen above the crescent of Turkey. The tidings that the Capsina was going to join the revolutionists with her ship had already spread through the town, and when next morning she went down to the quay to speak with the captains of the Spetziot vessels, she was like the queen bee to the swarm, and the people followed her, cheering wildly. Their voices were music and wine to her, and the thrill of exultation which belongs to acts of leadership was hers.

Fierce and fine too was the news from Spetzas: the people had risen, and after an immense meeting held on the quay had chosen a commander, and broken open the treasury in which was kept the annual tribute to the Ottoman government. The taxes had just been got in, and the treasury was full. With this money eight brigs were being armed and manned, and would set sail to Melos, at which island, as they knew, were several Ottoman vessels making their annual cruise of conscription for raising sailors. In such manner was the vintage of the sea to begin.

Round the Capsina and the Spetziot captains the crowd surged thickest. One of these, Kostas Myrrides, had a certain loud and straight-hitting gift of oratory, and the crowd gathered and swayed, and hung on his words. There had been erected for him a sort of rude dais made of a board placed upon two barrels, and from there he spoke to the people.

"The wine is drawn!" he cried; "to the feast then! Yet indeed there is no choice. Greece is up in arms, and before long the armies and fleets of the infidels will be on us. What will it profit you to stay still and watch? Do you think that the Turks will sit in justice and examine whether this man is an insurgent and the other is not? Is that their way of dealing? The justice of the Turk! You have heard the proverb and know what that means. The fire of war leaps from cape to cape and mountain to mountain. Kindle it here. Already has one of you, and that a woman whose name will not be forgotten, thrown in her lot with a glorious cause—Greece, the freedom of Greece!"

The shout rose and broke in waves of sound, only to swell and tower afresh when the speaker unfurled the new-blazoned flag, and waved it above them. Truly, if the Turkish ship of conscription had come in sight, there would have been short shrift for those on board.

The government of Hydra was in the hands of twelve primates, who were responsible to the Ottoman government for the annual tribute in specie (in itself but small), and also for the equipment and wages of two hundred and fifty able-bodied seamen yearly to the Ottoman fleet. To raise this more considerable sum a tax of five per cent. was levied on the income of every man in the island. Now the ship-owners were more than the bulk of the tax-payers, and it was clearer than a summer noonday that if they joined the revolutionists, unless the island revolution became general, or their ships met with immediate success, the Ottoman fleet would descend on the Hydra, and the Shadow of God would have a word for the primates, and a rope. Thus it came about that while the uproar was still growing and fermenting on the quay, the primates met together, and found grave faces. The Capsina, they considered, was primarily responsible for this consternating stroke, but to try to guide the Capsina back into the paths of peace, they feared, was like attempting to lead the moon with a string, and to quarrel with her was to quarrel with the clan, to whom she was as a god, eccentric, perhaps, but certainly unquestionable. The responsibility of debate, however, was not granted them, for before they could devise any check on the Capsina, a new and tremendous burst of cheering caused the president, Father Jakomaki Tombazes, to rise and go to the window. Three vessels were leaving the port, two being the Spetziot vessels, with the Greek flag blazoning its splendor to heaven, and as for the other, there was no mistaking the build of the *Sophia*. Tombazes gasped, then returned to the others.

"The Capsina has gone," he said. "And, by the Virgin," cried he, rising to the heroical level of the event, and striking the table with his fist, "she is a brave lass, and Hydra should be proud of her!"

This straightforward statement of the duty of Hydriots was not less abhorrent to the assembled primates. The Capsina had gone, the clan were shouting themselves hoarse on the beach, and, where an action of the Capsina was concerned, it was not less idle to argue with the clan than to employ rhetoric to a mad bull. The only courses open were to fly for safety to the mainland, join the revolutionists, or employ coercive measures with the rest, whereby they should not do so. Now the tax-collectors were necessarily of their party, for the necks of all the officials under the Turkish rule were, so to speak, in one noose, and there were also a number of old, sedately minded or retired men who would distinctly prefer to live out their lives in inglorious peace, unless matters were already in the fire, than to burn squibs, for in so small regard did the primates hold the revolution, under the very nose of the Shadow of God. But, look at it as they might, they were bound to confess that a sorrier party had never been got together. Even Tombazes, by his remark about the duty of Hydra, showed he was of no reliable stuff, and the primates seemed depressed. For the rest, the island was capering in exultant frenzy on the beach, at what the Capsina had done, and what they would do.

Tombazes, who as their president should have shown himself a pillar of prudence, alone of them all sat with a glistening eye, and smiled, showing his teeth in his black and scarcely gray-streaked beard. Then throwing his head back, he burst out into a great crack of laughter.

"The Capsina is finer than we all," he said. "What a girl! She is the only man among us, for all our long beards. Who knows she may not sail straight for Constantinople, force her way into the Sultan's presence, and set Michael at him. I can almost see her doing it, and indeed I should dearly like to. 'Hi, Michael, at his throat, boy!' she would cry. Yet I see her walking out again safe and leaving him lying dead like a broken doll, for I cannot imagine three armies of Turks stopping her. She would call them dogs and devils, and, the chidden dogs, they would tuck their tails away and only snarl. Yes, my brothers, this is not in order; I am but a fond dreamer. But let us come to the point. The Capsina beats us. Oh, she beats us! We need not waste time in making faces at that. But what next? Of course we must do our best to stop this rising, but, though I would not have it said by others, my heart is not wholly on our side, though my head shall be. Is not the Capsina stupendous?"

He rose again from his place, and hurried to the open window for another glance.

"They are all crowding on sail," he said, "but the Capsina's ship is first—first by half a mile, I should say. She is always first. Pre-eminently has she been first this morning. Yes, yes, I know, let us come to the point. Perhaps Brother Nikolas will give us his views," and the great burly man bent down his head to hide the inextinguishable joy of his face.

Brother Nikolas's views were short, sour, eminently depressing, and as follows:

The Turkish ships which were cruising for the conscription would be at Hydra before the end of April—that is to say, in considerably less than a month. Instead of two hundred and fifty able-bodied recruits they would find twelve, or perhaps eleven, primates—here his eyes looked lemon-juice at Tombazes —a quantity of unemployed tax-collectors, some elderly gentlemen, some women, and some children. This would probably be thought an unsatisfactory substitute. They could fill in the probable course of subsequent events for themselves, for one Turkish raid was very like another. He would suggest guarding the treasury at the risk of their lives, to show that they, at any rate, had no hand in the matter.

Others spoke in the same melancholy vein, and at the end Tombazes.

"The point, so I take it, is this," he said. "Unless we stop this movement, or, if we are unable to stop it, unless we run away for refuge to the insurgent armies in Greece or in other islands, we are certainly dead men. Brother Nikolas has suggested that we have a certain duty to the Turk; well, that is as it may be, but in any case we are at present the vassals of the Sultan, and for the sake of our own necks, this meeting, I am sure, would wish to repudiate the movement. It will be no manner of good, but we must let that be known. With your consent, I will send for the mayor, and make an official inquiry as to what the tumult is about, and where and why the Capsina has gone. Meantime, and with the utmost haste, I suggest that we stow the island revenues in the church. It may be difficult, but I think it will be possible if we do it quietly. The money will certainly be safer there."

The primates dispersed: some to mingle with the crowd, and try to allay this illicit enthusiasm, whereby certain men got infected with it; some to make arrangements for the funds of the national treasury being moved to the church; Tombazes alone, though burning to go down among the people, waiting in the room where they had met for his conference with the mayor, Christos Capsas. Indeed, he was in most unprelatical vein, and the meeting of the two was very cordial; you would have said they took the same side. Christos dwelt with extreme complacency on the expedition of the Capsina— it was like the clan, he said, to take the lead in adventure—and Tombazes, though officially he had bound himself to deprecate it, gave a halting lip-service only to the cause of the primates.

"And the men of the island, you say," says he, with a dancing eye, "are resolved to follow this—this most imprudent and ill-advised example set them by the Capsina? Man, do they realize what it means? Do they not know that the Turks will descend on those they leave behind—their women and their children?"

"Yet the women would have them go," said Christos.

"The more senseless they. Yet women are ever so. For what will happen to them? Are the Turks so chivalrous? And will Turks make kind parents to the children who will be fatherless?"

"Yet the children are sailing sticks and branches in the harbor, and throwing stones at them. 'This,' they say to one another, 'we will do to the Turks.'"

"By the Virgin, they are true Greeks, then!" shouted Tombazes, lustily, forgetting himself for a moment but his voice ringing true. Then with impatience: "What does it matter what the children do?" he asked. "It is a new thing to take counsel of the children before we act."

"Yet you asked me of the children," said Christos, smiling, "and, as you said, father, they are true Greeks."

Tombazes sat down, and motioned Christos to take a seat.

"You, then, are on the side of the women and the children," he said, "or rather, if you look at it aright, against them; for sure is it that you give them over to the Turks to treat—to treat as Turks treat women and children. Your son Christos a servant in the harem—have you thought of that?"

"I am on the side of the Capsina," said Christos.

Tombazes looked furtively round, as if to see that none other was there, walked slowly to the window, and came back again with quicker step. Twice he began to speak, twice stopped, but at the last he could contain himself no longer.

"And so, by all the saints, am I!" he cried. "See, Christos, I trust you, and this must not be known nor guessed. For sure I would, if I followed my desire, sail after that splendid girl—yes, swim to wherever she may go—with the Greek flag over me. Man, but my heart burned when I saw that. The cross above the crescent, and soon no crescent at all. Thus shall it be. But I and the others, and you, too, are put over these people, and we must make them consider what will follow. Nothing must be done wildly; because we are aflame with this wonderful, prophetic flag, tinder to that spark, we must not act as if the thing was done, as if the moment we take up arms, down go the Turks like the walls of Jericho; and in this, Christos, I am speaking with all the sincerity God gave me. No enthusiasm, no sudden rising will do the work; the fight will be long and bitter, and if a new and glorious thing is to spring up, it will be watered with tears and with blood—with tears of the fatherless and widow, and blood of the fathers. Tell me yourself, you are the father of a family, with a stake in peace; what are you meaning to do?"

"The Capsina has lent me the *Hydra*, which was to have sailed to Syria to-day with stuff for the Turkish governor. The stuff she has thrown overboard, and I sail to-morrow for Nauplia, where I shall get orders."

"She threw the Turk's stuff overboard? I would it had been Turks! Great is the Capsina!" and the primate capered barbarously up the room and down again. "And now I will go down to the people," said he. "You and I have a secret, Christos; but I wonder how long the devil will give me strength to keep it."

Down on the quay matters had fared more briskly than among the primates. A member and delegate of the Revolutionist Club, by name Economos, had landed with the ships from Spetzas, and had been preaching revolt and revenge to willing ears. Even before the departure of the Capsina, whose sails were now a gull on the horizon, he had begun enlisting volunteers, and before Tombazes reached the harbor, he was already at the head of an armed band, including several ship-captains, and was rapidly earning a cheap popularity by addressing the mob as "citizens of Greece."

Tombazes, who, for his ruddy face and burly heartiness, was popular with the people, made his way through to where the crowd was thickest, and instantly interrupted the man's speeches.

"Now what is this all about?" he cried, good-humoredly, pushing his way in. "What is all this disturbance? It is all most irregular. Ha, Dimitri, you should be driving out the sheep instead of wasting time on the quay, for all the world like a quacking goose that can't lay an egg! You, too, Anastasi, now you are a less idiot than some, tell me what this is about, and who is that holding a flag which I do not remember to have seen before?"

He made his way through the people up to Economos.

"Now, my good fellow," he said, "just stop preaching for a moment. We primates have a good deal of preaching to do, and so we have much sympathy for those who listen. Who are you, where do you come from, what's your business, and what's your name, and what are you talking about? Oh, you silly folk!" he cried, aloud, as a discontented murmur rose up. "You are all going to have fair play—that is why I am here. But just let me learn what it is all about. Melesinas, don't brandish your knife in that foolish way, or you will be cutting your own oaf's hand off!"

Economos paused, and realizing that there was nothing to be gained by insolence, seeing that this man was a friend evidently of the people, stepped down from the table on which he was standing.

"My name is Antonios Economos," he said. "I am an emissary from the Club of Patriots in Greece, and I am here to raise the revolt in Hydra against the Turk."

"That is all very well," said Tombazes. "You want ships and support, and for ships you want men, and for men money. Has the Club of Patriots supplied you with that?"

"The treasury—the national treasury!" shouted several voices.

Tombazes looked up quickly, and, springing forward with an agility which in a man of his bulk bordered on the miraculous, seized hold of a big fellow whom he had seen shouting and shook him till his teeth rattled in his head.

"Another word," he cried, "and I pop you into the harbor. You too, George, I saw you shouting too. If I tell your wife it will be but little supper you get. I am ready for you all, five under one arm and six under the other. Oh, I will teach you to interrupt when I am talking to another. Get back with you from the table, all of you, all of you. And you there, Yanni, bring me wine and two glasses, this gentleman and I have to talk together, and chairs—two chairs; and the sooner the rest of you silly quacking folk clear away, the fewer there will be for me to put into the sea, and that will save trouble for us all: for me, in getting hot on so warm a day, for there are fat lubbers among you; and for you, in having to change your clothes."

The crowd edged a little back, more good-humored than resentful, for they were accustomed to be treated like children by Tombazes, and the island knew him familiarly as "The Nurse." He was their doctor, a practitioner of heroic simples, sun and sea being the staple of his prescriptions, their spiritual consoler, herein also employing the less morbid remedies. He could sail a boat against the best of their seamen, and he had again and again, as they all knew, taken the side of the people against the greedy and grabbing primates. The wine and the chairs were brought, and he and Economos sat down, clinked glasses, and settled down to talk.

"You will have found dry work in all that talking," said Tombazes, "unless you are very fond of your own voice. Good wine is the gift of God, and this is not bad. Now I heard what that man shouted, and so did you. Now tell me straight, for this it will save trouble. Was it you who suggested that they should get the money from the treasury, or they?"

Economos, who had been playing the noisy demagogue all morning, and was quite prepared to play it again, if advisable, determined for the present to talk soberly.

"They suggested it," he said, dryly. "I'm willing also to tell you that it struck me as an admirable notion."

"Did it so?" said Tombazes, musingly. "Then you are more easily pleased than most men, for your idea of the admirable seems to me the silliest thing I have ever heard tell of. And as I am older than you, and a man of experience, it is likely I have run against many silly things in this world. Now, man, sit down; this is my way of speaking; no man in this island takes offence at what I say, for he knows that would not help what he has his hand to—aye, and he would be like to get his nose pulled, which is of the more immediate consequence. Now tell me how many ships do you mean to victual and put into commission with your admirable notions?"

"Four, to begin with," said Economos.

"Four, to begin with, says he!" exclaimed Tombazes, in a lamentable treble voice. "And how many to end with, and with what will you be paying the crews? Man, do you think you will find enough to keep them in pipes and tobacco with what is in the treasury? Four, to begin with!—save us all!"

"The crews will average sixty men each," continued Economos, "and that will make two hundred and forty. Every year the treasury pays the wage of two hundred and fifty men. I deal with facts, you see."

"Come, then, let's have facts," cried Tombazes, "and surely I will help you. It's facts the man will be wanting. Why, you must have a fever or an ague in your blood! You want bleeding, man, I see it in your eye. Do you think we collect the taxes for a whole year together?"

"I suppose what there is in the treasury will last us a month."

"Well, say it lasts a month," said Tombazes. "What then? You will return here for more money. Much will you find when you have taken from the island just those men who pay the bulk of the taxes. I'm thinking that your admirable notion is even sillier, if we look into it, than it appeared on the surface. And even the look of it on the surface made me think you had been better for blood-letting."

"See, father, listen to me," said Economos, with sudden earnestness. "Have you heard what has happened? Surely you have not, or you would not speak thus. Do you know that Kalamata has been taken by the Greeks, that the beacons of liberty have flashed from one end of the country to another? A free people have stood in the meadows round Kalamata and sung the 'Te Deum' for that great and wonderful victory. Is that not a thing to make the blood tingle? In the north, Germanos, archbishop and primate, has raised the revolt. The monks of Megaspelaion are up in arms; Petrobey and they of Maina have come forth like a herd of hungry wolves."

Tombazes' eye flashed.

"It is fit that you should tell me all you have to say for their mad scheme. Go on, man, go on. Tell me all you know. I—I can judge better so."

Economos suspected the truth, that the primate was all tinder to the flame, and, with a certain acumen, did not let him see this, nor did he at present tax him with it. Instead, he spoke of the plans of the revolutionists—how that the Turks were flocking into Tripolitza, from which, when the time came, there would be no escape; how essential it was to the success of the war that Greece should be cut off from the headquarters of the Ottoman forces. This could not be done till the coasts were in the hands of the insurgents, and their ships prevented fresh arms and men being sent into the country. That was the part of the Greek ports and islands. Spetzas had already joined; in Psara soon would the standard of revolution be raised; was Hydra, the largest and best-manned, she who should be both arms and sinews of naval Greece, to stand neutral? Indeed, neutral she could not be. If she was not with the insurgents the Turks would soon make her into an advanced point from which they could the more easily reach the mainland. She would be garrisoned; her harbor would be a cluster of Turkish ships—would that be a pleasant thing for the Hydriots? Their only safety was in fighting. Greece was in arms—what matter to the Turks if Hydra had joined the insurgents or not? Would the mob of soldiers and sailors spare them? Would they leave the Hydriots their houses while they camped on the hillside? Would their women be spared because they were loyal? And the danger to Greece was thus doubled. The Turks would be holding an eyrie from which to swoop in the midst of the patriots. "Indeed," concluded Economos, returning from his somewhat rhetorical language to colloquialism, "we will have no wasps' nests in the seat of our trousers, if you please."

This was too much for Tombazes, and motioning back the crowd, who had begun to encroach again, he spoke low to the other.

"I shall surely burst unless I speak," he said. "Do you not see how I am with you? Man, you are blinder than the worms if you do not see that. But if you drop a word of that till I give you leave, I swear by the lance of St. George and the coffee-pot which he made whole, that I will kick you till my foot is sore and you are less like a man than a jelly-fish! That treasury notion of yours is absurd. That I stick to, and for the reasons I gave you. Give it up, I ask you, for the present. Mark you, and listen to me. I am a traitor in my camp for a good cause, and I can help you. If the primates and others are assured you are not going to touch the national treasury—for its safety, they think, means their safety from the Turk—half the opposition will be withdrawn. You must raise money another way. Moreover, you want five times as much as there is in the treasury. And what is the use of four ships? Eh, that was what I meant when I said your notion seemed to me the silliest thing I have ever heard. Did you not see that? Ah, well, God made the blind men also! There are at least thirty in the harbor, which are all capable of carrying guns and of outsailing those lubberly Turkish tubs. You must have them all. And you must not leave the women and children here defenceless. You must organize a body of men who will guard the harbor and the town. Luckily there is no landing except this side the island. Afterwards, of course, you will add the money in the treasury to what must be collected by levying a tax. Milk the treasury dry, man. The money will be stored in the Church of St. George, and I shall have the key. Now mark the result of our conversation. I have persuaded you, so I shall tell the primates, and you the people, not to touch the treasury—that alone will quiet my party considerably. Propose to the people to levy a tax on all the capital in the island, and submit that to the primates as the only condition on which the treasury will be untouched. The people will give willingly, the primates unwillingly, but the money will be the same. Fill your glass; shake hands with me, and I will go to my party. I drink to the freedom of Greece, and to you. Viva!"

For the next two or three days negotiations went on between the primates and the people, and often Tombazes had occasion to wear a mighty grave face, whereby he should cloak the merriness of his heart. The part he was playing, as he assured himself, was the only way of fighting for the good cause, for had he openly joined the revolutionist party, the confidence which the other primates felt in him would be gone, and they would be the more eager to oppose tooth and nail to any proposals. But what they regarded as his diplomatic victory with regard to the national treasure, gave him a position of extraordinary security among them, and Economos, perhaps partly for his own ends, and the spurious credit which the people would give him of having successfully fought down the opposition of the primates, was equally anxious to conceal Tombazes' part in the affair.

At length a sum adequate to meet all immediate expenses was raised; the crews were all paid one month's wages in advance, with the prospect of prize-money won from the Turks, and the people seized on the national treasury. Tombazes' ill-suppressed delight at this step, which was conveyed to the primates in conclave, put him for the moment within an ace of exposure.

Fresh intrigues began; the primates, to make the best of a bad job, appealed to those sailors and captains who had formerly been in their employment, offering fresh berths in their own service; for many of them owned ships, and as the island was now pledged to the national cause, they, too, proposed to have a finger in the prize-money. Economos, on the other hand, failing to see how it was just that those who had opposed the scheme should take a share in it now, organized a revolutionary committee in whose hands should be the sole conduct of the war, and naturally enough did not appoint any primate on it. Eventually—for both sides were somewhat afraid of each other, and wished to avoid open collision—a compromise was arrived at. Those captains and men who had already definitely engaged themselves in the service of the revolutionists during the opposition of the primates, were forbidden to serve on the primates' ships. On the other hand, the ships of the primates were to be admitted to the fleet, and should be treated in the matter of prize-money with the others. Finally—and had the primates known the cause of this, there would have been angry men in Hydra—the command of the entire fleet was given to Tombazes.

On the morning of the 29th of April a solemn service was held in the church, and Tombazes read out the declaration of the independence of Hydra as part of the free state of Greece.

"It is determined by us," so ran the proclamation, "the primates and governors of this island of Hydra, to serve no longer nor obey the infidels who are the enemies of God and of His Christ, and of the blessed mother of Christ, and from this day we declare that we will make ourselves a free people of the realm of Greece. In the support of this resolve it will be our duty to fight for our wives, our children, our country, and we will fight till the death without counting the cost, and giving whatever we possess—our goods, our obedience, and our lives—to our country's cause. May He who is the Giver of Victory and has already given us the will to fight, strengthen our arms and deliver His foes and ours into our hands."

By the first week in May, such was the frenzy of expedition among the men, the Hydriot contingent, numbering twenty sail, was ready to go to sea. The eight brigs from Spetzas which had sailed to Melos to capture the Turkish conscription ships had put in at Hydra, uniting themselves with Tombazes' fleet, and reported complete success. The credit of the capture however belonged, as they acknowledged, to a strange ship that sailed as if by magic, and which no one knew. For as they were nearing Melos, intending to get inside the harbor where they knew the Turks were, and capture them before the Melian contingent got on board, and while they were still a couple of miles out to sea, the wind, which so far had been favorable, dropped, and the airs became so light and variable that they lay for two days like painted ships, taken back rather than making ground.

At this point, Tombazes, to whom the Spetziot captain was telling his tale, got up from his chair and waved his arms wildly.

"It was she—I know it was she! Thank God it was she," he cried. "Go on, man."

Captain Yassos looked at him a moment in surprised wonder.

"It certainly was a she," he said. "How did you know?"

"The spirit of prophecy was upon me!" cried Tombazes. "Finish your tale."

"It was our desire to take the ships, you will understand," he said, "before the Melian folk got aboard, while if we failed, they ran risk of being murdered by the Turks, for fear of their helping us. But it would seem God willed it otherwise, for He sent us no wind except as it were the breath of a man cooling his broth. A little mist, too, was rising seaward and spreading towards us, and when we who knew the sea saw that, we thought it impossible we could get ten miles in time, for the mist means a calm and windlessness."

"Oh, am I a boy who would be a sailor, that you tell me the alphabet of things?" exclaimed Tombazes.

"You will see it all makes the thing more marvellous," said the other, smiling, "so be patient with me. Well, we were cursing at the calm when suddenly, on our starboard quarter—my ship being to starboard of all the others—there came it seemed the shadow of a ship, white and huge, with all sails spread and coming towards us. Dimitri, my son, who was with me, said, 'Look, father, look!' and crossed himself, and I did the same. Now I am no left-handed man at ship sailing, but when I saw that ship moving slowly but steadily towards us while we lay like logs, I thought it no canny thing. She passed half a cable's length from us, and I saw her guns looking through the open ports, new so they seemed to me; and on her topmast, and I blessed the Virgin when I saw that, was the flag of Greece. One man stood at the tiller whose face seemed familiar to me, and by him stood a woman, tall, and like the morning, somehow, to look upon. In that still air I heard her say to him, 'A point more to starboard,' so it seemed that she was the captain, and as she passed us she waved her hand, and cried, 'Do you not wish a share in this, or am I to go alone? Come, comrades, follow, follow. I bring you the wind.'

"On her word the wind awoke, the slack ropes began to run through the blocks, and in a few seconds the sail was full. Up went our helm, and we followed. But it was like following a hare on the mountains to follow that great white ship. She swam from us as a fish swims from a man in the water, and before we had turned the cape behind which lies the harbor we heard her guns. Twice before we came up she had sailed round the largest of the three ships, pouring in broadside after broadside, the other replying clumsily and hardly touching her, and just as I, who was ahead of the rest, fired at one of the others, the ship she was battering struck its colors, and anchoring, she let down the boats, and with two boat-loads of her crew she put off to board them. Then those treacherous devils of hell under the flag of truce, you mind, again opened fire on her. But it seems she had calculated on that, and on the instant her ship blazed again, firing over their heads and raking the deck where the Turks were. This time, as I could see, they fired red-hot ball, and one, I suppose, struck the powder-magazine, for it was as if the end of the world came, and a moment after the Turk sank. The boarding party was not far from the ship, and the explosion showered boards and wreckage round them, but thereat they turned and rowed back again, their work being done for them. For me, I had my own affairs ready, and for ten minutes we blazed and banged at each other, but before it was over I looked round once, and saw already at the harbor's mouth the ship which had come out of the mist beating out to sea again. Now, father, you seem to know who that woman was; who was it?"

"Glory be to God!" said Tombazes. Then, "But, man, you are an ignorant fool. Who could it be but the Capsina of Hydra? But where has she gone? Why is she not with you?"

"I know not: she was gone before we had finished with the others."

With the combined squadron from Spetzas and Hydra had joined nine ships from Psara. There was half a day's trouble with them, for they refused at first to recognize the command of Tombazes, and said it was fitter that the three islands should cast lots, and let the choice of the admiral go with the winner. They had, they said, a most wary man of the sea among them, who had worked with the Russians and knew the use of the fire-ship. But the Spetziots had accepted Tombazes as commander of the two islands, and the Psariots were told that they might do the same or leave the squadron, and they chose the former, though ill-content.

They cruised northward, for knowing that news of the revolution had reached Constantinople and that the Sultan Mahmud was preparing to send a fleet to the refractory islands, they hoped to intercept this, and thus prevent punishment reaching their homes or fresh supplies putting into ports on the mainland. Several times they sighted Turkish ships, and thus two or three small prizes were taken. For ten days they met none but single ships, which, without exception, surrendered, often without the exchange of a shot; the crews were taken and sent back to Hydra or Spetzas, where they were prisoners; but these vessels being for the most part trading brigs of the poorer class, there was little booty to be divided among the captors.

The tenth day of the cruise saw the squadron off Cape Sunium, at the extreme south end of Attica. The day before they had run before a strong south wind, hoping to clear the promontory before night and get through the dangerous straits to the north of it by daylight. Until evening the heavens had been clear, but the night came on cloudy, starless, and calm, and fearing to pass the straits in so uncertain a light, for they were full of reefs, orders had been given to lie to and wait for day. But the currents of that shifting sea rendered it impossible to maintain position. The greater part of the squadron was caught by the racing flow of water that runs up northwest towards Peiraeus, and drifted safely but swiftly up the gulf. Of the remainder, all but two weathered Sunium and lay for shelter under Zea, where they remained till morning. But these two, finding themselves dangerously near the rocky south headland of Sunium, beat out to sea again before the breeze dropped, and by morning lay far out to the east of the others.

Day broke windless and calm, with an oily sea, big, but not broken, coming in from the south. The ships in the gulf had to wait for the land breeze to spring up: those off Zea who had passed Sunium lay to till the others joined them, but the two to the east, Hydriot ships, out of shelter of the land, had a moderate breeze from the north.

For two hours after daybreak they waited, but the others, out of reach of their wind, made no sign, and about nine o'clock they were aware of a Turkish ship coming from the north, and sailing, as they supposed, to the islands or to some Peloponnesian port. The two Greek ships were lying close together, it may be a cable's distance apart, and it was immediately clear to each that the Turk must be stopped, for the purpose of their squadron was none other than this. The admiral's ship, far away to the west, it was impossible to signal, and even if possible, ineffectual, for nought but a miracle would have brought up a land breeze at nine in the morning. So as in duty bound the two brigs, like sea swallows, put about, and hoisting the Greek flag went in pursuit of the Turk.

As they neared her it was evident that a day's work was before them, and Sachturi, the captain of one of the brigs, signalled to Pinotzi: "Ship of war," and Pinotzi signalled back: "So are we." Yanni Sachturi, the captain's son, a lusty, laughing boy of about eighteen, danced with delight as he read the signal to his father, and heard the order to clear for action. The ports had been closed, for a heavy sea had been running during the night, but in a few minutes the guns were run out, the men at their posts, and the pokers heating in the galley fire. Sachturi's vessel carried ten guns, four on each broadside and two in the bows; Pinotzi's only six, but of these two were thirty-two-pounders and heavier than any of Sachturi's.

The Turk was running due south, and Sachturi from the bridge, seeing that if they went straight for her, she would pass them, ordered that his ship should he laid two points nearer the wind, and Pinotzi followed his lead. In ten minutes it was clear that they were rapidly overhauling her, and in another half-hour they were but a short mile off. For a moment the Turk seemed to hesitate, and then, putting about, went off on an easterly tack. But here the Greek gained more speedily, and she, perceiving this, went off straight down wind again. This manoeuvre lost her more ground, and Sachturi and she were now broadside to each other when the Turk opened fire. Her aim was too low, and the halls struck the water some two hundred yards from the Greek ship. In spite of her imposing appearance Sachturi noticed that only five guns were fired, the balls from three of which ricochetted off the sea, and flew, two of them, just beyond the Greek's bows, the other clearing the deck without touching her. Sachturi's guns replied, but apparently without effect, and changing his course he made an easterly tack to pass behind her, for all her guns seemed to be forward. Pinotzi, who had heavier ordnance, ran up broadside, and he and the Turk exchanged a volley or two, but, owing to the heavy rolling of the ships and the inexperience of the Greek gunners at least, without doing or receiving damage.

Sachturi's guess had been correct, though why a ship-of-war had put to sea only half-armed he did not pause to consider, and, coming up within range, he let her have the starboard guns. But he had thus to lie broadside on to the sea, which made accurate aim difficult; and again putting her head to the sea, he ran on, meaning to use the two guns in his bows at close quarters.

For an hour or more it was the battle of the hawk and the raven. The two Greek ships skimmed and tacked about on the light breeze, sometimes getting in a broadside as they closed in, sometimes passing behind her stern, where she seemed to be unarmed. Twice Sachturi sailed round her, giving broadside for broadside, and at last a lucky shot cut the main-mast of the Turk in half, bringing down to the deck a pile of wreckage and canvas. They could see the men hauling away to clear the deck, when another shot from Pinotzi brought down the second mast, leaving her rolling helplessly, with only the mizzen standing. Sachturi had just rounded her stern, and had given another broadside, when the Turk fired, and a ball crashing through the bulwarks killed two sailors, and with them Yanni, who was just taking an order from his father to close with her and throw on the grappling-irons.

Sachturi did not move; but he set his teeth for a moment, and looked at Yanni. He was lying on his back, half his chest shot away, staring up into the sky. His face was untouched, and his mouth seemed to smile. He was his father's only son, and Sachturi loved him as his own soul.

In another ten minutes the grappling-irons were cast on to the Turk; twice they were thrown off, but the third time two anchored themselves in the ropes and blocks of the wrecked main-mast, and, though the Turks sought furiously to free themselves, in another minute the Greeks from Sachturi's ship were pouring over the side. Since Yanni had been killed he had only said three words, twice when the grappling-irons were thrown off, and he ordered them to be cast again, once as they boarded, "Spare none!" he had cried.

The order was obeyed. The Turks had exhausted their ammunition, and fought with knives only, charging down with undaunted bravery on the muskets of the Greeks, and when the deck was cleared the boarders went below. In a cabin they found an old man, dressed in the long white robe of a Mussulman patriarch, with the green turban of the sons of the Prophet on his head, playing draughts with a woman. And here, too, Sachturi's order was obeyed.

The booty taken was immense, for on board were presents from the Sultan to the Pasha of Egypt, and when the Turkish ship was no more than a shambles they brought it all on board Sachturi's vessel for division. They found him sitting on the deck, with Yanni's head on his knee. He was quite silent and dry-eyed; he rested his weight on one hand, with the other he was stroking the dead lad's hair.

CHAPTER III

The next fortnight's cruising was well rewarded by the prizes they took, but already symptoms of a dual control in the fleet, and thus of no control at all, had unhappily begun to make appearance. The primates were by no means disposed to forgive the slight which Economos had put upon them, and before long they devised a cunning and unpatriotic scheme of paying in public money, so to speak, their private debt to him. To a certain extent the immediate adoption of his naval plans among the sailors had been due to the hopes he put forward to the islanders of winning large prizes, and the primates, by making a main issue of this secondary desire among them, began to reinstate themselves in power. Much of the booty taken was to be divided on the return of the squadron to Hydra, and Economos, at the suggestion of Tombazes, proposed that one-half of the gains of the cruise should be appropriated to the prosecution of the war. This was an equitable and patriotic suggestion, but coming as it did from Economos the primates opposed it tooth and nail. Equally, too, did it fail to satisfy the more greedy and selfish of his supporters, who cared for nothing but their own aggrandizement.

Economos's proposal had been put forward one afternoon some three days after their return to Hydra, at the sitting of the revolutionary committee, which had been reorganized and included all the primates. Tombazes alone of his class supported Economos, but the matter was still in debate when they rose for the day.

The afternoon had been hot and windless, but an hour before sundown a southerly breeze began to stir, and before long word was brought by a shepherd who had been grazing his flocks on the hill above the town that he had seen a ship under full sail off the southwest, making straight for Hydra. It was known that a Turkish ship had escaped the fate of its consort at Kalamata, but the fleet, though they had kept a lookout for it, had seen nothing of it. Her fate they were to learn later. Tombazes hesitated what to do; the ship might be part of the Turkish squadron which had been cruising off the west coast of Greece; again, it might be the single ship from Kalamata. In the former case they had better look to the defence of their harbor, in the latter it might be possible to man a couple of brigs and give chase.

He determined, however, to wait a little yet; for no other ship had been sighted, and as long as there was but one it would be time to give chase when she declared herself more manifestly. So going down to the quay, where he would meet Economos and other commanders, he mingled with the crowd. Even in so short space the ship had come incredibly nearer, and even as he looked a livelier gust shook out the folds of her flag, and at his elbow some one shouted, "The Capsina; it is the Capsina! It is the Capsina back again!" The flag she carried was blue and on it was the cross of Greece, no crescent anywhere.

On she came, black against the crimson sky, crumpling the water beneath her forefoot. On the quay the crowd thickened and thickened, and soon there came to them across the water a cheer from the ship. At that all throats were opened, and shout after shout went up. For the moment all the jealousies and quarrelling were forgotten, the primates mingled their enthusiasm with the rest, feeling that but for the example so memorably set by the Capsina their pockets would be lighter by all the prize-money they had won; and even Father Nikolas, perhaps the sourest man God ever made, found himself excitedly shaking hands with Economos. After passing the southern point of the harbor the *Sophia* hauled down her mainsail, and three minutes afterwards she had swung round and her anchor chains were screaming out. Before she had well come into harbor fifty boats were racing out to meet her, then one of her own boats was let down, and they saw that tall girlish figure, preceded by Michael and followed by Kanaris, step in.

The elder Christos, with his son and daughter-in-law and grandchild, were the first on the steps when she came ashore. She kissed them affectionately, asking first after one and then the other.

"And what has been doing since I went?" she asked. "I have only heard that certain ships from Hydra have been stinging the Turks very shrewdly, but no more. For me I have not been idle, and two Turkish ships lie on the ooze of the deep sea, and one more I have taken to Nauplia; it will do penance for having served the Turk in now fighting for us. Ah, father," and she held out her hand to Tombazes, "or admiral shall I call you? Here is the truant home again."

But before the evening was out, though the enthusiasm of the people grew higher and higher as the Capsina's deeds went from mouth to mouth, the primates cooled, and Father Nikolas from being positively genial passed through all the stages of subacidity and became more superacid than one would have thought it possible for so small a man to be. For it appeared that Tombazes had dined with her and that she had wished to hand him over at once no less than eight hundred Turkish pounds for the "war fund." Tombazes had told her that at present there was no war fund, and that on this very day a proposal had been made for one, which would without doubt be vetoed on the morrow. At this it seemed that the Capsina stared at him in undisguised amazement, and then said, "We shall see!" Soon after a boy from her house came running into one of the cafés on the quay, which Economos frequented, and said that the Capsina wished to see him immediately.

Economos seemed disposed to finish his game of draughts, but his opponent, no other than the rejected Christos, who was getting the worst of it, rose at once, and swept the men back into their box.

"When the Capsina calls for us we go," he remarked, laconically.

"And when she sends you away you go also, but elsewhere," remarked Economos, who had heard of Christos's dismissal, and with this Parthian shot left the café in a roar.

The elder Christos was also with the Capsina, and when Economos entered she rose.

"You are doing what is right," she said, shaking hands, "and I am with you. So," and she looked severely at her uncle—"so will Christos Capsas be. Sit down. There is wine for you."

Then turning to Tombazes:

"It is quite out of the question not to have a war fund," she said. "On the mainland half of all that is taken goes to it, and the other half, remember, is divided among far more men in proportion to the prizes than we have here. Good God, man!" and she turned to Christos, "how is it possible that you did not see this? And you tell me you were going to vote with the primates. How is the war to be carried on thus? Is the war an affair of a day or two, to last no longer than an autumn's vintage? Already, you tell me, the national treasury is empty. Have you finished the war? for if so, indeed I have not heard the result; or how will you pay the men for the next cruise? How do the numbers go on the question? There are four of us here who will of course vote for the fund."

Tombazes appeared somewhat timorous.

"Capsina," he said, "it is not my fault, you know; but you must remember that you are not on the committee."

The Capsina laughed.

"That is not a matter that need trouble you," she said. "We will see to that to-morrow. The meetings are public, you say. Well, I shall be there—I mean to be on the committee, and of course I shall be. By the Virgin! it would be a strange thing if the head of our clan had no voice in affairs that so concern the island. It is fit also that Kanaris should be of the committee, for though he is a Psarian yet he serves on a Hydriot ship, and it is likely that I shall give him the command of another when I cruise next."

Even the blind faith with which Tombazes regarded the doings of the Capsina was disposed to question this, and Christos moved uneasily in his chair.

"Is it not a little irregular," he asked, "that one of another island should have a voice in the government of Hydra?"

"The war, too, is a little irregular," said the Capsina, "and only in the matters of this war do I propose he should have a vote. Now, father," she went on, "here is this man, one of a thousand, as I know him to be. He and I will fight any two of your ships, and knock them into faggots for the fire quicker than a man could cut them from a tree. He is of Psara, it is true, but he serves Hydra. And he shall have a voice in the matter of the fleet to which he now belongs."

With the admission of the Capsina and Kanaris into the committee, the conclusion would not be so foregone, so thought Tombazes, as it first appeared to him. For their admission he pledged himself to vote, and for the rest he trusted the Capsina.

Long after the others had gone Sophia sat where she was, lost in a sort of eager contentment. The home-coming, the enthusiastic pride and affection of her people, stirred in her a chord she had thought and almost hoped was forever dumb. The wild and splendid adventures of the last weeks, her ardent championship of her race, the fierce and ever growing hatred of their detestable masters, had of late made the sum of her conscious desires. But to-night something of the thrill of home was on her, more than once she had looked half enviously at the small ragged girls who stared at her as she passed, who were most likely never to know anything of the sweet sting of stirring action, but live inactive lives, with affection for ardor, and the care of the children for the cause of a nation. Michael lay at her feet, and she wondered vaguely if it were better to be as she was, or to sit at the feet of a master and be able to call nothing one's own, but only part of another. But to think barren thoughts was never the Capsina's habit, and her mind went forward to the meeting next day.

The meetings were held always on the quay. A table was set, round which sat the four-and-twenty members of the committee, and the people were allowed to stand round and listen to the official utterances. But after the pleasant freshness of hearing Father Nikolas say bitter things to Tombazes, and Tombazes reply with genial contempt or giggle only, had worn off, they were not usually very generally attended. But this morning, an hour before the appointed time, the end of the quay, where the meetings were held, began to fill, chairs and benches were in requisition, and Sachturi's father, the miser of Hydra, by report the richest man of the place, had given two piasters for a seat, which in itself constituted an epoch in the history of finance. By degrees the members of the committee took their places, Tombazes looked round with ill-concealed dismay at the absence of the Capsina, and called for silence. The silence was interrupted by a clear voice.

"Michael, Michael," it said, "come, boy, we are very late." And from the end of the quay came the Capsina, attended by Michael and Kanaris. She walked quickly up through the crowd, which made way for her right and left, stopping now and then to speak to some friend she had not yet seen, and still round the table the silence continued.

Father Nikolas broke it.

"The meeting has been summoned," he said, bitterly. "Am I to suppose it has been summoned for any purpose?"

But Tombazes had his eyes fixed on the Capsina.

"Is the meeting adjourned?" asked Father Nikolas, and the chairman smiled.

The Capsina by this time had made her way up to the table and looked round.

"A chair," she said. "Two chairs. Kanaris, sit by me, please."

She had chosen her place between old Christos and Sachturi, and the two parted, making room for the chairs. Kanaris sat down in obedience to a gesture from her, but she remained standing.

"I have a word to say," she began, abruptly. "Since the clan of Capsas has been in this island, the head of the clan has always had a voice in all national affairs. I have been prevented from attending the former meetings of this particular assembly, because I was perhaps better employed in chasing and capturing Turkish ships. And as head of the clan I take my seat here."

For another moment there was dead silence, and Father Nikolas, in answer, it would appear, to hints from his neighbors, stood up.

"This matter is one on which the vote of the committee is required," he said; "for, as I understand, by its original constitution it possessed the power of adding to its numbers. For myself—"

But Sophia interrupted him.

"Does any one here, besides Father Nikolas," she said, "oppose my election?"

"I did not say—" began Father Nikolas.

"No, father, because I made bold to interrupt you," remarked the Capsina, with dangerous suavity. Then, turning in her place, "This committee, I am told, was elected by the people of Hydra. There is a candidate for election. The chairman shall give you the name."

"The Capsina is a candidate for election," said Tombazes.

Among the primates there was a faint show of opposition. Father Nikolas passed a whispered consultation to his colleagues, and after some delay eight of them, amid derisive yells from the people, voted against her, but her election was thus carried by sixteen to eight. But there was greater bitterness in store for Father Nikolas.

The Capsina again rose, and the shouts died down.

"I have first," she said, "to make a report to the admiral of the Hydriot fleet, to which I belong, as to the doings of my crew and myself. We sailed, as you know, perhaps a little independently, but what we have done we have done for this island. On the second day of my expedition we sank a Turkish vessel, which was cruising for conscription in the harbor at Melos, with all on board. Perhaps some were picked up, but I do not know. On the eighth day we captured a cruiser off Astra, and Kanaris took her into Nauplia, where she will now enter the service of the Greek fleet. On the twelfth day we sank a corvette off the southern cape. There was a heavy sea running, and she went to pieces on the rocks. We have also taken a certain amount of prize-money, the disposition of which I will speak of later. But first there is another matter. Kanaris is by birth a Psarian, but he serves on my ship, and he is willing to continue to serve in the Hydriot squadron. It is right that he should have a voice in the affairs of our expeditions, for I tell you plainly if any man could sail a ship between the two Wolf rocks of Hydra, he is that man. He has been taken into the most intimate councils of the central revolutionary committee, and it is not fit that he should be without a voice here. Also before long he will be in command of the *Sophia*, when a new ship I am building is ready. Father Nikolas will now be good enough to tell us his reasons for his opposing my candidate."

Father Nikolas started as if he had been stung, but then recovering himself, "The Capsina has already stated them," he said. "This man—I did not catch his name—"

"If you reflect," said the Capsina, sternly, "I think you will remember that you did."

Father Nikolas looked round with a wild eye.

"This man," he continued, "is a Psarian. Is that not sufficient reason why he should find no place in a Hydriot assembly?"

"Surely not, father," said the Capsina, "for you, if I mistake not, are by birth a Spetziot; yet who, on that ground, would seek to exclude you from the assembly?"

"The cases are not similar," said Nikolas. "Thirty years ago my father settled here, while it is but yesterday that this Kanaris—"

"I was waiting for that," remarked the Capsina, absently.

A sound came from the chairman almost exactly as if somebody sitting in his place had giggled, and then tried unsuccessfully to convert the noise into a cough, and Father Nikolas peered at him with wrinkled, puckered eyes.

"I will continue," he said, after a pause in which he had eyed Tombazes, who sat shaking with inward laughter, yet not venturing to meet his eye for fear of an explosion. "For ten years I have sat in the assembly of primates, and any dissatisfaction with my seat there should have been expressed thirty years ago, some years, in fact, before she who is now expressing it was born."

The Capsina smiled.

"I think I said that no one would think of expressing, or even perhaps—well, of expressing dissatisfaction," she replied, "and I must object to your putting into my mouth the exact opposite of what you really heard from me."

"Your words implied what I have said," retorted Nikolas, getting white and angry.

"Such is not the case," said the Capsina. "If I were you, I should be less ready to find malignant meanings in words which bear none."

Here Tombazes interfered.

"Father Nikolas," he said, "we are here to discuss matters of national import, and I do not see that you are contributing to them. Kanaris, let me remind you, is a candidate for election."

Kanaris himself all this time was sitting quietly between the Capsina and Sachturi, listening without the least evidence of discomposure to all that was being said. He smiled when Nikolas suddenly blurted out the name of which he was ignorant, but otherwise seemed like a man who supports the hearing of a twice-told tale with extreme politeness. He was rather tall, strongly built, with great square shoulders, and his dress was studiously neat and well cared for. His hair, falling, after the custom of the day, on to his shoulders, was neatly trimmed, and his chin very smoothly shaven. In his hand he held a string of amber beads, which he passed to and fro like a man seated at a café.

Now, however popular the election of the Capsina had been with the people, it was soon clear to her that there was no such unanimity about Kanaris. The islanders were conservative and isolated folk, and they viewed with jealousy and resentment anything like interference on the part of others in their affairs. But for the adoring affection in which they held the girl, without doubt Nikolas's party would have won the day, and, quick as thought, the Capsina determined to make use of the people's championship of herself to gain her ends. She was of a quick tongue, and for the next ten minutes she concentrated the acidity of Nikolas on herself, provoking him by a hundred little stinging sayings, and drawing his attack off from the debate on to herself. At length he turned on her full.

"Already we see the effect of having a woman in our councils," he said. "An hour has passed, and instead of settling affairs of moment our debate is concerned with the management of the monastery rain-water and the color of my hair. This may be useful; I hope it is. But in no way do I see how it bears upon the conduct of the fleet. And it is intolerable that I should be thus exposed in the sight of you all to the wanton insults of this girl." His anger suddenly flashed out. "By the Virgin," he cried, "it is not to be stood! It was an ill day for the clan, let me tell them, when the headship passed into hands like that. I will not submit to this. A Hydriot is she, and where is the husband to whom she was betrothed? I tell you she cares nothing for Hydra, nor for the war, nor for any of you, but only for her own foolhardy, headstrong will."

"Is the Father Nikolas proposing that I should now marry Christos Capsas?" asked Sophia. "That is a fine thing for a primate to say, or is it not since he came to Hydra that my cousin Christos chose a wife for himself?"

Father Nikolas's face expressed an incredible deal of hatred and malice. "This must be stopped," he said; "this woman or I leave the assembly."

"The remedy lies with Father Nikolas," said the Capsina.

Nikolas paused for a moment: his mouth was dry with anger.

"It is not so long ago," he said, "that I heard Hydra proclaimed an independent state, and subject to none. Show me anything more farcical than that! Free, are we? Then who is this who forces herself and her creatures into our assembly? Are we to be the slaves of a woman, or her clan? I, for my part, will be dictated to and insulted by no man, or woman either. The clan of Capsas—who are the clan of Capsas? They are leagued together for their own self-seeking ends."

This was just what Sophia was waiting for. She sprang to her feet, and, turning to the people, "Clan of Capsas!" she cried. "You of the clan!"

In an instant at the clan cry there was a scene of wildest confusion. Old Christos jumped up; Anastasi overturned his chair and stood on the other side of Sophia; Michael raged furiously about in the ecstasy of excitement, and from the crowd that stood round men sprang forward, taking their places in rows behind the Capsina till their ranks stretched half-way down the quay.

Then the Capsina called: "The clan of Capsas is with me?"

And a great shout went up. "It is with you."

She turned to Father Nikolas.

"If you or any other have any quarrel with the clan, name it," she said.

Father Nikolas looked round, but found blank faces only.

"I have no quarrel with the clan," he said, and his voice was the pattern of ill-grace.

"Then," said Sophia, "again I propose Kanaris as a member of this committee."

The appeal to the clan had exactly the effect Sophia intended. It divided the committee up into those for the clan and those against it, and that strong and cheerful phalanx seemed to be terrorizing to waverers. Amid dead silence the votes were given in and counted, and Tombazes announced that Kanaris was elected by sixteen votes to nine.

The business of the war-fund then came before them, and this Sophia opened by handing over to Tombazes eight hundred Turkish pounds, that being half of the prizes of her cruise. Economos, who had been instructed by the Capsina, laid before Tombazes a similar proportion of his takings, and Sachturi and Pinotzi followed the lead.

Some amusement was then caused by Anastasi Capsas, who had been unlucky in the late cruise, gravely presenting to Tombazes the sum of twenty-five piasters, for all that he had taken was a small Turkish rowing-boat which he found drifting after Sachturi's capture of the Turkish ship, and which he had subsequently sold for fifty. Father Nikolas, it was noticed, did not join in the laugh. But a moment afterwards he rose.

"Perhaps the Capsina or the chairman will explain what is meant by the war-fund," he said. "At present I know of no such fund."

The Capsina rose.

"I hear that yesterday there was debate on this matter," she said, "and that Economos proposed that part of the booty taken should be given to a war-fund. Now it is true that nothing was said about this before the last cruise, but I understand that the money raised has been exhausted, and unless you consider that the war is over, I would wish to know how you intend to equip the ships for the next cruise. Or has Hydra tired of the war? Some of our ships have been lucky: Father Nikolas, I believe, took a valuable prize. It is easy, then, for him to defray the expenses of his ship for the next voyage. But with Anastasi Capsas, how will it be? For, indeed, fifty piasters will not go far as the wages of sixty men."

She paused a moment, and went on with growing earnestness.

"Let us be sensible," she said, "and look things between the eyes, as a man looks before he strikes, and not pretend there are no obstacles in the path. We have decided, God be thanked, to be free. This freedom can only be bought dearly, at the cost of lives and money, and by the output of all our strength. We are not fighting to enrich ourselves. Only the short-sighted can fail to see this, and the short-sighted do not make good counsellors. Can any one tell me how we are to man ships for the next cruise, how get powder, how make repairs to our ships? On the mainland they are contributing one-half of all that is taken to the service of the war. Would it become us to ask for funds from them—for, indeed, they are sore pressed for money, and many of them serve without pay or reward. What has Nikolas Vidalis got for his ten years' work, journeying, scheming, risking his all every day? This, as he himself said, the right to serve his country! Is he not wise to count that more worth having than many piasters? Have you heard what happened to the second ship from Kalamata, which put into Nauplia on its way to Constantinople, to bring back men and arms? Two boys followed it out into the bay at Nauplia, ran their caique into the stern, set fire to it, and saved themselves in their small boat. One was a son of Petrobey, the other was Mitsos Codones, the nephew of Nikolas; him I have never seen, but there is a song about the boys' deed which the folk sing. There is their reward, and where should they look for a better? Are we mercenaries? Do we serve another country, not our own? Is the freedom of our country to be weighed against money? But this I would propose—that after our next cruise, should anything of what we give now be left over when the men are paid and the ships fit for use again, let that, if you will, be divided. Only let there never be a ship which cannot go to sea, or is ill-equipped for want of money, which might have been ready had not we taken it for ourselves. Now, if there is aught to say against this, let us hear it. For me, I vote for the war-fund to be made up of half the takings of each ship."

The Capsina's speech won the day, and even a few of the primates went over to her side, leaving, however, a more malignant minority. At the end of the meeting the money was collected, and the Capsina was fairly satisfied with her morning's work.

It was two days after this that word was brought to Hydra by a vessel of Chios, that Germanos, Archbishop of Patros, had need of Economos. The latter had friends and relations in Misolonghi, and as there was a strong garrison of Turks there, it seemed wiser to get the soundings of the place, so said the archbishop, from a man who would move about unsuspected. Therefore, if his work in Hydra was over, let him come. Late that afternoon he had gone to see the Capsina, in order to find out whether any of her vessels were by chance going to Nauplia or some mainland port, and could put him on his way.

"For my work here is finished, or so I think," he said. "Only this morning, indeed, I met Father Nikolas, who alone has been more detrimental to the cause than even the Turks; but he seemed most friendly to me, and regretted that I was going."

The Capsina was combing out Michael's ruff after his bath, and was not attending very closely. But at these words she left the comb in Michael's hair and looked up.

"What is that?" she said.

"I met Father Nikolas an hour ago," said Economos; "he thanked me for all I had done here, and said that he had hoped I was stopping longer. In fact, I think he has quite withdrawn all his opposition."

Now the Capsina had excellently sure reason for knowing that the primate still harbored the bitterest grudge against Economos for having first proposed and eventually carrying the institution of the war-fund, and her next question seemed at first strangely irrelevant.

"Do you walk armed?" she asked.

"Not in Hydra."

She drew the comb out of Michael's ruff, and clapped her hands. The servant came in at the summons.

"I want to see Kanaris," she said. "Send for him at once."

She stood silent a moment or two, until the servant had left the room, and then turned to Economos.

"I don't really know what to say to you," she remarked, "or how to account for my own feelings. But it is borne in upon me that you are in danger. Nikolas friendly and genial to you! It is not in the man. He is genial to none. That he should be genial to you of all men is impossible. Afterwards I will tell you why. Come, what did he say to you?"

"He asked me to sup with him this evening," said Economos, "and I told him that for aught I knew I might be gone before."

"He asked you to sup with him?" said the Capsina, frowning. "God send us understanding and charity! But really—" and she broke off, still frowning. Then after a pause:

"Look you," she said, "I do not know much of Father Nikolas, but this I know, that you can have no enemy more bitter. He took, so you tell me, a valuable prize in this last cruise. It is you, so he thinks, who has deprived him of half of it, and certainly it is you and I between us who have done so. Now the man has good things in him. I am trying, you understand, to put together these good things, his certain hatred of you, and his asking you to supper. Did you notice how he winced when at the meeting the other day I said: 'You are a Spetziot, but *for that reason* we would not turn you out of our assembly,' I think he knew what I meant, though my words can have meant nothing but what they seemed to say, except to him, Kanaris, and to me. It is this: He is a primate, but he is married, and fifteen years ago the Turks carried off his wife, who is a cousin of Kanaris, from Spetzas. Now I believe that the one aim of his life is to bring her back. She is in Athens, and he knows where. Man, you have taken half the ransom out of his closed pocket, I may say. Does he love you much? And if a Spetziot does not love he hates, and when he hates he kills. Why, then, did he ask you to supper?"

"You mean, he intended to kill me?"

"Yes, I mean that," said the Capsina.

"The treacherous villain—"

"No doubt, but think what you have done. Now, without unreasonable risk to you, I want to be certain about this, for Nikolas, I know, will give trouble. I am going to send you off to-night in the *Sophia*, to be landed at Kranidi. But I want you to leave this house alone, and walk down to the quay alone. There is not much danger; your way lies through the streets, and, at worst, if my guess about Nikolas is right, he will try to have you knifed. He dare not have you shot in the town, but a man's throat can be cut quietly. Man, what are you afraid of? Indeed, I wish I was you. But here is Kanaris. Kanaris, did you see or speak to any one on your way up here?"

"Yes, to Dimitri, the servant of Nikolas. He was coming out of a shop."

"What shop?"

"Vasto's shop."

"They sell knives in Vasto's shop," remarked the Capsina. "Well, what did he say to you?"

"He asked if Economos was with you. And I said that I thought so."

"That is, then, very pretty. Kanaris, you are to take Economos over to Kranidi to-night. He will leave this house in an hour exactly. You will wait for him in that dark corner by Christos's house, and keep your eyes open. Why? Because Dimitri will not be far off, and he will try to knife him. Dimitri, I am afraid, must be shot. Economos will do the shooting, but he must not shoot towards the dark corner of Christos's house, or there may be a Kanaris the less. Mind that, Economos. If he shoots not straight, Dimitri will probably run down towards the quay, where he will mix with the crowd. It shall then be Kanaris's business to stop him. Or he may run up here. It shall then be my business."

Presently after Kanaris went down to the harbor to get the *Sophia* ready for sea. With a fair wind it was only two hours to Kranidi. The navigation was simple: a dozen men could work the ship, and they would be back before morning.

The Capsina took down two pistols, and proceeded to tell Economos what he was to do. He must walk straight to the quay and quickly. He must stop to speak to no man, and not fire unless attacked. She would be in the shadow of her own gate, Kanaris at the lower end of the street, where it opened on to the quay, so that should any attempt be made on his life the assassin would be hemmed in on both sides.

"Yet, yet," she said, hesitating, "ought I to warn Nikolas that I know? It seems a Turkish thing to do, to set a trap for a man. Really, I am afraid I should do

43

the same to you if I were he, only I think I should have the grace to kill you myself, for I cannot think I would have my dirty work done for me, and I should not be such a fool as to ask you to supper. I don't want this wretched Dimitri to be killed—I wonder what Nikolas has paid him? Yes, it shall be so; one who attacks in the dark for no quarrel of his own will be ever a coward. So shoot in the air, only to show you are armed, and leave Dimitri to me."

At the end of the hour Economos rose to go. The Capsina went with him to the gate, and from the shadow looked cautiously out down the road. The far end of it, a hundred and fifty yards off, opened on to the brightly lighted quay, and against the glare she saw the figure of a man silhouetted by the long creeper-covered wall to the right of the road.

"Yes, that is Dimitri," she whispered. "Begone, and God-speed. Don't shoot, except to save your own life. Run rather."

She stepped back under cover of her gate, and looked after Economos. He had not gone more than twenty yards when she heard a quick but shuffling step coming down towards her from above, and, looking up, saw Father Nikolas. Standing as she did, in a shadowed embrasure, he passed her by unnoticed, and went swiftly and silently across the road, and waited in the shadow of the opposite wall. He had passed so close to her that she could almost have touched him. Then for a moment there was silence, save only for the sounds of life on the quay and the rapid step of Economos, getting fainter every second. Then came a sudden scuffle, a shot, and the steps of a running man getting louder every moment. She was just about to step out and stop him, when Father Nikolas advanced from opposite. The man gave a little sobbing cry of fright, till he saw who it was.

"You have failed," said Nikolas, in a low voice.

"Yes, and may the curses of all the saints be upon you!" cried Dimitri. "You told me he went unarmed. You told me—Ah, God! who is that?"

The Capsina stepped out of the shadow.

"Yes, he has failed," she said. "And you, too, have failed. This is a fine thing for the Church of Hydra. Man, stop where you are. Not a step nearer. I, too, am armed. By God," she exclaimed, suddenly, rising an octave of passion and contempt, and throwing her pistol over the gate into her garden, "come a step nearer if you dare, you or your hired assassin—I am unarmed. You dare not, you dare not commit your murders yourself, you low, sneaking blackguard, who would kill men under the guise of friendship. You asked Economos to supper to-night, regretting he was going so soon: that would have been the surest way! Instead, you send another to cut his throat in the dark. You have failed," and she laughed loud, but without merriment. "A fine, noble priest are you! Hydra is proud of you, the clan delights in you! In the name of the clan I pay you my homage and my reverence."

Not a word said Father Nikolas.

"So you have no reply ready," she went on. "Indeed, I do not wonder. And for you, Dimitri, is it not shame that you would do the bidding of a man like this? Now, tell me at once, what did he give you for this?"

"If you dare tell—" whispered Nikolas.

"Oho! So there is perhaps something even more splendid and noble to come! If you dare *not* tell, rather," said Sophia. "Quick, man, tell me quickly."

The man fell on his knees.

"Capsina, I dare not tell you all," he said. "But I have a disgraceful secret, and Father Nikolas knew it. He threatened me with exposure."

The Capsina turned to Nikolas.

"So—this grows dirtier and more ugly, and even more foolish than I thought, for I did you too much justice. Devil I knew you were, but I gave you the credit for being cunning. It is not very safe for a man like you to threaten exposure, is it?"

And she turned and went a step nearer to him.

Father Nikolas, in a sudden frenzy, ran a couple of steps towards her, as if he would have seized her. For answer she struck him in the face.

"That for you," she said, suddenly flaming again into passion—"that for you; go and tell the primates that I have struck a priest. It is sacrilege, I believe, and never was I more satisfied with a deed. Run, tell them how I have struck you, and get me punished. Sacrilege? Is it not sacrilege when a man like you shows the people the blessed body and blood? You are afraid of man, it seems —for you dared not touch Economos yourself—but it seems you hold God in contempt. You living lie, you beast! Stand still and listen."

And she told Dimitri the story of Nikolas's marriage. Then, turning again: "So that is quits," said she, "between you."

Then to Nikolas: "Now go," she said, "and remember you are in the hollow of my hand. Will you come at night and try to kill me? I think not."

Nikolas turned and went without a word.

The Capsina saw him disappear, and then spoke to Dimitri.

"You poor, wretched creature!" she said. "You have had a lesson to-night, I am thinking. Go down on your knees—not to me, but to the blessed Jesus. I

45

forgive you? That is no word from one man to another. Go to the church, man, or to your home, or even here, and be sorry."

"Capsina! oh Capsina!" sobbed the man.

Sophia felt strangely moved, and she looked at him with glistening eyes.

"You poor devil! oh, you poor devil!" she said. "Just go by yourself alone somewhere and think how great a brute you are. Indeed, you are not a fine man, and I say this with no anger, but with very much pity. You had no grudge against Economos. Yet because you were afraid you would do this thing. Thank God that your fear saved you, your miserable fear of an ounce of lead. What stuff are you made of, man? What can matter less than whether you live or die? Yet it matters very much how you live and how you die. There, shake hands and go."

CHAPTER IV

The fleet put to sea again in the last week of May, cruising in the Archipelago, eager for the spring coming of the Ottoman ships. They took a northeasterly course, and on the 5th of June sighted a single Turkish man-of-war to the north of Chios. But it put about, before they were in range to attack, and ran before them to the mainland, anchoring in the harbor of Erissos, beneath the walls of the Turkish fort. To attack it there at close quarters meant exposure to the fire from the fort as well; moreover, the harbor was nearly landlocked, and thoroughly unsuited to that rapidity of manoeuvre by which alone these little hawks could dare attack the ravens of the Turkish fleet, for, except when the sea-breeze blew, it lay nigh windless. Tombazes could scarce leave it to sail south, but his plan of action was determined by the appearance, on the morning of the 6th of June, of more Ottoman ships from the north—a man-of-war, three frigates, and three sloops—and before noon news arrived from a Greek town called Aivali, farther up the Asiatic coast, that the garrison of Turks had been suddenly increased in the town.

Here, then, was work sufficient: the single Turk must not sail south, the fresh convoy of ships must be stopped, and help must be sent to Aivali. What this increase of garrison might mean, Tombazes could not conjecture, but he told off fifteen vessels to follow the Turkish ships, while the rest waited at Erissos to destroy the blockaded vessel at all costs and with all speed, and then sail on to Aivali. A meeting of the captains was held on the admiral's ship, and it was resolved to attempt the destruction of the Turk by fire. A Psarian in the fleet was said to know the use and handling of fire-ships, and one was prepared, but badly managed, and the only result was that two of its crew were first nearly roasted and then completely drowned. However, on the following day another Psarian volunteered to launch one, which was managed with more conspicuous success. The boat was loaded with brushwood, and brushwood and sails were soaked in turpentine. It set off from the fleet while it was yet dark, and, conveniently for the purpose, a white mist lay over the harbor. The air was windless, and it had to be rowed swiftly and silently up to the anchorage of the Turk. They had approached to within a cable's length when they were sighted from on board the enemy, but the captain of the fire-ship, Pappanikolo, knowing that a few moments more would see the work done, urged the men on, and drove his boat right into the bows of the Turk, contriving to entangle his mast in the bowsprit ropes. Then, bidding his men jump into the boat they towed behind, he set fire to the ship and rowed rapidly off. A few muskets only were fired at them, and they escaped unhurt. Not so their victim. In a moment the fire-ship blazed from stem to stern, pouring such vast clouds of smoke up from the brushwood, which was not quite dry, that it was impossible for those on board or from the fort to reach the seat of the flames. Many of the sailors jumped overboard and swam to land, but the ship itself burned on till the fire reached the powder-magazine and exploded it.

This being done, the remainder of the Greek fleet weighed anchor and went north again. While rounding Lesbos they met the ships which had pursued the rest of the Ottoman fleet returning. They, too, had shunned the Greeks, but with the south wind had escaped into the Dardanelles, where the Greeks had not ventured to follow. Most of the pursuing vessels had been of the primates, and the Capsina expressed her scorn in forcible language.

Aivali was a wealthy commercial town in the pashalik of Brusa and on the coast of Asia Minor. Since the outbreak of the war several similar Greek towns had been plundered by irregular bands of Turks, and the pasha, seeing that his revenues were largely derived from Aivali, for it was the home of many wealthy Greeks, was personally very anxious to save it. Thus the troops which, as Tombazes had been truly informed, had been sent there, were designed not for its destruction but its preservation. But the news of the destruction of the ship at Erissos had raised the excitement of the Turkish population at Aivali and desire for revenge to riot point, and already several Greeks had been murdered in the streets. Such was the state of things when Tombazes' fleet dropped anchor outside the harbor.

That night, under cover of the darkness, came a deputation to the admiral. Unless he helped them their state was foregone. Their protectors would no doubt guarantee them their lives, but at the sacrifice of all their property; but, as seemed certain if the Turkish population rose against them (for they had heard that irregular bands of soldiers were marching on the town), the luckier of them would be murdered, the fairer and less fortunate sold as slaves. They appealed to Tombazes to rescue them, and take them off on the fleet, and this he guaranteed his best efforts to do.

Aivali was built on a steep hill-side running up from the sea. The lower ground was occupied with wharves and shipping-houses, then higher up came the manufacturing quarter, consisting mainly of oil-mills, and on the crest of the hill the houses of the wealthier inhabitants. It was these which would be the first prey to the mob.

Early next morning Tombazes landed a company of soldiers to protect the families who embarked. The troops of the pasha, who wished to prevent any one leaving the town, replied by occupying a row of shops near the quay, and keeping up a heavy musket fire on the troops and the ships. Meantime the news that the Greek fleet would take off the inhabitants was over the town, and a stream of civilians had begun to pour down. The soldiers returned the fire of the Turks, while these were embarked in small boats and taken out to the ships; but the odds were against them, for their assailants were firing from shelter. But suddenly a shout went up from the fleet as the *Sophia* weighed anchor, and, hoisting her sails, came close in, shouldering and crashing through a line of fishing-boats, risking the chance of grounding. Then, turning her broadside to the town, she opened on the houses occupied by the Turks, firing over the heads of the soldiers and embarking population. The first broadside knocked one shop to pieces, and in a couple of minutes the Turks, most of the regular troops, were swarming out of houses like ants when their hill is disturbed, and flying to some position less exposed to the deadly and close fire of the *Sophia*.

Simultaneously the Greeks of the town, fearing that this occupation of the houses lower down by the regular troops should cut off their escape, in turn occupied some houses in the rear, and kept up another fire on them. Between the *Sophia* and them the troops were fairly outclassed, and the line of retreat for the population was clear again.

But this engagement of the regular troops with the Greeks gave the rabble of the Turkish population the opportunity they desired. They rushed to the bazaar and rifled the shops, spoiling and destroying what they did not take; and, after leaving the quarter gutted and trampled, made up the hill to the houses of the wealthiest merchants, from which the Greeks were even now fleeing, and captured not only goods, but women and children. Unless some speedy move was made by the troops, it was clear that the bulk of the population would escape or fall into the murderous hands of the rabble; and unable, under the guns of the *Sophia*, to make another attempt to hold the quay against the Greeks, they set fire to various houses in a line with the shore, that a barrier of flames might cut off the lower town from the upper. Meantime they collected again at the square which lay to the left of the town, with the purpose of making another formed attack on the troops on the beach. The Greek soldiers seeing this, as it was now hopeless to try to save the town from burning, themselves set fire to another row of houses at right angles to the beach in order to cut them off from the line of embarkation, and between the quay and the new position taken up by the Turkish troops. In a short time both fires, under the ever-freshening sea-breeze took hold in earnest.

Meantime boat-load after boat-load of the sailors had put to land; among the first, when the guns of the *Sophia* were no longer needed, being the Capsina and Kanaris, with some two dozen of the crew. They went up the town to help in protecting the line of retreat, and the fires being then only just begun, passed the oil-mills, and reached the wealthier quarter. The Turkish population, seeing they were armed, ran from them, and in an hour, having satisfied themselves that the upper quarter of the town was empty, turned back again towards the sea. But suddenly from some quarter of a mile in front of them rose a huge pillar of smoke and fire, and with it a deep roaring sound as if all the winds of heaven had met together. Kanaris first saw what it was.

"Quick, quick," he said, "it is an oil-mill caught! There is a whole row of them below us!"

They hurried on, but before they had gone many yards they saw at the end of the street down which they were to pass another vast volume of flame break out, sweeping across to the opposite houses in long tongues of fire. From inside the mill came a crash, and next moment a river of flaming oil flowed out and down the street. To pass that way was impossible, and they turned back to make a détour to the other side of the town, away from the quarter where the troops were assembled. But before ten minutes had passed a dozen more mills had taken fire, and when at length they had passed the extremity of the line of fire, and came out on the quay, it was to find the beach empty, and the boats no longer at the shore. The torrent of flaming oil had poured down the steep and narrow streets, and thence across the quay over on to the water, where it floated, still blazing, and a belt of fire some thirty feet broad lined the water along the bay. The charred posts on the edge of the harbor-wall were hissing and spluttering, sending out every now and then little lilac-colored bouquets of flame, and it was somehow across that burning canal that their retreat lay.

The Capsina stood still a moment and then broke out into a laugh.

"We shall get through tighter places together, Kanaris," she said. "See, the oil has already ceased flowing, but we cannot stop here. The troops may be down again. Look you, there is only one way. A run, a good long breath, a dive; if we catch fire, next moment the water will put it out—and up again when we are past the flames. It is not more than thirty feet."

Meantime the Turkish troops hearing that one party, at any rate, of the Greeks was still in the town, and thinking that all retreat by the beach was now cut off, had stationed themselves away to the left beyond the flames. The Capsina waved her hand to them.

"No, no, we don't go that way, gentlemen!" she cried, and next moment she had run the dozen scorching and choking yards across the quay and plunged into the flames. Kanaris followed, and after him the others with a shout. The Turks, seeing this, discharged their muskets at them, but ineffectually. A moment later a boat had put off from the *Sophia*, and, as they rose safe beyond the flames they were dragged on board dripping, yet strangely exhilarated and thrilled with adventure.

The deck of the *Sophia* was packed with men, women, and children rescued from the sacked and burning town, and strange and pathetic were their stories. Many did not know whether their families had been saved or not, for in the panic and confusion of their flight the children perhaps had been carried off in the boat from one ship, the parents in another. Some had come on board with nothing but the clothes they were in, others had dragged with them bags of money and valuables, but all were in a distraught amazement at the suddenness of the hour which had left them homeless. The sun was already sinking when the Capsina got back to her ship, but the glow of the sunset paled before that red and lurid conflagration in the town, and after dark, when the land breeze set in, the breath of it was as if from some open-mouthed furnace, and the air was thick with ashes and half-consumed sparks, making the eyes and throat grow raw and tingling with smoke. So, weighing anchor, they sailed out to the mouth of the harbor, some miles away from the burning town, where the heat was a little assuaged and the air had some breath of untainted coolness in it.

By next day the fire had died down, a smouldering of charred beams and eddying white ashes had taken the place of blazing houses and impenetrable streets, and once more the town was searched for any Greeks that remained. Some few were found, but in no large numbers; and that afternoon the fleet turned south again to give the homeless a refuge on one or other of the revolted islands. Many of the able-bodied at once enlisted themselves in the service of the revolutionists, others seemed apathetic and stunned into listlessness, and a few, and these chiefly among the older men and women, would have slunk back again, like cats, preferring a ruined and wrecked home to new and unfamiliar places.

Throughout August and September the fleet made no combined cruise; some ships assisted at the blockade of Monemvasia, others made themselves red in the bloody and shameful work at Navarin. Then for a time all eyes and breathless lips were centred on the struggle going on at Tripoli; the armies and ships alike paused, watching the development of that inevitable end.

Autumn and early winter saw the Capsina at Hydra, busily engaged in building another ship on the lines of the *Sophia*, but with her characteristic points even more developed. She was going to appoint Kanaris to command the old *Sophia*, and to sail the new one herself. December saw her launched, and about the middle of January the Capsina took her a trial-trip up as far as Nauplia.

It was one of those Southern winter days which are beautiful beyond all capacity of comprehension. There was a sparkle as if of frost in the air, but the sun was a miracle of brightness, and the wind from the southeast kindly and temperate. The sea was awake, and its brood of fresh young waves, laced here and there with a foam so white that one could scarcely believe it was of the same stuff as those blue waters, headed merrily up the gulf, and the beautiful new boat, still smelling aromatically of fresh-chiselled pine wood, seemed part of that laughing crowd, so lightly did it slip on its way, and with a motion so fresh and springing. From the time she left the harbor of Hydra till she rounded the point of Nauplia, her white sails were full and brimming with the following wind, and it was little past noon when they swung round to the anchorage.

All that afternoon the Capsina was busy, for there were many friends to see, and she spent some time on the Turkish ship which she had captured in the spring and which was being made ready for sea again; and all the time her heart was full, she knew not why, of a wonderful great happiness and expectancy. The busy, smiling people on the quay, the sparkle of the gulf, the great pine-clad hills rising up towards the fallen Tripoli, her own new ship lying at anchor in the foreground—these were all sweet to her, with a curious intimacy of sweetness. Her life tasted good; it all savored of hopes and aims, or fine memories of success, and she felt a childlike happiness all day that did not reason, but only enjoyed.

She was to sleep on board that night, returning to Hydra next day, and about the time of sunset she was sitting with Kanaris on the quay, talking to him and a Naupliot friend. The sky was already lit with the fires of the west sun, and the surface of the bay, still alive with little waves, was turning molten under the reflection. A small fishing-boat, looking curiously black against that ineffable blaze, was beating up to the harbor, and it gave the Capsina the keen pleasure of one who knows to see how well it was being handled. These small craft, as she was aware, were not made to sail close to the wind, but it seemed to her that a master who understood it well was coaxing it along, as a man with a fine hand will make a nervous horse go as he chooses. She turned to Kanaris.

"See how well that boat is handled," she said. "She will make the pier on this tack."

Kanaris looked up and judged the distance with a half-closed eye.

"I think not," he said. "It cannot be brought up in one tack."

The Capsina felt strangely interested in it.

"I wager you a Turkish pound it can and will," she cried. "Oh, Kanaris! you and I have something to learn from him who sails it."

The Capsina won her pound, to her great delight, and the boat drew up below them at the steps. It was quite close under the wall, so that they could only see the upper part of its masts, but from it there came a voice singing very pleasantly, with an echo, it seemed, of the sea in it, and it sang a verse of the song of the vine-diggers.

Up the steps came the singer, from the sea and the sun. His stature was so tall as to make by-standers seem puny. His black hair was all tousled and wet. He was quite young, for his chin and cheek were smooth, and the line of mustache on his upper lip was yet but faintly pencilled. Over his shoulder he carried a great basket of fish, supporting it freshly, you would say, and without effort, and the lad stood straight under a burden for two men. His shirt was open at the neck, showing a skin browned with the wind and the glare of the water, and the muscles stood out like a breastplate over the bone. His feet were bare and his linen trousers tucked up to his knees. And it was good also to look at his face, for the eyes smiled and the mouth smiled—you would have said his face was a smile.

The Capsina drew a long, deep breath. All the wonderful happiness of the day gathered itself to a point and was crowned.

"Who is that?" she asked the Naupliot, who was sitting with her.

"That? Do you not know? Who but the little Mitsos? Hi lad, what luck?"

Mitsos looked round a moment, but did not stop.

"My luck," he said. "But I must go first to Dimitri. I am late, and he wants his fish. For to-day I am not a free man, but a hireling. But I will be back presently, Anastasi, and remember me by this."

And with one hand he picked out a small mullet from his basket, threw it with a swift and certain aim at Anastasi's face, and ran laughing off.

So Mitsos ran laughing off, and a moment afterwards Anastasi got up too.

"We had better go," he said to Kanaris, "or the market will be closed, and you want provisions you say."

"Ah, yes," said the Capsina, "it is good that I have you to think for me, Kanaris, for I declare the thing had gone from my mind. Let them be on board to-night, so that we can sail with day."

The two went off together towards the town, and Sophia was alone.

"Some one from the sun and the sea"—her own words to Michael came back to her—"and you shall be his, and the ship shall be his, and I shall be his." The dog was lying at her feet, and she touched him gently with her toe.

"And will you be his, Michael? Will you be Mitsos's?" she said. "And what of me?"

Surely this was the one from the sun and the sea, of whom she had not dreamed, but of whom she could imagine she had dreamed, he who had gone at night and burned that great ship from Kalamata, returning, perhaps, as he had returned this evening, laughing with a jest for a friend and a ready aim, of whose deed the people sang. She had wondered a hundred times what Mitsos was like, but never had she connected him with the one of whom she spoke to Michael.

She rose from her seat and went to lean over the quay wall. She was convinced not in thought—for just now she did not think, but only feel beyond the shadow of doubt—that Mitsos was ... was, not he whom she looked for, her feeling lacked that definiteness, but he for whom she would wait all her life. He was satisfying, wholly, utterly; the stir and rapture of glorious adventure had seized him as it had seized her; the aims of their lives were one, and was not that already a bond between them? He was a man of his arm, and his arm was strong; a man of his people, and a man not of houses but of the out-of-doors. She had taken him in at one glance, and knew him from head to heel: black hair, black eyes, a face one smile, but which could surely be stern and fiery; for any face so wholly frank as that would mirror the soul as still water mirrors the sky, the long line of arm bare to the shoulder, trousers all stained, as was meet, with salt and sailing gear, the long, swelling line of calf down to feet which were firm and fit to run—surely this was he for whom she had been designed and built, and she was one, she knew, at whom men looked more than once. And her heart broke into song, soaring....

"UP THE STEPS CAME THE SINGER, FROM THE SEA AND THE SUN"

She stood up, a tall, stately figure, yet girlish, still looking out to sea. He had left his boat below the wall; he had said he would be back soon, and she meant to wait his coming. The wind was strong, and a coil of her glorious hair came unfastened, and she raised her hands to pin it up again; her skirt was blown tight and clinging against the long, slim lines of her figure, her jacket doubled back against itself by the wind, and like Mitsos, perhaps with thinking of him, her face was one smile.

The sun had quite set, but over the sky eastward came the afterglow of the day, turning the thin skeins of cloud to fiery fleeces, and flooding the infinite depth of the sky with luminous red. Behind her the town flushed and glowed, and the white houses were turned to a living gold. After a while she faced round again, for she heard steps coming, and seemed to know that it was Mitsos back again.

"Oh, Anastasi!" cried a voice, "but is there not a fool waiting behind that corner with a good fish to throw and waste? Take it home to your supper, man, and thank God for a dinner you have not earned except in that you have a large face easy to hit. Eh, do you think I cannot see you? You'll be thought a fine hand at hiding, will you?"

Mitsos advanced cautiously, for he was meaning to go to his boat, where he had left his coat and shoes, and the boat lay behind a corner most convenient for a hiding man. The Capsina was standing close by, and Michael bared his teeth as Mitsos came up.

"Fool, Michael!" said the Capsina; "is it not he?"

Then as Mitsos got within speaking distance—

"Anastasi has gone," she said; "you were over quick, were you not, at seeing him?"

Mitsos laughed, but paused a moment as Michael made the circuit of him, sniffing suspiciously.

"This is what I never entirely enjoy," he said, standing still. "Now no man can go sniffing round my bones and have a sound head on his shoulders. But there is less sport, so I take it, in fighting a dog. Ah, he is satisfied, is he? That is for the good. But where is fishy Anastasi?"

"He went to the market with Constantine Kanaris to buy provisions."

"Is Constantine Kanaris here?" asked the boy. "No, I know him not; but Nikolas Vidalis, the best man God ever made, and my uncle, knew him for a fine man. But why, if Kanaris is here she is here, for he serves with her."

"She! Who?"

"Who but the Capsina? I would give gold money to see her. Why—" Mitsos stopped short, and Sophia laughed.

"Thus there is double pleasure," she said, "for I, too, have often wished to see the boy of whom the people sing. Yes, I am the Capsina; why not?"

Mitsos's big eyes grew round and wide.

"What must you have thought of me?" he said. "But indeed I did not know—"

and he bent down from his great height and would have kissed the hand she held out to him.

"Not so!" she cried, laughing; "they of Maina and we are equal."

"That is true," said Mitsos, standing upright a moment; "but where is her equal who took three Turkish ships?" and bending again he kissed it.

"Yet a lad I have heard of burned a ship of war," said she.

Mitsos flushed a little under his brown skin.

"That was nothing," he said, "and, indeed, but for my cousin Yanni there would have been no burning." Then changing the subject quickly: "You came to-day only, Capsina? Surely you will not go again to-morrow." Then, "Ah," he cried, "but I, too, am going to sea, so I may say, with you, for I am to be of the crew of the Turk you brought in here. But you will have a fleet soon!"

"I cannot have too many brave men to work with," said Sophia. "But you under me! Lad, you could sail a double course while I sailed single. Though I have known you perhaps ten minutes, yet you have made me the richer," and she held out the Turkish pound she had won from Kanaris, telling him how she had gained it.

Mitsos grinned with pleasure.

"Well, I think I do know this bay," he said, "for indeed I must have been more hours on it than in the house. But, oh, Capsina, when will that Turkish ship you took be ready for sea, for indeed it eats my heart to go catching fish when I should be catching Turks."

"They tell me in six weeks," she said, "but they seem a little slow about it all. They want more speediness. See you, Mitsos," she said, then stopped.

Mitsos looked up.

"See you," she said again. "Kanaris after this takes command of the old *Sophia*. I want some one who knows the sea, and who is better at home on a ship than on his own feet, to be under me: or it is hardly that—to be with me, as Kanaris will tell you. Come. I sail from here to-morrow, or I will even wait for two days or three: or if that is not time sufficient for you—yet what do you want, for your hands and feet you carry with you?—you can join me as soon as maybe at Hydra. So. It is an offer."

"Then to none other shall it now be offered," said Mitsos. "And what shall I want with two days or three? See, I will sail home now on the instant across the bay, to say good-bye to those at home, and they I know will be blithe to let me go, or rather would think scorn of me if I stopped and went not; and what does a man want with two days or three days to sigh or be sighed over? For my life I could never see that. Oh, Capsina, may God send us great winds and many Turks! I am off now; I am a fool with words, and how gratefully I thank you I cannot tell you. And Dimitri has never paid me my day's wage. May he grow even fatter on it!"

The Capsina laughed with pleasure.

"You go quick enough to please me," she said, "and that is very quick. And I hope, too, I may be found satisfactory, for indeed you do not stop to think what sort of a woman I may be to get on with."

"You are the Capsina," said Mitsos, with sturdy faith.

"You find that good guarantee? So do I that you are Mitsos; little Mitsos, they call you, do they not? That will be the name you'll hear from me, for indeed you are very big."

"And growing yet," said Mitsos, going down the steps to his boat. "Well, this is a fortunate day for me. I will be at your ship again in three hours, or four, if this wind does not hold. My homage, Capsina."

"And mine, little Mitsos."

He shoved his boat out from the wall, and she stood with sails flapping and shivering till he pulled her out from under shelter. Then with a heel over and a gathering whisper of water she shot out into the bay, and faded, still followed by the Capsina's gaze, into the dim starlit dusk.

So he was coming—he. Surely there could be no mistake about it all. A stranger, she had seen a stranger at sunset on the quay, and her heart had embraced him as its betrothed. Only an hour, less than an hour, had passed, and as if to confirm the certainty, all arrangements had been made, and this very night he would be on her ship. Day after day they would range the great seas together with one aim and purpose.

How could it fail that that welding should leave them one? Had not her soul leaped out to him? How strange such a meeting was, yet not strange, for it was the inevitable thing of her life. How impossible that they should not have met, and met, too, at this very time, she in the height of her freedom and success—yet, oh, how ready to be free no longer!—he, just when he hungered to be up and throwing himself against the Turk. Michael, too, surely Michael knew, for when Mitsos was going off again, he had walked down to the bottom step above the water and watched him set off, wagging his tail in acceptance of him. She would have wagered herself and the brig and Michael that they were all going up to heaven.

Presently after came Kanaris from the market, and he whistled across to the ship that it should send a boat to take them off. He was surprised to find the Capsina still on shore, supposing she would have gone back to supper on the ship, or would be with some friend in Nauplia. Indeed, a friend had gone seeking her on her ship, bidding her to sup with him, but she, wishing still to be alone, had said she was just going home. This was half an hour ago, and she lingered yet on the quay with Michael for guard. As they sat watching for the boat, hearing the rhythmical and unseen plash of oars getting nearer, this struck Kanaris.

"You have supped, Capsina?" he asked.

She looked up.

"Supped?" she said. "I don't think I have. Indeed, I am sure I have not. I am hungry. I got to looking at the sky and the water, Kanaris, as one does on certain days, when there is no wind at sea, and it is certain I forgot about supper. Surely I have not supped. We will sup on the ship when we get back, and, as we sup, we will talk. Yes, I have been thinking a big cargo of thought. I will tell you of it."

They were rowed back across the plain of polished harbor water, and went on board in silence. Supper was soon ready—a dish of eggs, a piece of the broiled shoulder of a roe-deer, which the Mayor Dimitri had sent to the Capsina with a present of wine and cakes made of honey. And when they had eaten, Sophia spoke of her plans.

"Kanaris," she said, "I have found him who will take, your place when you have command of the old *Sophia*, as you will on this next cruise. Oh, be tender with her, man, and remember, as I have always said, that she must be humored. She will sail to a head wind if you do not overburden her, but too much sail, though no more than others carry, would ever keep her back. Ah, well, you know her as well as I do. What was I saying? Oh yes, Mitsos Codones, the little Mitsos, you know, will join me here; he who gained me a pound this afternoon. He sails with me in place of the Captain Kanaris."

Now the offer of the presidency of Greece would have been less to the taste of Kanaris than the command of the *Sophia*, and his gratitude, though not eloquent, was sincere. But presently after the Capsina, looking up, saw doubt in his eye.

"Well?" she said.

"It is this," said Kanaris, "though indeed it is no business of mine. Mitsos is but a lad, and, Capsina, what do you know of him? Surely this afternoon he was a stranger to you."

Sophia smiled, and with a wonderful frank kindness in her black eyes.

"And you, Kanaris," she said. "Did not a strange sea-captain come to Hydra one evening? Did he not talk with me—how long—ten minutes? And was not a bargain struck on his words? Was that so imprudent a job? By all the saints, I think I never did a better!"

"But he is so young, this Mitsos," said Kanaris.

"Am I so old? We shall both get over it."

Kanaris filled his glass, frowning.

"But it is different: you are the Capsina."

"And he is of the Mainats. That is as good a stock as ours, though our island proverb says we are the prouder. And, indeed, I am not sure we are the better for that, for I would sooner have Mitsos here than, than Christos."

The Capsina, it must be acknowledged, found an intimate pleasure in putting into plain words what Kanaris could not let himself conjecture in thought.

"Christos?" he said. "Well, certainly. And if, he being a cousin of yours, I may speak without offence, it would be a very bold or a very foolish man who would wish to have Christos only to depend on in the sailing of a war brig."

"And the sailing of my brig will be the work of Mitsos," said Sophia. "Oh, Kanaris, you have lost a pound, and how bitter you are made."

Kanaris laughed.

"Well, God knows he can sail a boat," he said. "My pocket knows it."

"Then why look farther for another and a worse?" said the Capsina.

Kanaris was silent; the Capsina had hinted before that she meant him to command the *Sophia* in the next cruise, but he had yet had no certain word from her. And, indeed, his ambition soared no higher, and to no other quarter —to command the finest brig but one in the island fleet was no mean thing; but it is a human failing common to man to view slightingly any one who takes one's own place, even when it is vacant only through personal promotion. Kanaris's case, however, was a little more complicated, for the Capsina was to him what he had thought no woman could have been. His habit of mind was far too methodical to allow him the luxury of doing anything so unaccounted for as abandoning himself to another; but there were certainly three things in his soul which took a distanced precedence of all others. Ships were one, destruction of Turks another, and the Capsina was the third. In his more spiritual moments he would have found it hard to draw up a reliable table of precedence for the three.

And certainly he was in one of his more spiritual moments just now, for there were no Turks about, his ambition to command a fine ship was satisfied, and the Capsina seated opposite to him had never so compelled his admiration. To-night there was something triumphant and irresistible in her beauty, her draught of sparkling happiness had given a splendid animation to her face, and that flush which as yet he had only associated in her with anger or excitement showed like a beacon for men's eyes in her cheek. But in her face to-night the heightened color and sparkling eye had some intangible softness about them; hitherto, when it had been excitement that had kindled her, she looked more like some extraordinarily handsome boy than a girl, but to-night her face was altogether girlish, and the terms of comradeship on which Kanaris had lived with her, uncomplicated by question or suggestions of sex, were suddenly and softly covered over, it seemed to his mind, by a great wave of tenderness and affection. The Capsina, the captain of the boat, the inimitable handler of a brig, were replaced by a girl. He had been blind, so he thought; all these weeks he had seen in her an able captain, a hater of Turks— a handsome boy, if you will—and he was suddenly smitten into sight, and saw for the first time this glorious thing. But Kanaris was wrong; he had not been blind, the change was in the other.

But here, coincident with the very moment of his discovery, was the moment of his departure, and he left her with another, a provokingly good-looking lad, the hero of an adventure just after the Capsina's heart, and the subject for the songs of the folk. Was not Mitsos just such as might seem godlike to this girl? In truth he was.

She filled his glass again, and he sat and drank in her beauty. She seemed different in kind to what she had ever looked before—her eyes beat upon his heart, and the smile on her beautiful mouth was wine to him. He looked, weighing his courage with his chance, opened his mouth to speak, and stopped again. Truly such perturbation in the methodical Kanaris touched the portentous.

The Capsina had paused after her question, but after a moment repeated it.

"So why look farther for another and a worse?" she said again.

"Don't look farther," he said, leaning forward across the table, and twisting the sense of her question to his own use; "look nearer rather. Look nearer," he repeated; "and, oh, Capsina—"

The smile faded from her mouth but not from her eyes, for it was too deeply set therein to be disturbed by Kanaris.

"What do you mean?" she said.

"It is that I love you," said he.

But she sprang up, laughing.

"Ah, spare yourself," she said. "You ought to know I am already betrothed."

"You betrothed?"

"Yes, betrothed to the brig. No, old friend, I am not laughing at you. You honor me too much. Let us talk of something else."

Mitsos meantime was on his way back to the Capsina's betrothed. He had sailed rapidly across the bay, and made the anchorage close to the house in no longer than half an hour. His father, Constantine, had died two months ago, and since then he and Suleima had lived alone. Just now, however, Father Andréa was with them, staying a few days on his way to Corinth, where he was summoned by the revolutionists, and Mitsos, going through the garden to the house, saw him walking up and down by the fountain, smoking his chibouk.

"Ah, father," he said, "I am late, am I not? But I must be off again. I met the Capsina to-day in Nauplia, and she has offered me a place on her brig—the place Kanaris held under her, or rather with her, she says. She sails to-morrow morning. Suleima is in the house?"

"Yes, with the child, to whom the teething gives trouble. This is very sudden; but, lad, I would not stop you, nor, I think, will Suleima. Go to her, then."

Suleima had heard voices, but she was trying to persuade the baby to go to sleep, while the baby, it seemed, preferred screaming and struggling. She was walking up and down the room with it, crooning softly to it, and rocking it gently in her arms. She looked up smiling at her husband as he entered.

"I heard your voice," she said, "and I would have come out, but I could not leave the adorable one. Poor manikin, he is troubled with this teething!"

"Give me the child," said Mitsos; and the baby, interested in his own transference from one to the other, stopped crying a moment, and Mitsos bent over it.

"Oh, great one," he said; "is heaven falling, or are the angels dead, that you cry so? How will you be able to eat good meat and grow like the ash-tree, unless there are teeth to you? And how should there be teeth unless they cut through the gums—unless, like an old man, you would have us buy them for you?"

The baby ceased crying at the deep, soothing voice, and in a moment or two it was asleep.

"It is wonderful," said Suleima, taking it back from Mitsos, and laying it in the cot; "but, as you know, I have always said you were often more a woman than all the women I have ever seen."

Mitsos laughed.

"A fine big skirt should I want and a double pair of shoes," he said. "And, oh, Suleima, but it were better for the Turks I had been just a chattering woman."

"Eh, but what a husband have I got," said she, pinching his arm. "He thinks himself the grandest man of all the world. But what is there you have to tell me?—for I read you like father reads a book—there is something forward, little Mitsos."

"Yes, and indeed there is," said Mitsos, "but what with you and the child, and all this silly, daffing talk, it had gone from my mind. But this it is, most dear one, that the Capsina is here, and she has offered me the post just under her on the new ship she has built, that one you and I saw put in this morning. Eh, but it is grand for me! She will sail to-morrow."

"To-morrow! Oh, Mitsos!" Then, checking herself. "Dearest one, but your luck is still with you. She is a fine, brave lass they say, and handsome, too, and, so Dimitri told me, her ship is the fastest and best in Greece. So go, and God speed you, and I will wait, and the little one shall make haste to grow! You will stop here to-night? No? Not even to-night? Come, then, I must look out your clothes for you at once, for you must have your very best, and be a credit to the housewife."

She held Mitsos's hands for a moment, and put up her face to his to be kissed.

"Blessed be the day when first I saw you!" she whispered.

"And blessed has been every day since," said Mitsos.

"Even so, dearest," and she clung to him a moment longer. Then, "Come," she said, "we must make much haste if you are to go to-night, and indeed you shall leave behind that shirt you are wearing, to find it clean and fresh and mended when you come back. I will not have you going ragged and untidy, and oh, Mitsos, but your hair is a mop. Who has had the cutting of it? Sit you down and make no more words, and be trimmed."

Suleima got a pair of scissors, and clapping Mitsos in a chair, put the light close, and trimmed and combed out his tangled hair, with little words of reproof to him.

"Eh, but she will think you a wild man of the woods, fit only to frighten the birds from the crops. Sure, Mitsos, you will have been rubbing your head in the sand, and it was only yesterday you were scrubbing and soaping all afternoon. Well, what must be, must. Shut your eyes now and sit still," and clip went her scissors along the hair above the forehead.

"It is like cutting the pony's mane," she went on. "Such horse-hair I never saw yet. Well, the stuffing is half out of the sofa-cushion, and this will all do fine to fill it again. Now, stop laughing, lad, or an oke of hair will fall down that throat of yours, and so you will laugh never more. There, you are a little less of a scare-man. Get up and shake, and then change that shirt and trousers."

In an hour Mitsos was ready, and with a big rug on his shoulder in which his clothes were wrapped, he and Suleima set off to the little harbor below the house. The boy was going with him in order to take the boat back again, but Mitsos had sent him on ahead, and he and Suleima walked slowly down to the edge of the bay beneath a sky thick sown with stars.

"Mitsos," she said, "it will be with a heavy heart and yet a very light one that I shall say good-bye; heavy because we love one another, and yet for that reason very light. And, however far you are from me, yet you are here always in my heart, and the child is daily more like you. And, indeed, how should I love one who sat at home and went not out on these great quests? Where should I have been now, think you, oh foolish one, if you had not gone catching fish and then Turks? so do not contradict me. And oh, Mitsos, I am going to say a very foolish thing for the last. You are so dear to me that I can scarcely speak of you to others, for so I seem to share you with them; and it would please me if I thought that you too would be very sparing of my name, for so I shall feel that, as on those beautiful nights together on the bay, we enjoyed each other in secret, and none knew. And now we are come to the boat—look!—and the boy has made ready. It is very bravely that I say good-bye to you, for with my whole heart I would have you to go. Oh, most beloved!"

For a minute, or perhaps two, they stood there silent, and though the smile on Suleima's mouth was a little tremulous and her eyes were over-brimmed, it was for very love that the tears stood there. And Mitsos kissed her on the eyes and on the mouth, and yet again; and though his voice was betwixt a whisper and a choke, his heart was light even as hers, and full of love.

The news of his coming was brought to the Capsina as they sat in the cabin by Michael's furious barking at the boat, which he heard drawn up alongside.

The Capsina got up when she heard that, and again her face so glowed that Kanaris wondered.

"That will be the little Mitsos," she said, "for a thousand pounds. He will want supper it may be," and she went on to the main deck to let a ladder down to him, for most of the crew were on shore still.

"Ahoy! ahoy!" shouted Mitsos from his boat. "Oh, Michael, be still! Am I a robber?" and he shouted again.

"Yes, I am coming," cried the Capsina, in answer. "It is you, is it not, Mitsos? Wait a moment, and I will let down a ladder to you."

Mitsos climbed up with his bundle on his shoulder, and bade the lad put back for home again. "So I am here," he said to the Capsina.

"And you are welcome—doubly welcome," said the Capsina, with a sparkling eye. "Oh, Mitsos, take care of your head. Are you not a size too large for my boat? I never thought of that. Come down to the cabin and have your supper; Kanaris and I have eaten, but we will sit with you."

She blew on her whistle, and gave Mitsos's bundle in charge to be taken to his cabin, and led the way.

"You know Kanaris? No?" she asked. "Ah, I remember you saying you did not. He is of the best of my friends. This way, little Mitsos. Here we are."

Though Kanaris had been disposed to think with jealousy of his successor, it was not in the nature of man to resist Mitsos. For he had all the ardor of a boy, as befitted his years, and with that an experience beyond them; and the modesty that comes from having done great deeds mixed with none of the conceit of the imagination that sees oneself acting greatly, should the chance come, and neither man nor woman could look in his face, as frank and cheerful as the eyes of a dog, and feel no impulse of friendliness. And Kanaris was not a man who from habitual reserve would distrust a friendly impulse when it came, and so it was that in half an hour they were all chatting together, like children, of ships and fish and winds and waves and the hundred healthy things that made the environment of the life of all of them. As the evening wore on they heard the crew coming merrily back from Nauplia, but they sat talking late, like friends who have met again.

Their three cabins were close together, and the Capsina, after showing Mitsos his, went to her own and sat there in the dark, too happy to think or sleep. She heard Michael's nails tapping along the wooden floor outside, and then with a soft thump he curled himself up outside her door, according to his custom. From Mitsos's cabin she heard the rattle of shoes, and soon after the partition wall between them creaked as he curled himself up in his berth against it. Then there was silence, and still she sat in the darkness of her cabin, looking out from the port-hole towards the quay of Nauplia, black beneath the stars, and seeing the lights from the town cast in long unwavering reflection over the calm water, and filled with a rapturous uncontent.

She was on deck next day, while yet night was mixed with morning, fresh as a flower, though having slept but little, and before six she gave the order to hoist sail, for a fair wind was blowing, and they could clear the harbor without need of boat or tow-rope. Day was coming infinitely clear and sweet; overhead there still burned a big star or two, which got paler and paler every moment till they seemed white and unluminous, like candles in the sunshine, and by degrees the pale primrose strip of sky in the east flushed with color before the upvaulting of the sun. The flush spread to the zenith, and was answered by the surface of the bay, and before they cleared the point of Palanede the sunrise was on them. She turned just as the first rays struck the ship, and saw Mitsos just coming on to the deck a few yards away; and the sun shining on her face, and Mitsos gladdening her eye, gave a radiance to her beauty that drew his eyes to her in a long gaze.

And in pain and rapture together she looked at him, and her heart exulted in its noble and self-rendered slavery.

For a moment neither spoke; then, and with an effort:

"So you have slept well, little Mitsos? And you do not repent our sudden bargain? There is time yet to put you ashore."

"I have slept all night and I repent nothing."

The Capsina did not answer at once, but looked out to sea, and wetting her finger, held it up into the wind and glanced at the compass.

"The wind is due north," she said, "and only light. The channel of Spetzas, through which we pass, is east-southeast. The distance you should know. Give the order, little Mitsos."

Mitsos smiled and scratched his head.

"Eh, but I do not know the ship," he said.

"Look at it, then."

Mitsos looked at the lines of the vessel, then at the canvas she was carrying.

"First hoist jib and halyards," he said. "We can carry more sail than this."

"And then?"

"Oh, Capsina," he cried, "but you want to find me ignorant! However, I should say, go right across to within a mile of Astra, squaring the sails ever so little, and then make the channel in one run. And now, God defend me from having said a very foolish thing."

"I think your prayer is heard," said the Capsina. "Therefore, it is time to have breakfast," and she called Mitsos's orders.

"Come down," she said; "the ship is running free and fine, and it will be an hour yet before we put on the second tack. Ah, here is Michael. He knows you, does he not? That always seems to me a thing of good omen, for indeed I trust Michael more than I trust myself. He welcomed Kanaris so, and I never had a better friend. Is Kanaris not up yet? He knows he is only a passenger now, and will have his lie in bed. Well, we will breakfast all the same."

When they had breakfasted, Sophia took Mitsos a tour of the ship. She was a brig of three hundred and fifty tons, very long for her beam, and deep-keeled. On her upper deck she carried six nine-inch guns—two forward under the forecastle, two amidships, and two astern. Both forward and stern guns were mounted on a carriage, which revolved nearly half a circle and looked from a very wide port, so that the stern guns could be trained on a point due astern, or be used for a broadside, or could fire forty-five degrees ahead, and the bow guns in the same way could fire straight ahead, or in any direction up to forty-five degrees behind them. The main-deck was armed in a similar manner with six guns, placed not directly below the upper-deck guns, but some ten yards horizontally from them, so that the smoke from the lower should not rise directly and interfere with the sighting of the upper. Mitsos, to the Capsina's great delight, saw and commended this arrangement, which was new to him. On the main-deck the forward and stern guns—four-inch, not six-inch—could not fire right astern or right ahead, but they had a wide broadside range. Below the deck the battery consisted of twelve guns, six on each side; the four guns in the centre of each side being of the same weight as those on the upper deck, but those in the bows and stern being four-inch guns. Thus in all she carried twenty-four guns—sixteen six-inch and eight four-inch—and it was a sight that made Mitsos lick his lips with blood-thirstiness.

"You would say she was a fortress," he said.

The two chattered like children over a new toy all their own, and Kanaris, who soon joined them, seemed to each to be like an elder who had outgrown enthusiasm; yet even to him the toy seemed flawless. The Turkish men-of-war and cruisers alike were contemptibly inferior in point of speed, and the men-of-war, which were armed with much heavier guns, carried all their strength in the broadside, while the Capsina's ship had two guns which could shoot straight ahead or astern, and six which could fire on either diagonal.

Meantime the ship was nearing Astra, and the wisdom or foolishness of Mitsos's tactics would soon be patent. But while they were still three miles off he turned to the Capsina.

"I have made a mistake," he said. "If we go about at once we shall still make the channel. For indeed she could go as an arrow goes."

The Capsina smiled with a thrill of pleasure in her ship.

"I won a pound over you yesterday," she said; "and if Kanaris will bet again, I will stand to win another. Give your orders, little Mitsos."

Kanaris looked incredulous.

"Kranidi is a very fine place," he said; "but I take it we want to sail between Spetzas and the land."

"Will you bet?" asked the Capsina.

Kanaris paused a moment, and heard Mitsos giving the order in a voice extraordinarily confident.

"I think I will not bet," he said.

After that there was the sailing-gear of the ship to be gone through. To Mitsos, used as he was to the big schooner sail, these square canvases seemed a thought unwieldable, but the foresails, the jib, and halyards had taken his fancy at once.

"It is a rein to a horse," he said; "it must go as you will."

"And it is according to your will that it shall go," said Sophia.

The hours of the golden day went by; they had made eight knots in the first hour, and nine in the second; and about ten in the morning, Kranidi, a grain of sparkling salt in the gray stretch of hill, appeared small and very distant. And at that Mitsos frowned.

"Again I was wrong," he said; "we might have put about a mile sooner. But, indeed, how was I to know?"

They were through the channel of Spetzas before noon; but presently, after the wind dropped altogether, and for a couple of hours, they lay becalmed on a windless sea, but swept slowly northward by the current running up the coast. The Capsina chafed at the delay, for though she would have waited two days or three at Nauplia, as she had said, for Mitsos, the loss of a few hours now seemed wholly disproportionate, for she was very eager to get off again on the fresh cruise. Kanaris remembered the morning he had spent with Nikolas on the Gulf of Corinth, and said to the Capsina:

"I was with Nikolas Vidalis in just such a position as this, and he said what seemed to me a very wise thing, Capsina: 'I am never in a hurry,' says he, 'when I am going as fast as I can.'"

"Ah, he was a man," said the Capsina; "but when did you ever know a woman who thought that? Why, it is only when we are going as fast as we can that we are in a hurry; if we are not going our quickest, we are not in a hurry."

Mitsos was lying on the deck, with his cap pushed over his eyes, and his back against the mast.

"That is not what Uncle Nikolas meant," he remarked.

The Capsina laughed.

"Wisest little Mitsos, explain to me, then."

"He meant—he meant—Oh, surely you see what he meant," said Mitsos, feeling too sleepy to express himself.

"Well, anyhow, his nephew is not in a hurry," said Sophia, looking at his lazy length.

"His nephew is completely comfortable," said Mitsos. "It is very good to be on this ship, and my bones are sweet to me."

Sophia felt a trifle irritated with him. It had been extraordinarily pleasant to her to see him make himself so readily at home the evening before, but just now she felt a little ill-used at his entire contentment with the brig and her and himself. She would have preferred a little feeling of some sort to any amount of pure content. But a moment afterwards he looked up quickly.

"There is a breeze coming," and he got up. "Yes, there it comes," he said, pointing southward. "We shall have to square sails till we get round again. Shall I give the order, Capsina?"

"Please." Then when he joined her again: "How did you know the breeze was coming, little Mitsos?"

"I don't know. Perhaps I smelt it. Really, now you ask me, I find I can't tell you."

"That is curious," said the Capsina. "I had heard there were men who could do that, but I put it down to folks' tales. Michael, I think, knows sometimes, and now I look at you I notice your nostrils grow big and small like a dog's."

"They are as God made them," said Mitsos, piously.

The Capsina laughed. "Oh, inimitable boy!" she cried. "Come, let us look round the ship again. Yes, it is good to be at sea, is it not? Here comes the breeze indeed. There! Did you see her shake herself as if she woke up suddenly, this beautiful shining ship, all ours! See how quickly she gathers way! We shall be at Hydra by five if this holds. Of course you will live with me there till we start, but I expect we shall be on the ship more than off. You might well have smelt the breeze, Mitsos, for surely it smells very good, and there is more to come, or I am the more mistaken."

It was still an hour before the sunset when they cast anchor in the harbor of Hydra, for the wind had got up and promised a stormy night. The clan welcomed the Capsina's new importation with fervor when they heard who it was; and certain of the primates wondered whether she would demand another seat in the assembly. But in truth the Capsina had other things to think of; for the Hydriot fleet was not going to cruise again till the spring, while she was going to make all speed to be off, with Kanaris on the *Sophia*, and she and Mitsos on the *Revenge*, for so had the new ship been named. And in these things there was much food for many thoughts.

CHAPTER V

The *Revenge* and the *Sophia* were ready for sea by early in February. Even the clan, who were accustomed to the habitual fever of the Capsina's energy, found themselves wondering whether she was a woman or a whirlwind. No job was too big for her, no detail too small, and she would be superintending the storage of the powder in the *Sophia* one moment, and the next would be half-way across to the anchorage of the *Revenge*, to see whether they had planed away the edge of her cabin door, which would not shut properly, and had sent from the wicker-makers the cages for the fowls. There seemed, indeed, to be only one person on the island, for the population were just tools in the hands of the Capsina—machines for lifting weights or stowing shot. She reduced her foreman to a mere wreck, for the unfortunate man had to stay up three consecutive nights doing the Capsina's business, and was roundly abused when she found him asleep after dinner the fourth day. Kanaris fared little better, and Mitsos alone seemed capable of dealing with the girl. She would find him sitting at a café after dinner smoking a pipe and playing draughts; and when she asked him whether he had done this or seen to that, he would say:

"I have worked ten hours to-day, Capsina, and I have not smoked ten minutes."

"Smoke, smoke!" cried the Capsina; "smoking and drinking is all that men are fit for!"

And Mitsos, with a face conspicuously grave, raised his voice and called for a pipe and a glass of wine for the Capsina, and an awed silence fell for the moment on those round, for this seemed little short of blasphemy; but the Capsina only glanced at Mitsos's demure face, burst out laughing herself, and was off again.

Kanaris and Mitsos lodged in her house, but until the last evening, when all was ready, and there was positively nothing left for her to do, she was never there except occasionally for supper and for sleep. Even on the last evening of all, as soon as supper was over, she started up.

"We are ready," she said; "why not sail to-night? What is the use of wasting time here?"

Mitsos, who had not finished, slowly laid down the mouthful he was raising to his lips.

"Oh, Capsina!" he said; "be it known to you that for my part I will not go till to-morrow. Yes, this is mutiny, is it not? Very well, put me in irons; but for the sake of all the saints in heaven, let me finish my supper!"

The Capsina looked at him a moment.

"Little Mitsos," she said, "you are a gross feeder."

And with that she sat down again, and filled both their glasses and her own.

"To the little Mitsos's good digestion!" she cried, and clinked her glass with his.

Mitsos smiled, but drank to his own digestion.

"And there is yet another toast," he said. "It is to the tranquil Capsina. Hurrah!"

They were going south round the capes, then north again, up the west coast of Greece, to cruise in the Corinthian Gulf, for there, as they knew, were Turkish vessels, which sailed from village to village along the coast, massacring and burning and destroying the Greek maritime population. The events of the last summer and autumn had made it clear even to that indolently minded enemy that if once Greece got command of the sea the war would be over, for on land the cause of the Revolution daily gained fresh recruits, and, if once the ports and harbors were in the hands of the insurgents, it would no longer be possible to send in fresh men and arms, except by the long and dangerous march through the disaffected mountains of north Greece. There, as the Turks had found to their cost, it was impossible to bring on a pitched engagement, for true to the policy of Petrobey, the villagers pursued a most harassing, baffling policy of guerilla warfare. The invaders could burn a village, already empty before their approach, but next day as they marched, suddenly the bare and rocky hill-sides would blaze, large bowlders would stream down the ravines and upset the commissariat mules, and during the livelong night dropping shots would be kept up, and a sentry, firing back at the uncertain aim of the momentary flash of a musket, would be bowled over from the other direction. But as long as the sea remained in the hands of the Turks they had little to fear; regiment after regiment could be poured into the country, and the end would be sure. With this object, several Turkish vessels were cruising among the clustering villages on the gulf, burning ships and depopulating the men of the sea. But it was an ill day for them when the news of their doings came to Hydra. It had been arranged that some fifteen brigs should follow the Capsina in the spring, and part would close the mouth of the gulf while the others joined her. Tombazes had in vain urged her to wait, for no Turkish fleet would be sent out from Constantinople till spring; the Greeks would have the start of them leaving Hydra, and no sane man would think of cruising in the winter. But all remonstrance was useless, for the Capsina only said:

"Then I suppose Kanaris, Mitsos, and I are mad. That is a sore affliction, father. Besides, you would not have us stop; Turkish ships, you know, are in the gulf."

For more than a week after they started they were the butt of violent and contrary winds, but the Capsina was impatient of delay no longer. Indeed, on the surface she was "the tranquil Capsina" to whom Mitsos had drunk, and he at any rate had no cause to know of the unrest that stormed below her tranquillity. They had set out from Hydra about eleven of the morning, and almost immediately after leaving the harbor they had taken a somewhat different course to the *Sophia*. She made a wider tack to port, while the *Revenge* sailed closer to the wind, and after they had turned the southern end of the island, and there was open sea, with the main-land lying like a cloud to the west, Sophia and Mitsos left the bridge. Just as they went down she looked round: Kanaris was far away to the offing, Hydra was sinking down to the north, there was only sea and Mitsos. And with an uncontrollable impulse she held out her hands to him.

"At last!" she cried, and before the pause was perceptible—"at last we are off!"

She loved these fierce winds and heavy seas which kept them back; it was a fierce and intimate joy to her to wake at night and know that Mitsos was there, to wake in the morning for another day of that comradeship, which was in itself already the main fibre of her life. The huge gray seas from the south hissed and surged by them, with dazzling, hungry heads of lashed foam, now and again falling solid on the bows with a shower of spray, and streaming off through the scuppers back into the sea. The wind shrilled and screamed through the rigging; the buffeted ship staggered and stood straight again, then plunged head-foremost with a liquid cluck and crunch into the next water-valley; the bowsprit dipped in the sea, then raised itself scornfully with a whiff of spray twenty feet above the crest of the wave; and every wave that beat them, every squall that whistled aloft, every flash of raking sunlight that fled frightened across the deck was for the two of them; they stood side by side, wrapped in tarpaulins, and watched the beautiful labor of the ship; they sat in the swaying, rolling cabin, and it was like a game to pluck at the food as it bowed and coquetted away from their hands; like a game, too, the scramble and rush across the deck, laid precipitously towards the seas rushing by, or the house-roof climb up it as it rose staggering to the next billow, or the watching Michael as he toiled or slipped after them, sometimes sliding gravely down on his haunches, sometimes doing tread-mill work up the wet incline; but for one of them at least the game was one at which the stake was serious. They would amuse themselves with the most childish sports, watching themselves to see who could stand the longest on one foot when the ship was pushing and shouldering its way along through the cross sea, the one finding pleasure in such things because he was just a boy with a double portion of animal spirits, the other because anything that was shared with him was passionately well worth doing. Often and often Mitsos wondered that this was the same girl who had nigh driven the Hydriots to death, doing more than any of them, yet indefatigable; and she that this was the Mitsos who had brought hot death to that Turkish ship in the harbor at Nauplia.

For three days the southwest wind blew half a gale, and the sky was one driven rack of scudding rain-clouds. Sometimes a squall would sweep across the sea, the torrent hissing audibly into the water, and more loudly than the scream of the wind as it approached. The windward sea would become a seething caldron; the broken wave-tops were scarce distinguishable from the churning of the rain—all was furious foam. Then the squall would charge slanting across the deck, pass, and perhaps for half an hour the wind would seem to moderate, but again the humming of the rigging would change to a moan, and the moan to a shriek; and so another night they would sail, scarce making any way, but, tacking wide out to sea, return again, having won but a dozen miles in half a dozen hours. All the time the *Sophia* kept a wider and more seaward course, now and then getting close to them at the end of her starboard tack, and then standing out again.

But on the fourth morning they woke to a sky washed clean by the rain, and of an incredibly soft blue. The gray, angry waves became a merry company of live beings which sparred in jovial play with the ship. The wind was still fresh, but it had veered round to the north, and mid-day saw the two ships close together, rattling along close-hauled in the channel between Cerigo and Cape Malea. To the south the island lay green and gray and fringed with white, and, to the north, promontory after promontory, each grayer and bluer than the last, melted into the bay of Gythium. It was a morning on which those in whose veins the joy of life is flowing are conscious from toe to finger-tip, from finger-tip to the end of the hair, of the indubitable goodness of life, and the smallest thing was a jest to them, and the largest a jest also. Michael, in particular, caused many mouthfuls of laughter; for his dinner was thrown out of its bowl by a sudden lurch of the ship, and he ran after the various bones as they rolled away, growling and ill-pleased, till he too was laid on his back, and picked himself up with the air of not being hungry and having fallen down on purpose. And the perception of the shallowness of this seeming, combined with a half-swallowed piece of orange, reduced Mitsos to a choking condition, and the Capsina thumped him on the back.

"Thank you, yes, I am altogether recovered," says he; "but, oh, Capsina, you have a very strong arm."

"Little Mitsos, it was for your good," said the Capsina, a thought sententiously, setting her white teeth in the peel of her orange.

"I suppose so; things that are good for one, I have noticed, make one a little sore."

"What do you know about things that are good for you?" asked she.

"That only; that they make one sore. For indeed I do not think that things that are good for one *are* good for one. You understand?" he added, hopefully.

"Perfectly," said the Capsina, and they laughed again, causelessly.

The evening brought calmer weather, and to them somewhat calmer spirits, and that night after supper they talked quite soberly.

"Oh, but it is a strange world," said the Capsina; "to think that a week ago I had never set eyes on you, and now—well, there is no one in the world I know better. I have taken you as I found you, and you me; we have asked no questions of father or mother, and here we are. Oh, it is a strange world!" she said again.

Now there was perhaps no subject in the world to which Mitsos had dedicated less thought than the strangeness of the world. So he waited in silence.

"Is it not so?" went on Sophia. "What could have been less likely than the chance that put your boat in to Nauplia that night, and on the one tack. For, indeed, if you had taken two tacks, and so I had lost my pound to Kanaris, I should not have stopped there."

"Then should I at this hour have been catching the little fish in the bay," said Mitsos, "and that is only worth the doing when there is nothing forward. Yet I like the bay," he added, thinking of Suleima, "for I have had many good hours there. See, there is Taygetus, all snow! You would say she was a bride," he added, with an altogether unusual employment of metaphor.

He got up and leaned over the bulwarks looking out to the north, where the top of Taygetus appeared above a bank of low-lying cloud, itself bright in the evening sunshine. The sea had gone down considerably in the last hour, and they moved with a steady swing over the waves, no longer torn and broken. In the lessening wind they had been able to put on all sail, and the ship, with its towers of fresh snowy canvas, seemed like some great white seabird, now skimming, now dipping in the waves. From where she sat, Sophia could see the sky reddening to sunset under the arched foot of the main-sail, and when the bows rose to a wave Taygetus would appear as in a frame between the ship and the sail. Mitsos was leaning on the side, in front of the main-mast, bareheaded and blown by the wind, his face turned seaward, so that she saw only the strong clear line of brow and cheek. And the sight of him, listless, contented, and unconscious of her, filled the girl with a sudden spasm of anger and envy. The last week, which had so welded itself into the essentials of her life, seemed no more to him than the sound of the wind which had buffeted them, or the hiss of some spent wave which had struck them yesterday; she had been mad, so she thought, to have so let herself go, abandoning herself like that to the childish pleasure of the hour. It seemed the one moment incredible that he had not guessed that this child's-play was something far different to her, at the next impossible that it should have seemed to the boy to be anything else. They had played, laughed, chattered together, and to him the play had been play, the laughter and the chattering mirth only. Yet she counted the cost and regretted nothing, and waited with an eager patience for the fierce deeds in which their hands would be joined, and therein surely draw closer to each other. The affection and delighted comradeship of the boy was hers; hers too, so she promised herself, should be the keener, inevitable need for her when they did a man's work together.

That evening they passed round Cape Malea, keeping close in to the land, and Mitsos, as they turned northward, watched with all the pleasure of recognition the near passing of the coast where he and Yanni had made their journey with the messages for the mills. Sophia listened eagerly to the story, making Mitsos tell over again of the fight in the mill, and she sat silent awhile after he had finished.

"That explains you," she said at length; "for these last days you have been just a child, but I suspect that when there is work forward you are made a man; and there will soon be work forward for you and me, little Mitsos," she added to herself.

Two days after this they were nearing Patras and the entrance to the Corinthian Gulf, and being no longer in the open and empty seas, it was necessary to use some circumspection in their advance. They lay to some eight miles outside Patras, and Kanaris came on board to consult. The fortress

74

of Patras was in the hands of the Turks; but they would give this a very wide berth, so Kanaris suggested, and pass Lepanto, another Turkish fortress in the narrows of the gulf, at night. It was there the greater risk awaited them. Lepanto was a heavily armed place, the gulf was less than three miles broad, shoal water lay broad on the side away from the fortress, and the channel close below its walls. Further, it was ludicrously improbable that either the *Sophia* or the *Revenge* would be allowed a passing unchallenged, for indeed the resemblance of either to peaceful trading brigs was of the smallest. But Sophia, with the support of Mitsos, demurred: it were better to seek a weed in a growing cornfield than to go into the gulf without some guidance as to the position the Turkish cruisers were in, but beyond doubt Germanos or some other of the revolutionists at Patras could give them information.

"For, indeed," said the Capsina, with asperity, "I have not come a pleasure sail in a little rowboat with a concertina to sing to."

"But do you mean to put in to Patras," asked Kanaris, "and say to the Turks who hold the fort, 'Tell me where is Germanos, for I wish to know where the Turkish cruisers are'? Will they not guess your business when they see the ship?"

"No, I shall not do that," said the Capsina, "nor shall I put out a great notice in Greek and Turkish that all may read, saying I am the Capsina and carry four-and-twenty guns. Oh, speak," she said, turning to Mitsos, "and do not sit as round-eyed as an owl at noonday!"

Mitsos grinned.

"Never mind the compliments," he said, "and give me time, Capsina, for it is my way to think slow."

"If they know that you are at Patras," continued Kanaris, "word will go to the Lepanto, and we shall see nought of the gulf but the bottom of it."

"And so will the little Mitsos be among his little fish again," said the Capsina.

"The devil take the little fishes!" said Mitsos. "Why will you not let me be, to think slow, and tell you some very wise thing in the end? I shall go think by myself." And he went forward.

"How can you be so imprudent, Capsina?" said Kanaris. "Yes, I am at your orders completely: I need not remind you of that, and where you go I go. But you have ever told me to say my mind."

"You are quite right," said the Capsina, "but we will wait to hear what this slow thinker says."

In ten minutes or so Mitsos returned, still owl-like, but, so said the Capsina, with a blush of intelligence on his face.

"I am thinking I shall have to be a peasant lad again, with a mule and a basket of oranges. For I take it that both you and Kanaris are in the right, Capsina."

"The oranges will help us very much," remarked the Capsina, but the owl still sat in Mitsos's eyes.

"For thus," he continued, "even as in the days of the mill fight, I will go into Patras and find Germanos and speak with him."

"But how are you to get to Patras?" asked Kanaris.

"I have in my mind that there is a place called Limnaki, three miles this side Patras, and the foulest spot God ever made, being one pestilent marsh. Now my thought is that our brig could sail close in there, while the other waited about on the alert. That shall be this afternoon, and before it is dark I can be with Germanos. Then he will tell me where these Turks are in the gulf, and before morning I shall be at Limnaki again. So far I am with the Capsina, but then let us do as Kanaris says, and pass the guns of Lepanto at night."

"Hoot, hoot! so the owl speaks!" said Sophia; "and I think the owl is right. You know Germanos, do you not, little Mitsos?"

"Surely. I was at Tripoli."

It was so arranged, and Kanaris returned to his ship, while the *Revenge* put about, and in an hour's time had got close in to the shore opposite Limnaki. It was a starved little village, feverish and unhealthy, and the chance of Turks being there was too small to reckon with. Mitsos got into peasant's dress, and as time was short, omitted the oranges and the mule, and after being landed quietly, set off an hour before sunset over the hill towards Patras. Barefooted, and with a colored handkerchief for a cap, he passed without remark through the gate of the town, and mingled with the loiterers in the market-place.

The citadel of Patras was still in the hands of the Turks, and the Turkish garrison there, and the Greek revolutionists who held the monastery hill both lived in a state of semi-siege, while meantime the rest of the Greeks and Turks in the town continued to pursue the usual trade, finishing up six days out of the seven with a little mutual massacring in the streets; and Mitsos's object was to get to the Greek camp without involving himself in any street row. The monastery was but a quarter of an hour's walk from the square, and he reached the outposts of the Greek lines in safety, and demanded to be taken at once to Germanos. He gave his name, and stated that he was on the business of the Capsina.

Germanos received him immediately with kindness and courtesy, though the little Mitsos, remembering the affairs at Tripoli, was as stiff as the soul of a ramrod. But, to Germanos's credit be it said, his manner suffered no abatement of geniality, and when he had heard Mitsos out, he spoke:

"There are nine Turkish vessels in the gulf," he said. "Three are coming along the north coast, and left Lepanto only two days ago. They attacked a village called Sergule yesterday, and, I should think, would move on again to-day or to-morrow. Three more were at Corinth two days ago, and, I have just heard, were going northward; the other three are somewhere along the south coast, but I do not know where. But how are you going to get in, little Mitsos?"

"We are going to sail in," said Mitsos, curtly.

Germanos looked at him a moment in silence. Then, "That is not very courteously said, little Mitsos," he answered. "Yes, I know you think that has passed which passes forgiveness. Yet Nikolas forgave me, did he not, and do you not know that I was sorry and ashamed, and did I not say so publicly? That was not very easy to do. But I do not wish to interfere; if you desire to know more that I can tell you, you are welcome to my knowledge, and, if you will, my counsel; if not, I can only regret that I can be of no more service to you, and wish you God-speed—that with all my heart."

Mitsos stood a moment with eyes downcast. Then with a wonderful sweet frankness of manner he spoke:

"You are right, father," he said, "and I am no better than a sulky child. I ask your forgiveness."

"You have it very freely, nephew of Nikolas, for indeed Nikolas forgave even me," said the proud man.

Mitsos's face dimpled with a smile, both genial and sorry.

"So, that is good," he said. "Well, father, here we are, still outside the gulf, and we want, if we can, to pass in to-night, so that they in Lepanto shall not see us."

Germanos thought a moment.

"I can help you," he said, "and it is pleasure to my soul to do so. You do not see all your difficulties. You can depend on getting past Lepanto with the land-breeze in the evening, which blows off the hills out of Lepanto, and a little up the gulf. Now the land-breeze drops by an hour after sunset, and so by then, therefore, must you be past Lepanto. That is to say, you must pass Patras in broad day. You will be seen from the citadel, a man on horse will reach the straits before you are there, and word will go across to the fortress. It is now after sunset, and it is hopeless to attempt it to-night. But to-morrow I can help you, and this promise I give you, that to-morrow afternoon we make a sortie, and hold the two city gates on the east, so that no man passes out. Thus word cannot be sent to Lepanto. For, believe me, if you are seen, as you must be seen passing here, the straits will be guarded, and you will never get in. But, little Mitsos, what a scheme! Is it the Capsina's? For how will you pass out again; for when once they know you are there, the straits will be guarded. They have ships at Lepanto."

"In a month the fleet leaves Hydra," said Mitsos; "till then we have plenty of work in the gulf. But that is a wise thought and a kind one of yours, father."

Germanos got up and walked about; he was much moved.

"If this is the spirit of the people," he said, "it will be no long time before not a Turk is left in Greece."

"The people are not all as the Capsina, father," said Mitsos.

"It is splendid! splendid!" cried Germanos. "Whenever did a man hear of so noble a risk? To shut herself up in a trap for six weeks, fighting like a wild beast at bay. And, indeed, there is cause; five villages already have been exterminated—they are no more. We on land cannot touch the ships. None know where they will come next, and it is out of possibility to garrison all the villages of the gulf. God be praised for giving us such a girl!"

"Indeed there is none like her," said Mitsos. "But it is borne in upon me that she is waiting off Limnaki, and she does not like waiting."

"I will have you seen safely out of the town," said Germanos, "for, indeed, we cannot spare you either, little one. How is the wife and the baby?"

"The one is as dear as the other," said Mitsos, "and they are both very dear."

Mitsos was escorted out of the town and set on his way by a dozen men, to defend him from the street brawls, and before midnight he was down again on the shore at Limnaki, where he found the boat waiting to take him off. The Capsina had come ashore, and was pacing up and down like a hungry animal. Mitsos told her how he had sped; she entirely approved the primate's scheme, the ship was got under way, and they went north again, with a fitful and varying breeze, to join Kanaris.

All next morning they lay some eight miles out to sea, waiting until the time came for them to move up the gulf. A west wind was blowing, and now one and now the other beat a little out to sea, in order to keep their distance from the land. On the Capsina's ship an atmosphere of nerves was about, for all the men knew what they were to attempt, and the waiting was cold matter for the heart. Mitsos alone possessed himself in content and serenity, and smoked a vast deal of tobacco. Michael had caught the prevailing epidemic, and followed the Capsina about on her swift and aimless excursions fore and aft with trouble in his eye.

At length the Capsina came and sat down by Mitsos, who had chosen a snug berth under the lee of the forecastle, where he was sheltered from the wind and warmed by the winter sun.

"Have you ever bathed on a cold day?" she asked.

"On many," said Mitsos. "But why?"

"Is there not a moment before one jumps in?" asked the girl, and she set off again to look to the ammunition for the thirtieth time that morning. Mitsos smoked on and soon she returned, having forgotten that for which she had gone.

"It is all this arranging that is a trouble to me," she said. "Had you not gone to see Germanos and take precautions, I should have been as calm—as calm as you, for, indeed, I know nothing calmer. The devil take that silly scheme of yours, Mitsos. But to know that he is taking measures for our safety, and we have to wait till his measures are taken—oh, it beats me!" she cried. "And there are other things."

Mitsos's eye roamed over the sky for inspiration and noticed the sun.

"It is time for dinner," he said; "in fact, it is already late, and my stomach howls to me."

A singing west wind had been blowing all day, and promised to usurp the air of the land-breeze; but, not to run risk, about four o'clock the Capsina signalled to Kanaris, and they both hoisted sail and went eastward. The wind was still holding; they made good sailing, and half an hour before sunset they were off Patras. They were not more than a mile out to sea, and it was possible in that clear air to make out that something unusual was going on. The fort seemed deserted, but they could see lines of men, moving slow and busy like ants, lining the western wall. Now and then a spit of smoke would come from the citadel, followed after an interval by the drowsy sound of the report, and once or twice a long line of white vapor curled along the city wall, and the rattle of musket-fire confirmed it. It was clear that Germanos was as good as his word.

The sun had already set half an hour when they neared Lepanto, but a reflected brightness still lingered on the water, and as they approached they had the lights of the town to guide them, and the Capsina put on all sail. The strength of the wind had risen almost to violence, and Mitsos, standing with the Capsina on the poop, more than once feared for the masts, or to hear the crack of the mainsail. Once he suggested taking a reef in, but the Capsina paid no attention. All afternoon the girl had been strange and silent, as if struggling with some secret anxiety, and Mitsos, seeing she gave no account of it, refrained from asking. Kanaris's orders were simply to follow, but when they had passed the fort, and still the Capsina neither spoke nor moved from her place, Mitsos again addressed her, but with some timidity, for her face was iron and flint.

"We are safe past," he said. "Where do—"

But she interrupted him vehemently.

"Get you below," she said; "this night I sail the ship."

Mitsos wondered but obeyed, and sat up awhile in the cabin; but the ship still holding her course, as he could tell from the rapid swishing of the water, about nine he went to bed. Later the sound of the anchor-chain woke him for a moment, and he waited awake, though laden with sleep, for a minute or two, in case he was wanted. Then there came the unmistakable splash of a boat lowered into the water and the sound of oars. At that he got up, threw on a coat, and went on deck.

It was starlight and very cold; several sailors were standing about, and he asked one of them, who took the duty of first mate, where they were. Dimitri pointed to a faint glow along the shore.

"That is—that was Elatina," he said.

"And what was Elatina?"

"A village the Turks have burned. The Capsina is being rowed there," he said, "and as she got into the boat I saw she was crying."

"Crying? The Capsina?"

"Yes; it was the village her mother comes from," said Dimitri, who was a Hydriot.

Mitsos hesitated a moment, but reasoning that as the Capsina had said nothing of this to him it was a thing outside his own affairs, he went back to bed again.

He woke again in the aqueous, uncertain light of dawn, and in the dimness made his way on deck. The water was a mirror, the sky hard and clear as some precious stone. The Capsina was not returned to the ship; she had been gone ashore all night, and none on board knew anything of her. The boat she had disembarked in had been back once during the night to take more men: they supposed she was trying to save some whom the Turks had left for dead.

Kanaris's ship was lying close, and after taking some coffee, Mitsos rowed across to consult with him. He advised going ashore, and though Mitsos hesitated at first, for if the Capsina had wanted him she would have sent for him, they went together.

The long line of houses along the harbor was still smouldering—though for the most part they had been skeletons of dwelling-places, built only of wood —a heap of charred and blackened beams. Sometimes a breath of moving air came down from the mountain behind, and fanned the burned heaps into a sullen glare of glowing charcoal, or blowing off a layer of white ash, showed that the fire still lived beneath. A row of mimosa-trees fronted the houses, their leaves all singed and wilted with the heat, and as the two landed on the quay the dawn breeze awoke and blew straight down to them across the burned town, hot and stifling, and, what gave to Mitsos a sudden pang of intimate horror, with the smell of burning wood was mingled a smell as of roasting meat. Here and there from a heap of charred ruins protruded a blackened leg or arm, or the figure of a man or woman lay free from the fallen timbers, but with hair consumed to its roots, and holes burned in the clothes, a crying horror and offence to the purity and sweetness of morning. Once, on their way up that street of death, Mitsos turned to Kanaris with ashen lips. "I think I cannot go on," he whispered, but after a moment or two he mastered himself and followed the other. The ghastly hideousness of the sight, now that his blood danced with no fever of war nor was his heart shadowed by an anxiety fiercer than this indiscriminate death, touched some nerve which the shambles at Tripoli had left unthrilled. Here and there from the waters of the harbor the masts of some sunken vessel pricked the surface, and the slope of the beach was strewn with the wreckage, not of ships alone. And by degrees Mitsos's cold horror grew hot with the fiery lust for vengeance; and steeling himself to look and feed on the sight, before long he looked and needed no steeling. The color returned to his lips and inflamed his face, his eye was lit from within with the thought of what should swiftly follow. For beyond a doubt this was the work of the three ships that had sailed from Lepanto only a few days before, and, indeed, they must have been gone not yet a full day.

Curious and pitiful was it to see the dogs still guarding a pile of burned beams which their instinct told them was home; they had returned, no doubt, when the fierceness of the fire was over, and now lay in front of the consumed houses, growling at Kanaris and Mitsos as they passed, or, if they came close, springing up with bared teeth ready to attack. At one house a great gaunt dog rose as they approached and stood with hackles up, snarling; the poor brute stood on three legs, for the fourth was broken and hung down limply. And, seeing that, a sudden poignancy of compassion at this faithfulness in suffering stung Mitsos to the quick, and, drawing his pistol, he put the beast out of his pain.

As yet there had been seen no sign of the Capsina or her party, but the noise of the shot reached them, and next moment two of the sailors came at a run round a corner some small distance up the street. They waited on seeing who the new-comers were, and Kanaris and Mitsos came up with them.

"Where is she?" asked Mitsos.

"At the house of her mother, clearing what is fallen to see if there are any left alive."

Mitsos and Kanaris followed, and, passing through two short streets of ghastly wreckage, found themselves at the house. It was larger than most, and built of stone, so that while the walls still stood the inside was one piled mass of burned beams and fittings of the floors and staircase. As they came near four sailors emerged out of the door with the charred burden of what had been a man. This, covered with a cloth where the face had been, they laid with others like it a little distance off.

The Capsina had kept with her some half-dozen of the men, with whom she was clearing the beams and débris, having sent the remainder off to other houses. She was hacking furiously at a beam too heavy to drag away except in pieces when Mitsos entered. Her dress, hands, and face were all blackened with the work; one hand was bleeding, and round the wrist was wrapped a bandage of linen. Seeing Mitsos, she stopped for a moment and wiped the sweat from her forehead. No tears or sign that she had been weeping was in her eye, only a savage and relentless fury.

"So you have come," and she looked up. "Ah, it is day already," and she quenched an oil-lamp that was burning by her. "I was going to send for you and more men when day broke, for it was no good coming at night. I only stayed because I could not go away. Send for more men from our ship, little Mitsos, and you, Kanaris, from yours, for we must make speed, leaving only a few there and a few on the shore, who will send word if the Turks are seen. And let those on board be in readiness to sail at a moment. Ah!" she went on, with a sudden lifting of her hands indescribably piteous, "we should have come straight through Lepanto and chanced everything. Then, perhaps, we might have saved the place. This," and she clasped her hands together and then threw them apart—"this was the house from which my father took his bride. Ah, ah!"—and she took up her axe and fell to hewing at the beam again, like a thing possessed.

It was no time to waste words, and as soon as the fresh contingents came, some with axes, others with ship's cutlasses and capstan-bars, or anything that would help clear the wreckage, Mitsos and Kanaris went off and began searching the houses for those who might still be alive. They found that the massacre had taken place and been done with thoroughness before the burning began, and the devil's work had been carried out coolly and systematically. At the end of the street leading up out of the village towards the mountain there had evidently been some sort of combined stand made by the villagers, for there the corpses lay thick; and higher up on the path lay others who had run for their lives, only to be shot down by those infernal marksmen as they climbed the steep hill-side. But an hour's search was rewarded by Mitsos finding one man who still breathed, but who died not half an hour after; and farther on, in the front room of a house, he discovered a woman lying dead, while on her breast lay a baby, alive and seemingly unhurt, who pulled at its mother's dress crying for food.

Then he turned and searched the houses opposite on the other side of the street, but found nothing that lived, and so came back to the church, which stood with doors open, and being built of stone throughout, the Turks had not attempted to fire.

To make the search thorough, though not expecting to find any one there, he entered, and then stopped with a quick-drawn gasp.

No pillage had been done there, the place was orderly and quiet; a row of little silver lamps untouched and lighted hung across the church above the low altar-screen; a big brass candlestick stood on the left, filled with the great festa tapers, still burning. Only from the great wooden crucifix which stood above the altar the carved Christ had been removed, and in its place, fastened hand and foot by nails and bound there by a rope, was the figure of a young man, naked.

Mitsos paused only for a moment, crossed himself, and without speech beckoned to the others. The door of the altar-screen was locked, but putting his weight to it, he burst it open. Then, with three others, he mounted onto the altar, and lifting the cross from its place, laid it on the floor. The figure on it lay quite still, but there was no other mark of violence on it than the rents in the hands and feet made by the nails, and even as Mitsos wrapped a piece torn from his shirt round one of them to get a firmer hold, the lad stirred his head and opened his eyes.

"Fetch Kanaris," said Mitsos, to one of the men; "he has skill in these things."

One by one the nails were loosened and the limbs freed, and Mitsos carried the lad down the church out into the fresh air, where he propped him up against the door. The blood had clotted thickly round the wounds, and though the withdrawal of the nails had caused it to break out afresh, Mitsos managed to stay the flow by bandaging the arms and legs tightly where they joined the body, as Nikolas had taught him to do. The lad had fainted again, but one of the sailors, a rough Hydriot fellow down whose cheeks the tears were running, though he knew it not, had spirits with him, and poured a draught down the young man's throat, and in a little while he moved one arm feebly. Another had found his clothes laid by the altar, and Mitsos tenderly, like a woman, wrapped these round him as well as he could without jarring him, and then, lifting him gently off the stones where they had set him down, laid him across his knees, supporting his head on his shoulder.

Before long Kanaris came, washed and bound up the wounds, and, as the life began to run more freely and the hopes of saving him increased, arranged a litter with leaves and branches strewn on an unhinged door, and had him carried down to the ship.

When he was gone Mitsos went back into the church, and putting the carved image back onto the cross, set it again in its place above the altar. Then for that he had committed sacrilege in standing there, he knelt down before he left the church.

"Oh, most pitiful!" he said, "if I have sinned Thou wilt forgive."

When he got outside again the rest of the men had gone back to the work, but he paused on the church steps a moment, blind with pity and hate and the lust for vengeance, and with a heart swelling with a horror unspeakable. The wounds of that living image of the crucified should not cry to deaf ears. The very sacrilege that had been done seemed to consecrate his passion for revenge, to lift his human hate and pity into a motive of crusade for the wrong done to Christ. Blasphemously and in hideous mockery those incarnate devils had turned their inhuman cruelty into a two-edged thing, cutting at God and man alike. And with the Capsina feeding hate in the ruins of her mother's home, and Mitsos feeding hate at the house of God, it was likely that their ship had not been named amiss.

The work was over an hour or two before the sunset. The Capsina had found in her mother's house nothing but the dead, but, elsewhere, two women who were still alive, but died before the noon; Kanaris had found none, so that from what had been a flourishing village two days ago there were left only the young man with whom they had preferred to commit outrageous blasphemy, leaving the body to a lingering death rather than to kill, and the baby untouched by some unwitting oversight. Only a few bodies of Turks had been found—the thing had been massacre, not fight. As the Capsina and Mitsos were going down to the ship again in silence, he saw her turn aside to where a dead Turk was lying under a tree. She stamped on the face of the dead thing without a word, and followed by Mitsos, stepped into the boat that was waiting for them.

No sooner had all got on board than the Capsina gave the order to start. But before they had gone half a dozen miles the breeze failed, and, for the night was close upon them, they lay to waiting for the day, fearing that if a breeze sprang up in the night they might, by taking advantage of it, overshoot those for whom they were looking. The lad the Turks had crucified was on

Kanaris's ship, where he would receive better doctoring than either Mitsos or the Capsina had the skill to give him, but the baby was on the *Revenge*.

They had not tasted food since morning, the Capsina not since the night before, and they ate ravenously and in silence. Once only during their meal did the Capsina speak.

"When I have hung those who did this thing," she said, "I may be able to weep for my own dead."

But when they had eaten, and were still sitting speechless opposite each other, a little wailing cry came from the cabin next them, and the Capsina rose and left the room. Presently after she brought the baby in, rocking it in her arms, and before long the child ceased crying and slept, and Mitsos, looking up, saw the girl weeping silently, with great sobs that seemed to tear her. And at that he got up and went on deck, thinking that it would be the better to leave her alone with the baby.

He awoke before dawn next morning to a haunting sense of horror and excitement, to which by degrees awakening memory gave form, and only throwing on his coat, went up. A thick white mist hung over the bay higher than where he stood on the deck, but it seemed to be not very thick, and strangely luminous. So he climbed up the rigging of the mainmast as far as the cross-trees and looked out. The sky was cloudless—a house of stars—in the west the moon was pale and large. They were not more than a mile from a rocky headland, which peered out darkly into the white mist farther down; perhaps a mile away another pointed a black finger into the water, and between the two the line of coast was lost, and Mitsos rightly supposed that they were opposite some bay. Then suddenly, with a catch of his heart, his eye fell on a couple of masts which rose pricking the mist scarcely half a mile distant, and looking more closely he saw the masts of two other ships, one to the right, the other to the left, a little farther off. And with fierce excitement he climbed down and went to the Capsina's cabin. In a moment, so quickly that she could not have been asleep or undressed, she came out to him with a finger on her lip.

"Hush!" she whispered, "the baby is asleep. What is it, Mitsos?"

"Three ships are lying not far from us," he said. "I make no doubt they are the Turks. You can see their masts from the cross-trees; on deck there is white mist."

"Where are they?"

"Between us and land, which is a mile off, on the entrance of a bay."

"Is there wind?"

"Not a breath; but when day wakes the wind will wake with it, and the mist will lift. The sun will be up, I should think, in an hour. There is the smell of morning already in the air."

The Capsina paused a moment, thinking intently, and went out on deck.

"Praise be to the God of vengeance!" she said. "Oh, Mitsos, pray that our revenge may be complete. See, this is what we will do. As soon as the wind comes we sail round them into the bay, Kanaris attacks them on this side. Send across to Kanaris at once. Saints in heaven, but how are we to find him in the mist? Go aloft again, lad; see if you can spy his masts: he cannot be far, for when we lay to last night he was close by us, and look out to see if there is a sign of wind coming."

Mitsos returned speedily. "He is not a quarter of a mile from us to seaward," he said, "and it is already lighter, and I see where we are: the farther cape is just this side Galaxidi. And oh, Capsina, there is a great black cloud coming up from the west; the wind may be here before the sun."

In a few minutes the *Revenge* was all alive, though silent and soft-footed, making ready, as a cat makes ready for its spring. A boat had put off for Kanaris's ship with Mitsos in it, who was to explain what their tactics were to be. All that they could be certain of was to take the *Revenge* in between the land and the Turks, for they would get the breeze first, while Kanaris waited outside to stop them if they would not engage but tried to escape across the gulf. If they stood their ground he was to close in on them.

Mitsos was back again in less than twenty minutes, but already the jib, halyards, and upper and lower yards had been set, in case the wind came down on them, as so often happened in that narrow sea, in a squall; the men were all at their posts, the cutlasses and muskets were laid out in depots on the deck, if it came to a hand-to-hand fight, and the Capsina was on the bridge. Dimitri, who was a kind of first mate, being directly under Mitsos and the Capsina, was standing with her, and even as Mitsos joined them there came through the still thick mist the shiver of a sigh, and the jib flapped once and again. Then from down the gulf, without further warning, the squall was upon them; in a moment the mist was rent and torn to a thousand eddying fragments, the *Revenge* heeled slowly over to the wind and began to make way. For a short minute sea and land were as clear as in a picture; they saw Turkish ships lying half a mile off, to the northeast, at the mouth of the bay, and next moment the rain fell like a sheet. But that glimpse had been enough; there was room and to spare to pass between the nearer headland and the ships, and the Capsina pointed without speaking, and Dimitri roared his order to the men at the tiller. The *Revenge* trembled and struggled like a thing alive; once the tiller broke from the two men who held it, and she sheered off straight into the wind again; but next moment they had it fastened down and they tacked off northeast, and for a minute the rain ceased as suddenly as it had begun, and the ship threshed on through the ruffled water, gathering speed.

The men were ready at the guns, but the order had been not to fire till they were broadside. Already they could see a stir and bustle on the nearest Turk, and sailors were putting up the jib, as if to run out to sea. Then it seemed they sighted the *Revenge* bearing down on them, and they hesitated a moment, and presently after Mitsos saw two or three ports being opened. But they were too late; by this time the *Revenge* was broadside, and all three batteries poured a deluge of shot into her, slipped past her like a swan, and fired again as she crossed their bows, leaving the three Turks, as the Capsina had intended, between her and Kanaris.

Once in the bay, the face of the squall reached them not so violently, for they were under shelter of the promontory close to which they had passed; but the Capsina ran on some half-mile before putting about. Of the Turkish ships they could see that the middle one, lying too close to the one on the leeward of it, had, in trying to put out to sea, fouled the other, and Kanaris observing this, hauled up his halyards, beat up a little way against the wind, and then, turning, fired a broadside into them. Meantime, the ship first attacked, whose foremast had been shot in two by the Capsina's broadside, had cut away the wreck and was making for the open sea, and seeing this the *Revenge* was put about, and making a wide tack to eastward, passed near the two which had fouled each other, and got in two rounds, with only the reply of one. Kanaris, whose business it was to stop any of them getting away, instantly put about to head the escaping ship, but the other slipped by him, and the two beat out to sea together.

The Capsina saw this.

"He will overhaul her in two miles," she said to Mitsos; "and now to our work again," and her face was grimmer than death and hell.

The other two ships were now free; but they saw at once that the one which had received the fire both of the *Revenge* and Kanaris was already doomed, and from minute to minute as they overhauled them she was visibly settling down with a cant to leeward. There was no doubt that she had been struck by one or the other below the water-line, and, indeed, as they neared her they could see the pumps vomiting water down her sides. She still carried sail, for they seemed to hope to get near the land before she foundered, but her sails dragged her farther over, until from the deck of the *Revenge*, now some three hundred yards distant, they could see both lines of bulwarks, with a strip of deck in between. Then they saw them begin to lower the boats, and at that the

Capsina gave the word to fire, and Mitsos, thinking on the deeds of the day before, felt his heart laugh within him. At that range the heavy guns of the brig were the sentence of destruction, and their whole broadside went home, sweeping the decks and tearing fresh holes in her side. Already the list was so great that she could no longer reply, and as they neared her the Capsina again gave the command to fire.

Then was seen a disgraceful thing; for the second ship, still untouched, put about, leaving her companion a wreck at the mercy of the *Revenge*. But indeed there was little to be saved, and the Capsina, seeing the tactics of the other and not wishing to waste shot now the work was done, put down her helm and, passing by the bows of the disabled ship, went in pursuit. The other carried two stern guns, and she opened fire, but both balls hummed by harmlessly—the one missing altogether, the other just carrying off a few splinters from the starboard bulwarks; and in answer the *Revenge* sheered off a moment into the wind, which was still shifting to the north, and replied with the three starboard guns of the upper deck. One shot went wide, but of the two others the bow gun made a raking gash in the stern of the chase, and that amidships, which fired a little after, took the rudder, smashing the rudder-post below the juncture with the tiller, leaving her simply in the hand of the wind. In a moment she swung round from her course and pointed straight across the bows of the *Revenge*.

On the instant the Capsina saw her chance, for in a second or two she would cross close.

"Let go the helm!" she shrieked; "get ready to fire starboard guns."

The tiller banged against the side, and the *Revenge* swung round into the wind, while every moment the two ships got closer to each other, and at a distance of not more than a hundred yards they were broadside to broadside. Then:

"Fire!" she cried.

For a moment they neither saw nor heard anything through the wreaths of their own smoke. Then, as the wind dispersed it, they saw the great ship a wreck on the water. She heeled over till the yard-arms dipped and the sails trailed in the water. The deck, they could see, was covered with men holding on, as if to prolong the bitterness of death, to whatever they could catch. Some climbed up the mast, others clung to the bulwarks, some jumped overboard. But the Capsina scanned it all with hungry eyes, and, as if unwilling to leave the feast, gave an order to shorten sail, and in the slackening speed ran to the stern of the *Revenge* to look her last on the drowning men.

Then she turned to Mitsos.

"We may leave them, I think," she said; "they are more than a mile from land."

Kanaris and his charge were out of sight, and the *Revenge* put about to the ship she had left before. She was sinking fast, but they saw that the crew had manned some half-dozen boats, which were rowing to land, and the Capsina called Dimitri.

"Sink all," she said.

The hindermost boat was not more than two hundred yards ahead, but the Capsina delayed her fire. Then, as they got within fifty yards of it, she walked slowly and calmly to the side of the ship, and spoke in Turkish.

"We are more merciful than those who crucify," she cried. And then, "Fire!"

The other boats seeing what had happened, and resolving, if possible, to sell their lives more dearly, got ready their muskets. But the Capsina saw this, and while they were out of musket range:

"The bow guns for the rest," she said. "It is good target practice."

Five out of the six boats had been sunk, and they were already preparing to fire on the sixth when a sudden pity came over Mitsos.

"Look," he said, "there are women in that boat!"

The Capsina shaded her eyes for a moment against the glare of the water.

"Turkish women only," she said.

"But women!" cried Mitsos, with who knows what memories of one who had lived in a Turkish house.

"There were women in Elatina," said the Capsina. "Fire!" Then turning to Mitsos: "Are you a woman, too?" she said—and suddenly her voice failed as she looked at him. "Mitsos, little Mitsos!"

And he looked at her, biting his lip to check the trembling of his mouth.

"Even so," he said, and turned away.

The first squall had blown over, and an hour of checkered sunshine succeeded; but in the west again the clouds were coming up in wind-tormented ribbons, and they had only just cleared the bay when a second hurricane was on them. For some three-quarters of an hour the wind had been slowly shifting into the north, and the wreckage of the ship they had sunk at the mouth of the bay had drifted a little out to sea, and they cut between drift-wood and masts and here and there a man still afloat. Where Kanaris and the third ship were they had no certain idea, but it was impossible for the clumsy Turkish ships to tack against a violent wind without having the masts crack above their heads, and this one, as they knew, was without its foremast, and must have sailed nearly down wind. The second squall was even more violent than the first, and the *Revenge* scudded out to sea with only jib and halyards flying. As they got farther from the funnel of land down which the wind came, the force of it decreased a little, and they hoisted the upper yards on the mainmast. But for an hour or more they raced across a choppy and following sea, obscured by driving squalls of rain, before they sighted either. All this time the Capsina had hardly spoken, and Mitsos, standing by her, was as silent. But as they came in sight of the two ships, both running before the wind, she stamped on the bridge.

"Hoist this foresail!" she cried.

Mitsos looked up: the ship, he knew, was carrying as much sail as she could.

"You will lose your mast," he said.

The Capsina turned on him furiously.

"Let us lose it, then!" she cried.

"And you will go none the faster," he said. "More sail will only stop the ship."

"That is what they say," she remarked. "They say it pulls a ship over, and makes the bows dip. What do you advise, little Mitsos?"

"By no means hoist the foresail. Even if the ship can carry it you will go the slower," he said. "Is it an order?"

"Yes."

Then suddenly she turned to him.

"Do not judge me," she said, "for indeed I am not myself. When this is over, if God wills, I shall be myself again. Oh, lad!" she cried, "have you water or milk in your veins? Do you forget what we saw yesterday?"

Mitsos looked at her a moment, and caught something of the burning hate in her eye.

"I do not forget," he said. "But the women—oh, think of it!"

"I too am a woman," said Sophia.

Then, after a pause: "Ah, but look; is not the ship worthy of its name? See how she gains on them! Oh, Mitsos, go below if you will, and take no part in this. But I must do what I must do. Surely God is with us. Do you forget what

91

you saw in the church? You do not. Neither do I forget the house of my mother."

Again the rain came on, a cold scourge of water, and in the lashing fury of the downpour both ships were again lost for a while.

Then there followed a raking gleam of sunshine, which struck the gray of the sea, turning it to one superb blue, and already they could see the figures of men on the ships. Kanaris was on the port side, trying evidently to head the Turk, and if she came on to give her a broadside, or if she declined to drive her back. The sea was rising every minute, and the three ships rolled scuppers under, and it was evidently out of the question for him, in such a sea and at the distance they were apart, to fire at her.

The Turk had made a good start against Kanaris, and though the *Sophia* was overhauling her, it was clear that she was no tub, and as they were both running before the wind, it was more a question of which ship could carry most sail than of seacraft; and for another mile or more they ran on, the two pursuing ships gradually gaining on the enemy, but not very rapidly. It was evident that she was making for some port on the southern side of the gulf, perhaps where she expected the second trio of Turkish ships, and it was this the Capsina wished to prevent. But the Turk saw that both were gaining on her, and knowing that the opposite coast must be at least nine miles off, hoisted the mainsail. The Capsina started in amazement as she saw the great canvas go up; the mast bent like a whip for a moment, but stood the strain, and she scudded off.

"It is desperate," she said to Mitsos; "she cannot stand it. In ten minutes she will be ours."

The Capsina was right; only a temporary lull could have let them get the sail up, and before many minutes the squall came down on them again; the mainmast bent, and then, with a crash they could hear from their ship, broke, and a great heap of canvas encumbered the deck.

"Two points to starboard!" said the Capsina. "Get ready to fire port guns!"

More rapidly than ever the distance diminished; the *Revenge* creeping up on the starboard side, the *Sophia* holding her course to port, until at length the doomed ship was nearly between them, and on the moment the Capsina gave the word to fire, and the broadside crashed into the Turk. A moment after Kanaris fired, and the Turk replied with a broadside to each. The Capsina did not wait to reply again, but sailed past her, and then put the helm hard to port, risking masts and sails, so that the ship swung round with her broadside to the Turk's bows some five hundred yards off. Kanaris, who kept his distance, fired again, and section by section, slowly and with deliberate aim, the

Capsina volleyed at her bows. Steady shooting was impossible on such a sea, but some of the shot they saw went home, one hitting the bowsprit, and several others crashing through the bulwarks and raking the ship lengthways. No fire answered them, but her broadside replied twice or thrice to Kanaris, doing some damage.

The Turk was now practically a log on the water, and the Capsina, knowing there was time and to spare, made a wide tack off into the northeast, and returning on the opposite tack again closed up with the Turk from behind, putting a broadside into her stern.

At that there was only silence from the Turk, and the Capsina closed in again on the starboard quarter, signalling Kanaris to do the same on the port side, and as they approached they saw that the decks were strewn with dead. A company of men were marshalled forward with muskets, who separated into two companies, and manned the bulwarks on each side, waiting for the ships to come to a closer range.

But the Capsina laughed scornfully.

"I would not waste the life of a man on my ship over those dogs," she said. "Train the bow guns on them and do not sink the ship. Kill the men only."

The wind was abating and the sea falling, and in a quarter of an hour of the eighty or a hundred men who had been left they could only see sixteen or twenty. But these continued firing their muskets coolly and without hurry at the approaching ships, and a couple of men on the *Revenge* were wounded and one killed.

"I should not have thought Turks were so brave," said the Capsina. "Be ready with the grappling-irons! Port the helm! And be quick when we get in. Fifty men with muskets man the port side. Keep up the fire! Keep under shelter of the bulwarks all of you!"

The *Revenge* slid up to the Turk's starboard quarter, and as they got within a hundred yards the Capsina gave orders to furl all sail; as the distance lessened, the irons were thrown, the ropes were pulled home, and the two ships brought up side by side.

A dozen Turks or so were still gathered in the bows, but as the crew of the *Revenge* swarmed the deck, they laid down their muskets and stood with arms folded. One of them, in an officer's uniform, was sitting in a chair smoking.

He got up with an air of indolent fatigue, still holding the mouth-piece of his pipe.

"I surrender," he said, in Greek. "Where is your captain?"

The men made way for the Capsina, and she walked up the deck between their lines.

"I am the captain," she said.

The man raised his eyebrows.

"Indeed!" and he laughed softly to himself. "You are too handsome for the trade," he said. "You are better looking than any of my harem, and there are several Greeks among them. Well, I surrender."

"For that word," said the Capsina, "you hang. Otherwise perhaps I should have done you the honor to shoot you."

The man blanched a little, and his teeth showed in a sort of snarl.

"You do not understand," he said. "I surrender."

"You do not understand," she replied. "I hang you. For my mother was of Elatina."

She came a step nearer him.

"If it were not that I hold the cross a sacred thing," she said, "I would crucify you, very tenderly, that you might live long. Oh, man," and she burst out with a great gust of fury, "it is you and what you did in Elatina that has made a demon of me! I curse you for it. There, take him, two of you, and hang him from the mizzen yards. Do not speak to me," she cried to the captain, "or I will smite you on the mouth! It is a woman you are dealing with, not a thing from the harem."

In a moment two men had bound his legs and pinioned his arms, and, with the help of two more, they carried him like a sack up the rigging and set him on the yard. Then they made fast one end of the rope to the mast and noosed the other round his neck, while the Capsina stood on the deck, unflinching, an image of vengeance. And at a sign from her they pushed him off into the empty air.

Mitsos gave one short gasp, for though he would have killed a man, laughing and singing as he drove the knife home, in fight, his blood revolted at the coldness of this, and he turned to the Capsina.

"You say you are a woman!" he cried. "Is that a woman's deed?" and he pointed to the dangling burden.

"He insulted me," said the Capsina, "and I repay insults. As for the rest, shoot them," and she turned on her heel, with her back to Mitsos, and he could not see that her lip was trembling.

But it was not at the hanging or the shooting that she trembled. She had sworn she would avenge the death of those in Elatina—for to her these were not prisoners of war, but murderers of women—and that she did without flinching. But Mitsos's words recalled her to herself, and thinking inwardly of the child's-play on the ship with him, she wondered if it were possible that this stone which seemed to be her heart could ever be moved again to tears or laughter, or that Mitsos could smile again or jest with so cold and cruel a girl. And at that thought she turned to him piteously.

"Oh, Mitsos, it is not me, indeed it is not!" she cried, passionately. "Take me as I am now out of your remembrance, for pity's sake, and think of me only as I was before. I will be the same again; I will be the same. Ah, you don't understand!"

CHAPTER VI

The prize was divided equally between the two ships, as it had been agreed that all taken on this cruise, by whichever ship captured, should be shared in common, after one-half had been appropriated to the fund for the war, out of which the wages of the crew were paid. Evidently the spoils from Elatina had been carried on this ship, for they found many embroidered Greek dresses, several vestments, presumably from the desecrated church, and a considerable sum of money, packed in hampers. The *Revenge* had hardly suffered at all in the encounter, but a hole had been stove high in the bows of the *Sophia*, some five yards of bulwark had been knocked into match-wood, and the round-house was a sieve. They had also lost eight men killed, and from both ships some thirty wounded. Under these circumstances it was best to put in at Galaxidi for repairs, and, as the crew would not now be sufficient for the handling of the ship in case of a further engagement, for the raising of a few recruits. Kanaris himself had a graze on the wrist from a musket-shot as they were getting to close quarters, but the hours had been sweet to him, and his cold gray eyes were as of some wild beast hungry for more.

The Capsina examined the gear and sailing of the prize with scornful wonder. "A good hole for rats to die in," was all her comment. But there were half a dozen serviceable guns and a quantity of ammunition, the latter of which they divided between the two brigs. She would have liked to remove the guns also, for, apart from their use, she felt it would be a pleasant and bitter thing to make them turn traitors to their former owners, but there was no tackling apparatus fit for such weights, and they had to be left. But as she had no notion of letting them again fall into the hands of the Turks, she set fire to the ship before leaving it, and saw it drift away southeastward, a sign of fire, with its crew of death, its captain still dangling from the foremast and swinging out from right to left beyond the bulwarks as the ship rolled. There was a gun loose in the deck battery, and they could hear it crashing and charging from side to side as the unruddered vessel dipped and staggered to the waves, with flames ever mounting higher. Then another squall of impenetrable rain swept across the sea, and they saw her no more.

The Capsina had intended to escort Kanaris as far as Galaxidi, on the chance of other Turkish ships being about, but when they came near and saw that the coast was clear, she turned off into the bay where they had fought that morning to see if there was anything left of either of the other two ships worth picking up. But she found that both had sunk, one in deep water, the other in not more than fifteen fathoms, and through the singular clear water they could see her lying on her side, black and dead, while the quick fishes played and poised above and round her. The sight had a curious fascination for the girl, and, after putting about, she lay to for an hour under shelter of the land, while she rowed out again to the spot and leaned over the side of the boat, feeding ravenously on the sight, angry if a flaw of wind disturbed the clearness of it. But to Mitsos, though his heart could be savage, the poor ship seemed a pitiful thing, and he wondered at the fierceness of the girl.

They reached Galaxidi before the evening and the land-breeze fell, and the Capsina, who had cousins there, went ashore with the baby, intending to leave it there, for, indeed, on the brig they had but little time or fit temper for a child that should have been still lying at its mother's breast. She heard from her friends of a young mother who would perhaps take charge of it, for her own child, a baby of three days old, had suddenly died, and the Capsina herself took it there, nursing it with a singular tenderness, and jealous of all hands that touched it.

"See," she said to the mother, "I have brought you this to care for. I am told that your own baby has died. It seems like a gift of God to you, does it not? Yet it is no gift," she added, suddenly; "the child is to be mine. But I will pay you well."

The young woman, no more, indeed, than a girl, came forward from where she had been sitting, and looked at the baby for a moment with dull, lustreless eyes.

Then suddenly the mother's love, widowed of its young, leaped into her face.

"Ah, give it to me," she cried, quickly. "Give it me," and a moment afterwards the baby was at her breast.

The Capsina stared for a little space in wonder and amazement, then her face softened and she sat down by the girl.

"What is your name?" she asked.

"Catherine Vlastos," and her voice caught in her throat; "but Constantine Vlastos, my husband, is dead, and the little one is dead."

Again the Capsina waited without words.

"Tell me," she said, at length, "what is it you feel? How is it that you want the child? It is nothing to you."

"Nothing?" and the girl laughed from pure happiness. "It is nothing less than life."

"You will take it for me?"

"Take it for you!" Then, as the baby stirred and laid a fat little objectless hand on her breast: "You are the Capsina," she said, "and a great lady. They tell me you have taken three Turkish ships. Oh, that is a fine thing, but I would not change places with you."

Sophia rose from her seat, and walked up and down the room.

"You loved your husband?" she said, at length. "Was that why you loved your baby, and why you love this baby?"

"I don't know. How should I know?"

Sophia stopped in her walk.

"And I love the baby, too," she said, "and I know not how or why. Perhaps only because it was so little and helpless, for, indeed, I do not like children. I don't want to leave it here. Yet I must, I suppose. Will you promise to keep it very safe for me? Call it Sophia, that is my name; and, indeed, it has a wise little face. I must go. Perhaps I shall call here again in a few weeks. Let me kiss it. So—I leave money with you, and will arrange for you to be supplied with more."

She turned to the door, but before she was well out of the house she came back again and looked at the baby once more.

"Yes, it is very curious," she said, "that I should care for it at all. Well, good-bye."

Mitsos, meantime, had gone across to Kanaris's ship, where they were busy with repairs. The squalls had blown themselves out, and sky and sea were a sheet of stars and stars reflected. The work was to go on all night, and he had to pick his way carefully between planks and hurrying workmen, doing the jobs by the light of resin flares. The resin flares brought the fishing into his mind—the fishing those dear nights on the bay, and the moonlight wooing and winning of Suleima. How strange that Suleima should be of the same sex as this fine, magnificent Capsina—Suleima with all her bravery and heroism at the fall of Tripoli, woman to her backbone, and the Capsina, admirable and lovable as she was, no more capable of being loved by him than would have been a tigress. Yet she had sobbed over the little crying child—that was more difficult still to understand. And Mitsos, being unlearned in the unprofitable art of analysis, frowned over the problem, and thought not at all that she was of a complicated nature, and then felt that this was the key to the whole situation, but said to himself that she was very hard to understand.

He found Kanaris dressing the wounds of the lad who had been crucified. Healing and wholesome blood ran in his veins, for though they had been dressed roughly, only with oil and bandages, they showed no sign of fester or poisoning. The lad was still weak and suffering, but when he saw Mitsos coming in at the cabin door his face flushed and he sat up in bed with a livelier movement than he had yet shown, and looked up at him with the eyes of a dog.

"I would rise if I could," he said, "and kiss your hands or your feet, for indeed I owe you what I can never repay."

Mitsos smiled.

"Then we will not talk of that," he said, and sat himself down by the bed. "How goes it? Why, you look alive again now. In a few days, if you will, you will be going Turk-shooting with the rest of us. Ah, but the devils, the devils!" he cried, as he saw the cruel wounds in the hands; "but before God, lad, we have done something already to revenge you and Him they blasphemed, and we will do more. How do they call you?"

The boy was sitting with teeth tight clinched to prevent his crying out at the painful dressing of the wounds, but at this he looked up suddenly, seeming to forget the hurt.

"Christos is my name," he said. "That is why they crucified me. Oh, Mitsos, do you know what they said? They looked at me—you know how Turks can look when they play with flesh and blood—when I told them my name, and one said, 'Then we will see if you can die patiently as that God of yours did.'"

The lad laughed suddenly, and his eyes blazed.

"And though I wince," he said, "and could cry like a woman at this little pain, yet, before God, I could have laughed then when they nailed me to the cross, and set me up above the altar. I cannot tell you what strange joy was in my heart. Was it not curious? Those infidel men crucified me because my name was Christos. Surely they could have had no better reason."

Kanaris had finished the dressing of the wounds, and the boy thanked him, and went on:

"So I did not struggle nor cry at all; indeed, I did not want to. Then soon after, it was not long I think, hanging as I did, the blood seemed to sing and grow heavy in my ears, and my head dropped; once or twice I raised it, to take breath, but before long I grew unconscious, supposing at the end that I was dying, and glorying in it, for I knew that the Greeks would come again and find me there, and the thought that I should be found thus, with head drooped like the wooden Christ, was sweet to me. And they came—you came—" and the lad broke off, smiling at the two.

Mitsos's throat seemed to him small and burning, and he choked in trying to speak. So for answer he rose and kissed the boy on the forehead, and was silent till again he had possession of his voice.

"Christos," he said, and involuntarily, with a curious confusion of thought, he crossed himself—"Christos, it is even as you say. For it seems to me that somehow that was a great honor, that which they did to you, though to them only a blasphemous cruelty."

Mitsos paused a moment, and all the dimly understood superstitious beliefs of his upbringing and his people surged into his mind. The half-pagan teaching which suspected spirits in the wind, and saw gods and fairies in the forest, strangely blended with a child-like faith which had never conceived it possible to doubt the truths of his creed, combined to turn this boy into something more than human, to endow him with the attributes of a type. He knelt down by the bed, strangely moved.

"It is I," he said, "who should kiss your hands, for have you not suffered, died almost on the cross, where wicked men nailed you for being called by His name?"

Mitsos was trembling with some mysterious excitement; and his words were so unlike anything that Kanaris had suspected could come from him, that the latter was startled. His own emotions had been far more deeply stirred than he either liked or would have confessed, and to see Mitsos possessed by the same hysterical affection frightened him. He laid his hand on his shoulder.

"Get up, little Mitsos," he said; "you don't know what you are saying. See, the Capsina has gone on shore; you will have supper with us. We will have it all together here, as I have finished the doctoring. You feel you can eat to-night?" he said, turning to the boy.

Christos smiled.

"Surely, but you and Mitsos must feed me," and he looked with comic contempt at his bandaged hands.

"That is good," said Kanaris, and, clapping his hands, he told the cabin-boy to bring in supper for the three.

Mitsos's serene sense soon came back to him, and he wondered half-shamedly at himself, and thought of his previous excursion into the kingdom of hysterics, which he had made after the fight at the mill. Certainly Christos was human enough at supper, and they put victuals into his mouth, and in the vain attempt to ply him with wine simultaneously, brought him to the verge of choking.

Mitsos found the Capsina waiting up for him on the *Revenge* when he got back. She was sitting idle, a thing unusual, and she looked as if she had been crying. But she smiled at him, though rather tremulously, as he entered, and pointed to a seat, and all Mitsos's amazed horror at the hanging was struck from his mind.

"Oh, Capsina," he said, "you do not know how sorry I feel for you. Surely you were no more than just to those on the Turkish ships, and indeed this is no time for gentleness. You have been thinking of those that—that were in Elatina?"

The Capsina nodded.

"Of them, and, oddly enough, of the baby, which I have left here. How is the lad they crucified? You have seen him?"

"Yes." Then in a whisper, "Is it not strange?" he said; "his name is Christos."

"Oh, Mitsos! Was that why they did thus to him?"

"Yes. They said they would see if he could die as patiently."

The Capsina flushed, and her eyes were fire.

"Then may Christ never forgive me if I do not revenge this thing by blood and blood and blood! Here and by this I vow," and she laid her hand on the little shrine at the end of the cabin, "that if ever I stay my hand or spare one of those accursed enemies of Him, that that day shall be the last day of my life, for indeed I shall not be worthy to live and breathe pure air of His making. So I swear. And may all the saints of heaven, and may the blessed Christ, and the thrice-holy mother of Christ, help me to keep my vow!"

She knelt a moment before the shrine, crossing herself, and then turned to Mitsos.

"We will take the lad with us, if he will come," she said, "for I think that the blessing of God cannot fail to rest on the ship that carries him. I will go and see him in the morning. And now, little Mitsos, let us go to bed, for it has not been a very quiet day for us; and for me, I could sleep like a child tired with play. Good-night, lad. I thank God every day for that meeting of ours."

She held his hand in hers for a moment, with a gentle pressure, looking at him with great shining eyes and smiling mouth.

"Good-night," he said; "and oh, Capsina, I bless God for that meeting, too, and as far as there is strength in me I will help you to keep your vow. It is even so; they are the enemies of the Christ, and He has graciously made to us for Him. Yet—yet, do not hang a man again. For somehow it seems to me poor manners to add insults to death, and to insult is what Turks do."

Sophia looked at him, silent, then laughed, passing her hand wearily over her eyes.

"And as you are of the Mainats, and I of the clan of Capsas, you think we should have fine manners. Oh, little Mitsos, you are a boy of the very oddest thoughts. Well, be it as you say. I was angry when I did that, and indeed we have no time for anger, for the sword does not feel angry when it strikes. It only strikes, and strikes true. So."

CHAPTER VII

From the moment of entering the Gulf of Corinth one precaution was of primary necessity to the success of the Capsina's expedition, and that was that no word of the coming of her ships should go about between the various Turkish ships in the gulf. Their good fortune had determined that the nine ships which they knew were there were separated into groups of three, and she felt confident that her two could tackle three. But supposing word went about, and the remaining six mobilized, the position would be serious enough to steady even those two brigs full of tigers.

It was practically certain that the Turkish garrison of Lepanto had before this received news from Patras of their entrance into the gulf, and if so only the most dire stress of circumstance would drive the Capsina to attempt to pass again, except at night, for the channel was altogether commanded by the heavy guns of the fortress, and she preferred the windy waters of the gulf, with room to turn and manoeuvre, to that tight-rope of a way. Hitherto all had gone well, for of the three ships they had encountered neither man, woman, or child would do aught else than toss with the ooze and tangle of the gulf, and tell their tale to the fishes; and a further point in their favor was that only a very few villages on the shore had Turkish garrisons, so that any combined movement to drive them into a corner would be difficult of execution. Their safety chiefly lay in expeditious action, and their danger in the escape of any Turkish ships which might manage, after being attacked by them, to join the others.

Now the Capsina's recklessness was of the more judicious kind, or, rather, it may be said that she was prudent, except when the occasion demanded a free disregard of possible consequences; it was clearly a poor economy to save a little time and go to sea with ships not thoroughly up to the mark, and she waited with a rebellious patience until the *Sophia* was altogether fit for action again. The folk of Galaxidi regarded her more in the light of some splendid incarnation of the spirit of insurrection than a woman, and to them, as to Mitsos, Christos was almost a sacred thing. Men and women came in shoals on to the *Revenge*, where the Capsina had caused him to be moved when he was enough recovered, and looked with a kind of religious awe at the lad whom the infidels had crucified. And the great pride the boy took in what had been done to him was inspiring to see.

But the Capsina's impatience found a bridle in directing and superintending, with Mitsos and Kanaris, the establishment of a fort at Galaxidi which should command the harbor. Galaxidi boasted one of the few well-sheltered harbors on the gulf which could for certain be reached by a well-handled boat in stormy weather, for while the harbor at Aegion faced nearly north and was impossible to make in a northwesterly gale, and the harbor at Corinth had so narrow an entrance that, with a heavy cross sea, a ship was as like as not to be shouldered on to the breakwater, at Galaxidi the harbor faced south, and had a wide entrance protected from the violent westerly winds by the long headland, on the other side of which lay Elatina. Otherwise, the shore for several miles was rocky and inhospitable, and no enemy's ship, as the Capsina saw, could take Galaxidi unless it first had possession of the harbor, and it was on the end of the promontory which commanded it that she caused the defences to be begun.

Heretofore the whole of this coast district had taken no part in the work of the Revolution, and the bloody scheme of the Turks was to wipe out those fishing villages one by one, so as to secure themselves against the possibility of such movements in the future. Such had been the fate of Elatina; for such a fate, no doubt, had Galaxidi been devilishly designed, when the two Greek brigs overtook and spoke with the designers thereof.

On the second day of their stay there, when even the Capsina had been forced to be prepared to stop at least a week, she and Mitsos prowled about the quay and harbor like whelps on some sure trace of blood, how rightly no future was to prove.

"It is a death-trap, little Mitsos," said the girl. "See, this is my plan. Let us put up a big shed on the quay, for all the world like a Turkish custom-house, with the Turkish flag over it, if you will—don't frown, Mitsos, you seem to think that it is our mission to render the Turkish nation immortal—a flag to give confidence, as I was saying. But it shall be no custom-house, or rather a custom-house where the dues are rather heavy, and of our sort. Thus, supposing by some devil's luck either of those two companies of ships escape from us, we can at least do our best to head them towards Galaxidi."

"Where they will see their own flag flying," put in Mitsos. "Eh, but I am a partner with a tigress."

"And I with a ba-a-lamb, it seems," went on the girl, with a glance at this fine-grown ba-a-lamb. "Thus they will sail in unsuspecting, and all the fiends in hell are in it if ever they sail out," she concluded, with a sudden flare.

"There is more to it than that," said Mitsos. "We are in this gulf for a month, or more than a month maybe. It is well to have a place for breathing in. It is sure that we cannot get out of the gulf until the coming of the fleet, or so I think. Well, with a fort here in the hands of the Greeks, we shall not need to."

The Capsina stood silent a moment surveying the harbor, with her head a little on one side.

"It is by no means a rotten egg we are trying to hatch," she said, at length. "The mayor, who is my cousin, shall dine with us to-day, and there will be much talking. Go back to the ship, lad, and smoke your pipe. That is what you want."

"Am I so stupid this morning, then?" asked Mitsos.

"There is no mellowness in tobacco," said she, sententiously, quoting a Greek proverb. "No, you are not stupid, but I have other business in which you have no share."

"And what is that?"

"And who will have made the little Mitsos my confessor?" said she, drolling with him. "Well, father, I am going to see the baby."

"The blessing of the saints be on your work, my daughter," said Mitsos, with prelatical solemnity. "But you are never away from the baby, Capsina. Am I to be superseded?"

She flushed a little.

"Not from my affection," she said, with secret truth; "only in the matter of advice, I claim a right to consult another." And she turned and walked briskly away from the quay.

The mayor, Elias Melissinos, was a little withered man, with a face the color of a ripe crab-apple. His eyes, bright and black like a bird's, peeped out from a great fringe of eyebrow, and seemed the very hearth and home of an infernal shrewdness. He was the first cousin of the Capsina's mother, but thought nothing of his connection with the clan, remarking with much truth that the same God made also the vermin, and the tortoises upon the mountain. But as he had grave theological doubts as to whether it was God or the devil who had made the Turks, he was a suitable ally. He ate his dinner peeking and peering at his food, and swallowing it gulpingly like pills, with a backward toss of his head, occasionally glancing at Mitsos, who fed Christos and himself alternately, and asking sharp little questions. When they had finished they went on deck, and Elias sucked at his pipe like a grave little baby, while the Capsina made exposition.

"See, cousin," she said, "Mitsos and I have examined the quay, and we both think that it is easily defensible and hard to take. There is already a big shed on there; you will have to build another one on the promontory, opposite; between them they will command the harbor like a two-edged sword."

"You will be putting guns on the sheds, maybe?" asked Elias, briskly.

"There would not be much advantage to us in building the sheds and leaving them totally empty," remarked Mitsos.

"Yes, but my dear cousin," said Elias, "where are the guns to come from? For I never yet authentically heard that they grew on the mountain-side. Muskets we have and plenty of them, but I am thinking that before a Turkish ship gets within musket-shot our sheds will be spillikins and match-wood; and, if it comes on to rain, the muskets will get rusty; but, indeed, I don't know that there will be any other result worth the mentioning."

"You can have two four-inch guns from the *Revenge* and two from the *Sophia*," said the Capsina, "for we are a little overarmed if anything. What say you, Mitsos?"

Mitsos scratched his head.

"I say that I wish there were not so many good guns lying at the bottom of the Gulf of Corinth," he said.

"Where do they lie?" asked Elias.

The Capsina sprang up.

"Indeed, the little Mitsos has no wooden head, though he thinks slower than snails walk, cousin. One ship and all its guns lie in fifteen-fathom water, not a mile from land, in the bay westward from the point of Galaxidi. I could lead you there blindfolded. Can you raise them, think you?"

"We can try," said Elias. "But if your brigs are over-armed——"

"They are not overarmed!" cried the girl. "I wish we had more guns."

Elias bowed, with a precise little smile on his lips.

"The mistake is mine," he said. "I was wrong when I thought I heard you say so. Please continue, cousin."

"For the expenses, I will provide out of the money we have put aside for the war fund," continued the Capsina. "How much have we, little Mitsos? Oh, is there nothing you know? In any case there is enough. Then you want men. Are there plenty here who are ready to take up arms?"

"They are ready to stand on their heads, cousin, if you bid them," said Elias.

"Good; now about the attempt to raise some of those guns," and she plunged into details of rafts and gear and divers and tackling, leaving, it is to be feared, both her listeners in a state of bewildered confidence in her powers to draw the moon to the earth if so she wished, but confused as to the methods she purposed to adopt.

In such ways the Capsina drew a curb on her impatience to be gone again, and derived a certain satisfaction in curtailing the hour of Mitsos's tobacco smoking. The six guns, after an infinity of trouble and the swamping of two rafts, were raised and towed to Galaxidi; the corn-mills were put to grind powder, a black flour of death; another shed was run up opposite the quay, and loads of earth and sand to be packed in corn sacks were stored as a protection for both forts. The quantity indicated, as Mitsos pointed out, an outrageously impossible harvest; but, as the Capsina retorted, Turkish ships coming to raid a town do not usually pause to consider whether the preceding summer has been weather suitable for the crops.

But the Capsina having put these preparations in train, intrusting their complete execution to Elias, stayed not an hour after the *Sophia* was again fit for sea, for every hour wasted meant an hour's risk to some perhaps defenseless village, and eight days after their arrival they put to sea again eastward, touring round the gulf, and leaving Galaxidi humming like a hive of bees.

For several days they made but little way, the winds being contrary or calm, and the hours were the first hours of the cruise lived over again. With the help of two crutches Christos was soon able to limp about the deck, and, as his boyish spirits reasserted themselves, became pre-eminently human, showing only a dog-like affection for Mitsos, who fussed over him insistently. The thing both pleased and enraged the Capsina; half the time she was jealous of the lad, but for the rest found it suitable enough that the little Mitsos should have rescued him, and that the rescued should agree with her in his lovableness. When the deck was wet and Christos's crutches showed a greater aptitude for slipping than supporting, Mitsos would take him and carry him across to some sheltered place, where the three would sit by the hour, talking and laughing together.

On one such evening, following a day of fretful and biting rain, the sky had cleared towards sunset, and they were tacking out to sea for a mile or two under a northeasterly wind, to anchor, as soon as the land-breeze dropped, at the end of the second tack, making, if possible, a dark wooded promontory which lay due east. The Capsina always kept as near as possible to the shore, so as not to run the least risk of missing the Turkish ships, which, as they knew, were going from village to village, and a watch was kept for the enemy's ships, the Capsina offering a prize to the sailor who first sighted them.

Mitsos had come slipping and sliding across the deck with Christos in his arms, and a sudden roll of the ship had come near upsetting them.

"So, hereafter," said Mitsos, "you shall shift for yourself, Christos, for you put on the weight of a sack of corn every day. You didn't hurt yourself, did you?"

"Not in any way."

"Are you sure?"

The Capsina burst out laughing.

"Oh, little Mitsos, that I should compare you to a hen. But a hen with one chicken, no other—you and Christos."

Mitsos sat down and filled his pipe and Christos's.

"Well, I know one who clucked considerably over a baby," he said. "And I like taking care of people. There's your pipe, lad. Open your mouth."

The Capsina laughed again.

"Chuck, chuck, chuck," said she.

"Well, let me have two chickens, then," cried Mitsos. "What can I do for you, Capsina?"

"You can be my very good comrade."

"Surely, I hope so. But let me fuss for you. Christos is getting well, and I must take care of somebody."

"Well, you can tell me if it is time to put about."

"Eh, but I didn't bargain that I should have to get up," said Mitsos, raising himself foot by foot, and looking out. "Well, yes, we shall make that promontory on the next tack, and then we can lie to. Nothing been seen of the devils, Dimitri?"

Dimitri shrugged his shoulders.

"Well, we'll put about. You'd best move, Christos. When we go on the other tack you'll get wet there."

"It is of no consequence whether I get wet," remarked Sophia.

"Well, come along, then," said Mitsos. "I'll carry you across first."

Sophia hesitated.

"Help me up, then," said she, and laughed.

Mitsos bent down, gathered her up, and staggered across the deck with her, half laughing, half puzzled.

"Eh, but God made you a big woman," he said. "Why, Christos is half your weight. Steady, now."

But the Capsina slipped from his arms.

"Oh, Christos; it is always Christos!" she cried. "There, go and fetch him, little Mitsos! He is trying to walk himself, and he will get a fall."

Mitsos stared a moment, but obeyed, and the Capsina finished the journey across the deck alone, and stood looking out over the sea for a moment with a flushed face and a hammer for a heart. A thrill of tremulous exultation shook her, and unreasonably sweet she found it. The thing had been nothing—he had taken her up as he would take a child up to help it over a brook, but for a moment she had lain in his arms, with his face bent laughing into hers, and the very fact that this had meant no more than the shadow of nothingness to him gave her a sense of secret pleasure to be enjoyed alone. She had felt the sinews of his arm harden and strain as he lifted her—her own arm she had cast, for greater security, round his neck. She had felt on her wrist the short hair above his collar, for since they had come to sea he had cut it close, saying that the salt and spray made it sticky. And at that physical contact the last shred of unwilling reserve went from her.... She was his, wholly, abandonedly....

In a few moments Mitsos returned with Christos's long legs dangling from his arms, and for an hour more they sat together beneath the lee bulwarks, while the ship started on its last tack. The sun was already a crimson ball on the sea, and the mountains on the north of the gulf were obscured in a haze of luminous gold which seemed to penetrate them, making them glow from hither. A zigzag line of fire was scribbled across from the horizon to the ship, and from the sheets of spent foam which flung themselves over the weather-side as the brig shouldered its way along through the great humping seas, the spray turned for a moment to a rosy mist before it fell with a hiss white and broken on the weather-deck. With a crash and a poise the bows met the resounding waves, then plunged like a petrel down the sheer decline of the next water valley, and the black promontory which they were already opposite, with its fringe of foam, rose and fell like the opening and shutting of a window over the jamb of the bulwarks. The land-breeze was steady and not boisterous, and hummed like a great sleepy top in the rigging. Mitsos sat on the deck with his back to a coil of rope, facing the other two, his face turned rosy-brown by the sunset, and the Capsina, looking at him, knew the blissful uncontent of love. And the sunset and the sea died to a pearly gray; one by one the stars pierced the velvet softness of the sky, until the whole wheeling host had lit their watch-fires, and presently, after the brig passed the promontory, the white sails drooped and were furled, and the whole world waited, silent and asleep, for the things of the morrow.

They were now nearing the easternmost end of the gulf, and about twelve of the next day they could see dimly, and rising high in heaven, the upper ridges of Cithaeron—"a house of roe-deer," so said Christos. The sea-haze rose, concealing the lower slopes, but the top was domed and pinnacled in snow, clear, and curiously near. All the coast was well known to Christos, for his father had been a man of the sea, trading along the shore. Vilia, so he told them, was the chief village at the gulf's end; the immediate shore was without settlements, except for a few cottages which clustered round certain old ruins, walls, and high towers, so he said, big enough for a garrison of Mitsos's men; and thus his ears were pulled. Porto Germano was the name of the place, because a man of outlandish language, so it seemed, and of guttural voice, had made great maps of the place. "There are only walls and towers," said Christos; "yet he spent much time and labor over them, and gave money to those who held machines and tapes for him, writing many figures in a book, and talking to himself in his throat."

Mitsos and the lad were sitting aft as Christos delivered this information in a half-treble staccato voice, with an air of sceptical innocence, and shyly as to a demigod. The Capsina had left them and gone forward, but she returned soon to them with a quicker step and a heightened color.

"Mitsos," said she, "come forward. No, come you, Christos, for you are sharp-eyed, and you, little Mitsos, signal to Kanaris that he join us."

"Is there, is there—" began Mitsos.

"Oh, little Mitsos!" cried the girl. "But there will be blood in the sunset, if God is good. Go you and signal, lad; and come forward, Christos. It seems I have won my own prize."

They were some six miles off the eastern shore of the gulf, running before a favorable wind, and after Mitsos had signalled to the *Sophia*, which was between them and the north coast, on the port tack, and had seen her put about on the starboard tack in answer, he went forward to join the Capsina and Christos.

Right ahead and close in to land they could see the masts of three ships, but the hulls were down. The moment was critical, for the ships were evidently at anchor, as no sails were spread, and they were close in shore. Thus, every minute, perhaps, was murder and rapine to some Greek village. It was possible that they had only just come, and that the Capsina was in time to save a village. Again, it was possible that the infernal work was even now going on, even that it was over.

The Capsina stood in thought for a moment only.

"It is this," she said to Mitsos. "We are certain that Vilia is the village they are making for. Vilia is how far inland, Christos?"

"Two hours and a steep way through pine-woods."

"Thank God for the pine-woods. Look, Mitsos, they will have meant to leave the ships at anchor while they raided Vilia, but beyond any shadow of doubt they will have left some part of their crews on board, who will, of course, give the alarm if Greek ships are seen approaching. We have to get between their ships and the men they have sent up to Vilia. There is no village on the mountain-side except Vilia, Christos?"

"None."

"How are we to do it?" asked Mitsos. "The moment they see us they will send after their men."

"There is no time to lose," said the Capsina, quietly. "Hoist the Turkish flag," and she looked at Mitsos as if questioningly, and Mitsos met her gaze.

"Yes," he said, "it is one of the things I do not like, and I am unreasonable. There is no other way of getting in, and all things are right to save Vilia. I would turn Moslem if so I could kill more of them. Oh, Capsina, I quite agree with you. I will even hoist it myself. How comes it you have one?"

"Because I am one who looks beyond to-morrow," said she, much relieved. "I made it in Hydra myself."

The signal was made to Kanaris, and a few moments afterwards they saw the Turkish flag run up on the *Sophia*. The wind still held, and the *Revenge* took a reef in to let the *Sophia* join her, and by the time the hulls of the Turks had risen above the horizon line of water, the two were sailing close together.

They approached quickly, under a steady and singing west wind, and before two o'clock they could already see the thin line of cutting ripples breaking on the shingle, and yet from the Turkish ships came no sign. They lay at anchor some furlong from the shore, it would seem deserted.

The Capsina's orders were to be ready to fire on the word, but if possible to pass the Turkish ships without firing a shot and cast anchor between them and the shore. Her object was, if the men had landed to take Vilia, to cut them off from their ships, which, if possible, they would capture; but at present there was no means of telling in what state things were; only the deserted appearance of the Turkish ships argued the probability of the raid having set forth. The Capsina, if this probability should prove true, had given orders, signalling them to Kanaris, to leave one-third of the men on the ships and land with the rest in pursuit of the Turks, for if, as was now certain, since the brigs had been allowed to approach so close, they had no suspicion that armed ships of the Greeks were in the gulf, they would have attacked Vilia with all their available men, leaving a handful only on their ships.

As they came alongside, with sails already furled, moving only by their impetus and ready to swing round and cast anchor, a Turk strolled across the deck of the ship nearest to the *Revenge*, and, leaning carelessly on the bulwarks, shouted in Turkish, and for answer had only the hiss of the lapping water and the sight of Mitsos's unfezzed head, for the Capsina had told the rest to keep out of sight; and as the appearance of a woman on the bridge would have seemed odd to even those indolently minded folk, she had left Mitsos alone there, while she crouched in concealment behind the bulwarks. At that suspicion seemed to awake, and he popped his head down and was seen no more, and a moment afterwards, just as the anchor of the *Revenge* splashed plunging into the sea, two shots were fired in rapid succession from the Turk's bow gun, which was pointing out to sea and evidently aimed at neither the *Sophia* nor the *Revenge*.

110

At that the Capsina jumped up.

"That is a signal," she cried; "there is no time to lose! Down with the devil's flag and up with the cross!"

A great cheer went up from the men as the blue-and-white ensign was hauled up the mast, for, like Mitsos, they put the hoisting of the crescent among the things they "did not like," and in three minutes the first boatloads were on their way to the shore. Along the beach were drawn up the boats in which the Turks had landed, guarded only by a few men, who, as the Greeks drew near the shore, fled incontinently into the olive-groves that grew down to within fifty yards of the sea, and climbed to the foot of the pine-forests of the upper hills.

"Let them run," said Mitsos, "for I could ever run faster than a Turk," and he vaulted clean and lithe over the boat's side, and pulled her in through the shallow water to the shore. "Eh, Capsina," he added, "but it won't do to let those boats stop there, else the men will be embarking to their ships again when we chase them, and sail off with our prizes. Dimitri, see that as soon as we have gone all boats are taken away from the shore and tied up to the *Revenge* or the *Sophia*."

"So shall it be," said Dimitri. Then: "Oh, most beloved little Mitsos, cannot I come with you?" he asked; "for I should dearly like to hunt the turbaned pigs through the forest."

Mitsos shook his head.

"It is the Capsina's order," he said, "and we must not leave the ships without good garrison. But," and his eyes twinkled, "when I am after some fat brute, who trips in the brushwood, and calls on the prophet who shall be very slow to help, I will think of you, Dimitri. Meantime you have your hands full. Board the Turkish ships, one by one, with three-quarters of the men from the *Sophia* and *Revenge* together, for they have no boats, and cannot reach us, and make ready supper, for I doubt we shall get no dinner to-day, except only food for joy. They will not have left more than half a dozen men on each ship."

"And those half dozen?" asked Dimitri, completing the question with a look.

"Yes, it must be so," said Mitsos. "And now off with you!"

The second boatload and the third came racing to land, and using for greater expedition the deserted Turkish boat to disembark the men, in less than half an hour the whole contingent, some four hundred and fifty, were ranged ready to start. Mitsos had in vain endeavored to persuade the Capsina not to come with them; they would have a run fit to make a man burst, he said, up the hills, and at the end God knew what rough-and-tumble fighting. But the girl, breeched like a man, and carrying musket and pistol, scornfully refused to be left behind, and, indeed, she seemed fit for any work. Mitsos looked at her with candid admiration as she trotted briskly along up the slope from the beach by his side, and:

"It is like being with Yanni again," he said. "When the lad found his legs too short for the pace, why, he would lean on me, so," and he drew the Capsina's arm within his own, and bade her give him of her weight. And the Capsina, flushed and panting a little, did as he told her.

Mitsos had been intrusted with the ordering of this raid of the raiders, and he called a halt as they got to the edge of the pine-wood, and repeated his instructions. The men were to form a long open file on each side of the path leading up the hill, so that should the Turks have turned and scattered through the woods on the signal of recall they might not slip past them. Fifty men were to stop there on patrol at the edge of the wood so as to intercept any who might have passed the advanced body, who, if they marched through the pine-wood which extended to within a mile of Vilia without encountering the enemy, were to form again on the open ground.

"And this, too," said Mitsos, in conclusion, with a voice of most joyful conviction: "the Turks are certainly a work of the devil. Therefore, it is entirely our business to hate them and to kill them. This is the last raid of these men. God has willed it so, and has made them short of leg and the more easily overtaken, short of arm and the easier to deal with at close quarters. Therefore"—and he raised his voice—"open out right and left as I gave the order."

And the men, with mouths full of laughter at the little Mitsos's homily, opened out.

The pine-wood through which they hoped to hunt the "turbaned pigs" grew thick and tall above them, and the ground was muffled with the fallen needles. Here and there, in spaces where the pines grew thinner, sprouted a tangle of scrub and brushwood, but for the most part the ground was bare of undergrowth. The track, a cobbled Turkish road, wound round the contours of the hill, and thus those in the wood on each side had to march the more slowly, allowing for the deviousness of the path. The morning was as if borrowed from the days in the lap of spring; the mid-day sun shone with the cheerfulness of April, peeping like a galaxy of warm-rayed stars through the clusters of needles on the pines, and the west wind, fresh and vigorous from the sea, gave briskness to the going of the blood. Glimpses of the snows of Cithaeron far and high in front carried the foot on after the eye, and the steepness of the ascent melted fast under vigorous feet. As the line went forward up the mountain-side, the sea, like a friend, rose with it, as if to watch and guard its foster-children, till a ravine cut crossways through the mountain hid that cheerful presence from the eye though its crispness lingered in the limb. Here the trees grew somewhat thicker, a spring had flushed the hill-side with a more stubborn growth of low creeping things, and owing to the windings of the road those who marched on either side were hanging on their footstep to allow the followers of the path to keep up with them, when the Capsina beckoned to Mitsos, who was forcing his way through a belt of young poplar which grew in the open. He paused, and, seeing what she had seen, crawled into cover of the pines and passed the word down to halt, and that those on the path should leave it for shelter of the bushes.

The slope of the ravine opposite them was thickly covered with trees, but high upon it, three hundred feet above them, and a mile away, was a little group of glittering points, winking and flashing among the trees, like the dance of the sun on water, and moving down towards them. Now and then, as if the sun had disappeared behind a cloud, they would be hidden from sight by a thickness in the pines, to burst out again in a fleet of bright moving spots where the ground was clearer. The advancing line of the Greeks had halted, those on the path had made concealment of themselves under the trees; and but for the bright specks opposite the mountain-side seemed tenanted only by the whispering pines, and only watched by a few high-circling hawks.

The Capsina was standing by Mitsos, and the lad's eyes blazed with a light that was not the fury of hate which the burned ruins of Elatina had kindled, nor veiled by the softening of pity for a man hung at his own yard-arm, but the clear, sparkling madness of the joy of fighting—the hungry animal joy of scenting the desired prey.

"Oh," he whispered, and "oh," again, and with that he looked up and saw the circling hawks. "They will be nearer before night," he said, "and fat with pickings. It is all as clear as sea-water, Capsina, and easier than smoking. We wait here exactly where we are, but closing up a little, and very still, till the Turks strike the bottom of the ravine below us. Then a volley, perhaps two, and, for they will break and scatter, then every man to feed his own knife and pistol. If it please you, I will give the order."

"And think you Vilia is safe?" asked the Capsina.

"Oh, woman, how can I tell? But, safe or not, there is nothing to do but what we are doing. We only know that the devils are not in Vilia now and are coming to us. We deal with them first. Is it an order?"

"Surely."

Mitsos passed the word right and left and sat down, taking no notice of the girl, but drawing his finger along the edge of his long knife. Once or twice he drove the point tenderly and lovingly into the bark of a tree, but for the most part sat smiling to himself, purring, you would say, like some great cat. Suddenly he turned to the Capsina.

"Get you back to the ships," he said. "This is no work for a woman that we have on hand. I would not have a woman see it."

The Capsina laughed softly.

"In truth, little Mitsos, you know not much about women. Who told you that women have soft hearts and fear blood? Some man, no doubt, for it is not so."

"It will not be fit for you," said Mitsos again. "Will you not go back?"

"Certainly I will not."

Mitsos sat still a moment frowning.

"It is true that I do not know much about you. But—"

"But then I am not like a woman, you think?" asked the girl, with a sudden anguish at her heart.

"Yet I would there were more women like you," said Mitsos. "So be it, then. Look, they are getting closer."

Meantime the Greek line had closed up, and Mitsos stole away in cover of the trees to give the orders. The signal for firing was to be one musket-shot from the Greek line, given by himself. If the Turks stood their ground, the firing was to continue; if they broke each man was to be his own general, and his business was to kill. Turks were good marksmen, but they were slow of foot; and the wood was thick, and knives were the gift of God. The Greeks would collect again (and Mitsos smiled like an angel militant), when the work was done, in the place they now occupied.

Then came the space of quivering delay, when men could have found it in their hearts to shriek aloud with the straining tension, pulling like pincers at their flesh, while they were compelled to stand still and watch in silence that little glittering patch dancing and shining down the mountain-side. Mitsos for his own part was conscious of no thought but an agonized desire for tobacco, and to Kanaris the fact that he had left three if not four piastres lying loose on his cabin table was the source of an immeasurable regret; a stray lock of the Capsina's hair, which had escaped from her cap, and blew now and again against her cheek, was an annoyance of nightmare intensity, but all watched the growing, glittering patch. In another ten minutes it was nearly opposite them on the hill-side in front, some quarter of a mile away, and they could see that the men were hurrying along, half running, half marching unencumbered by booty or captives; and at that Mitsos drew a sigh of relief, for he knew that they had not reached Vilia when the signal of recall turned them back. Then he took his musket up from the ground where he had laid it, and holding it ready, with finger on the trigger, looked round at the Capsina.

"It is nearly over," he whispered. "Indeed, I am in a hurry to-day," and she smiled in answer.

Slowly and now with perfect steadiness, though five minutes before his hand had been like some ague-stricken thing, he raised the musket to his shoulder, and picking out one of the foremost men who were coming down the path opposite, kept him balanced on the sight of the gun, for, with the thriftiness of his race, he saw no reason why his signal to the others should not be in itself of some little use, and as the man stepped on to the little arched bridge that crossed the stream below, fired. The man spun round and fell, and a volley from right and left indorsed his shot.

He shook some powder out of his flask into his hand.

"That is a good omen," he said. "Oh, Capsina, I am most exceedingly happy!"

The Turks had halted for a moment, and a few fired wildly into the trees. A bullet struck the ground at Mitsos's feet, burying itself in the pine-needles, and the lad ripped up the ground with his knife, and put the bullet he was going to ram home on the top of his charge into his wallet again.

"To be returned," he said, and fired, and there was joy in his heart.

A second rather straggling volley came from the almost invisible Greeks, and at that the Turks stood no longer, but broke in all directions, some following the stream in its course to the valley, some charging up the hill where the Greeks were posted in order to get back to the ships, some rushing up the hill-side again in the direction of Vilia.

"Shall we go, little Mitsos?" said the Capsina, as if she would ask him to take a turn about deck.

They were standing not far from the path, and Mitsos for answer pushed the Capsina behind a tree.

"Fire at those coming up the path," he said, "and for the sake of the Virgin remember that I am in the brushwood not far in front," and he jumped over a low-growing bush.

About fifty Turks had kept together, and were coming up the path towards them at a double. Some two dozen Greeks had already begun running down the path after the others, and there were a few moments' tussle and fighting, two or three falling on both sides, but the Turks struggled through them and hurried on. Mitsos, the Capsina, and a few others fired coolly and steadily at them from cover, but they soon passed them and were lost in the wood behind. Mitsos threw his musket down.

"The knife and pistol for me," he said. "Come. The patrol outside will talk to those."

For the first few minutes the odds were largely against the Greeks, for many of the Turks, despairing of escape, had hidden themselves in clumps of brushwood, which, as the Greeks came on, spurted and bristled with fire, and some number were wounded, but a few only killed. But when once they got the ambushed Turks out of the nearer hiding-places, and on the move again, the odds were vastly the other way. The trees were so thick that, as Mitsos had seen, muskets were of little use, and it was hand-to-hand fighting, or pistols at close quarters. Pistols, however, required reloading, and time was precious, for the main object was to prevent the Turks from reforming, or gaining open ground where they could make an organized resistance. But knives were always ready to the hand, and needed no charging but the arm-thrust, and in a little while only occasional shots were heard, and hurrying steps slipping on the muffled floor of pine-needles, or the short-drawn gasp of the striker or the groan of the struck. Now and then a couple of figures, with perhaps two more in pursuit, would hurry across a piece of open ground, and but for that a man on the slope opposite would have seen only the hill-side, green and peaceful, and heard the whispering of the trees above his head, or what he would take to be the sound of the wild boars routing and tramping in the undergrowth, and have suspected nothing of that dance of death raging under the aromatic pines. He would, perhaps, have noticed that the hawks were wheeling in large numbers, and very silently, without their usual shrill pipe, above the trees, and would have said truly to himself that there was carrion somewhere below them.

Mitsos and the Capsina had kept close together, but Kanaris, cool and business-like as ever, had lost them almost at once among the trees, for he had turned aside a moment to investigate a musket-barrel which pointed out of a clump of oleander by the stream, and had been rewarded for his curiosity by having his hair singed by the fire which passed close to his temple. Mitsos had paused a moment and laughed as he saw Kanaris draw back a step or two and jump with knife raised into the middle of the clump.

He shouted "Good-luck!" to him, and turned in time to see the Capsina fly, like some furious wild-cat, holding her pistol by the barrel in one hand and her long knife in the other, at a man who was crossing her between two trees just in front. He saw the Turk's lips curl in a sort of snarl, and he put his hand to his belt a moment too late, for the next the Capsina's knife had flickered down from arm's-length to his throat, and the butt of her pistol caught him on the temple. He fell sprawling at her feet, and she had to put one foot on his chest as purchase to pull the knife out again.

"Yet she is a woman," muttered Mitsos to himself, and, wheeling round, "Ah, would you?" he cried, and another Turk, rushing at the Capsina, who was still tugging at her knife, got Mitsos's weapon between his shoulder-blades.

The girl turned. "Thanks," she said. "I owe you one. Pull my knife out for me, little Mitsos—pull; oh, how slow you are!"

Even in so short a time the tide had completely turned, and the Turks were but as game driven from one cover to another. The Greeks who had gone off in pursuit of those who had fled down the bed of the stream were returning, for no more of them were left to be slain, and the fight was centring round a copse of low-growing trees more in the open and higher up the hill. The majority of those Turks who were not yet slain had taken refuge here, and already the place had proved expensive to the Greeks, for more than twenty lay dead round it. The brushwood was so thick that it was impossible to see more than a yard or two, and while a man was forcing his way in after some Turk in front of him, a shot would come from the right or left, or from closer at hand a knife would lick out like a snake's tongue, and while he turned to his new enemy, the pursued became the pursuer.

Such was the state of things when Mitsos and the Capsina came up. The latter had received a nasty cut across her left arm, and Mitsos had tied it up roughly for her, being unable to persuade her to stop quiet out of harm's way while the work was finished. But she refused, laughing wildly, for drunkenness of blood was on her, and the two went forward together.

She paused a moment some fifty yards from the edge of the copse. From the ground above it every now and then a Turk would make a dash for the cover, sometimes getting through the Greeks, who were fighting on the outskirts, sometimes knifing one on his way, or more often falling himself; and once from behind them a man ran swiftly by, cutting at Mitsos as he passed, and disappeared with a bound into the trees. The Capsina looked round at the dead who were lying about, and her face grew set and hard.

"What fool's work is this?" she cried. "We are in the open, they in shelter. Smoke them out."

She caught up a handful of dry fern, and firing a blank charge into it obtained a smouldering spark or two, which she blew into flames. Half a dozen others standing near did the same, and fixing the burning stuff on her knife she rushed forward to the very edge of the ambush, while from without half a dozen muskets cracked the twigs above her, and rammed it into the heart of the thick tangled growth. Other fires were lighted along the west side of the copse, the dried raffle of last year's leaves caught quickly, and the wind took the flame inward. The greener growth of spring cast out volumes of stinging smoke, and when the place was well alight she drew off the men, stationing them round the other three sides, advancing as the flame advanced, for escape through the choking smoke and fire was impossible. Then, at first by ones and twos, the Turks came out like rabbits from a burrow, some bursting wildly out and occasionally passing the line of Greeks, some standing as if bewildered and trying to steal away unobserved, others running a few steps out and then turning back again. An hour later the whole copse was charred ash and cinders.

It remained only to search for the dead and wounded of the Greeks. The dead, whom they accounted happy, they buried there on that smiling hill-side, so that the preying beasts of the mountain and the carrion-feeding birds might not touch them, but only next spring the grasses and flowers would grow the more vivid on their resting-places; the wounded they carried back tenderly to the ships. And how thick the Turks lay there the hawks and eagles know.

CHAPTER VIII

The fourth day after saw the two brigs returned in peace to Galaxidi again, an expenditure of time which had cost the Capsina much misgiving and impatience, but for which to the reasonably minded there was an undeniable necessity. For the crews of both ships had lost somewhat heavily in the battle at Porto Germano, and even the girl herself was bound to admit that they wanted more men. Again, they had on their hands three empty Turkish vessels, all fully equipped for war, which they could not leave behind lest they should again fall into the hands of the enemy, and which it would have been a glaring and inconceivable waste to destroy. For there was on board a large quantity of ammunition and shot, three or four hundred muskets, and, in all, eighteen guns; and, though the Capsina grumbled that the powder was damp and the guns would burst if used, and even offered to stand forty paces in front of each of them in turn while Mitsos fired them at her, her remarks were rightly felt to be merely rhetorical, and to express her extreme impatience at the enforced delay and nothing further. So Mitsos was put in command of one Turkish ship, Dimitri of another, and Kanaris's first-officer of the third; Christos, chiefly because he rashly expressed a wish to be transferred with Mitsos, was retained by the Capsina on board the *Revenge*, and he stepped ashore at Galaxidi looking battered. "God made the tigers and tigresses also," was his only comment to Mitsos when the latter asked how he had fared.

The Capsina was already vanished on some hurricane errand by the time Mitsos had brought his ship to anchor, and Christos and he being left without orders or occupation took refuge in a café, where they sat awhile smoking and playing draughts, for outside the day was nought but a gray deluge of driven rain. To them at a critical moment in the game entered the Capsina, and words adequate for the occasion failed her. But Mitsos, seeing that her eye betokened imminent chaos, took a rapid mental note of the position of the remaining pieces on the board. Then he said, hurriedly, to Christos: "It's my move, remember, when we get straight again," and stood up. Christos shrunk into a corner.

"Mitsos Codones, I *believe?*" remarked the Capsina, with a terrifying stress on the last word, and a burning coldness of tone.

"And I believe so, too," said Mitsos, genially.

"Whom I engaged to play draughts in low cafés," said the Capsina, with a wild glance, "and to waste his time—Oh, it is too much," and the draughtsmen described parabolas into inaccessible places. "God in heaven! is it not too much," cried the girl, "that I have to go hunting you through the villages of Greece, up and down the Lord knows where, to find you playing draughts with that pigeon-livered boy? And the *Revenge* is pulling at her hawser, while Mitsos plays draughts; and the Greeks are being murdered all along the coast, and Mitsos plays draughts!"

An interminable grin spread itself over Mitsos's face. "And the Capsina, I doubt not, goes to see a strange baby, while the Greeks are murdered all along the coast. And the *Revenge* strains at her hawser, and the Capsina spends her time in abusing her own first officer," he said. "Oh, Capsina, and where is there a choice between us? Do not be so hasty; see, I shall have to pick up all these draughts, for finish the game I shall and will, and as you very well know we do not start till to-morrow. It was my move, Christos, and these pieces were so—eh, but there is another. Is it up your sleeve, Capsina?"

The Capsina glared at Christos a moment as if she were a careful mother who had discovered him luring a child of hers into some low haunt and directed the torrent of her grievance against him.

"Never did I see such a lad," she said; "if you were of the clan I should set you to the loom and the distaff like the women. He would sit and look at the sea by the hour, Mitsos; he would throw bread to the gulls. Gulls, indeed!"

Mitsos fairly laughed out.

"Oh, Capsina," he cried, "sit down and watch us play. There is nothing we can do, you know it well. The new men have volunteered—Kanaris had the choosing of them; you settled that yourself, and the *Revenge* cannot start before morning. Then how does it assist the war to stamp up and down through the villages of Greece, as you say, and call me and Christos bird-names? There, I am cornered; I knew that would happen; and the pigeon-livered wins. Move, pigeon."

Mitsos shook back his hair from his eyes and looked inquiringly at the Capsina.

"Does not that seem to you most excellent sound sense?" he said.

The Capsina stood a little longer undecided, but the corners of her mouth wavered, and Mitsos, seeing his advantage, clapped his hands.

"Coffee for the Capsina!" he cried to the shopman. "Is it not so, Capsina?" He fetched her a chair. "Now watch us finish, and then Christos will play you, and I will take your side. Thus we stand or fall together, and may it ever be so with us. Christos is the devil of a cunning fellow, for be it known to you I am pretty good myself, and see what there is left of me."

"Oh, fool of a little Mitsos!" said the girl, and she looked at him a shade longer than a friend would have done and sat down.

"There came a caique in from Corinth this afternoon," she said, "with news of the other three ships, and with news, too, from overland—from Nauplia!"

Mitsos paused with his finger on a piece.

"What is the news?" he asked.

"The three Turkish ships tried to put in there, but they could not make the harbor."

"No, I mean the news from Nauplia?"

The Capsina looked up, raising her eyebrows.

"Are they at home so dear? Yet you have been with me a month now, Mitsos, and except only that you want to say good-bye to those at home before starting, I know not if you have father or mother. And it is bad manners," said she, with her nose in the air, "to ask for what one is not given."

"But what is the news?" repeated Mitsos.

"Good news only: the town is blockaded by land and sea, so that no Turk can go out or in. The Greek women and children with the men who do not serve —but there are few such—all left the town the night before the blockade began and have encamped on the mound of Tiryns. But in the spring the

Turks will send a fresh army south, in time, they hope, to raise the siege."

"Praise the Virgin!" said Mitsos; "but Nauplia will be starved out before that. I move, and my king goes as straight as a homing honey-bee into the mouth of the pigeon-livered. But there is no other way, oh, your Majesty!"

The Capsina laughed.

"Surely there has never been a lad yet so single of purpose," she said. "To him there is nothing in all the world but a little wooden king."

"Even so, if only the news from Nauplia is good!" said Mitsos, smiling half to himself, "and if the little Turks will be kind and sail northward to us."

"Yet still you do not tell me," said the girl, "and I will throw my manners away and ask. Have you a mother, Mitsos?"

"No, nor father either," and he stopped, remembering what he and Suleima had said to each other as they walked beneath the stars down to the boat.

"Then who is it who is so dear?" she asked, and with a sudden uprising of anxiety waited for the answer.

"It is Suleima!" said Mitsos, "the little wife, and he the adorable, so she calls him, the littlest one."

The Capsina stared a moment in silence.

"So," she said, at length, "and you never told me that! Little Mitsos, why have you so greatly made a stranger of me?"

She rose from where she sat, and with that the flame in her eyes was quenched, and they were appealing only as of a chidden dog.

"Indeed, Capsina," and again "Indeed," he said; but the girl turned quickly from him and went out of the place, leaving her coffee untouched, into the dark and rain-ruled night.

She walked up the quay and down again, hardly conscious of the driving rain. On the right the water below the harbor wall hissed and whispered to itself like an angry snake under the slanting deluge. The *Sophia* and *Revenge* lay side by side some two hundred yards out; from nearer in she could hear the rattle of the crane which was unloading the Turkish ships which they had captured, and a great oil flare under the awning flickered and flapped in the eddying draughts. The wind kept shifting and chopping about, and now and then the drippings from off the houses would be blown outward in a wisp of chilly water across her, and again the spray from the peevish ripples in the harbor would be cut off and thrown like a sheet over the quay. But in the storm of her soul she heeded not, and that chill and windy rain played but a minor part in the wild and bitter symphony of her thoughts. At first it seemed an incredible thing to her: ever since she had seen Mitsos come up out of the sunset from his boat, her conviction had been unchanged, that this was he, the one from the sea and the sun, who was made to fulfil her life. As if to put the seal on certainty, that very night he had joined her on the ship; they had tossed together to the anger of the Ægean, together they had played like children on a holiday, and they had been together and as one, comrade with comrade, in the work to which they had dedicated themselves. Comrade to comrade! That was exactly Mitsos's view of it, but to her the comradeship was her life. Yanni, the cousin of whom he had often spoken, Kanaris, the lad Christos— she was to Mitsos as they were, perhaps a little less than they, for she was a woman.

Oh, it was impossible! God could not be so unkind. She who spent her days, and risked her all—and oh, how willingly!—fighting against His enemies, was this her wage? Who was this Suleima? A Turkish name by the sound. Some moon-faced, pasty girl, no doubt, fat, fond of sweet things, a cat by the fire, what could she be to Mitsos? The littlest one, Mitsos's son—and at the thought impotent, incontinent jealousy and hatred possessed her soul. Mitsos was not hers but another's, pledged and sealed another's—and she walked the faster. Michael, who had accompanied her without murmur, since such was the duty of a dog, stood a moment under the protecting eaves of a house, with his head on one side, looking at her in reproachful protest, for even his shaggy coat was penetrated by the whipping rain. But she still walked on, and he shook himself disgustedly from head to tail and went after her. Opposite the café again she hung on her step, looking in through the rain-slanted window-panes. Mitsos was bent over his little wooden kings, absorbed and sheltered, while she was outside rain-drenched, with anguish for a heart. Ah, what a humiliation! Why could she not have lived like the other women of her class, have married Christos the cousin, and long ago have settled down to the clucking, purring life, nor have looked beyond the making of jam, the weaving of cloth, marriage among the domestic duties? She had thought herself the finest girl God had made, one who could treat with scorn the uses and normal functions of her sex, one who had need of no man except to serve her, one who thought of woman as a lower and most intensely foolish animal, whose only dream was to marry a not exacting man, and settle down to an ever-dwindling existence of narrowing horizons. Yet, where were all those fine thoughts now? She had sailed her own ship, it was true, and sent a certain number of the devil's brood to their account, but what did that profit her in the present palpable anguish? Her pain and humiliation were no less for that. The clucking women she despised were wiser than she; they at any rate had known what they were fit for; she alone of all had made a great and irrevocable mistake. She, the Capsina, was brought down to the dust, and Mitsos played draughts with the little wooden kings. Her flesh and blood, her more intimate self, and that childish need for love which even the most heroically moulded know, cried out within her.

Then pride, to her a dominant passion, came to her rescue. At any rate none knew, and none should ever know, for thus her humiliation would be at least secret. She would behave to Mitsos just exactly as before: not one tittle of her companionship, not an iota of her frank show of affection for him should be abated. And, after all, there was the *Revenge*, and—and with that, her human love, the longing of the woman for the one man came like a great flood over the little sand and pebbles of pride and jealousy and anger, and she cried out involuntarily, and as if with a sudden pang of pain, bringing Michael to her side.

They had reached the end of the quay; on one side of the road was a little workman's hut, erected for the building of the Capsina's "custom-house," and, entering, she sat down on a heap of shingle, which had been shot down there for the making of the rough-cast walls of the building. Michael, cold and dripping, but too well bred to shake himself when near his mistress, stood shivering by her, with a puzzled amazement in his eyes at the unusual behavior of the pillar of his world. The girl drew him towards her, and buried her face in his shaggy, dripping ruff.

"Oh, Michael, Michael!" she sobbed, "was not one to come from the sea—all sea and sun—and we, were we not to be his, you and I and the brig, and was not heaven to fly open for us? Indeed, it is not so: one came from the sea and the sun, but it was not he. I was wrong. I was utterly wrong, and now the world holds no other."

The rain had ceased, and from outside came only the sullen drumming of the waves breaking on the shingle beyond the harbor, followed rhythmically by the scream of the pebbly beach, dragged down by the backwash, and the slow, steady drip from the sodden eaves. Suddenly these noises became overscored with the rise and fall of voices, and the Capsina drew Michael closer to her and hushed his growling.

"So, indeed, you must not mind, Christos," said Mitsos's voice, "for there is none like her. Her eyes but grow the brighter for the excitement, when, to tell the truth, my heart has been a lump of cold lead. It is an honor to us that we are with her, that she trusts us—she even likes us—which is more than she did for any of those in Hydra. Eh, but it will be rough to-morrow. Look at the waves! I suppose she has gone back to the ship."

"I expect so," said Christos; "let us go, too, Mitsos."

"No, but wait a minute. There is nothing like the sea at night, unless it be the Capsina. It is strong, it is ready to knock you down if you come too near, yet it will take you safely and well if you only make yourself—how shall I say it? —make yourself of it. The fire-ship—did ever I tell you about the night of the fire-ship? Of course I did not, for I never told any but Uncle Nikolas, nor am I likely to, except to one only. Yes, so it is; I admire her more than I admire the rest of this world rolled into one—always, so I think, I would do her bidding. She might chide me—I would crawl back to her again; I would even bring Suleima, too, on her knees, if so it pleased the Capsina. She must know Suleima. I feel she does not know me, nor I her, until she knows Suleima. Well, come; let us get back. I think the good news from Nauplia must have made me drunk. Surely I was anxious and knew it not. Did I ever tell you how the Capsina and I … Oh, she is of finer mould than all others!" And the voices were caught and drowned in the riot of the sea.

Obedience, admiration, liking—that was all. And she would have given them all at that moment—for at that moment the devil and all his friends were lords and masters of her soul—for one flash of the human longing and desire of flesh and blood felt by him for her. No matter in what form it came, a moment's heightened color, the sudden leap of the enchanted blood, an involuntary step towards her, hands out-stretched, and eyes that longed, she would have given all for that; let him hate her afterwards, or be as indifferent as the Sphinx, to have once called out that which must call itself out, yet never tarries when its own call comes, would be sufficient for her. That he should for one second forget Suleima, remembering her, that he should be unfaithful to Suleima and before the accuser could pronounce the word turn faithful again, would be enough. And the evil thoughts suddenly shot up like the aloe loftily flowering, and she clutched Michael till the dog whimpered.

She drove not her thoughts away, but picked those bright and evil flowers, pressing them to her bosom: she tended them as a shepherd tends his sheep, and like sheep they flocked into her soul, on the instant a familiar abiding-place. If Suleima should die; better even if she should not die, but live bitterly, for, no doubt, she too loved him. He would come to her, how well she could picture in what manner, great and awkward and burning and beyond compare, saying little but letting all be seen. Not content with that picture, she went on to put specious, despicable words into his mouth. Suleima, he should say, would soon get over it; for him he was simply one of the sea, and Suleima hated the sea; she would live with Mitsos's friends—a man's friends were always kind to women who had wearied him. No, it was not her fault nor his either—she had wearied him, he had wearied of her. Besides, he loved. And even as she imagined him saying such sweet and terrible things, her heart rose against him, and her better self spat out like an evil taste the false image she had conjured up of him.

Sullen and windless rain began again outside, and fell hissing and spitting like molten lead into the harbor water, yet somehow to her it was a baptism and a washing of the soul. And she rose, and with quick step and firm went back to opposite the *Revenge*, and blew her whistle for the boat. And strangely sweet and bitter was it to hear Mitsos's voice shouting an order, and to see him beneath the flare bareheaded to the rain clamber quickly down the ship's side into the boat and row with all the strength of those great limbs to come and fetch her, himself and alone.

Almost before the sun was up next morning they prepared to put to sea. The rain had again fallen heavily during the night, but it ceased before daybreak, and Mitsos, stumbling sleepily on deck, was soon awakened by the chilly breeze from the mountains which should take them out of the harbor. The deck was dripping and inclement to the bare feet, and his breath trailed away in clouds like smoke in the cold air. Land and sea and sky were all shades of one neutral gray, more or less intense and strangely sombre. The tops of the hills to the west were pale and pearly, reflecting the more illuminated clouds eastward, and deepened gradually without admixture of other color into the lower spurs and ridges behind the village. The sea which had grown calm again during the night was but a mirror of the low-hanging clouds overhead, and to the south it faded so gradually and with so regular a tone into the sky that the horizon line eluded the eye. Even the ripple which broke against the wall of the quay seemed in the misty air to be woolly in texture, as if drawn from the ooze of the bottomless sea and to have lost the sparkle of foam. But early as he was the Capsina had come on deck before him, and before he had stood more than a few seconds on the bridge she joined him, nodded him a greeting in silence, and they waited side by side, Mitsos occasionally shouting an order while the ship cleared the harbor mouth.

Then Mitsos yawned, stretched himself, and rubbed his eyes.

"This is no proper hour," he said; "it is neither night nor morning, even as the jelly-fish is neither plant nor animal; and oh, Capsina, but it is extraordinarily cold."

He turned and looked at her, and something arrested his gaze. She had slept but little, but the added touch of pallor only lent a more potent brilliance to her black eyes; the courage of a resolution but newly taken was there, and the animation which effort to be herself gave her. She had twisted a brilliantly colored shawl round her head, but her hair just loosely coiled showed in two broad bands over her forehead, and it was wet and sparkling with fine drops of condensed mist. Surrounded on all sides by the endless gray of the enormous morning she seemed to him more vivid than ever, and her beauty, for he was a man with eyes and blood, rose and smote him. Then throwing back his head he laughed for very pleasure, not from the lips only, but from head to heel—the whole man laughed.

"But you are splendid," he said; "indeed, there is none like you!"

She looked up at him quickly; was this the leap of the blood, the sudden step nearer which she had told herself would be sufficient for her? And again, more quickly than the upward sweep of her eyelids, she indorsed that thought. But even before she looked her heart told her that it was not thus he spoke of Suleima, nor thus he would speak to her. The admiration in his voice, the involuntary tribute so merrily paid, all the appreciation he gave, all that he had to give, but one thing only, did not make up that little more, which is so much. For he was not, so she thought, one who would make pretty speeches, or play at love-making with one woman while he thought of another, and, indeed, she would not have accepted such a travesty of the heart's deed. But let him come to her but once, were it only with a glance, or a handshake, involuntary and inevitable—that was a different matter. And she answered him without pause, speaking from the heart, while he thought she spoke from the lips only.

"Indeed, little Mitsos," she said, "but you are very sleepy. Surely you are but half awake, and are dreaming of Suleima."

Mitsos laughed.

"Surely Suleima would not know me if I spoke to her like that," he said.

"What, then, do you say to Suleima?"

"Oh, nothing, or a hundred things, all sorts of foolishness; for some mornings she will do nothing but stare at the baby by the hour and just say at the end that it will be a tall lout like me, and for answer I say it will be like to its mother. Other mornings she will be shirt-mending and do no more than grunt at me. Yet you and I, too, talked only silly things for the first week of our voyage, Capsina, so there is excuse for Suleima and me."

The Capsina turned away a moment with a sudden gasping breath. "Look, the sun is up," she said, "and it is getting warmer. Also our coffee will be getting cold. Come down, little Mitsos. And is the lazy Christos abed yet?"

"He shall soon not be," said Mitsos, taking a flying leap down the stairs. "Ohé, Christos!" he cried.

But Christos appeared to be not yet on deck, and Mitsos went down to his cabin, and a moment after cries for mercy mingled themselves with the Mitsos's voice raised in solemn reproof.

"Is it not a shame," he said, "that the Capsina and I should have our eyes grow dim with the midnight watches and the Greeks be murdered all along the coast, as she herself said, while you lie here—no, away comes that blanket thing—and that we should burn our fingers making coffee for those fine ladies who lounge in bed? This shall not be, indeed it shall not. Christos, there are more uses for a slipper than to put on a foot; them shall you learn. Lord, what a wardrobe of clothes the lad has! it is enough for a Turk and his harem. Here is a red sash, if it please you, and a gay waistcoat; a razor, too—what in the name of the saints does the smooth-faced Christos want with a razor? Suleima will be wanting me to buy her a razor next, or perhaps the little Nikolas. Let go that rug, Christos, and be turned out of bed cool and peaceful, or sharper things will be done to you. Now be very quick, for I shall continue to drink coffee, and thus there may be none left in ten minutes, for I do not drink slowly."

Mitsos, having once spoken of "the little wife" to the Capsina, spoke of her more than once again that morning, and to his secret surprise he found the girl extraordinarily sympathetic, and as if much pleased and interested in being told of her. And this was beyond measure an astonishing thing to him, for heretofore his intercourse with her had been either of adventure past or to come, or they had, as at first, been no more than two children at play. But any matter touching the heart had been so remote from the talk on the board that Mitsos had never thought of her as a human woman, one to whom these things could or rather must be of any concern. She, to her bitter cost, had seen him merely as a great, strong, and silly boy, boyish altogether, though to her a magnet for the heart; and of the more intimate lore of man and woman, so she had planned it, they were to learn together. And the surprise to him of finding that she was clearly willing to hear him talk thus was perhaps hardly less strong than the shock to her of finding that he had known too well what she had thought they would learn together. And thus, with a strange flush of pleasure to the boy and a new bond between them, he told her of the ride from Tripoli, the finding of Suleima at home. Only of the anguish of the night of the fire-ship he spoke not at all. There was no intimacy but one only close enough for that. So to all the admiration and affection he felt for the girl, this added a tenderness to his thoughts of her, and without knowing it the knowledge of the thing itself, which had severed them irrevocably in the Capsina's mind, was the very cause of a new tie binding Mitsos to her, and the strands of it were of a fibre more durable and more akin to that which she now despaired of than any that had bound them yet.

They sailed a southeasterly course, for the ships that had put out from Corinth had gone, according to their information, north, and it was not unlikely that they were on their way to join the three which the Capsina had already accounted for at Porto Germano, and which were now being made ready, in hot haste, to take the sea again under the flag of the cross instead of the crescent. It was at any rate certain that they would keep close to the coast, unless driven out to sea by bad weather, destroying as they went, and thus the Greeks had a winning chance of falling in with them at the narrow end of the gulf. But after a breezy morning, at mid-day the wind had died down and they lay a mile or so off shore, with canvas flapping idly, and Mitsos whistled the "Vine-digger's Song" to stir the heavens, but the wind came not for all his whistling.

The day continued gray and unseasonably cold; from time to time a little sprinkle of mingled sleet and rain pattered on the chilled deck, and Mitsos stamped up and down the bridge cursing the delay of the dead wind, for as soon as they had settled the remaining three vessels their work in the gulf would be over, and he had a hundred schemes whereby they might pass the guns of Lepanto and be off. They had already been six weeks on the trail, and now, as he knew so well, the warmer March winds and the blinks of spring sunshine would be beginning to open the flowers of the plain of Nauplia. For himself flowers were no great attraction, but Suleima, accustomed to the luxuriant Turkish gardens, had planted row upon row of scarlet anemones under the orange-trees, and it seemed to Mitsos that Suleima's flowers were among the fundamental things of the world. Long winter afternoons he had spent in a glow of grumbling content at her womanish fads in digging up the roots on the hill-side, and evening by evening he had come back again grimed with soil and washed with the winter rains, and with a great hunger in his stomach, while Suleima turned over the spoils of the afternoon, always saying that there were not yet near enough. Once out of the gulf he would go home again, if only for a week or two, for the Capsina, as she had told him, was meaning to join the Greek fleet on its spring cruise, and till it started on that even she confessed there was no further work to hand.

Towards evening the sleet, which had been continuous all the afternoon, grew intermittent between the showers, and the air was hard and clear as before a great storm; fitful blasts of a more icy wind scoured across from the north, and Mitsos, feeling the sea-weed barometer which hung in the cabin, found it moist and slimy. Supper was ready, and on the moment the Capsina came down flushed with the stinging air.

"More rain," said Mitsos; "I wish the devil might take it to cook the grilling souls of those Turks we have sent him. The sea-weed is as if you had dipped it in an oil-jar."

The Capsina felt it.

"You have a trick of smelling the wind, Mitsos," she said. "Can you smell the wind?"

"I have smelled strong wind all day, and it has not come for all my smelling," said Mitsos, sulkily.

As if to exculpate the deceptiveness of his weather, almost before they had sat down the rigging began to sing, and before Mitsos had time to get on deck the song was a scream. The Capsina followed him, and he looked rapidly round.

"Still north," he said; "and may the saints tell us what to do! Look there;" and he pointed over the hills above Galaxidi. The sun had not quite set—a smudge of dirty light still smouldered in the west. To the north the sky lowered blackly, and a tattered sheet of cloud was spreading and ripping into streamers as it spread over the heavens. Even as he spoke a snake's tongue of angry lightning licked out of the centre of it, followed at a short interval by a drowsy peal of thunder.

"We must beat out to sea," he continued. "God knows what is coming; the wind may chop round, and Heaven save us if we are within two miles of shore!"

But the Capsina felt suddenly exhilarated. The prospect of some great storm which should take all their wits to fight braced her against her secret trouble. Here was a more immediate employment for her thoughts.

"Out to sea, then, while we may!" she cried. "Oh, Mitsos, it is a fine thing to be in the hand of God and all His saints! But what if the Turks slip by us?"

"There will be rocks and big waves for the Turks," said Mitsos, laconically. "Hoist jib and staysail; she cannot stand more than that. Where are Kanaris and the *Sophia*?"

"Kanaris is as wise as we, and will get sea-room for himself," said the Capsina. "There, that is done. Come back to supper, little Mitsos."

Mitsos looked round again.

"I think not yet," he said; "but go you down. I will stop here till there is a spoonful or two more water between us and land."

"I am with you," said the girl, and they began pacing up and down the deck together.

Night fell like a stroke of a black wing feathered with storm-cloud. As a sponge with one wet sweep will wipe out the writing from a slate, so that black cloud in the water sucked the light from the sky, and the wind screamed ever higher and more madly. Once again the angry fire licked out and was gone, and the thunder clapped a more immediate applause, and with that they were the centre of an infinite blackness. Land, sea, and sky were swallowed up and confounded in one terrific tumult of unseen uproar. Fast as the brig scudded before the storm, the waves seemed ever to be going the faster, as if to reach some terrible rendezvous where they would wait for her. In Mitsos's mind the present fear was that the wind would veer, as so often happens on those inland seas, and before they were sufficiently far from land would be forcing them back on to the lee shore. Then he knew there would be before them a night's work of battling with the wind that yelled in exultation as it took them back, of losing ground inevitably, and of desperately fighting every inch until the storm blew itself out.

Half an hour passed and they were still running out to sea, when, suddenly, the wind shifted westward, and the ship for a moment trembled and shook as if she had struck a rock. The two men at the tiller knew their work, and in a moment had the struggling tiller jammed down, and the *Revenge* checked like a horse, and again slowly made way on the starboard tack.

And at the sight of the obedience of the ship, more like some intelligent beast than a thing of wood, a great thrill of pleasure struck the Capsina. "Well done!" she cried. "Well done, dear ship!"

Then the sky above them burst in a blaze of violet light, and Mitsos, in that flash, though half-blinded, saw two things—the one a ship, some two miles distant, as far as he could judge in that glance, and straight before their bows on the troubled and streaky sea, the other a great gray column rising like a ghost from the waves, not more than four hundred yards away, and which was the more dangerous, he knew.

The Capsina, too, had seen it, and called out to him:

"Saints in heaven! What is it? What is it?" she cried. "No, not the ship—the other. Is it the spirits of those from Elatina?"

But Mitsos was no longer there. He had seen that great gray column, and known it for a water-spout, and, without a moment's pause, he had rushed forward and told them to load the six-pounder in the starboard bow. Ammunition was stored forward, and, though it seemed to him that he waited through the suspense of a lifetime, in a few seconds the gun was loaded, and he waited again, the fuse in his hand.

The darkness was intense; from the blackness came only the hoarse scream of the wind and the threats and buffets of the sea. But soon he saw against the blackness the glimmering column of gray, and he could hear above the riot of the storm a drip as from a thousand house-roofs. It came on in a slightly slanting direction, and, waiting till it began to cut across the muzzle of the gun, he fired.

And with a crash of many waters the gray column vanished.

The Capsina had followed him forward, and as the smoke cleared away he saw her eye dancing, and she slapped the brazen side of the gun.

"There will be more work for you to-night!" she cried. "Well, Mitsos, gone is the gray ghost. But the ship remains."

Mitsos sat still a moment, the strain and responsibility of his aim left him unnerved. But almost instantly he recovered himself.

"You will give chase to-night?" said he, incredulously.

"Why not?"

"Because God is blowing a great gale. There is no light, and who knows where we shall drive to?"

Again the violent sheet of flame blazed from the cloud overhead, and the Capsina laughed.

"No light? Is that no light, when the clouds are bursting to give it us? I saw her quite plainly then. Oh, lad, what is the wind for except to sail on? Would you chase the Turks in a calm? There again!"

Now whether it was from the mere infection of the excitement which possessed the Capsina, or whether his nerves were strung by the electricity in the air to that shrill pitch when a man will do and dare anything, in any case something of the irresponsible recklessness of the girl was on Mitsos, and it seemed to him a fine piece of play—something between a dream and a drunkard's idea—to go a-hunting of Turks in this wild storm. The flashes of lightning, repeated and again repeated with redoubled quickness, kept showing them the ship which, since they first sighted it, had furled all sail and lay rolling on the water simply weathering the storm. The *Revenge* was carrying jib and staysail, and while the Turk drifted eastward, was rapidly diminishing the distance between them.

Mitsos rubbed his hands exultantly.

"She will be as safe as a hare in a gin," he said, "when once we get her between us and the land, for no power on earth will let her sail out in the teeth of the wind. But, Capsina, where is the *Sophia*, and where are the other two Turks?"

"Signal the *Sophia*," said the girl; "Kanaris will be on the watch, and if he is near enough to hear our signals he will soon know what we are about."

The two stern guns on the upper battery accordingly were fired in quick succession, this being the signal agreed on with Kanaris, and before long they saw the answering flash of two guns on their starboard, and five seconds afterwards heard the report.

"He has beaten out farther to sea," said Mitsos, "for, indeed, he is more prudent than we are. Well, we are alone in this piece. The Turks, they say, are afraid of ghosts by night, and so, for that matter, am I. They shall see a phantom ship, and it will speak with them."

The *Revenge* was still going south at about right angles to the wind, and as the coast trended eastward was every moment getting more sea room. The Turk, as they knew, was drifting due east, but for five minutes or so after the word to run out the guns was given no lightning broke the black and streaming vault, and they waited in thick, tense silence for another flash. But while above them the clouds remained pitchy and unilluminated, once and again to the south there came a flash distant and flickering like the winking of an eye, showing that another storm was coming up from that quarter.

Mitsos stamped with angry impatience.

"That is what I feared," he said; "the wind will shift farther south and we shall have to look to ourselves. Holy Virgin, send us a flash of lightning and west wind for half an hour more."

He and the Capsina were standing together on the bridge, Mitsos bareheaded and tangle-haired to the streaming rain, she with the brilliantly colored shawl wrapped round her head. Once he shifted his position, and putting forward his hand on the rail to steady himself, laid it on the top of hers, and she could feel the blood pulsing furiously through the arteries in his fingers. She stood perfectly still, not withdrawing her hand, and, indeed, he seemed unconscious that it was there. At last what they had been waiting for came; a furious angry scribble leaped from west to east over their heads, and peering out into the darkness they saw the Turk to leeward of them, some four hundred yards distant. At that Mitsos grasped the girl's hand till she could have cried out with the pain.

"There she is!" he cried. "We have her. We have her. Let go the helm and be ready to furl the sails on the instant. Oh, Capsina, this hour is worth living."

But the tumult in the girl's mind did not allow her to speak; the moment was too crowded even for thought, and she could only strain her eyes in the darkness to where they had seen the Turk. She felt not mistress of herself, and Mitsos, as she knew, was nigh out of his mind. Who could say what the next hour might bring? Death, shipwreck, victory, lightning, love, and madness chased each other through her brain. Meantime the ship, left to itself, spun round like a top into the wind, and under the hurricane that followed it dipped and fled like a bird born and bred to tempest after the other. But after a few headlong seconds Mitsos cried the order to furl all sail, and the canvas came dripping and streaming onto the deck. The men were at the guns with orders to fire the moment the lightning showed the ship, and as the spark leaped through the clouds again the forward guns on the port side of the *Revenge*, from all three decks, added their bellowing to the succeeding thunder. Anything approaching to accurate shooting was out of the question. They had some two seconds, for the flash was vivid and far leaping, for the sighting, and they simply fired into the heart of the loud and chaotic darkness.

Mitsos saw the Capsina standing not far from him after the first round, behind the fore-port gun on the main deck, and he took a step across the reeling ship to her side.

"Oh, Capsina, assuredly we are both madder than King Saul!" he said, "yet I find it glorious, somehow."

"Glorious!" and the girl's voice was trembling with passion and excitement. "I am living a week to the minute. Ah!" she cried, as another flash flickered overhead. "Again, again!"

The wind fell a little, but the violence and frequency of the lightning doubled and redoubled, and the guns answered it. The thunder no longer broke with a boom on some distant cloud-cliff, but with a crash intolerably sharp and all but simultaneous with the light. Some cross-current in the sea had swung the bows of the *Revenge* more southward, and Mitsos sent Christos flying aft to tell the stern guns on the port side to be ready to fire. From the enemy, in reply to their two first discharges, had come no response, but at the third they were answered, and a couple of oversighted balls went whirring overhead through the rigging like a covey of grouse. Then came two flashes of lightning in rapid succession, and by the second they could see a hole crash open in the side of the Turk from the balls they had fired by the light of the first. There was not time, nor near it, to load the guns twice, yet the Capsina in the frenzy of her excitement cuffed one of the gunners over the head, calling him a slow lout. The man only laughed in reply, and the Capsina laughed back in answer. Again and again the heavens opened, and this time a ball from the Turks came in through the port-hole of one of their guns, breaking the muzzle into splinters and ricochetting off on to the man to whom the Capsina had just spoken. He was shot almost in half, but his mouth still smiled, showing his white teeth. The ball which had killed him whistled on, striking a stanchion on the starboard side and plopped out again overboard, and Mitsos, with a great laugh, threw his cap after it.

Then came the end; the ships were at close range, and a ball from the *Revenge*, delivered from a port gun, struck the Turk just on the water-line, opening a raking tear in her side, and when next they could see her she was already listing to starboard, and with the rattle of the thunder mingled hundreds of human voices. The giddy, complete drunkenness of blood was on them; all the men laughed or shouted, or went back to their supper and drank the health of the dead and their portion in hell; and Mitsos, forgetting all in the frenzy and fury of culminated excitement, opened his arms, and flung them round the Capsina and kissed her as he would have kissed Yanni at such a moment.

"Another, another!" he cried; "thank God, another shipful will feed the fish of the gulf!"

"Mitsos, oh, little Mitsos!" cried the girl, and she kissed him on the cheek and on the lips.

The next moment they had started asunder, knowing what they had done, and the Capsina, burning with an exulting shame, turned from him and, without a word, went to her cabin.

CHAPTER IX

During the four months of Mitsos's absence the progress of the war in the Peloponnese had been checked by a thousand petty and ill-timed jealousies on the part of the chiefs and primates, and more than ever it was becoming the work of the people. It had been agreed in the preceding autumn that the Peloponnesian senate instituted at Tripoli should be dissolved at the fall of that fortress, which took place in October, and that a national assembly, now that the war was a business in which the whole nation, north and south alike, had taken up arms, should direct the supreme conduct of affairs. But this suited very ill with the greed and selfish ambitions of many of the military leaders and primates. Their places in the Peloponnesian senate were assured, and having a voice in its transactions, and for the most part a singular unanimity of purpose, their object being to get as much plunder as possible, it was not at all their desire to be superseded in power by deputies chosen from the whole of Greece. But until the national assembly was formed all power was vested in them, and with a swift insight—cunning, to use no uglier word, rather than creditable—they passed a resolution that the deputies to the national assembly should be elected by themselves.

Now the prince Demetrius Hypsilantes, though weak and indecisive, and altogether incapable of initiative action, had, at any rate, in the Peloponnesian senate that power which an honest and upright man will always hold in an assembly where the ruling motive is personal greed. But his curiously infirm mind clutched, like a child with a bright toy, rather at the show of power than at power itself, and now that the development of the war, with the demand for a more representative assembly, threatened to deprive him of that, he threw in his lot with the primates and captains of the Morea, preferring to retain the presidency of the Peloponnesian senate, and to be a *roi mort*, rather than take a subordinate part in the national assembly. For it seemed certain that Prince Mavrogordatos, who had been appointed governor-general in northwest Greece, would be elected President of Greece, and this for more than one reason. In the first place, he had not as yet shown himself too patently unfit for the office, while Hypsilantes had; in the second place, the Peloponnesian senate was far too heavily faction-ridden to co-elect out of their own body except on the barest majority against other candidates singly; and, in the third, they unanimously preferred to have as a president a man who, it was understood, would go back to his command in north Greece, leaving them to their own control, which was just equivalent to no control at all.

This national assembly met at Epidaurus in January; it shouted itself hoarse over many high-sounding declarations, loud and empty as drums; it conferred titles and honors; it devised banners and legislative measures, all highly colored, it presented Kolocotrones, the old chieftain and leader of an enormous and disorganized band of brave and badly armed men, with a brass helmet and the title of commander-in-chief in the Morea, and congratulated itself on having put things on a firm and orderly basis. Furthermore, it resolved to take the fortress of Nauplia without loss of time, with the effect that in May the siege was still going on, without any prospect of a calculable termination. Mavrogordatos, elected President of Greece and confirmed in his command of the northwest province, went back to his duties, and engaged on a series of futile manoeuvres which, as he had no acquaintance of any kind with military matters, ended in a disastrous defeat at Petta. Hypsilantes chose a new aide-de-camp in place of Mitsos, who had departed without leave to the Gulf of Corinth with the Capsina; and Kolocotrones put on his brass helmet and went on small marauding expeditions, returning now and then to Nauplia to see how the siege had got on, as a man watches a pot over a slow fire. Such were the main results of the great council of Epidaurus, and thus passed the days from January to May; till May the Greek fleet was idle, though a dozen ships at double pay blockaded Nauplia by sea in order to prevent its relief by the Turkish fleet, which every one very well knew was still at Constantinople. On land the lower town was in the hands of the insurgents, who, however, made no attempt to take the fortress, but waited for nature, in the shape of starvation, to act unaided. Petrobey, disgusted at the appointment of Kolocotrones as commander-in-chief, retired with the growling Mainats into his own country to wait till, as he hoped, the voice of the people should recall him, or, if not, until some one should be appointed commander-in-chief whom he could with honor serve under. For Kolocotrones, so he openly said, had brought dishonor on Greece by his disgraceful trafficking with the besieged in Tripoli, and was no more than a brigand chief weighing the honor of the nation against piasters, and finding the piasters the worthier.

Suleima was busy to and fro in the veranda and garden of the house, one May afternoon, her hands full, as behooved a good housewife, with the woman's part. The littlest one, now seven months old, was tucked away in his cot for his mid-day sleep, under the angle of shadow cast by the corner of the veranda, and every now and then Suleima would pause in her work and let her eyes rest on him a moment. The child slept soundly, one creased little hand lay on the wicker side of the cradle, a pink little nose pointed absurdly to the roof.

"He is altogether quite adorable," said Suleima to herself, pausing to look, and with a smile of utter happiness went back to her work.

The other corner of the veranda was covered with wooden trays, over each of which was stretched a confining sheet of gauze. In the trays were spread fresh shoots of mulberry-leaves, on which reposed hundreds of silk-worm moths of the fairer and fatter sex busy laying eggs, as in duty bound, and, it must be conceded, fulfilling their duty with the utmost profuseness. The males, smaller and rather duller in color, fluttered about against the gauze or walked drone-like across the leaves, taking rude short cuts over their wives when they happened to find those estimable women in their way. Outside the gauze on the floor of the veranda lay another tray full of shoots of mulberry-leaves eaten bare by the broods of young caterpillars already hatched, or still covered with the eggs, which looked like a rash of minute gray spots. Suleima was behindhand with her work, for the eggs should have been transferred to the mulberry-trees before they hatched, and she moved quickly backward and forward from the row of young trees in the garden which spring had clothed in their new gowns of green, carrying the egg-laden twigs in her hand. These she either tied to the living shoots or, where the foliage was thicker and no sudden gust of wind could blow them away, she merely put it in the middle of the growing leaves. Round the trees, below the lowest output of branches, was painted a band of lime to prevent the caterpillars straying. She sang gently to herself out of a happy heart as she moved on her errands, stopping every now and then on the step from the veranda, and looking out over the shining shield of the bay towards Nauplia with eyes eager for the ruffling land-breeze which should bring a ship, which she waited for, climbing up wave after wave against it as a man climbs a ladder rung by rung.

Outside in the garden the air was still windless, and the trees stood with leaves drooping and motionless as if in sleep. Only near the fountain the alder, whose finer fibre perceived a moving air where others let it pass unnoticed, whispered secretly to itself. The spring had been late in coming, but in a day, so it seemed, the sun grew warm and sluices of mellow air were flung open to flood the land, and from hour to hour the anemones and little orchids had multiplied themselves by some vast system of progression along the hill-side as the stars grow populous in the heavens at the fall of night. Already Suleima's red anemones, sheltered from north winds by the house, and more forward than those fed by the thinner soil of the moorland, were over; one blossom only still held its full-blown petals, and to Suleima it seemed a thing of good omen that there should be just one left for Mitsos on his return. For this morning the *Revenge*, recognizable by its area of canvas, vaster than that of other ships, and the raking line of its bows, and flying the Greek flag, had been sighted out in the gulf, from the village of Tolo, heading for Nauplia. But to the sea-breeze had succeeded a dead calm, and she was yet some three miles out, mirrored in the sea as still as a ship in a picture till the land-breeze should awake. Father Andréa had set off for Nauplia after the mid-day dinner to welcome Mitsos home, and to catch a glimpse of the Capsina.

All afternoon the *Revenge* lay dozing on an unwrinkled sea. There was not breeze enough even to make the sails shiver and flap; you would have said the wind was dead. To the Capsina and Mitsos it was strange to lie idle thus, without even the occupation of considering their plans for the morrow, and the girl at times half hoped that the wind would soon come which would bring them to Nauplia and part her from Mitsos, half felt that the interminable procession of days would be only hour after impossible hour without him. The memory of that moment when, forgetting Suleima indeed, yet not remembering her except as in the hour of victory a comrade's heart goes out to a comrade, he had taken her into his arms, was like some devouring thirst which made dry her soul. She was too just to blame him for it; the fierce exultation of that night of battle and thunder had been all that prompted him. At such times a man would kiss a man, and so, and in no other way, had he kissed her; he had but overlooked the fact that she was a woman, had been ignorant she was a woman who loved him. She had returned to him a minute afterwards to find him shy, ashamed, awkward, and knew as well as if her thoughts were his own what was in the lad's mind. He wanted to apologize, thinking that he might have offended her, yet hesitated, lest he might solidify the matter for offence; perhaps he even feared that she imagined he was thinking so light of her as to treat her to a little love-making. Now the Capsina felt sure of the ancestry, so to speak, of that embrace; she was not offended;

137

she knew he was not making love to her, and with a delicate simpleness almost too straightforward to call tact, she had entered into conversation with him so quickly and naturally that he was at his ease again.

But, justice of God, the difficulty and the unfairness of it all! That wild, fierce joy which filled Mitsos at the sinking of the Turkish ship was paid for not alone by those drowning cries, but by her also, and heavily. She had succeeded too well, so she told herself, in her assumption of a perfectly natural manner. Had Mitsos's sudden action been dictated not by the excitement of that moment, but by the spasm of heat of a man for a woman, she had shown herself too disregardent, she had taken it too lightly; she had treated him, so he must have thought, as a boy who had been merely rude to her, but whose rudeness she had overlooked. And she laughed out at the thought, and Mitsos raised his eyebrows and asked what the matter for amusement was.

They were alone, for Christos had been left with his cousins at Patras now more than a week ago. They had passed the guns of Lepanto by night, after hanging about ready to fight their ships if they attacked, but out of range of the fort guns, for nearly a week. But one evening, after the sea-breeze had failed, a sudden wind had got up after midnight, in obedience to the Greek proverb that says, "On the first of spring the wind alone is contrary," and they had sailed out, passing close under the guns of the fort, reaching Patras before daybreak. Certainly the wind had been divinely punctual, for the very next day every sense said that winter was over. March and April had been cold and rainy, smiling sometimes through their tears, but for the most part scolding months, full of peevish weeping. But then, with the early days of May, the change came. The Primavera scattered her flowers broadcast over the land, and every land-breeze was sweet with the promise of budding woodland things. Bees, more than once when they were farther than a mile from land, had flown busy and drunken across the deck, and the superstitious sailors had told the Capsina that surely some very good thing was on its way to her.

To-day they had dined on deck, and after dinner Mitsos, in a ferment of restlessness at the sight of home, had gone more than once to the side of the ship, sniffing to find if he could smell the wind. But the wind yet tarried, and now he had stretched his lazy length along the deck, his head supported by a coil of rope, and smoked his narghile as he talked. He had just received his share of the prize-money—more than a hundred pounds—and this large sum was weighing on his mind when the Capsina's laugh broke in upon his meditations, and he roused himself.

"Talking of the prize-money—" he began.

"Which we were not doing," said the Capsina.

"Then let us do so now. It is thus: I do not want it, for it was not for that I came, and I would rather that you gave it to the war fund."

The Capsina turned a little away and played with the end of a rope lying near her.

"Then why was it you came?" she asked, unable not to give Mitsos the opportunity her heart knew he would not take.

He frowned.

"Why? Why?" he repeated. "Was there not reason enough, and are not the reasons justified? Or"—and he smiled—"or shall I make pretty speeches to you?"

"The Virgin defend me!" said the Capsina, with leaden calmness, again shrinking from what she had encouraged. "But you are absurd, little Mitsos. Are you to go home to—what is her name?—to Suleima empty-handed, and have no fairing for her and the baby?"

"Oh, Suleima wants no presents," said he.

"You mean she will be so happy when she sees you that—Oh, saints in heaven!" she broke off.

Then, as Mitsos stared at her with the quiet, habitual wonder with which he regarded her sudden outbursts as common phenomena:

"You think she will be so pleased to see you she will have no thought for aught else?"

Mitsos blew out a great blue cloud of smoke before he replied.

"It is thus," he said. "Had Suleima been away all this time, what, think you, should I have cared what she brought me so long as she brought herself? And I think—yes, I think it is not different with her."

"Oh, you men-folk make me mad!" she cried. "Little Mitsos, you are just exactly like my cousin Christos, and that, I may tell you, is no compliment from my lips. He could not understand, his mind was simply not able to appreciate how it was that I preferred the sea, and the brig, and—and Michael, to marrying him. 'What more can the girl want,' says he to himself, 'than to have a husband such as me?' And, indeed, you think, like Christos, that a woman has no other wish. Is a woman not a human thing? Because Suleima is so fortunate a girl as to have this great, fine Mitsos for her husband, is there nothing else in the world she can desire?"

The Capsina brought the words out like hammer-blows on an anvil. Then she went on hurriedly, reverting to the main topic.

"About the money," she said; "if you won't take it as prize-money, take it as wages, for, indeed, I think you are worth your pay, though lazy and given to tobacco, and I am not dissatisfied with you. Not—not as wages, for the Mavromichales, you say, have never accepted wages. The more fools they. Take it as a present from me. Does that offend you? I see it does, for you make a moon-crescent of your mouth. Then give it to Suleima as a present from me. It offends you still, for though you make your mouth straight, your nose is in the air. But, before God, little Mitsos, you are the queerest and the proudest lad I have ever seen. You should have been of the clan of Capsas."

"That you might treat me as you treated the cousin Christos, to whom I am so like? The words are from your own mouth, Capsina, not from my moon-crescent, as you are pleased to call that where I put my food."

The Capsina flushed ever so slightly.

"Ah, you talk nonsense," she said, quickly. "I do, too, being a woman; I know it; but that is no excuse for you."

Mitsos took the pipe out of his mouth and made a mock bow.

"What the Capsina does is good enough for me to do," he said.

The girl smiled back at him, her heart beating a little quicker than its wont, and sat for a moment silent, watching him as he lounged lazily with down-dropped eyes, stirring up the live charcoal which burned in the bowl of his narghile.

"Oh, it is a queer people the good God has made," she said. "I am of the clan of Capsas, you of the Mainats, and never have Mainats and Capsiots gone hunting together before. Why are we made so—you a Mainat, I a Capsiot? For, indeed, little Mitsos, you are more like the clan than Christos. Think if I had married Christos! I should have been, like the others, long before this day counting the eggs the hens have laid instead of the Turks that I have killed, and cooking the supper, and talking like one of a company of silly sparrows in a bush. Why is it that one thing happens to me, and not another? Why did you meet Suleima? Why—"

And her voice was a little raised and tremulous, and she stopped abruptly, though her silence half strangled her. She seemed unable to exchange an ordinary word with him without letting her sex obtrude itself. If she was never to be aught but a comrade to Mitsos, it would be something, at any rate, to make him know how much more he was to her. Her fierce, full-blooded nature, accustomed to impose its will on others and to exercise no control on itself, if baffled in the first respect might at least realize the other. She was hurt; each day of her life hurt her; at least, she could cry aloud. But the mood passed in a moment: Mitsos was full of the thought of Suleima, whom he would see that evening. He would think her mad, or worse; and still, he would not care. She would cease even to be a comrade to him.

Mitsos had not noticed the raised voice nor the abrupt breaking off. He was dimly suspicious that the Capsina was making metaphysical remarks to which politeness required an answer, and he frowned and shook his head hopelessly to himself, there being no subject of which he knew less. But the sudden introduction of Suleima into the question made things clearer.

"Suleima?" he said. "Why did I meet her? Oh, Capsina, how could it have been otherwise? Tell me that. For I could not be myself without her. Oh, I cannot explain, for God, in His wisdom, made me a fool!" he cried, and he puffed away at his pipe.

"And tobacco is always tobacco," remarked the Capsina, justly enough.

They sat in silence a while longer, and then the girl got up from where she was sitting and strolled towards the bows of the ship, which pointed up the gulf. She could see the ruddy-gray side of the fortress hill Palamede which stood up five hundred feet above Nauplia, but the town itself lay out of view behind a dark promontory which ran rockily out. The sea was perfectly calm and of a translucent brilliance, clear as a precious stone, but soft as the air above it. Fifteen fathoms below lay the sandy bottom of the gulf, designed, here and there, like a map, with brownish-purple patches of sea-weed, and between it and the surface, poised in the water, drifted innumerable jelly-fish and medusæ, shaped like full-blown balloons, with strange, slippery-looking strings and ropes trailing below them. Some were pink, some of a transparent and aqueous green, some rustily speckled like fritillary flowers, but all, as in a stupor of content, drifted on with the current of warm water settling into the bay. Now and then a shoal of quick fish would cross, turning and wheeling all together like a flight of birds, their burnished sides glittering in the sun-steeped water, or stopping suddenly, emblazoned, as if heraldically, on the green field. A school of gulls were fishing behind, dipping in and out of the water for chance fragments from the ship. Mitsos, lying at ease on the deck, with his pipe in his mouth and his cap pushed forward to shield his eyes from the sun, seemed to excel even the jelly-fish in content, and to the girl it appeared that she alone, of all created things, was of an uneasy heart. That evening they would reach Nauplia. News of their coming would before now have gone about, and she tingled at the thought of the welcome they would get together. Not only for her would those shouts go up, but for Mitsos with her, thus sounding with more than double sweetness to her ear. And when the shouting and acclamation were over she would go back to the ship, and Mitsos would go to Suleima. She hated this girl whom she had never seen, and mixed with her hatred was an overwhelming curiosity to see her.

Mitsos finished his pipe, got up thoughtfully foot by foot, and strolled towards where she was standing leaning over the bulwarks. He was getting impatient for the coming of the tardy wind, but judged it to be on the first page of good manners that he should keep his impatience private. Also he wanted to let this girl know in what admired esteem and affection he held her, and his tongue was a knot when he sought for words. Day after day they had run the same fine risks, their hearts had beat as one in the glory of the same adventures, they had laughed and fought and frolicked like two lads together, welcoming all that came in their path; and yet he could not take her arm and let his silence speak for him. Even Yanni had never been more ready and admirable of resource, more ignorant of what fear was, more apt and suited to him, nor more lovable, as comrades love. She had all the live and fighting gifts of his own sex, yet in that she was a woman he felt that they were the worthier of homage, and that he was the more unable to pay it.

His bare-footed step was silent across the decks, and he came close to her before she knew of his coming. And after spitting thoughtfully into the water, leaning with both elbows, awkwardness incarnated, on the bulwarks next her, he spoke.

"Oh, Capsina," he said, "how good a time I have had with you! And will you make me a promise, if it so be you are one-tenth as satisfied as I? It is this: If ever again—for now, as you know, with this siege of Nauplia and the Turks coming south, my duty is here—if ever, at some future time, you have need of one who hates the Turks and will act as your lieutenant or your cabin-boy, or will, if you please, swim behind your ship or be fired out of your guns, you will send for me. For, indeed, you are the bravest woman God ever made, and it honors me to serve you."

And once again, as on the night he joined the ship, he took of his cap and bent to kiss her hand.

Mitsos blurted out the words shyly and awkwardly, in most unrhetorical fashion, yet he did not speak amiss, for he spoke from his heart. And the Capsina stood facing him, and, holding both his hands in hers, spoke with a heart how near to bursting she only knew.

"I make you that promise," she said, "and I need not even thank you for all you have done. And, oh, little Mitsos—this from me—if you should suggest we sail the ship to hell together and fire on Satan, I would help hoist the mainsail, for, indeed, you are the best of boys."

And she turned suddenly, with a quivering lip, and looked out to sea.

Presently after, just before sunset, the land-breeze began to blow, and they ran a three-mile tack towards the far side of the gulf, and from there, helped by the current that sweeps into the bay, they made a point a short mile outside

Nauplia. Then, standing out again, they ran a short tack, and not long before the dropping of the wind cast anchor a cable's-length from the quay. Straight in front rose the lower town, on the side of the steep hill, pierced with rows of lights, as if holes had been knocked in the dark. Higher up, but below the Turkish walls, gleamed the fires of the Greeks who were besieging the place, and supreme and separate, like a cluster of stars, hung the lights at the top of Palamede. News of their coming had gone about, for the blockading ships cheered them as they passed, and all the length of the quay were torches and lanterns, hurrying to the steps where they would land, growing and gathering till they seemed one great bouquet of red flowers reflected in long snake-like lines on the water.

As soon as they were at anchor the Capsina and Mitsos were rowed to shore, and as they neared the quay, seen clearly in the blaze of the torches, the shouting broke out and swelled till the air seemed thick and dense with sound. The Capsina was the first to step out, and the folk crowded round her like bees round their queen. But she stood still, looking back, and held out her hand to Mitsos, and they went up the steps—the same steps up which he had come "from the sea and the sun"—hand in hand. Those who had never seen her, and knew her name only, having heard as in some old chivalrous tale of the wonderful maid who had chased the Turkish ships like a flock of sheep, crowded round to catch the glimpse of her, and her heart was full to brimming with the music of their acclamation. Yet the touch of Mitsos's hand was a thing more intimate and dearer to her.

Among the first was Father Andréa, and holding a hand of each:

"Now the Virgin be praised, you have come!" he cried. "And oh, little Mitsos, is it well?"

"Surely there is not much amiss," said he. "And again, is it well?"

"She waits for you impatiently content," said he, "and the child waits."

The crowd broke way for them to pass on, but surged after them as they walked in a babel of welcome and honor. Some pressed forward to touch Sophia's hand, other old friends crowded round Mitsos, pulling him this way and that, kissing him and almost crying over him, and the whisperer whispered and the gossips made comments.

"Eh, but what a pair would they have made!" said one. "They could pull the Sultan from his throne," and the speaker spat on the ground at the accursed name.

"The little Mitsos has grown even littler," said another. "See what a pillar of a man. And she, too; she is higher than his shoulder, which is more than you will ever be, Anastasi, till God makes you anew, and most different. Look at her face, too; no wonder the cousin in Hydra was loth to lose her."

Still hand in hand the two passed on to the mariner's church on the quay, where, as in duty bound, they offered thanks and alms to their name-patrons for their safe coming; and having finished their prayers they stood for a moment, silent, at the church-door.

"You will not sail to-morrow?" asked Mitsos. "You will come and see the home? May I not come for you in the boat in the morning?"

Sophia hesitated a moment.

"No, I cannot come," she said. "I sail to Hydra to-morrow, for I, too"—and she smiled at him naturally—"I, too, have a home. But surely we shall be together again, if you will. If this report of the Turks moving south is not true, we shall want you by sea, and speedily. Kanaris—you—me! Lad, the Turks will not be very pleased to see us again. So good-bye, little Mitsos; get you home."

And without another word she turned from him and went back to the ship.

Mitsos's way lay eastward, through the lower town, and many tried to make him stop awhile and tell them of the big deeds.

"Yes, but to-morrow," he would cry. "Oh, dear folk, let me go," and he had fairly to run from them.

The moon had risen, and the familiar homeward road stretched like a white ribbon in front of him. The bay lay in shining sleep; from the marsh came the ecstatic croaking of frogs, and the thought that they had stayed so long in one marsh made Mitsos smile. From the white poplars came the song of love-thrilled nightingales, and white owls hovered and hooted and passed, and now and then a breeze would blow softly across the vineyard, laden with the warm odors of spring and the smell of growing things. But he went quickly, for his heart's desire was a spur to him, and stayed not till he came to the garden-gate; and ere yet he had lifted the latch Suleima had knowledge of his coming, and they met, and the love which each had for the other brimmed their very souls.

CHAPTER X

The town of Nauplia itself lies on the north side of a tortoise-shaped promontory of land swimming splay-fashion out into the gulf. The upper part of this, surrounded by walls of Venetian fortification, was held by the Turks; the lower part, including the quay, by the insurgent Greeks. Behind the town, away from the sea, rose the rock on which was built Fortress Palamede, sharp, supreme, and jagged, like a flash of lightning, also in Turkish hands. A flight of steep, break-neck steps, blasted in many places out of the solid rock and lying in precipitous zigzags, communicated by means of a well-defended but narrow passage, battlemented and loopholed, with the citadel of the town proper. The south side of this promontory needed but little watching, for no man could find a way down crags which imminently threatened to topple over into the sea. On the west a water-gate communicated with a narrow strip of land giving into the shallow water of the bay, where no anchorage was possible. On the north the lower town was in the hands of the Greeks, whose lines of beleaguer stretched from the western end of the quay to the base of Palamede. On the east the only outlet was a small gate in the passage leading between Palamede and the citadel.

Now Nauplia was one of the strongest and, in the present state of affairs, quite the most important fortress in the Peloponnese still in the hands of the Turk. It communicated with the main arteries of war in the country; the harbor was well sheltered, defended by the town, and would give admirable anchorage to the the fleets of Europe, and the Sultan Mahomed, with his quick, statesmanlike sagacity, had seen that all his efforts must centre on its retention in Turkish hands. With Nauplia securely his, he could at will continue to pour fresh troops into the country, and there could be but one end to the war.

Had the Greeks acted with any singleness of purpose or the most moderate promptitude after the fall of Tripolitza in the previous October, Nauplia might have been taken without difficulty, but they let slip this opportunity. Instead they distributed honors and titles, and banners and tokens—a thing to make the more patriotic dead turn in their graves—and the Turks were in possession of a well-watered fortress, and had only to hold out till the fleet relieved them by sea and the army, which, under the command of the Serashier Dramali, had received orders to march straight to Nauplia, at the end of Rhamazan, drove off the besiegers.

April in the plains was somewhat rainless, and May unseasonably hot; and though the springs in the fortress did not run dry, yet the torrid weather made itself felt in the garrison of the sun-scorched Palamede. But the fleet, as was known, would set out in May, and Dramali would leave Zeituni, where he was encamped, in the first week of July. By the end of July, therefore, relief would be certain.

In the Greek lines much cheerfulness and nonchalant good-humor prevailed.

During April the Turks had made two sorties, which were repulsed with but little loss to the besiegers and at a heavy price to the besieged, and the latter now seemed inclined to wait for relief, trusting to the admirable fortifications which defended them and a certain growing slackness on the part of the besiegers, rather than make another attempt. Hypsilantes, an excellent field-marshal when there was nothing to do, treated the chiefs with a courtly condescension, and frequently entertained them at dinner; while Kolocotrones, with his new brass helmet and a hearty raucous voice, went hither and thither, often leaving the camp for a week at a time on some private raid, and swelled and strutted already with the anticipation of a plentiful plunder. For the Greeks considered their own ships as adequate to stop any fleet the Sultan might send from Constantinople, and thought it impossible that the garrison would hold out until the coming of the army.

Mitsos, the truant aide-de-camp, chiefly conspicuous hitherto by his absence, reported himself the morning after his return to Prince Hypsilantes, who, taking into consideration what he and the Capsina had done, was pleased to accept his lack of excuses and poverty of invention with graciousness, and further gave him furlough for a week, on the granting of which the lad posted back to Suleima and the silkworms. And that evening, when the child was gone to bed and Father Andréa had charged himself to see that nothing caught fire, and that no changeling fairy—a vague phantom terror dreaded and abhorred of Suleima's soul—malignantly visited the cradle of the littlest, the two went off for old sake's sake in the boat, Mitsos with the fishing spear and resin, to visit the dark, dear places of the bay. The land-breeze was steady, and the moon already swung high among the stars, and from afar they could see the white wall that both knew. As they passed it, Suleima clung the closer to Mitsos.

"How strange it all seems," she said, "to think that I was there year after year, not knowing of any but old Abdul and the eunuch—oh, a pig of the pit!—and Zuleika and the others. And now they are where?"

"In hell," said Mitsos, promptly, and with all the cheerfulness of unutterable and welcome conviction. "Yanni sent Abdul there himself at Tripoli. Oh, a fat man. His cheeks were of red jelly, you would say, forever wobbling. I pray I may never be a jelly-man."

Suleima laughed.

"Yet there were good things even in Abdul, though not of his intention, but his age rather," she said; "for instance, he was very calm and lazy, and he let us do as we liked, and never troubled us. Indeed, I think he hardly spoke to me six times. Yet had I been there a year longer, who knows? For latterly he used to look at me with his mole's eyes."

Mitsos frowned.

"Don't speak of it," he said, sharply; "he is in hell; even for me that is enough, and for me enough is not a little."

They tacked out to sea again after passing the white wall, for they were going across to the sandy bay where Mitsos used to fish. Nauplia, with the fires of the besiegers and besieged, gleamed like a low cluster of stars at the mouth of the bay, and the island, with its old Venetian castle on it, stood up a black blot against the glittering company. Towards Tripoli the hills were clear and black, and cut out with the exquisite precision of a southern night. Now and then from the town a sudden roar, soft and muffled with its travel over the water, would rise and die away again, but for the most part only the whisper of the severed water or the tap and gurgle of a wavelet crushed by the bows broke the silence. Then putting to land, Mitsos, with his spear and light, poked among the rocks for fish, while Suleima sat on the warm, dry sand watching him. And it seemed to both that the romance of the wooing was not yet over.

But to the beleaguered garrison of Nauplia scorching days and dewless, unrefreshing nights went by in hot procession, and by the middle of June, though the Greeks were not aware, the besieged knew that unless relief came within a few days surrender was imminent. Remembering in what fashion the Greeks had kept the treaty of Navarin, they had but little confidence in the observation of the terms of any capitulations they might make; but remembering, too, scenes of traffic, what Germanos with bitter truth had called "the market of Tripoli," they hoped that their lives might be spared, perhaps until the approach of the army, if they stipulated that until the capitulation was finally signed they should be supplied with food by the besiegers, though at famine prices.

Now Ali, the Governor of Aryos, being supreme in Argolis, was the superior of Selim, the commander in Nauplia, but as there was no possibility of his conferring with Ali through the Greek lines, the proposed draft of the treaty of capitulation had to be drawn out by him. He was a shrewd man, busy and cunning, and the terms he proposed showed that he had not failed to intimately acquaint himself with the character of the chiefs who besieged the place. Accordingly, one day in the last week of June, Mitsos, who had returned to his duties as aide-de-camp, came to Hypsilantes saying that a white flag was flying over the northern gate, and that the Turkish commander wished to confer with the head of the Greek army.

Now at that time Kolocotrones was absent from Nauplia with a large band of his irregular troops, and in his absence, since nothing whatever had previously occurred during the siege which demanded strength in the hand or thought in the head, Hypsilantes had always been given a supremacy of courtesy, in virtue of his original mission from the Hetairia, and that this business should have occurred while Kolocotrones was away—though without doubt if, when the latter came back, he found fault with what Hypsilantes had done he would revoke his acts—was honey to the prince, who still clutched at the show of power. So calling together the other chiefs and members of the national assembly, he intimated to them what had happened, in beautiful language, and Mitsos was forthwith sent with a flag of truce in his hand to conduct Selim to Hypsilantes.

Selim was a brisk, lively little person, who conducted conversation, you would say, more by a series of birdlike, intelligible chirrupings than by human talk, and, more abstemious in his ordinary life than his countrymen, he had suffered less from the sparing rations they had been on for the last fortnight. The gate was opened as soon as Mitsos approached it, and Selim came trotting out, as pleased with his flag of truce as a child with a new toy, and twittered away to Mitsos, as they went back to Hypsilantes' quarters, with the utmost vivacity in rather imperfect Greek.

"And it's pleasant indeed," he said, "just to take a walk down these streets again, even if his highness and I can come to no terms and I am sent back like a hen into that infernal cage, though indeed it's little fattening we get there. And how old may you be, and how long have you been a rebel to his majesty?"

He looked up sharp and quick in Mitsos's face like a canary, and the lad smiled at him.

"Ever since the beginning of the war," said he; "and, indeed, you may have seen a fine blaze my cousin and I made not so far from here?"

"What, the ship that was burned going out of the harbor?" asked Selim. "You did that, Mishallah? If we meet again, not under the flag of truce, there will be high blows."

And, as Mitsos laughed outright, "Do not be so merry," he said. "I could reach up as far as that big chest of yours and send the sword home."

"And what should I be doing the while?" asked Mitsos, "whistling a tune and looking the other way?"

The little man frowned.

"Maybe you would have had a poke at me, too. No, I'm not denying it."

Hypsilantes and the other members of the assembly then at Nauplia were awaiting their arrival. These consisted of two primates, both greedy and mischievous men; Poniropoulos, who had been turned out of the camp at

Tripoli for intrigue with the besieged, but whom affinity of interest had ingratiated with Kolocotrones. He had, like the others, collected together a corps of savage, undisciplined men who were too large a factor in the army to leave unrepresented in the assembly. In addition, there were a couple of other captains no worse and no better than he. Selim had known very well with whom he was to deal, and his proposals were greeted by eyes which gleamed with the prospect of speedy and ample gains. And here is his offer, how correctly calculated those eyes bore witness:

1. That the Turks should surrender the fortress, their arms, and two-thirds of their movable property.

2. That the Greeks should give them safe conduct out of the place, and further, hire neutral vessels, which should convey them to Asia Minor.

3. That the Greeks should supply them with provisions till the vessels were ready, upon which Clause 1 of the capitulation should be put into effect.

4. That hostages should be given on both sides for the fulfilment of the treaty.

And thus for the time the siege of Nauplia was at an end and the market of Nauplia began.

Selim made his offer and withdrew, but there was little need of that, for he was scarce out of the room when a whisper and a nod of perfect comprehension went round the chiefs, and being immediately recalled, he was told that his proposals were accepted.

"And I will see," said Hypsilantes, with a grand air, "that arrangements for the ships to convey you away are put in hand at once. Meantime——"

But Poniropoulos interrupted.

"May I have your highness's permission," he said, with a great hurry of politeness, "to supply the citadel with bread?"

"Certainly," said Hypsilantes, not seeing the man's meaning, "and it were well to put that too in hand at once."

But Selim was the sharper, and he leered at Poniropoulos, if a canary can be said to leer, with a twinkle of perfect comprehension in his eye.

"I doubt," chirped he, very clearly and loud, "that bread is most expensive in Nauplia."

And Poniropoulos scowled at him, for he had meant that it should be very expensive indeed.

So the terms were accepted, and Hypsilantes parted in a dignified manner from the Turk, and the latter went back to the citadel.

Poniropoulos, with hands itching for the touch of gold, took prompt and characteristic measures. He went straight to the nearest baker's, bought the whole of the bread he had in stock, staying only to haggle over a few piasters in the total, and not caring even to go back to his quarters for his own beast, hired a mule and hurried up the path with plying stick to the citadel. The baker, Anastasi, Mitsos's friend, stood for a moment wondering what was in the wind, when the solution struck him; and being a man born with two eyes wide open, saw that there was large profit to be made here, but no reason why the "Belly," as they called Poniropoulos, should be monopolist therein; and running out, he conferred with other bakers in the town, and it was unanimously and merrily agreed that all bread sold directly and indirectly to the "Belly" should be at just three times the price of the bread sold to others, and that if this did not satisfy him, why, he might make bread himself, and be damned to him.

The news spread rapidly—it could hardly have failed to spread—for before an hour was up the camp presented the dignified spectacle of various captains and primates bargaining and arguing over wine and olives with the shop folk, and literally racing each other to the citadel, where they sold their produce at starvation rates, laughing to themselves that Kolocotrones at any rate was out of it. Mitsos, who was buying fish in the market for himself, was pointing out to the shopman the impropriety of selling stale fish to a man with a nose, when the primate Caralambes came in to buy all the fish, he could find. And Mitsos, grinning evilly:

"This is a fish I would have bought," he said, "but it is not so fresh. We make you a present of it. You will get five piasters for it above, for the use of the church."

Kolocotrones returned after a few days, and entirely approved of the terms. Hypsilantes was engaged in his usual finicking and dilatory manner upon hiring ships for the embarkation of the Turks, according to treaty, but Kolocotrones told him that he need trouble himself no more about that, as he himself would see to it. But it was thus that he saw to it: Three ships which had been already engaged he dismissed with a certain compensation, saying that they would not be needed, and turned from the hiring of ships to the more immediate and lucrative pursuit of selling provisions to the half-starved garrison. The ships could be hired afterwards, and then there was a penny to be turned in the matter of passage-money.

The longer this traffic went on the better were both sides pleased. For the Turks, every day brought the arrival of relief forces nearer, and every day the captains reaped a golden harvest. There would be time, so thought Kolocotrones, to see about getting the ships when the new army drew nearer, and in any case the treaty of capitulation held, for the Turks, when the ships were ready, were bound to deliver over the fortress, their arms, and two-thirds of their movable property. And again the captains licked their lips.

Meantime the end of Rhamazan had come, and Kanaris, who with the Capsina had joined the Greek fleet in the eastern sea, had paid the Turks a visit which should cause them always to remember Rhamazan, 1822. The Greek fleet under the Admiral Miaulis had encountered the enemy off Chios, and the latter had retreated to the Gulf of Smyrna. There they had engaged the Greek in a desultory and ineffectual cannonade for a day or two, the Greeks not venturing in under the guns of the fort which protected the fleet, and the Turks not caring to sail out and give battle in earnest. Eventually the Greeks retreated to Psara, and the Turks again anchored off Chios, some six miles from the entrance to the Gulf of Smyrna.

All the last day of Rhamazan gala preparations went forward on board the ships for the solemn celebration of Bairam, and before night fell watchers were stationed on the main-tops of all the fleet to look for the first appearance of the new moon, which was the beginning of the feast. As the sun went down lines of bright-colored lanterns designed with their light the rigging of all the ships, the more conspicuous and the most bedecked being the eighty-gun ship of the captain, Pasha Kara Ali, who entertained for the feast the chief officers of the fleet. The deck was a house of Syrian tents and awnings, and troops of dancing-girls were in waiting to amuse the guests. As a salute to the end of the Rhamazan, ten minutes before sunset all the guns of the fleet volleyed again and again, till the air was thick with the smoke of the firing. Then, as the last echo died away, for a space there was silence, while all waited for the word. Suddenly, from the mast-heads, it was cried, "The moon, the moon of Bairam!" and the jubilant cry, wailing and mournful to western ears, was taken up by every throat. On board the flag-ship of Kara Ali all waited, standing at their places at the tables till the word was cried, and at that they reclined themselves, and the feast began.

Now many had noticed, but none had thought it noticeable, that all day there had lain close to the entrance of the Gulf of Smyrna, as if unable to get in, two small Greek ships. As soon as dusk fell and their movements were obscured, they changed their course. They carried, each of them, a cargo of brushwood soaked with turpentine, and their sails were steeped with the same. Kanaris, a straw in his mouth, for he could not with safety smoke on a fire-ship, commanded one, and Albanian Hydiot the other. The wind held fair, and Kanaris went straight for the ship of Kara Ali, and favored by the land-breeze blowing freshly off the coast, towards which the bows of the ship were pointing, ran his bowsprit straight through a port as near the bows as possible, set light to his ship with his own hands, and jumped into a boat that was towed behind. In a moment the flames leaped, licking from stem to stern of his caique, and driven by the wind, mounted like a flicked whiplash up the sails and in at the open ports. The awning on the quarter-deck caught fire, and being dry from the exposure to the hot sun all day, burned like timber. And Kanaris, having exchanged the straw for a pipe, rowed back to a safe distance, and watched the destruction of the ship with his habitual calm.

"It will burn nicely now," he said.

He saw a few boats launched, but into them poured so hurried and panic a flight of men and women that they were overloaded and sank. Other escape there was none, for the flames, driving inward and with a roaring as of bulls in spring, rendered it impossible to reach the seat of the fire. From overhead the blocks were falling from the rigging, and when boats began to arrive from other ships of the fleet, the heat of the flames and the fierce licking tongues which shot out at them rendered it impossible to approach; and the ship, with all on board, excepting only a few who jumped overboard and were picked up, perished. Kara Ali, as he was putting off in a small boat, was struck on the head by a falling spar. He died before they reached the shore.

Now the Sultan's orders had been curt. He had himself sent for Kara Ali before the fleet set out, and removing his jewelled mouth-piece a moment from his lips, said: "To Nauplia. Kosreff succeeds you if there is disaster. You have my leave to go." And he put the mouth-piece back into his mouth again, and turned his back on Kara Ali. Now Kosreff was at Patras, having been in charge of the western fleet the autumn before, and the captains of the other vessels had but little choice left them. They were bound to Nauplia, but there was no admiral. It was clearly their part to pick up the admiral at Patras, and then go back to Nauplia. There was always a little uncertainty, in acting under Sultan Mahomed, as to what was the right thing to do; but if a man did the wrong thing, it was not at all uncertain what the consequences would be, and no one felt at all inclined to take on himself the responsibility of handling the fleet when the Sultan had signified that Kosreff was to do so. And next day the fleet weighed anchor and set off for Patras, leaving Nauplia to take care of itself till their return.

Now the Serashier Dramali, the commander of the land army, was in receipt of orders just as peremptory. He was to wait at Zeituni till the end of Rhamazan, and then, as soon as the horses, according to the immemorial custom, had eaten the green barley of the fresh crops, was to go straight to Nauplia, where he would overwhelm and defeat the Greek force besieging it by land. There, too, he would meet the Sultan's fleet, which would drive off the Greek ships and throw provisions into the town. Such an attack, if delivered according to orders, said the Sultan, with a somewhat sinister stress on the word "if," could not conceivably fail of success.

Now the executive government of Greece was so busy mismanaging a hundred unimportant affairs that it had left the one thing needful quite undone, and the landforce of Dramali passed without opposition right through Eastern Greece, and reached, on the 17th of July, the isthmus of Corinth. Here the Acro-Corinth was in the hands of the Greeks, and defended only by a small guard; for the place was impregnable on all sides but one, and well supplied with provisions and water. But the commander, named Theodrides, no sooner saw the long lines of brilliant Turkish cavalry beginning to deploy on the plateau below the fortress, and marked the infantry mounting the steep ascent to the gate, than a sort of panic fear, unjustified though he knew indeed nothing of military matters, seized him. He gave orders that all the Turkish prisoners in the town should be murdered, and himself led the way out of the fortress by an almost impracticable path to the east, and with his gallant band made for the mountains, spreading the news that the Turks were in numbers as the sand-fly in August. Then, without a blow, Acro-Corinth fell into Dramali's hands.

He had long held the valor of the Greeks in unmerited contempt, but since he started from Zeituni it seemed that his contempt was not so ill-deserved. As he marched through the narrow gorge of Locris and Doris not a hand had been raised to stop him. On the hills north of Corinth the guards had fled at his approach. Here, at Corinth, at the sight of his troops a fortress nigh impregnable had been given up, as if by a tenant whose lease had expired to the incomer. The fleet, he supposed, would meet him at Nauplia, and without delay he decided to push on with his whole army there, leaving only a small garrison in Corinth.

He pointed contemptuously to the murdered prisoners. "Look," he said, "that is all these dogs do; they have the madness, and they shall be done by as they have done!"

And indeed it seemed that his contempt was very well merited.

The main road from Corinth to Nauplia, through Argos, lies up a long hill-side, passing at length into a barren and mountainous region set with gray bowlders and only peopled with lizards. Thence, gaining the top of a considerable ridge, it lies for the space of five miles or so in a narrow, downward ravine, called the Dervenaki, before it emerges into the plain of Argos. A riotous water passed down this, and the road crosses and recrosses by a hundred bridges—sometimes lying close to the torrent, at others climbing hazardously up the flanks of the ravine. On either hand the hill-side rises bowldersown and steep, too near the precipitous to let large trees get a grip of the soil; and between the gray stones grew only the aromatic herbs of the mountains. Even the hawks and eagles, looking from aloft for prey with eye that would spy even a mouse in a crevice, cut not their swinging circle in the sky above it, for no living thing, except the quick lizards, find food there. Three other roads besides, but less direct, crossed these hills between Corinth and Argos—two to the east, and westward one.

Through this Dervenaki Dramali marched rapidly. He found it altogether unguarded, and his scouts, who made casts to the east and west, reported that the other roads were clear also. At that Dramali's contempt began to breed want of caution, and instead of occupying Nemea and Aghionores, villages which commanded two of the other roads, and leaving troops to keep the pass and his communication with Corinth open, he went straight on with his whole army through the hills and on into the plain of Argos.

Meantime, at Nauplia and Argos, the supreme government had continued to display the imbecility usual with it. Ali, of Argos, had been allowed to enter the fortress of Nauplia, though without provision or arms, and he had at once arrested the Greek secretaries who were registering the property of the Turks. The Greeks had taken no steps to secure ships for the embarkation of the Turks, and had, consequently, failed to do their part of the treaty. The Greeks' hostages he retained as pledges for the Turkish hostages in the hands of the Greeks; for the rest, he supposed that the Turkish fleet would arrive from day to day. Dramali, he knew, had reached Corinth, and would push on at once.

The members of the central government of Greece were at the time at Argos, where they were chiefly employed in promoting each other unanimously to various lucrative appointments, and causing what they called the national archives to be written—a record of the valor of some of them, and the judicious statesmanship of others, the remainder. Among such business they had just appointed Prince Hypsilantes to be president of the legislative board, which made a quantity of regulations about the prevention of punishment of crime in the new Greek republic, and enjoyed handsome salaries. Hypsilantes, who had wit sufficient to see that their only object was to deprive him of his military command, was still debating what course to take, sitting about the time of sunset in the veranda of his house, which looked towards the Dervenaki, when he observed a quantity of little bright specks issuing therefrom. This being not a natural phenomenon he looked again, and the specks redoubled. At that he got up with a smile.

"I fancy the legislative measures will wait," he said to himself, and went across to the council chamber, where the ministers were already assembling for the purpose of mutual appointments. He went to his place, bowed, and pointed out of the windows. "I would draw your attention to this, gentlemen," he said.

For a moment there was silence, and then a babel of confused and incoherent cries went up from the terror-stricken lips of the legislative and executive boards. Metaxas, a consummate lawyer, was the first to run from the room; Koletres, unequalled in the knowledge of conveyancing, called lamentably on the Virgin and followed. At a stroke, on the scent of danger, the red-tape rule, and the grabbing greed which called itself patriotism, banished itself and fled. Ministers, senators, lawyers, and what not, ran incontinently to take refuge on the few Greek vessels which lay opposite Argos; the alarm spread like the east wind in March through the town, and women and children, some with bundles of their property snatched hastily up, rushed out in all directions to find safety, some with the blockading Greeks at Nauplia, some in the neighboring villages, others in the mountains. Many fugitives from towns on the coast which the Turks had sacked were in the place, and these, remembering the red horrors from which they had but lately escaped with bare life, left behind them the scanty remains of their property and, like rabbits remorselessly ferreted from one burrow to another, fled in the wildest confusion. Encamped in the square, crowding the poorer quarters, were hordes of camp-followers who had been drawn here by the prospect of the fall of Nauplia—wild men of the mountains, attended by great sheep-dogs, almost less savage than themselves. These being of able body and for the most part unencumbered by families or property, but very willing to become encumbered with the latter, spent a fruitful hour while the Turkish troops were still creeping from the entrance of the Dervenaki across the plain in plundering the houses of the wealthier citizens who had abandoned them, preferring to make sure their escape than to risk it for the sake of their goods. Among others, the secretary of state, Theodore Negris, a bibliophile, gave no thought to the small library of valuable books he had brought with him to Argos, supposing that the seat of government would be there, if not permanently, yet for a considerable time; and a Laconian camp-follower, entering his house after his flight, and unwilling to leave behind what might be of value, packed the most of the books in a sack and slung them over a stolen horse. But the horse fell lame, and the man wishing to push on to the hills, thought himself lucky to sell it, books, lameness, and all, for two dollars to a Greek officer who was in need of an animal to carry water for the troops at Lerna.

Night fell on a scene of panic and confusion. The last of the sunset had shown the van of the Turks no more than four miles off, with arms glistening red in the fire of the evening sky, moving steadily, though without hurry. The advance-guard of cavalry was already clear of the pass, and after an interval the main part of the army had been seen defiling out of it. They would enter the town in not more than two hours. Any one with a horse to sell, and a pistol to protect himself and it, could sell the beast for its value told a hundred times. Mules, oxen even, and calves were laden with valuables and kicked and goaded along the roads, away from the quarter from which the Turks were advancing. Had the executive council possessed the slightest authority or power of organization, much of this wild struggle for escape could have been avoided, but the executive council were hurrying like scared hares down to where a couple of Greek ships lay in the bay. There, too, were disgraceful things to see: more than one boat sent to convey the fugitives on to the ships was swamped by the stampeding crowds; others, private speculators, refused to take the panic-stricken folk on board, except at the payment of thirty piasters per head, and in one case only was the revolting greed properly punished, for a couple of men having agreed to pay the stipulated sum, were taken on board and straightway tipped the owner over his own gunwale into the water, and, heedless of his bubbling remonstrances, filled the boat with fugitives, denying him a place in it, and spent the next two hours in plying to and fro between the ship and the land.

But, meantime, the Greek garrison at Argos, consisting mainly of Albanians, had behaved with the utmost quietness and decency, and waited for orders. Hypsilantes, it was known, had been summoned by the terror-stricken council to join them in his new capacity of legislator on the ships, and he had returned answer that he would do no such thing; his place was where he could be useful, and as soon as the alarm was given, he, with Mitsos in attendance, Kolocotrones, Niketas, and a few others, met, and deliberated hastily what to do. It was quickly decided to destroy all the grain and forage in the town—as it was impossible to stand a siege—fill up the wells, and retire to Lerna, a heavy and small Greek camp, some two miles off on the sea-coast, defended on one side by the mountains, on one by the sea, on another by a large belt of swampy ground, which cavalry could not well pass. The Turks would hardly go on to Nauplia leaving them unattacked in their rear; if, on the other hand, they attacked, Lerna was well defended, and the dreaded Turkish cavalry at least were useless.

Above Argos, just outside the town, stands the Larissa, an old Greek fortress, subsequently built up by the Venetians. The hill it crowns is very steep and difficult of access, and it is well supplied with water. It was a matter of the first importance that this should not be let to fall, as had happened at Corinth, into the hands of the Turks, and a small body of volunteers, among whom was Mitsos, threw themselves into this, determining to hold it as long as possible. What artillery the Turks had they did not know, but unless they had heavy field-guns, there was a reasonable hope that for a time, at any rate, they could defend it successfully, and be another deterrent to the Turkish advance on

Nauplia.

Meantime, while they were busy taking up as much provision as they could lay hands on, the rest set to with destroying forage, and generally making the place untenable; until a picket stationed at the Corinth gate gave the alarm that the Turks were near, at which all but those who were to keep the Larissa set off through the now deserted and silent streets for the new camp at Lerna.

All through the hot hours of the summer night the seemingly endless procession of Turks continued to enter Argos. One by one their watch and cooking fires were kindled until the town, empty an hour before, twinkled with lights. Dramali's troops numbered not less than ten thousand men, nearly the half of whom were cavalry. And at present he intended to keep this formidable force at Argos, until the fleet appeared which should bring provisions and supplies to Nauplia by sea. He could then make a simultaneous assault by land, as the Sultan had so curtly intimated, and establish his headquarters there. But until the fleet arrived he could do nothing which might help Nauplia, for he had to forage for his own supplies, and could throw none into the beleaguered fortress. And the fleet, it will be remembered, had already passed Nauplia going to Patras to fetch the new captain, Pasha Kosreff, in place of the victim of Kanaris's fire-ship. But of this Dramali knew nothing, and waited for its appearance to deliver the *grand-coup* in the manner prescribed to him at Constantinople. News of the taking of Argos by the Turks had blazed like stubble-fed fire through the Peloponnese. The incompetent and useless administration had gathered their skirts and fled, and the war once more was in the hands of the people, commanded, it might be, by many avaricious and greedy men, but by no cowards.

And as a thunder-cloud collects on some grilling afternoon on the hills, so from all sides did sullen bands, full of potential fire and tumult, gather and grow on the mountains round. To attack the Turks, with their great force of cavalry, on the plain was no sane scheme, and the lesson had been taught at Tripoli, and taught thoroughly. But, though no attack was made on the Turks, it was soon found that Dramali, with Heaven-sent stupidity, had neglected to hold the range of hills over which he had come, and gradually the Greeks amassed a force high on the four roads which crossed from Corinth. Niketas, with not less than two thousand men, was intrenched in the easternmost road, and murmured softly to himself the words he had learned from an English sailor, "This is dam fine!" and Kolocotrones, finding Lerna inconveniently crowded, removed to the mountains to the west of Argos.

And all waited—wild beasts, hungry.

For the time all party and personal jealousy ceased. Petrobey, with a thousand Mainats, came from the south and joined the Greek force assembled in the main camp, and the scornful clan, it was noticed, were very silent, as their habit was when there was work to the fore. He had a long conference with Hypsilantes, and to their council came Krevatas, a primate from the country of Sparta, a man made of blood, courage, and hatred, who would go about among the soldiers, seeing visions by day and night, and exclaiming, "The Lord is a man of war!" He had but little other conversation, and cried thus very frequently. Like Hypsilantes, Petrobey saw that there was no object to be served in attacking the Turks in Argos. Supposing the fleet came, and Dramali moved to the capture of Nauplia, they would have to attack then. If, on the other hand, something, as was now possible, had delayed the fleet, it was certain that Dramali's supplies could not last him very many days, for the Turks were foraging far and wide both for corn and provender for their horses, and when he retreated to Corinth, as he must needs do, the fleet not coming, there were the hills he had left unguarded to be passed, and Petrobey's blue eye danced, like the sun on water, and Krevali's exclamation was fit commentary.

Twice in the first day of his occupation Dramali directed an attack on the small band of some five hundred men in the Larissa, but finding that it was no easy matter to storm it, and thinking perhaps that the place was ill-watered and the defenders would surrender, shrugged his shoulders, and left it, as the Greeks had left Nauplia, to the slower but not less sure process of starvation. But Petrobey saw the immense strategical advantage of the place. Dramali could hardly advance to Nauplia, leaving a well-fortified citadel in his rear, into which the Greeks would pour as soon as he left Argos, and he insisted that the garrison should be increased.

"They may be as fierce as hawks and as swift," said he, "but their numbers are too small. Also, if we can throw men into it, we can also throw provisions. The lad Mitsos will be glad of that: he would eat a roe-deer as I eat an egg— at one gulp."

Yanni, who was with his father, looked up.

"Oh, if it is possible, let me go among them," he said, "for my place is with Mitsos."

Petrobey, another of whose sons had been killed that year in a skirmish, looked at the boy.

"Benjamin, too," he said, half smiling, half with entreaty. "Yet did he not come back safe to his father? So be it, Yanni. Now, let us talk how it is to be done. We will go on dear Nikolas's plan, and say all the impossible things, and so take what is left."

"Daylight," said Yanni, promptly.

"A great noise," remarked Hypsilantes, with the air of a man who says a good thing.

Petrobey laughed.

"So much is certain," he said. "But then comes a difficulty. If by night, as like as not the lads will think it is an attack from the Turk. Thus will Benjamin come home, shot through the head by his very dear friend Mitsos."

"Cannot we call to them as we approach?" said Yanni. "Or wait. Oh, father, cannot we signal during the day from the hills behind?"

Petrobey nodded.

"Not so bad," he said, "but of the men there, who knows the signal tongue?"

"Mitsos and I did signalling work at Tripoli."

"So you did. It is worth trying. Now the attention of the Turks on the night you enter, if the signalling goes well and enter you do, must be elsewhere. Perhaps your highness would conduct a skirmishing party with much noise and bush-firing and swift running away in the opposite quarter."

"I?" asked the prince, and a sudden glow of courage exalted the man. "I should sooner be of those who attempt to enter the Larissa."

Petrobey looked at him approvingly.

"It is an honorable service," he said, "and the Larissa is a steep hill. I then will see to the other. Now Yanni, off with you, and a nice, warm walk you will have. Get you to the hill behind the Larissa and signal till you attract their attention, or until your arms drop off like figs over-ripe. It is yet early, so say that a relief party will make the attempt to enter the citadel to-night, an hour before moonrise. They will climb the back of the hill, or wherever they find it unguarded. Those inside will know best the disposition of the Turkish troops."

The hours went on through the suffocating calm of mid-day, when no breeze stirs the still and stifling air, and the Greek camp at Lerna, lying against the mountain-side, was a bakehouse of heat. In the low, marshy ground below, among the vineyards and melon-patches which stretched down to the bay, they could see companies of Turkish soldiers, guarded by their cavalry, picking the grape-leaves as fodder for their horses, while the men gathered the only half-ripe fruit for themselves. Once a band of some fifty approached to within five hundred yards of the outworks which had been thrown up round the mills where the Greeks lay, and the Mainats on guard snarled and grumbled like caged lions who long to smite and crack the heads of those who look through their prison-bars. But the cavalry were too close to risk an attack, which must have ended in trampled flight and knifing, and they could only store up their hate for future use. On the other hand, the Greeks were equally secure, for the broken ground near the camp, intersected by channels and banks for irrigation, and further defended by the steep water-eaten banks of the torrent-bed of the Erastinus, now summer-dry, rendered the approach of the Turkish cavalry impossible, and a combined attack of Dramali's infantry would have been necessary to drive them out of their secure position. Such an attack Dramali could not afford to make: the object of his expedition was the relief of Nauplia, and until that was effected he dared not risk defeat. Several small skirmishes had indeed taken place, but Petrobey, pursuing his policy of keeping his men out of the reach of cavalry, had always forbade them to follow retreating Turks into open ground. Furthermore, the two Greek vessels moored not far off covered the open space which was near the bay across which the Turks must advance, and, in case of any massed attack, were ready to open fire on them. Meantime Petrobey, though burning to be at work, found a certain shrewd comfort in watching the Turks eating the unripe melons. "They are cool for the mouth," he said, "but burning fire in the bowels." And, indeed, before many days a sort of dysentery broke out among the Turkish troops, which added to the difficulties and hazards in which, as Dramali was soon to find, he had placed his army.

Kolocotrones had left Lerna to take up his position on the hills before Petrobey, with his Mainats, arrived, and it was to below an outlying post of his camp that Yanni climbed to signal to those in the Larissa. The day was extraordinarily hot, and his way lay over long, palpitating flanks of gray bowlder-covered hills. There all vegetation had long ago been shrivelled into brown, ashy wisps of stuff, though up higher, near the point to which he was making, a spring which gushed from the mountain-side still flushed an acre or two of cup-shaped hollow below it with living vegetation. The great green lizards alone seemed not to have been turned brown by the drought, and slipped pattering over the bowlders into cracks and crevices as Yanni passed. Overhead the sky was a brazen wilderness, deserted of birds, and the air over the hot mountain trembled and throbbed in an ague of heat. But Yanni went fast and very cheerfully. He carried no arms, for the Turks never went beyond the plain, and it was a healthier heat to walk just in linen trousers and shirt, open from neck to waist, than to lie sweltering in guard and under arms in the camp at the hills of Lerna.

An hour's climb gave him elevation sufficient to be able to see over the outer circuit of walls on the Larissa, and show him the sun-browned tops of the hill peopled with the tiny, living, moving specks of the garrison who held it. Below the base of the hill the lines of Turkish tents formed a circuit nearly complete, but at the back, where the rocks rose almost precipitously, there was a break in them. Whether the hill was accessible or not at that point he did not know—evidently the Turks seemed to think not—but if he succeeded in attracting the attention of the Greeks in the citadel, he could learn from them where was the best place to make the attempt. He had brought with him a strip of linen for the signalling, but finding the distance was greater than he anticipated, he saw that it would be too insignificant an object to be noticed, and, stripping off his shirt, he made wild waving with it, signalling again and again, "Mitsos! Mitsos Codones!"

For five minutes he stood there, with the sun scorching his uncovered shoulders like a hot iron, without attracting any attention; but before very much longer he saw a little white speck from the top of the citadel, also waving, it would seem, with purpose.

"Oh, Mitsos, is it you?" he said, aloud, and then repeated "Mitsos" as his signal, and waited.

The little speck answered him. "Yes, I am Mitsos," it said. "Who are you?"

Yanni laughed with delight.

"Yanni," he waved, "your cousin Yanni."

"Have the clan come."

"Many okes of them, under father. We are going to send a party to support you in the citadel to-night, an hour before moonrise. Be ready." There was a pause, and Yanni, forgetting that he was rather over a mile off, shouted out, "Do you see, little Mitsos?" and then laughed at himself. Soon the waving began again.

"We can hold the place, I think, but we are short of food."

And Yanni answered:

"Oh, fat cousin, we bring much food. Where shall we make the attempt?"

"From the back, between where you are standing and me. It is steep, but quite possible for those not old and fat. It is where you see no Turkish tents. Who is in command?"

"Hypsilantes."

"I am laughing," waved Mitsos, "for I see his big sword tripping him up. Go very silently. If the alarm is given, and the Turks attack you, we will help from above. Good-bye, Yanni; it is dinner-time, and the littlest dinner you ever saw."

Yanni put on his shirt again, and, seeing that Kolocotrones' outpost was not more than two hundred feet above him, though concealed from where he stood by a spur of rock, he bethought himself to go up there and get a drink of wine before he began his downward journey—for his throat was as dust and ashes—and also give notice of the intended relief. He found that Kolocotrones was there himself, and was taken to him.

That brave and avaricious man was short of stature, but of very strong make, and gnarled and knotted like an oak trunk; his face was burned to a shrivelled being by the sun, and he wore his fine brass helmet. Unlike Petrobey, who was scrupulously fastidious in the matter of clothes, cleanliness, and food, he cared not at all for the things of the body, and was holding a mutton-bone in the manner of a flute to his mouth, gnawing pieces off it, when Yanni entered. The old chief remembered him at Tripoli, and though he was on the most distant terms with the clan, who regarded him with embarrassing frankness as a successful brigand, he nodded kindly to the boy.

"Eat and drink," he said; "talk will come afterwards," and he would have torn him a shred of meat off the flute.

"Surely I will drink," said Yanni, seating himself, "for indeed it is thirsty work to stand in the sun. No, nothing to eat, thank you."

Kolocotrones poured him out wine into rather a dirty glass and when the boy had drank, "What is forward?" he asked. "Are you of Maina come?"

"A thousand of us. To-night we are sending a relief force to those in the citadel. I have been signalling to Mitsos with my shirt from the hill-side."

Now when money was not in the question, Kolocotrones was the most enthusiastic of patriots. There was certainly nothing to be got from the citadel, and he dropped his mutton flute and struck the table a great blow with his hand.

"That is very good," he said. "My compliments to the clan, and to Petrobey. Lad, but I have these Turks in the hollow of my hand. The fleet still comes not, and without the fleet how shall they relieve Nauplia, where already the besieged purchase food from the besiegers; they cannot hold Argos more than a week now, for here, too, their food is failing. Then they will try to get back to Corinth. All the hills are guarded, and I shall be there for them. Oh, I shall be there! and where would all of you be without old Kolocotrones to think for you, ay, and act for you when the time comes?"

Yanni was half amused, half offended, at the arrogance of the old chief, and took another great draught of wine, some bitter stuff; but, as Petrobey said, "That fellow cares nothing for what he eats, save that it should be meat; and nothing for what he drinks, save that it should be wet. Then answer me. Why did God give us a palate?"

Kolocotrones took another chew at his mutton-bone and tilted back his helmet a little, showing a bald forehead.

"Panos—my son Panos will be with me," he continued, "and the lad and I will chase them like sheep and kill them like chickens. Also there will be much gold."

And his eyes grew small and bright like a bird's.

Yanni's scornful young nose was in the air by this time, but his manners forbade his saying just what he thought of Panos, and he rose to go.

"I am cooler," he said, "and less dusty in the throat. I will be going back. Indeed, I think I would have paid weight for weight in gold for that wine."

"I wish you had," chuckled Kolocotrones, whose humor was of the most direct. "But it is a free gift, lad, and I do not grudge it you."

Yanni saluted and retired. Once out of the camp he executed a sort of war-dance of scorn down the mountainside.

"A free gift!" he muttered. "A free gift, indeed! What else should a draught of sour wine be? Thank God, I am of Maina, and not of that stock. I would sooner keep a khan than be that general or his pasty son."

And Yanni, bursting with indignation, went scrambling down the mountain-side, thinking how fine it was to be a Mavromichales.

The arrangements for the relief party were not long in making. Petrobey, as soon as night fell, was to lead a band of Mainats towards the southeast of Argos—an uneven tract of ground, full of bushes and marsh, and much intersected by dikes—where the cavalry could not be utilized against them. They were to advance as close as they safely might to the gate of the town, fire, and run away, come back and fire, and generally give color to the idea that a noisy and badly planned attack was being delivered from that quarter. The effect of this would be to make the enemy alert and watchful of movements in that direction; in any case, their eyes and ears would not be too keen on the Larissa, which was quite on the opposite side of the town. Orders were given that if they were pursued in any number, they should run away, scattering as they went, but return again and keep up the disturbance till the moon rose. By the rising of the moon the relief party would already have made good their entrance into the fortress, unless they had been repulsed, and there was no longer any necessity for the others to dance about like will-o'-the-wisps in the marshes. It would be dark by nine, and the moon did not rise till midnight, so that the others would have ample time to cross the two miles of plain which lay between them and the Larissa in the cover of the dark, and do their best. The relief party, consisting of between four and five hundred Mainats, were nominally under the command of Hypsilantes, but Yanni alone, having seen from the mountain the lay of the ground on the far side of the Larissa, and alone knowing the disposition of the Turkish blockading lines there, was to act as guide. The object of the expedition being in the main to get supplies into the fortress, they took with them a flock of goats, all carefully muzzled so that they should not bleat to each other, and on the back of each goat was a hamper of loaves. "Quite like little men on a journey," said Yanni. Round the beasts the men marched in a sort of hollow oblong, thus forming a pen for them. When they came near the lines of the Turks a small reconnoitring party was to be sent on to see if the steep rocks were practicable and unguarded. If so, they should make a dash for these, dragging two or three goats with them, which, once past the Turkish lines, they would unmuzzle, so that the others, hearing them bleat, might follow. It was impossible to take sheep, for the way up the rocks, though practicable for men and, therefore, for goats, might not be so for the less nimble animals. The whole expedition, its striking irregularities, its hazards, its remoteness from anything commonplace, was after the hearts of the clan, and they grinned to each other as the goats, with their luggage strung on their backs, were driven into their living pen and the door formed up between them.

They had to go slowly, for the leading and retention of the beasts was not very easy, and before they had marched half a mile they heard shouts begin from the opposite quarter of the town and knew that Petrobey's party had got to their dancing. Soon the black, gigantic walls loomed nearer, sharp cut against the blue-black of the star-sown sky, and they halted behind a bluff of upstanding rock, while Yanni and some others moved forward to examine the ground. A hundred yards farther on they got a good view of the Turkish camp-fires, so that they could tell, roughly, the disposition of the troops, and here they halted in council.

"It is even as Mitsos said," whispered Yanni. "There is a great gap in its lines, and that is, no doubt, where the steep rocks came into the plain. He said a man could climb there, and I told him the Prince was coming, at which he laughed, thinking he would trip up. Shall we do this?"

Kostas Mavromichales, the brother of Petrobey, shook with suppressed laughter.

"The assault of the goats," he said. "Oh, a very fine plan! I thought of it."

They were about four hundred yards from the Turkish lines, but the ground, evilly for their purpose, was level and without cover, and the more speedily this was passed the better. The gap in the lines was about three hundred yards in width; immediately above them the rocks began. Once there, every one must find his own path, the leaders dragging forward an unmuzzled goat or two to encourage the others. It was agreed that Kostas and Yanni should take one between them, Athanasi and Dimitri a second, and two other Mainats a third.

These whispered arrangements made, they hurried back to the others and gave them what they had seen. The six goat-draggers were to be in the first line, who, as soon as they reached the rocks, would take off the muzzles, and then climb and scramble on as fast as might be. If they were seen or heard before they got close up to the lines, it was very unlikely they would be able to get in at all, for it passed the wit of man to fight and drive goats simultaneously; and it was worse than useless to get in without the goats, for thus there would be the more mouths to feed, and nought to feed them with. So "with the goats or not at all" was the order.

The ground was hard with the long heat, and they moved forward as silently as possible, but accompanied as they went by the sharp, swift pattering of the goats' feet drumming like a distant tattoo. To the right and left of them twinkled the rows of fires, but straight ahead where the rocks went up there was sheer untenanted blackness. They marched quickly, and every man besides looking to his own steps had to give an eye to the goats nearest him; but carrying their muskets horizontally and at the full length of their arms, these formed a useful though rough barrier. Already they were between the lines of camp-fires, and the black rock was close ahead, when the report of a musket sounded from the left, a bullet from a one-sighted gun sang above their heads, and a voice shouted a Turkish something. At that Yanni paused, and with his knife cut the string muzzle of one of the goats.

"Catch hold of the other horn, Uncle Kostas," he whispered, "and run. Pinch the devil and make him talk. Holy Virgin, if it is a dumb goat! Pinch him, oh, pinch him!"

Yanni gave a great tweak to the goat's ear as he ran forward dragging him, and the beast bleated lamentably and loud. Meantime the other two goats had been served in like manner and made shrill remonstrances, and the herd passed on through the opening made in the front ranks, after the sufferers.

"Oh, it is done," panted Yanni; "here are the rocks. Good God, they are steep! By the hind leg, uncle, lift it. So. We have got a prize goat, I think. There is another shot. But we shall be up before the sentries have given the alarm."

The other men opened out a little, still forming a barrier to the right and left of the herd, to prevent them straying till they gained the rocks, and then went up hand over hand on the face of the cliff. The face of the hill, though steep, was firm and reliable, with good hold for hands and feet, and in a few minutes the Mainats were scattered over the ascent, the men black and almost invisible against the dark cliff, and the dappling of the trotting goats only showing vaguely and uncertainly. Below in the Turkish lines they could see men stirring, and a few shots were fired at the hindmost of them; but so swift had been their passage, and so scattered their climbing of the rocks that they were already in the higher bluff before the Turks realized what had happened. From above, ahead, came heart-broken bleatings, and that was all.

Mitsos since the sun went down had been peering into the darkness over the citadel wall, and hearing the shots supposed that the relief party was passing the Turkish lines and that the alarm was given. Immediately he heard the bleatings of the goats, and, like the Turks, saw only a moving company of gray specks. A party was ready to make a sortie, but as there were but a few shots he waited.

"It is undoubtedly they," he remarked; "but in what fashion are they coming?"

And he went down to the gate, and looking through the window of the chamber saw the specks coming nearer. Before long the foremost were close, and he shouted "Yanni."

And from the darkness Yanni found just enough breath to shout: "Yes, yes, open the gate! Come on, brute."

Mitsos grinned, thinking that the words were to him.

"Surely little Yanni will be sore to-night," he said to himself, and with two others unbarred the gate. Next moment Yanni and Kostas rushed through struggling and panting, each with a horn of the mishandled goat, and the frightened, pattering herd poured after them. The other men had kept behind the beasts, and to right and left were shepherding them; and as soon as the last had passed in the gates were closed again.

Yanni flung himself on the ground, utterly blown, and too exhausted to notice Mitsos.

"Never again! oh, never," he panted, "will I drag a goat up the Larissa. So— don't ask me. Oh, I shall burst."

Mitsos had broken into a roar of hopeless laughter, which was taken up by the hungry garrison, and while Yanni was recovering he and the rest herded the goats together again, and rations of bread were given out, and a few goats killed.

Then having secured a great chunk of bread himself, he came back to Yanni, who was sitting up, still rather breathless. Kostas, with his fat red face, had not yet reached convalescence, but lay large and palpitating on the ground.

"Yanni, oh, little Yanni!" said Mitsos, "but I am one joy to see you. The goats too. It was a miracle of a plan. Yanni, when did you come? You will sleep with me to-night. Oh, there is the Prince."

And Mitsos stood up, and saluted the Prince with a twinkling eye, for he himself was a deserter; and the Prince's face was in patches of red and white, comical to the irreverent, and his breath whistled untunefully in his throat as he drew it. Mitsos fetched him a piece of sacking to sit on, and stood respectfully by him as he paused to get his breath.

"My aide-de-camp," said the Prince at last, smiling, "I had to come to you as you persisted in going away from me."

This was undeniably the statement of the case, and Mitsos waited a little sheepishly, and the Prince continued.

"But we will look it over," said he, getting up, "even a second time. For, indeed, little Mitsos, they would have made a legislator of me, for which I have no call, neither abilities therefor, or inclination, and I would rather be with the people. Show me, please, where I can sleep, and give me first some water, for I am tired and as thirsty as sand with climbing those rocks. Eh, but I have done a finer work to-night than I ever did in the councils of the senate!"

Mitsos soon found quarters for Hypsilantes, of the roughest, to be sure, and it was curious to him to see how the Prince took a sort of childlike pleasure in having to sleep in a shed, on a heap of sacking, with a crust of bread, a little very tough goat's-flesh, and a draught of water for his supper. His face quite lighted up at the thought that he was playing the soldier in earnest.

"This is better than swords and medals, Mitsos," he said, as the latter brought him the food. "There shall be no more honors and decorations for me or from me, for, indeed, there is no help in those things. I should have done better by scrambling up rocks and dragging goats with the others from the first. Listen at the lads singing! I would sing, too, for the lightness of my heart, had God given me a note of music in my throat."

Mitsos left him and went out to find Yanni, whom he had not seen since the taking of Tripoli. The Mainats had fraternized most warmly with the other part of the garrison, and they were lounging and leaning together on the wall, looking towards Argos, when Mitsos came out. The moon had not yet risen, and the party under Petrobey were still out on the far side of the town. But the sky had brightened with the approach of moonrise, and though the plain lay still sombre and featureless, except where the flash of muskets drew a line of fire across the dark like a match scratched but not lit, the bay had caught the gathering grayness of the sky, and lay like a sheet of dull silver. Across the water the lights of Nauplia looked like some huge constellation of stars growing red to their setting, and in the town below they could see that the Turks were on the alert, and little patches of men as small and slow as insects now and then crossed the streets which lay stretched out below them, hurrying towards the southeastern gate. The goats, relieved of their burdens, stood penned near, visible in the firelight which the men had lit to cook the flesh, adapting themselves with the nonchalance of their race to their new conditions, some still sniffing inquisitively at the ground, two or three fighting and sparring together, others lying down half asleep already with ears just twitching. Yanni was among the other men, and when he saw Mitsos coming, left the group, went towards him, and taking his hand, walked off with him to the other side of the citadel.

"Oh, Mitsos," he said, "what need of words? As soon as I knew you were here the devils of the pit could not have held me back. And you—tell me that Suleima has not made you forget me."

Mitsos put his arm round the other's neck.

"Not even Suleima," he said, "nor yet the littlest one, your godson, whom you have never seen, nor yet the Capsina, with whom I have spent more days of late than with Suleima. Did I not swear the oath of the clan to you, and that very willingly, and not a thing to be sworn lightly? And do we not love each other?"

Yanni gave a happy little sigh.

"So that is well," he said. "So now, tell me of all that concerns you. What of the Capsina, for I heard of the deeds in the gulf?"

"Indeed it is difficult to tell you of the Capsina," said Mitsos, "for never have I seen any one to compare with her. The soul of a man, I think, must have been given her; also she is as beautiful as—as Suleima, at least so another would say. Do you remember the journey we went together, Yanni? Well, my cruise with her was like that. Of all women I have ever seen I love one only, and yet I think I love the Capsina in the way I love you."

"And she?" asked Yanni.

"Oh, she likes me," said Mitsos. "I am sure she likes me, else we could not have got on so well together. We used to play and laugh like children, and everything was a joke—that was when we first started, and before she knew of Suleima."

"Why did you not tell her of Suleima?"

"Oh, that was some dear nonsense of Suleima's own. Then one day I did tell her, because she asked me straight who were they at home."

"What did she say?"

"I forget. Nothing, I think. Oh yes, she asked why I had treated her like a stranger, and not told her. I remember now; it puzzled me that she said that. Christos and I were playing draughts at the time, and I remember she went out soon after, though it was most wet and stormy."

Yanni whistled low and thoughtfully to himself, and Mitsos continued:

"I expect she will be soon at Nauplia when the fleet comes. Oh, she is splendid. You shall see."

He pointed down the hill where the relief party had come up.

"Do you see there?" he cried. "There are lights moving at the bottom of the hill, and men. They are drawing their lines more closely where you came up. There will be no passing them next time."

Yanni spat contemptuously over the wall.

"Who cares for the cross-legged Turk?" he said. "I saw Kolocotrones to-day. He says they are in the hollow of his hand. His hand, Mitsos! A dirty hand it is. He gnaws a mutton-bone, holding it in greasy fingers, and licking them afterwards, and drinks sour wine. Why should a man live like a pig when there is no need?"

"Because he has a pig's soul, even as the Capsina has a man's soul," said Mitsos. "Yanni, we must go Turk-sticking on the mountains when we get out of this. There will be plenty of Turks to stick."

"When will that be?"

"When the Turks have no more to eat, or when the fleet arrives, whichever happens first. You see, it is like this: The fleet still comes not, and without the fleet how shall they relieve Nauplia, not having sufficient food themselves. If the fleet does not soon come, they will have to make their way back to Corinth. Meantime, on the mountains, between here and there, every day fresh Greeks collect. How many men has Kolocotrones with him?"

"Ten thousand, he says," said Yanni, "but he always says ten thousand."

"May his saints have made him speak truth at last!" said Mitsos. "Then there are Mainats. How many?"

"A thousand," said Yanni, "and Niketas is already encamped on the hills with two thousand. Oh, Mitsos, it is a nice little trap we have ready for the devils!"

Mitsos suddenly felt in his pouch.

"Tobacco—oh, tobacco!" he cried. "Yanni, not a whiff has been in my mouth for three days, when the tobacco was finished. I will sell you my soul for tobacco. Surely you have some."

Yanni pulled out a roll of it.

"Halves," he said. "Cut it, Mitsos, and remember the saints are watching you!"

Mitsos ran across to the still glowing fire and fetched a light.

"The Capsina said I thought about nothing but tobacco," he remarked, "and indeed I do think about it a good deal. What was it we were saying? Oh yes, we stop here till there is no more food, and then we cut our way out, somehow. There will be broken heads that day. I pray mine shall not be one of them. But if the Turks move first we garrison the place and leave men here sufficient to hold it, and follow the Turks to Nauplia, if this fleet comes, or up into the mountains towards Corinth."

"You will join the Mainats again when we move?" asked Yanni.

"Surely." He paused a moment, frowning. "Yanni, it is absurd of me, but again I am disquiet about Suleima. I ought to have learned by now that God watches her very carefully. But supposing the Turks go towards Nauplia, the house is on the way."

Yanni laughed.

"And Father Andréa, maybe, will run away, leaving Suleima there. Oh, it is very likely," said he. "It is time to go to bed, Mitsos. Where do you sleep?"

"I will show you. There is room for two. Oh, I am a guard for the last two hours of the night, and you will have the bed to yourself. But surely at sunrise I will come back, very full of sleep, and I shall fall on you. Thus you will be flat."

A long barrack-room stretched from near the gate up the north side of the citadel, already nearly full of men stretched, some on the ground, others on sacking, asleep. The night was very hot, and the atmosphere inside was stifling. Mitsos sniffed disgustedly.

"This will not do," he said. "We will fetch the sacks and lie outside. Tell the guard, Yanni, that when my watch comes I shall be asleep by the gate, so that they may wake me."

Other men had come to the same conclusion as Mitsos, and on their way to the gate they passed many stretched out still and sleeping on the dry, withered grass. The moon had long since risen, and the plain was flooded with white light. The fire near the gate had died down, and only now and then a breath of wind passing over the fluffy ashes made them glow again for a moment. A little farther they passed the goat-pen against the wall, and two or three goats looked up inquisitively as they walked by out of long, shallow eyes. The sentry was opposite the gate as they came up, and Mitsos showed him where he would be in a deep embrasure of the wall, where a projecting angle stood out, leaving a dark corner sheltered from the glare of the moonlight. They threw down the sacking here and arranged it lengthwise, making a bed broad enough for two. Mitsos had brought his thick peasant's cloak with him, and this formed an admirable pillow, for the night was too hot to need it as a covering. He kicked off his shoes and unbuttoned his shirt, so as to let the cool night air on to his skin, and as his pipe was not yet finished, he sat and talked to Yanni, who lay down.

"But it is hot beyond endurance to-night," he said, "and you will see towards mid-day to-morrow, when there is no shelter for a fly, how fine a grilling-pan is this Larissa. The land is no place for a man to live; he should be on the sea year in and year out."

He beat out the ashes of his pipe.

"Yet it is good to be together again, Yanni," he said, lying down. "And now it is sleeping time. I wish the devil would fly away with sentry duty at night."

Three hours later the sentry came to wake Mitsos, and Yanni, who was not asleep, got up gently.

"I will take Mitsos's duty," he said. "Yes, I am Yanni Mavromichales, who came in to-night."

The man grunted sleepily and turned in, wondering whether, for any consideration in the world, he would take a night watch out of turn.

CHAPTER XI

But with the increase in the number of the garrison the flock of goats dwindled like patches of snow when the spring had come, and after a three days' grilling on the rock, and a calculation which showed that there was food for the whole number of men for only three days more, it was judged more prudent that, since the Turks showed no signs of meditating another assault, half the garrison should cut their way through the Turkish lines and go back to the Greek camp at Lerna and return again with fresh supplies of food. The Turkish fleet, meantime, had not appeared, and it seemed certain that the army would not hold Argos much longer. Forage and food were getting daily scarcer and more distant of gathering, and many men were stricken down with a virulent dysentery and fever, arising, no doubt, from their constant expeditions into the marshy ground and the unripe fruit which they plucked and ate freely. And day by day the Greeks continued to collect on the mountains.

It was decided that the original occupiers should go, for many of them were hardly fit for longer service after their ten days on that gridiron rock; but a few Mainats—and among others Mitsos—sturdily declared that they would not leave the place while there was a piece of goat's-meat or a loaf of bread remaining. Hypsilantes also, whose untrained body felt the heat and the coarseness of the scanty food most severely, was, after many fruitless attempts at persuasion, induced to be of the evacuating party. His object was already gained: he had thrown in his lot with the people, turning his back on the idle and cowardly senators; and it was important, until more food was obtained, to have as few mouths as possible to feed, provided that those who remained could hold the place in case of attack.

Fortune favored their escape, for before sunset on the night on which this partial evacuation was fixed a wrack of storm-clouds, scudding out of the sea from the south and spreading over the sky with a rapidity that promised a hurricane, brought in their train a noisy night of storm. By nine o'clock the rain had come on in torrents, with thunder and lightning, and in the headlong pelt they marched silently out of the gate, and crept down the hill-side towards the Turkish lines. These had been now drawn round the rocks where the Mainats had entered three nights before, and as they had to cut a way through the enemy somewhere, it was best to choose a place where there should be quicker going than down the goat-path. To the left of the rocks the hill ended in a steep earth-covered slope, below which were the lines, and this point most promised success. Under cover of the storm they approached unheard, and then quickening up, they ran down the last slope, which, under the tropical downpour, was no more than a mud-slide. Between the alleys of tents were lanterns, somewhat sparsely placed, and by good fortune the first Greeks who entered the lines came straight upon one of these, round which were two or three sentries. The sentries were neatly and silently knifed before any had time to raise the alarm or fire, and still at the double, the Greeks passed the second line of tents into another parallel passage. Here they were hardly less lucky. A shot or two was fired, and the alarm was given; but under that blinding and deafening uproar of the elements the Turks ran hither and thither, over tent-ropes and into each other, and without loss of a single man the Greeks gained the plain beyond.

Twice during the following week Petrobey attempted to force his way by night through the Turkish lines, which now closely invested the Larissa, for the taking in of fresh supplies to the troops there, but both times without success. The Turks had drawn off a number of troops from the town to strengthen those blockading the citadel, and they were on the lookout for these expeditions. Yet still the fleet did not appear, and it was becoming a question of hours, almost, how long Dramali could remain in Argos, for the intense heat of the last days had withered the scanty forage of the plains, and the men were in no better plight. But meantime the main object of the citadel garrison had been effected. Dramali had been delayed at Argos, not caring to leave this for towns occupied by the Greeks in his rear, instead of pushing on nearer to Nauplia. The Greeks had now collected in force in the hills. But if Dramali was nigh provisionless, the garrison was even more destitute; and on the morning after Petrobey's second attempt it was found that the provisions were coming to an end and, almost worse than that, the water supply was beginning to run short. They had hoped that the tropical storm of a week ago would have replenished the wells, but the sources lay deep, and the thirsty soil absorbed the rain before it penetrated to the seat of the spring. The only difficulty was how to get out.

That evening they had come to the end of the meat, there were only a few loaves left, and the water that day had been muddy and evil tasting; and Mitsos, as they sat round the remains of their scanty meal, tried to persuade himself that Petrobey would have advised their continuing to hold the place, for to propose that they should evacuate was a bitter mouthful. But the more prudent, and so to him less savory, council prevailed. The Mainats were sitting about, gloomy and rather dispirited, and none felt equal to the courage of saying they had better go. Mitsos had been selected by a sort of silent vote to the command, and they waited for him to speak. During a long silence he had been lying full length on the ground, but suddenly he sat up.

"Oh, cousins of mine!" he said; "it is not pleasant to say it, but it shall be said. Assuredly, we cannot stop here any longer. There is no more food, but little water, and that stale and full of the well dregs, and the others have tried twice to get in, and failed. It remains for us to get out."

The Mainats who were close and heard his words grunted, and those farther off came to find out what was forward. Mitsos repeated his words, and again they found a response of grunts. At that he lost his patience a little.

"This is not pleasant for me," he said. "You seem to want to stay here, and you make a coward of me for my thoughts. So be it; we stay. Much good may it do any one."

Kostas raised himself on his elbow. His fine fat face was a little thinner than it had been.

"Softly, little Mitsos," he said. "Give time. I am with you."

"Then why not have said so?" asked Mitsos, in a high, injured voice.

Yanni, sitting close, bubbled with laughter.

"Oh, dear fool," he said, "do you not know us yet? I, too, am with you. So are we all, I believe."

"If it is so, good," said Mitsos, only half mollified; "and if it is not so, very good also."

The clan suddenly recovered their spirits wonderfully. One man began whistling; another sang a verse of the Klepht's song, which was taken up by a chorus. Two or three men near Mitsos patted him on the back, and got knocked about for their pains, and Yanni was neatly tripped up and sat on. Mitsos also regained his equanimity by the use of his hands, and turned to Kostas.

"Is there no word for 'yes' among you but grunts only?" he asked. "Well, let it pass. We must go to-night. Every day the defences are strengthened; and as for that sour bread, thank God, we have done with it," and he picked up the few remaining loaves and hurled them over the fortress wall.

"I am better," he said, "and we will grunt together, cousins."

Now at the back of the Larissa, some hundred yards from the rocks up which the Mainats had climbed, there lay a steep ravine, funnel-shaped, cut in the side of the hill from top to bottom. It ended at the bottom in a gentler slope, and being a very accessible place, since the night surprise it had been closely guarded. The sides of it were sharp-pitched, and a stone dislodged from the top went down, gathering length in its leaps till it reached the bottom of the hill. Kostas had discovered this, for one morning, leaning over the battlements, he had idly chucked a pebble over, and watching its course, saw it fall on the top of a Turkish tent below and, being sharp, rip a hole in it, and Kostas laughed to see that a man popped quickly out, thinking, perhaps, that it was a bullet from above. At the head of this ravine, close to the citadel walls, rose a tall pinnacle of loose, shaly rock. This, too, Kostas had noticed.

His proposal was as follows: A mine should be laid in this rock, with a long fuse. As soon as this was done they should all descend the hill with silence and despatch, keeping on the two ridges that bounded this ravine, and getting as close as possible to the Turkish lines, wait.

"Then," continued Kostas, with admirable simplicity, "will nature and gunpowder work; for the rock will blow up with the gunpowder, and nature will lead the large pieces very swiftly down the ravine. One pebble brought a man from his tent; how many will be left when a mountain falls? We shall be in safety, for stones do not climb steep sides; and when the stones have passed, we will pass also."

Kostas looked round, and knowing the Mainats better than did Mitsos, found encouragement in their grunts, and the grunts were followed by grins.

"There will be broken heads," said Yanni, sententiously, "yet no man will break them. What does the great Mitsos say?"

Mitsos reached out a large, throttling hand.

"There will be a broken head," he remarked, "and I will have broken it. It is borne upon me that Uncle Kostas is the great one. When shall we start?"

"Surely as soon as may be, since Mitsos, in his wisdom, threw the rest of the bread away. We have first to bore a big hole in that rock; five men can do that, while we collect all the powder there is left. We shall need none, because we bolt hare-fashion, and there will not be time for fighting. Also the portion of rock to fall must be very great."

"Then let five men go out very silently now," said Mitsos, "and begin. Let some one watch on the wall, and when we have finished open the gate and come out very gently. Then we will set the fuse and go. Anastasi, collect the powder from each man's horn, and bring it out when it is collected. I go for the boring. Who is with me?"

Mitsos got up and went off with four other volunteers to drill the rock. They chose a place behind it, and away from the ravine, so that the loosened pieces might not fall and perhaps lead to extra vigilance on the part of the Turks. The rock was soft and crumbly, and though the night was a swelter of heat, a hole was drilled without very much labor. By the time it was ready the powder had come, and was carefully rammed in. Mitsos laid a long train of damp powder in sacking, making a fuse of about ten minutes' law, and when all was ready he whistled gently to the watcher on the wall. A moment afterwards the gate was put softly ajar, and the men filed out. He waited till the last had emerged, and then set a light to the train.

The night was not very dark, for although the moon was not yet risen, the diffused light of the stars made a clear gray twilight. But the two ridges of the ravine down which they climbed were rough with upstanding bowlders, and by going very cautiously and quietly, it was easily possible to approach the lines without being seen. Indeed, the greater fear was from the hearing, for the dry stones clanged and rang metallically under their feet, and as they began to get nearer the men took off their mountain shoes, so that their tread might be the more noiseless. Already the foremost were as far as they thought it safe to go, and in silence the others closed up till the shadow of each bowlder was a nest of expectant eyes. The air was still and windless; each man heard only the coming and going of his breath; above them was not a sound except that from time to time a bird piped with a flute-like note among the rocks. The strain grew tenser and yet more tense; now and then a murmur would come drowsily up from the Turkish lines, and the bird piped on. Mitsos was only conscious of one perplexing doubt: would the bird be killed or not?

Suddenly, with a roar and crash and windy buffet, that which they were waiting for came. The crash grew into a roar, which gathered volume and intolerable sound every moment, and in a great storm of dust the shattered rocks passed down the ravine, the smaller pieces leaping like spray from a torrent up the sides, the larger coiling and twisting together like the ropes of water in a cataract. They passed with a rush and roar down on to the Turkish lines below, and as the tumult went on its way there mingled with it the noises of ripped canvas, broken poles, and human cries. Close on the heels of this avalanche came the Mainats; from the tents near men were fleeing in fear of another shower of stone coming; the path of the rocks themselves lay through the lines as if cut by some portentous knife. None thought of stopping them; the lanes through the camp passed like blurs of light, and keeping to the edge of the path cut by the rocks, they reached the plain without a shot being fired at them. But they did not halt nor abate the pace. Though they carried muskets they were without powder, and but for their knives defenceless, and, without even waiting to fall into any sort of formation, they struck out over the plain towards the lower hills at the base of which the camp at Lerna stood.

The vigilance of the Greeks was of another sort to that of the Turks, and knowing that they would run a most considerable risk, if they approached the camp without giving warning, of being shot, they halted some three hundred yards off, and Mitsos yelled aloud.

"From the citadel," he cried, "Greeks of Maina!"

A shout answered him; and now that they were beyond all reach of pursuit, they went the more quietly. The sentries at the first outpost had turned out in case of anything being wrong, but in a moment they were recognized and passed.

Petrobey met them.

"So Benjamin has come home," he said, kissing Yanni. "And oh, Mitsos, you have come to friends."

All that week the Turks in Argos and the Greeks at Lerna and on the mountains waited, the one for the Ottoman fleet to appear, the other for that which should certainly follow on its non-appearance. Already, so it was rumored, some of the Turkish cavalry horses had been killed to supply food for the men, and the Greeks heard it with a greedy quickening of the breath. One morning two ships appeared suddenly opposite Nauplia, and it was feared they were the first of the Turkish ships, but Mitsos announced they were the *Revenge* and the *Sophia*, though why they had come he knew not. The hills round were a line of Greek camps, waiting, like birds of prey, for the inevitable end. Down at Lerna the men were growling discontentedly at the waiting; the hot, foul air of the marshes smote them, but they swore they would smite in return. And thus in silent and hungry expectation the first week of August went by.

At length, on the morning of the 6th, the end came. When day broke it was to show the long bright lines of Albanian mercenaries who formed the advance-guard of Dramali's army, marching across the plain northward towards the guarded hills. From Lerna, lying low, they were only visible when they began to reach the foot-hills of the range towards Corinth, and by that time the cavalry had begun to leave the north gate of Argos. Instantly in the camp there was a sudden fierce outburst of joy and certain vengeance. The hills were guarded, the Turks in a trap; it only remained to go.

The hills between Argos and Corinth were rough and bowldersown. The main pass over them, called the Dervenaki, lay due north from Argos, and was that over which the Turks under Dramali had come. This, however, had now been occupied five days before by a large body of Greeks from the villages round —hardy men of the mountains, as leaderless as a pack of wolves, and fiercer. They had taken up a senseless position too near the plain and below the gorge through which the road passed, and which was narrow and easily held. The Albanians, therefore, the advance-guard of the force, seeing that the pass was occupied, turned westward towards the village of Nemea by another road, which joined the Dervenaki again, after a long détour, beyond the gorge. Kolocotrones with his son Panos and some eight thousand Greeks were in possession of Nemea, and news that the advance-guard, consisting of about a thousand Albanians, was approaching was brought him as he sat at breakfast in his brass helmet.

Now the Albanians were not Turks, but Greeks serving as mercenaries under the Sultan. Many of them had relations and friends among the Greeks, and a year ago, at the siege of Tripoli, a separate amnesty had been concluded with them, and they had not been prevented from going home. Moreover, they were excellent men of arms and poor. All these things Kolocotrones considered as he debated what to do. While he was still debating the first rank of them came in sight. He looked at them for a moment, and then turned to the scouts who had brought the news.

"May hell receive you!" he snarled. "They are Greeks."

They were Greeks; every one knew that. They were allowed to pass unmolested. They were also poor, and that Kolocotrones knew.

Besides the Dervenaki and the Nemean way to the west, two other possible roads led over the pass, both to the east. Of these one lay parallel with the Dervenaki, and only five or six hundred yards from it, till nearly the top of the pass. The roads then joined and, after running for some half-mile one on each side of a narrow, wedge-shaped hill, became one. Farther away, again to the east, lying in a long loop, was a third road. Both of these branched off from the Dervenaki before coming to the spot where the irregular Greeks on that pass were encamped. The road farthest away to the east was held by the English-speaking Niketas. He had with him two thousand men, including many Mainats.

The advance-guard of the Turks preceded the main army by some half-hour. Dramali rode with the second body of cavalry, and when he saw the Albanians take the western road, which he knew was held by Kolocotrones, he burst into a torrent of Mussulman abuse. He had been betrayed, sold, bartered; these Albanians were in league with the Greeks. So he ordered an advance up the shortest and most direct road—namely, the Dervenaki. His scouts soon returned saying it was held by the Greeks, and Dramali turned eastward into the parallel road, which appeared to be untenanted. A low ridge divided the two, and as he crossed it he was seen by Niketas's outposts. He, without a moment's hesitation, divided his band into two parts. With one he crossed the road Dramali was taking, and took up a position near the top of the pass on the steep, wedge-shaped hill that separated it from the Dervenaki, and on the road itself, blocking it. To the others he gave orders to hang on the right flank of the Turks as they advanced northward. Of the Turks, now that the Albanians were separated from them, the greater part of the cavalry came first as an advance-guard; the most of the infantry followed. Between them marched an army of luggage-mules, with tents and all the appurtenances of Turkish warfare, mules and camels carrying embroidered clothes, gold-chased arms, money, women, and behind, again, the lesser part of the cavalry and the remainder of the infantry.

Meantime the men in camp at Lerna, more than half Mainats, had seen the road the Turks had taken, and were in pursuit. Now that it was seen that the Turks were in retreat, and had no thought of attempting the relief of Nauplia, since the fleet had not arrived, there was nothing to be gained by continuing to hold the Larissa; it was better to concentrate all forces on the hills over which the Turks had to pass, if so be that they passed. The cavalry they had seen had gone first. It was no time to think of prudence and security, and they dashed through Argos and its empty and silent streets and out to the right at the tail of the Ottoman forces, risking an attack as they crossed the plain. But Dramali had no longer any thought of attacking. Those doomed lines with their trains of baggage-beasts moved but slowly, and Petrobey reached the outlying foot-hills before the rear of the Turks had left the plain.

The pass on each side of which Niketas's troops were posted narrowed gradually as it went, and near the top where they waited it was just a road, flanked on the left side by the steep promontory of hill, on the other by a stream riotous only in the melting of the snows, but now a mere starved trickle of water. Beyond that was a corresponding hill, covered sparsely with pines, which grew up big among big bowlders of white limestone, lying like some petrified flock of gigantic sheep. The day had broken with a pitiless and naked sky, and as the sun rose higher it seemed that the world was a furnace eaten up with its own heat. Niketas himself with some hundred men had already taken up his position on the left side of the pass through which the Turks would come on the steep turtle-backed ridge dividing it from the Dervenaki. Another contingent was on the road itself, employed in heaping up a rough wall of stones across it to shelter themselves and delay the advance of the cavalry vanguard. On the right of the road were the remainder of Niketas's troops, some five hundred in number, dispersed among the pines and bowlders of the hill-side, which rose so sheerly that each man could see the road, as it were a stage from the rising tiers of theatre-seats, and shoot down on to it. Petrobey sent Yanni forward to find Niketas and ask him where he would wish the fresh troops from Lerna to be posted, and the answer came back that they were most needed in the road to help the building of the barricade and stop the first cavalry charges. Those already there were under Hypsilantes and the priest Dikaios; would Petrobey take council with them? It was possible also that a reinforcement would be needed on the right of the road; if so, let the Mainats be divided. He himself had sufficient men to hold the hill on the left, and it was all "damn fine." Finally he wished Petrobey good appetite for the feast; Mainats he knew were always hungry.

The Turks were still half an hour away, and Petrobey led his troops down on to the road from off the uneven ground of the hill, so that they should make more speed, and in ten minutes they reached the place where the rest were building the barricade. Here all set themselves to the work: some rolled down stones from the slopes into the valley, others fetched them from the bed of the stream, while those on the road carried them to the site of the growing wall and piled them up. Now and then a warning shout would come from the hill-side, and a rock would leap down, gathering speed, and rush across the road, split sometimes into a hundred fragments and useless, but for the most part— for the limestone was hard—a valuable building stone. Eight or ten men, like busy-limbed ants at work, would seize it and roll it up to the rising barricade, piling it on top if not too heavy, or using it to form part of a buttress. But their time was short and the wall was but an uneven ridge across the road and stream, four feet high or so in places, elsewhere only a heap of stones, when it was shouted from the outposts that the cavalry was approaching, and the men ceased from their work and, gathering up their arms, retreated to behind the improvised barricade and waited.

To the left of the road, and below the barricade, rose the wedge of hill on which Niketas's contingent was stationed. They were drawn up in five ranks of about two hundred men each, in open order, with a space of some thirty paces between the last three ranks, so that, owing to the steepness of the ground, each man commanded a view of the road and each rank could fire over the heads of those in front. The ground, however, was of a more gradual slope as it approached the road, and the first rank lay, sheltering themselves as far as possible, among the bowlders not twenty paces from the road itself; the second rank, five paces behind it, knelt; and the third stood. On the right of the road the hill was too rugged and uneven, being strewn with bowlders and sown with shrubs and trees, to allow of any formation, and was in fact one great ambuscade, the men being hidden by the trees and stones. Here and there a gun-barrel glistened in the sun, but a casual passer-by might have gone his way and never suspected the presence of men. A bend in the road, some two hundred yards below, concealed the barricade and its defenders from the Turks.

The vanguard of the Turks halted a moment, seeing that the hill to the left of the road was occupied, and then set forward again at a brisk trot, meaning perhaps to go under fire along the road commanded by Niketas and then, wheeling at the top of the pass, attack him, and thus enable the rest of the troops to march through the ravine while they were engaging its defenders, and reach the open ground which lay beyond. Just before the first ranks reached the bend in the road Niketas opened fire on them, but they did not wait to return it, and putting their horses into a canter swept round the bend.

At that the hill-side on their right flank blazed and bristled, and every shrub and stone seemed to burst into a flame of fire. On each side the Greeks, at short range, poured a storm of bullets into them; at each step another and another fell. Suddenly from in front the Mainats from between their barricades opened fire; retreat was impossible, for the whole of the cavalry were now advancing from behind; to stop meant one congestion of death, and they spurred savagely on. In a moment they were at the wall. Some leaped the lower parts of it, alighting, it seemed, in a hell of flame; others were checked by the higher portion, and their horses reared and wheeled into their own ranks; others passed through the stream-bed, or putting their horses at the wall of defenders as at a fence, found themselves faced by the rear rank of Mainats, who were waiting patiently higher up the road till they should have penetrated into their range.

Meantime the check given to the first division of the cavalry at the barricade had resulted in a congestion all down the advancing lines. The second division had closed up with the first, the third with the second, and on the heels of the cavalry came the infantry. Dramali, who was stationed in the rear still, almost on the plain of Argos, had ordered them to advance, at all costs, till they gained the top of the pass, whence they could intrench themselves on the open ground, and every moment added a crust to the congealment of destruction. The masses of those moving on from behind pushed the first rank forward and forward, all squeezed together, and pressing against the wall of barricade, as a river in flood presses against the arches of a bridge. At two or three points it had been entirely broken down, and through these—now free for a moment, now choked again with the bodies of horses and their riders—a few escaped through the first ranks of Mainats and into the road beyond, raked indeed by the other ranks, who held the pass higher up, but no longer exposed to the full threefold short range fire from Niketas, the barrier, and those in ambush on the left. Already the wall of dead and dying was heaped higher than the barricade that the Mainats had raised, and the horses of the Turks who forced their way through trampled on the bodies of the fallen. But pass they must, for they were forced forward, as by some hideous, slow-moving glacier, by a stream of dead and living. Here and there a dead horse carrying a dead rider was borne on upright and unable to fall because of those who pressed so closely on each side, the rider bowed forward over the neck of his horse or sprawling sideways across the knee of his fellow, the horse's head supported on the quarters of the beast in front or wedged between it and the next. More terrible even was some other brute, wounded and screaming, but unable to move except as it was moved and carried along for some seconds perhaps, till two or three of those in front forced their way through the breaches in the barricade of horses and riders and gave it space, so that it fell and was mercifully trampled out of pain and life.

For five deadly minutes they pressed on hopelessly and gallantly, while the leaden hail hissed from either flank and from in front into the congested horsemen; but at the end the Turks broke and fled in all directions, some up the hill where Niketas's troops, still untouched and unattacked, were stationed, others up the hill-side opposite, which still spurted and blazed with muskets. There every bush was an armed man, every stone a red flower of flame. But the rush could not be stopped any more than a rush even of cattle or sheep can be withstood by armed men. The Turks fled, scattering in all directions, northward for the most part towards Corinth, where they would find safety, and the Greeks troubled not to pursue, but shot as a man shoots at driven deer. Almost simultaneously with the breaking of the troops, those of the cavalry who had passed the first ranks of the Mainats who guarded the wall, once of stones, but now a heap of men and horses, succeeded, in spite of the steady fire of the rear ranks and with the cool courage of desperation, in clearing some sort of passage round by the stream-bed, which was now fuller than it had been, but red and with a froth of blood, and through this some four hundred of the cavalry passed. They drove the Mainats from the barricade with much slaughter, forcing them up the two hill-sides which bounded the ravine, and charging forward passed the other ranks without sustaining heavy loss, and made their way into the open ground, reaching Corinth that night.

Dramali's cavalry had been divided into two parts, the larger of which formed the vanguard. Of these four hundred had passed through that valley of death, of the rest the red and fuller flowing stream gave account. Behind them had followed the first division of the infantry, some three thousand men, now scattered over the armed hillsides, and behind again the baggage mules and camels. Dramali himself rode with the second division of the cavalry, some three hundred yards behind, and the rear was brought up by the remainder of his foot-soldiers. He himself had been checked in the lower part of the pass by the congestion in front, and waited in vain to move again. Aides-de-camp were sent off to ascertain the cause of this contravention of his orders, but before any came back, the sight of the hill-sides, covered with flying men, brought him quicker and more eloquent message.

He paused a moment, then in nervous anger drove his spurs into his horse, and checked it again, biting the ends of his long mustache.

"Why do they not go forward?" he said. And again, "Why are they scattering?" Then, with a sudden spurt of anger, "Oh, the dogs!" he cried; "dogs, to be chased by dogs!" But the fire in his words was only ash.

He looked round on the calm, impassive faces of his staff, men for the most part without the bowels of either mercy or fear, who would meet death with as perfect an indifference as they would mete it out to others. The absolute nonchalance of their expression, their total disregard of what might happen to them, struck him into a childish kind of frenzy, for he was of different make.

"If we push on, we all die," he said, in a sort of squeal; "and if we turn back, what next?"

At that the officer near him turned his head aside, hiding a smile, but before Dramali had time to notice it a fresh movement of the Greeks from in front made up his mind for him. Those under Niketas, on the left of the pass, were seen pouring down off the hill on to the road, and almost before the Turks saw what was happening had cut his army in two, drawing themselves up just behind the baggage animals, hardly three hundred yards in front of the second division of the cavalry with whom Dramali rode. That was enough for the Serashier. Dearly as he loved his battery of silver saucepans, his embroidered armor, and all the appliances of a pasha, he loved one thing better, and that at least was left him; he was determined to save it as long as possible.

"Back to Argos!" he screamed. "Let the infantry open out; the cavalry will go first." And putting his spurs to his horse he fairly forced his way back, and not drawing bridle, rode through the scorched plains which he had passed that morning, and by twelve o'clock was back at Argos again.

On that afternoon and all the next day he remained there in a feverish stupor of inaction, crying aloud at one time that Allah was dead, and the world given over to the hands of the infidels, at another that the ships were already at Nauplia, and that he would march there. Then it would seem that the world only contained one thing of importance—and that a certain narghile of his with a stem studded with turquoise and moonstone—and that this had fallen into the hands of the Greeks. Let them send quickly and say that he would give an oke of gold for it, and two Greek slaves of his which had been taken at Kydonies: one was sixteen, and the other only fourteen; they were worth their weight in gold for their beauty only, and Constantine, the elder, made coffee as it could only be made in paradise. Let Constantine come at once and make him some coffee. Anyhow, Constantine and coffee were left him, and nothing else mattered.

Two days later the remnant of the Turkish force again started for Corinth. This time Dramali, who had abated a little his contempt for the Greek dogs, making up the complement in fearful haste, took the precaution to send forward an advance-guard during the night, who should find out if any of the passes were unoccupied. The Greeks under Niketas, who were in no hurry to engage the Turks again—for, since their escape was impossible, they could afford to wait—were still holding the pass which the Turks had attempted to cross two days before, and the reconnoitring party of Dramali found the road farther away to the east unoccupied. Niketas, when it was seen which way they were going, hastened across to secure a repetition of what had gone before, and making his way over the hills, again stopped the advance. But the road here was wider, lying between hills less easy to occupy, and the Turkish cavalry, by a brilliant charge, won their way through and escaped to Corinth, abandoning the remainder of the infantry and the rest of the baggage. On them the Greeks settled like a cloud of stinging insects, and that evening Constantine, the coffee-maker of paradise, exercised his functions in the house of his father, a refugee from Kydonies, who had taken service with Niketas.

Thus the great scheme came to an end, a pricked bubble, a melting of snow in summer. No ships had yet appeared off Nauplia, and Dramali's invincible army, which waited for them, had come and gone. The eager, hungry eyes of those besieged in Nauplia starved and watched in vain, and to the hungry mouths the food was scantier. Slowly and inevitably the cause of the people, in the hands no more of incompetent leaders, was gaining ground against the intolerable burden of those heartless and lustful masters, and link by link the chain of slavery was snapping and falling as the husks burst and fall from corn already mature and ripe.

CHAPTER XII

The *Sophia* and the *Revenge*, as Mitsos had seen, had come to Nauplia a week ago, but neither he nor yet the Capsina herself could have fully explained why they remained there. Indeed, the girl seemed to be wrestling with some strange seizure of indecision. She would determine to go after the Turkish vessels which had sailed, for Patras; again, she would say that she would remain blockading Nauplia till it was taken. She had heard that Mitsos was with those who held the citadel of Argos, and it seemed impossible to her to leave Nauplia until he was out; then, when news came that the defenders had joined the camp at Lerna, there was still another reason that detained her. She felt she must see Suleima; why, it puzzled her to say, except that some fever of jealous curiosity possessed her. Yet the days went by, and every day saw her unable to do that most simple thing—namely, to walk up to the white house which had been pointed out to her, a magnet to her eyes, say she was the Capsina and the very good friend of Mitsos, and be received with honor and affection, both for her own sake and for his. Meantime no urgent call bade her leave Nauplia; the Turkish fleet would soon be back from Patras, and it was as well to wait here as to go cruising after them; only it was unlike her to prefer to wait when to cruise after them would have done as well. They must certainly pass up the Gulf of Nauplia, and those narrow waters were a model battle-field for light-helmed ships like hers, and cramping to the heavy and cumbrous Turkish vessels. Thus she told herself, as was true, that in all probability, even if there had never been a lad called Mitsos, she would have waited there. Then fate, pitying her indecision, took the helm out of her hands and steered her straight for Suleima, and in this wise.

It was the evening after Dramali's first evacuation of Argos. All morning they had heard the sound of firing coming drowsily across the water, and before noon had seen the body of Turks who, with Dramali, had escaped back to Argos across the plain again, but as yet there was no certain news of what had happened. But about five of the afternoon more authentic tidings came: there had been a great slaughter; the Turks had broken and fled, the most towards

Corinth, but that some hundreds of them, this being unknown to Niketas, had collected on the hills, and despairing of getting through to Corinth, were marching towards Nauplia, with the object, no doubt, of seeking safety—and starvation had they known it—in the citadel.

Now, though this was a mad and impracticable scheme, yet there was great disquietude in the news. The women and children of the Greeks who were besieging Nauplia were largely gathered on the hill of Tiryns, some two miles from the gate, and defenceless. Tiryns lay on the route of the Turks, and three hundred yards farther up the road away from Nauplia stood the white house.

The Capsina was on the quay when the news came, the impassive Kanaris with her. She sent him off at once to the ships with orders to bring both crews back armed, leaving only a few in charge. Already women and children from Tiryns were beginning to pour, a panic-stricken crowd, with all they could carry of their household gear, into the town, with confirmation of the approach of the Turks. A shepherd lad feeding his sheep on the lower hills had fled before them, leaving his flock behind him; there were not less than three hundred of them.

The Capsina's men were the first to start; another contingent drawn off from the besieging troops were to follow. They were to march straight to Tiryns and guard the place through the night, and in the morning they would be relieved. There still remained many Greek women and children there, and the place was also a sort of hospital for sick men from Argos and Corinth; and the Capsina's eye blazed.

"Women, children, and wounded men!" she cried, "a tit-bit for Turks!"

Kanaris had done his utmost to persuade her not to come with them. If the news was true, and the Turks attacked Tiryns, there would be wild, hazardous fighting in the dark, each man for himself, no work for a woman. There were no sort of fortifications or even houses at the place; the people lived in wry-set rows of pole booths, roofed in with branches and maize-stalks. The Turks would enter where they pleased. But the girl only laughed.

"It is as well to die one way as another," she said, "and this is one of the better ways. Besides, I mean to sail the *Revenge* many times yet. Oh man, but I killed five Turks at Porto Germano; and had it not been for Mitsos, the fifth would have killed me. I was happy that day. If God is good, I will kill five more. One was as big as you, Kanaris, and fatter by half."

The sky was already growing dusky red with sunset when they set off. The land-breeze had set in shrill and steady, rattling the dry maize-fields, whistling in the stubborn aloes and cactuses along the road, and whispering in the poplars. Here and there they passed little knots of women flying into Nauplia, all with the same tale. The Turks were undoubtedly coming, and there were still many left in the town; they had been seen not two miles off, and that ten minutes ago.

A gaunt set of apparitions awaited them at the place, men shaking with fever, leaning on crutches, with bandaged arms and swathed heads. Some few only had muskets, the most part short knives, but many only stakes of wood, pointed and hardened in the fire. A crowd of women and children, crying and bewailing themselves, hung about them, unable to make up their minds to face the perils of the dark road into Nauplia, and convinced that Turks were in ambush there. They clung to the men, now beseeching them not to desert them, now begging them not to fight but to surrender. What chance had they against three hundred armed men?

To these the sight of the Capsina and her sailors was like a draught of wine.

"Praise the Virgin," cried one, "it is the Capsina!" And she fell on the girl's neck, sobbing hysterically.

The Capsina disengaged herself.

"There is no time to lose," she said to Kanaris. "Take the women off, and put them in the centre. The attack will be from the north; at least they come from there. These men are useless. Man!" she cried, turning to one, "if your arm shake so, you will as like cut off your own head as the head of a Turk. Get you with the women. You too, and you!"

The second contingent from Nauplia had not yet arrived, and even while the Capsina spoke a man from a farm near, half dressed and bleeding from a wound in the hand, rushed in saying that the Turks had pillaged his house. He had escaped from there with a sword-cut; they were not two hundred yards off. The last of the women were pressing into the centre of the town, and there was only one child left, a boy about three years old, who was clinging, with howls, to his father, a gaunt, fever-stricken man, but capable of using a knife. The Capsina spoke to the child.

"Father will come to you if you will go with the others," she said. "Oh laddie, let go of him. Take charge of the child," she said to the last of the women. "Mind, I leave him with you."

She paused a moment, listening. Above the whistling of the wind could be heard the tramp of feet along the road.

"The others are not here yet," she said. "These feet come from the north. To your posts along the huts by the north, three men together! There are no other orders except to kill; that only, and to save the women."

The men filed off quickly, but without confusion, but before more than half had gone there came a sudden rush from outside, and a band of Turks poured up the narrow lane of booths. For a few moments the two crowds surged together without fighting-room, then they broke up right and left into the narrow alleys, fighting in groups. The Capsina found herself wedged up in the crowd, a Turk between her and the door-post of one of the huts, each staring wildly at the other, and neither able to move. Then, as the pressure behind grew greater, the door-post gave under the weight, and they both tumbled headlong in. The Capsina's pistol went off wildly in the air, a musket-bullet whistled by her, and the hut was suddenly full of smoke. She had fallen straight across the man, but in a moment she struggled to her knees and stabbed fiercely at something soft below her. The soft thing quivered and was still, and something warm spurted onto her hand with a soft hot gush.

At that the madness of fresh blood took possession of her, and she laughed softly, a gentle, cooing, cruel laugh, like in spirit to the purring of a wild cat which has killed its evening meal and is pleased, not only with the thought of the satisfaction of its hunger, but with having killed. She stayed still a moment, the silent centre of the shouting confusion outside, waiting to see if the man moved again. Outside the fight had surged and wavered and moved away, and though she was on her feet again in less than a minute from the time when she and her prey had fallen together headlong into the hut, she looked out to find the little alley, where the first rush had been made, empty except for a few forms which lay on the ground, and a Turk who was leaning against the post of a hut opposite, in the shadow of death. His side had been laid open by a sword-cut, and he was trying, but very feebly, because he was already a dead man, to stanch the flow of blood. Looking up he saw the Capsina, his mouth gathered in a snarl, and with an effort he raised his pistol and pulled the trigger. But it had already been fired, and he threw it from him with a grunt of disgust and took no more notice of her. And she laughed again.

Listening, she heard the turmoil of the fight sweeping away round to the east of the hill, and she was just about to dash off again to rejoin the rest when up the lane by which the Turks had entered came a woman with a baby in her arms. In the dim light of the stars and the grayness before the rising of the moon the Capsina could not clearly see her face, only she was tall. The baby was hidden under the shawl in which her head was wrapped; she carried it on her left arm, and in her right hand she held a pistol. Then catching sight of the Turk opposite propped against the hut door, she paused a moment and pushed noiselessly but with all her weight against the door of another hut, seeking shelter.

The Capsina came out of the shadow and beckoned to her.

"Here, come in here," she said; "but why are you not with the other women?"

The woman sank down in a corner of the hut, and then swiftly got up again.

"What is it here?" she said. "There is some one here!"

The Capsina laughed again.

"Limbs and a body," she said. "A Turk. I killed him. Where are you from?"

"From a house near," she said. "I left it in haste, and had to hide in a ditch till the Turks passed. I saw the Greeks from Nauplia enter here, and I thought I should be safer with them than on the road."

A question was on the Capsina's lips, but at that moment a Turk came by within a yard of the door of the hut, and seeing a comrade lying opposite, spoke to him. The Capsina had drawn Suleima into a corner, but stood herself opposite the door. She saw the wounded Turk raise his head feebly and point at the door of the hut where she was, and on the instant the other put up his musket in act to fire. But the Capsina was the quicker—had the man passed by, she would not have risked a shot, for she and Suleima were alone there, but she guessed what that pointed finger meant—and while yet the man's musket was but half way to his shoulder, he fell, shot to the heart.

She handed back the pistol to Suleima, with her case of powder and bullets, while the child crowed with delight at the flash of the fire.

"Give me your pistol," she said, "if it is loaded, and load mine again if you know how. That child should be a soldier some day."

She stepped swiftly out of the hut, and without a quiver of a muscle pointed the pistol at the wounded Turk's head.

"I should have shot you at once," she said, and then with the smoking pistol in her hand stepped quickly back into the hut, leaving the thing fallen forward like a broken toy, thinking only of her unasked question.

Still she could not frame her lips to it, and Suleima having loaded the pistol handed it back to her.

"You have save my life and that of the littlest and dearest," she said. "I kiss your hand for it, and thank you from my heart."

But the Capsina drew her hand quickly away.

"I could do no less," she said, shortly, "but I want to ask you—"

Suddenly the child broke out into a little wailing cry, and Suleima turned to it.

"Oh littlest Mitsos," she said, "hush you, my little one. The father never cried when he was such as you."

The Capsina stood quite still, and suddenly her throat felt dry and burning.

"The child's name is Mitsos?" she asked, in a whisper.

"Surely, after the name of his father."

The two girls could not see each other in the darkness of the hut, but for a moment Suleima thought she felt the other's hand touching the baby lightly, and there was silence for a space.

"You did not seem frightened when you came in here," said the Capsina, at length.

"I had no time or thought to spare for fright. I had the child with me."

A great burst of shouting broke out at the moment, and the Capsina rose to her feet.

"It is the others from Nauplia," she said.

Then from no long distance her name was called out, and she went to the door of the hut.

"Kanaris—is it Kanaris?" she cried. "I am here and safe."

Kanaris ran up, breathless and bloody, and more enthusiastic than his wont.

"It is all over," he panted; "we have driven them out of the village, and the rest from Nauplia are seeing to those who have escaped. Surely you bear the good luck with you, Capsina."

"That is as God wills!" Then lowering her voice: "I am attending to a woman in here, a Greek. Take command of the men, Kanaris, and leave me here. We stop here till morning, and let a good watch be kept. Ay, man, I have killed three Turks, one with the knife and two with the pistol."

Then she went back into the hut again and sat down by Suleima.

"Your name is Suleima, then," she said, in a cold and steady voice, "and your husband's name Mitsos Codones?"

"Surely," said Suleima. "Oh littlest, hush you, and sleep."

"Give me the child," said the Capsina, suddenly, with a cruel choking in her throat; "let me hold it. Children are good with me."

She almost snatched the baby out of Suleima's arms, and in the darkness Suleima, wondering and silent, heard her kissing it again and again, and heard that her breath sobbed as she drew it.

In truth the stress and tempest of the impossible battling with the heart's desire had burst on the girl. At one moment she wondered that her hand did not take up the loaded pistol that lay beside her and kill Suleima as she sat there, and at another that she loved the woman who was loved of Mitsos, and could have found it in her heart to kiss her and cling to her as she had clung to the baby. So this was she whom so strange a pathway had led to her, this Suleima, whom she had seen so often in the visions painted by her imagination. She had pictured herself a hundred times meeting Suleima, killing her, and passing on with the road clear to Mitsos at the end of it. She had pictured Suleima coming to her for safety from the Turks, she had heard herself say: "You come to me for safety?" and laughing in her face at the thought and turning her back to where some hell of death received her. She had seen Suleima a dull hen-wife, fond of Mitsos, no doubt, and clever at the making of jam. What she had not seen was a woman, motherly like this, yet not afraid, a pistol in one hand, the little one on the other arm. Here they were, sitting together in the deserted hut, they two and the baby and the dead Turk, who sprawled on the floor, and yet she fulfilled none of these visions. The knowledge that Suleima had heard her name called by Kanaris, the suspicion that she had betrayed herself, troubled her not at all; the child was Mitsos's, and she devoured it with kisses.

Suleima sat silent, and by degrees the Capsina grew more quiet. Her breath came evenly again, and only now and then a sudden sob caught in her throat. Suleima had heard Kanaris call the other's name, and the truth and solution of the situation were instantly flashed into her mind. Her sweet and womanly nature, her utter trust in Mitsos, and the enthusiastic honor in which she held the Capsina for her brave deeds, struck out of her mind all possibility of jealousy, and she was only sorry, deeply and largely sorry, for this wonderful girl with whose name all mouths were full. At last, not being very clever and being very honest, she laid her hand on the Capsina's knee.

"I am so sorry," she said. "Believe me, I am very sorry."

The Capsina sat perfectly still and rigid for a moment, and then with a sudden spasm of ungovernable anger her hand leaped out and she struck Suleima on the face.

"You lie!" she cried. "Take back the baby. You lie!"

Suleima took the baby and got up. The blow, delivered in the dark, had nearly missed her, but her ear was tingling with the Capsina's fingers as they flashed past. The other sat still.

"Capsina," she said, "you have saved my life. I am wholly yours to command at any time. I can say no more. Good-night, and may the Holy Virgin watch over you."

She moved a step towards the door of the hut and would have gone out, when suddenly the gates of the Capsina's heart were flung wide.

"Ah, no, no!" she cried; "Suleima, wait. What can I do? I am sorry and ashamed—I who have never been ashamed before. Wait; do not go. Sit down. Where did I strike you? Indeed I did not mean it; my hand came and went before I knew it. Sit down again—and first, you forgive me?"

Suleima came back, and knelt by the girl.

"Forgive you? That is easily done, and it is done. The thing was not," she said, "and the fault was mine. I should not have said that. See, take the baby again. That will show, will it not, that there is nothing between you and me?"

The Capsina took the baby again, and began to sob hopelessly and helplessly. Suleima sat close to her and put her arm round her.

"It comes ill from me to say it, Capsina," she said, "but we both love the lad; and is not that a bond of union between us? And he—you should have heard him speak of you! If ever I could be jealous, it would be of you I was jealous. There is none in the world to compare with you he says."

"Ah, what does that matter?" sobbed the girl. "It is not that I want. It is he. Strike back if you will. It is monstrous I should say that to you. Oh, baby! littlest Mitsos! Mitsos! Mitsos!"

And she fell to kissing the child again.

"I have been a brute, a brute!" she wailed. "I would have taken him from you if I could. I would have tempted him, only he was not temptable. Often and often I would have killed you, often I have killed you in my thoughts. How can you trust me? I am unclean. How can you let me touch the child? I shall defile it. Take it back! No, let me hold it a little longer. It does not know who I am. Do not teach it to curse me."

Suleima laughed gently.

"It is an ignorant little one, and knows little," she said, "but he can say 'father' and 'mother,' and one other word. How quiet the child is with you, Capsina. Sometimes he fights me as if I was a Turk. Wake, little Mitsos. Say 'Capsina.'"

From the darkness came a little treble staccato pipe:

"Cap-sin-a."

"Mitsos taught him that," continued Suleima. "When he was home from the cruise with you, he would sit with the little one in his arms for an hour at a time, saying 'Capsina, Capsina,' to it. Ay, but it is a great baby I have for a husband!"

The girl rocked the child to and fro gently.

"Say it again, little one," she whispered, "say 'Capsina.' I know not why that is so sweet to me," she continued to Suleima, when the child had piped her name again, "but somehow it seems to put me more intimately with him and you. Surely he would not have taught the child my name if he was not my friend. So clearly can I see him doing it, sitting there by the hour smoking, and lazier than a tortoise. Indeed, he is a baby himself; we used to play child-games on the *Revenge* when we sailed from Hydra, and laughed instead of talked."

"He has told me," said Suleima—"he has told me often!"

After that they sat for a while in silence. Now and then one of the women of the village would go by the illuminated square of the door, or one of the Greek sentries would pass on his round, whistling softly to himself. Otherwise the world was a stillness. The moon was risen, and little bars and specks of light filtered in through the roof of branch and bough. The body of the Turk, still lying where he had fallen, sprawled in the other corner, but neither of the women seemed to notice it. An extraordinary sense of effort over had possession of the Capsina; she had betrayed herself, and that to the one woman in the world to whom she would have thought it impossible to speak. Her pride, her strong, self-sufficient reserve, her secret, which she thought she would have died to keep, had been surrendered without conditions, and the captor was very merciful. She was tired of struggling, she had laid down her arms. And it was wonderfully sweet to hold Mitsos's child…. It was not easy for her to speak, but when a reserved nature breaks down it breaks down altogether, and when she spoke again she held nothing back.

"Even so," she said. "I loved him as soon as I saw him, and I love him still. But in this last hour I do not know how a certain bitterness has been withdrawn; perhaps the bitterness of hatred which was mixed up with it, for I hated you, and you were part of Mitsos. That is your doing—you would not let me hate you, and indeed it is not often that I am compelled like that. And now, Suleima, get you home. I will send a couple of men with you to see you safe; but the Turks are gone. There is no danger."

"You will come with me, Capsina?" asked the other. "Will you not sleep at the house to-night?"

"I must wait here with my men." She hesitated a moment. "But do you ask me? Do you really ask me?"

"Ah, I hoped you would come," said Suleima, smiling. "You will come, will you not? Did I not hear you tell Kanaris he was in charge this night?"

"And may I still carry the little one?"

"Will you not find him heavy?"

"Heavy? And do you never carry the little one because he is too heavy?"

And she got up quickly and moved towards the door. There Suleima paused a moment.

"Shall we not say a word for those whom you have killed?" she said. "It is kinder, and they will offend us no more. So send peace to their souls, thrice holy Mother of God!"

She crossed herself thrice, and followed the Capsina out. The moon had already risen high towards the zenith, and shone with a very pure, clear light. Like a caressing and loving hand, it touched the sun-dried and bowlder-sown ground between them and the road; it was poured out like a healing lotion over its roughness, and lay on it with a cooling touch. The noises of the night joined in chorus to make up the one great silence of the night. A bird fluted at intervals from the trees, frogs croaked in the marshes below, an owl swept by with a whisper of white wings and a long-drawn hoot. Below lay the bay, an unemblazoned shield of silver, and on the left hand the fires of the Greeks round Nauplia pierced red holes in the dark promontory. A falling star, ever a good omen to the peasants, shot and faded in the western sky, and the stream that ran through the vineyards towards the marsh spoke quietly to itself, like one talking in sleep. And something of the spirit of the stillness touched the Capsina's soul. The great impossible thing was not less impossible nor less to be desired, but she had not known till now how aggravating and chafing a thing it had been to feel this wild, vague hatred against Suleima. That had gone. She could no more hate this brave, beautiful girl, who had treated her with so large and frank a courtesy, with such true and stingless sympathy, than she could have hated Mitsos himself. Only an hour ago it would have seemed to her that pity or sympathy from Suleima would be the crown of her rank offence; now it was a thing that soothed and strengthened. Her pride did not disdain it; it was too gracious and large-hearted to be disdained. And the baby slept against her heart, that baby with its three words—father, mother, Capsina.

The two passed through the garden and into the veranda. The house-door was open, as Suleima had left it in her flight, and on the threshold she paused for the Capsina to enter first.

"You are welcome," she said; and then, in the courteous phrase she had heard in Abdul's house; "The house is yours."

Suleima would have made a bed for the Capsina in Father Andréa's room, who was away in Nauplia, but the girl asked if she might sleep with her, and instead they went together to Suleima's room. A big double mattress on a wooden frame was the bed; a little cot for the baby stood at the foot of it. Mitsos's great plank washtub stood in a corner, and there was a press for clothes. The moon shone full in at the window, making a great splash like a spill of milk on the floor, and there was no need for other light.

"THE SPIRIT OF THE STILLNESS TOUCHED THE CAPSINA'S SOUL"

Suleima was tired and soon fell asleep, but the Capsina lay long with eyes closed, but intensely awake. A mill-race of turbulent, unasked-for thoughts whirled and dashed down the channels of her brain; she clinched her hands and bit her lips to keep them away—to keep her even from crying aloud. The blood and flesh of her, young, tingling, and alert, was up in revolt, lashing itself against the hard, cruel bars of circumstance. She ought never to have come here to sleep where he had slept; she had done a stupid and sweet thing, and she was paying for it heavily. At last she could stand it no longer, and rising very quietly for fear of disturbing Suleima, she dressed again and let herself out of the house.

The hour of her weakness was upon her, and she lived back into the years of childhood, when one thing will make the world complete and its absence is an inconsolable ache. Like a child, too, she abandoned herself to the imperativeness of her need; nothing else would satisfy; nothing else was ever so faintly desirable. Yet she could only stretch out her hands to the night, every fibre of her tingling, and the silent cry, "I want, I want!" went up beseechingly, hopelessly, into the indifferent moonlight, a dumb, dry litany of supplication, not only to Heaven, but to all the cool sleeping earth; to tree, bush, stream—all that knew him. But after a while she saw and scorned herself. Where were all the great schemes and deeds in which she shared? Was their magnificence a whit impaired because she, an incomparably small atom, was in want of one thing? And by degrees made sane, and weary with struggle, she came to herself, and going back into the house, lay down again by Suleima; and when morning came Suleima was loath to wake her, for she slept so sound and peacefully, so evenly her bosom marked her quiet breathing.

Waking brought an hour of sweet and bitter things to the girl; washing and dressing the boy was almost wholly sweet, and never before had that sunny child of love been so laughed over and kissed. The Capsina showed what was to the experienced mother the strangest ignorance of the infant toilet, and even the adorable creases in his own pink skin and the ever-new wonder of his ten divisible and individual toes palled in grave interest to the owner before these new and original methods. Sweeter even than that was the unprompted staccato, "Cap-sin-a, Cap-sin-a," "like a silly parrot," so said Suleima. Indeed, the girl was truly a woman, though the profound judge, Mitsos, had given her a sex all to herself, and the little household duties so lovingly done by Suleima were a keen pleasure to her to watch and assist in. And after they had breakfasted she still lingered.

"Let me wait a little longer," she said to Suleima; "but I will not wait unless you promise to do all you would do if I was not here."

So Suleima, to whom the mending and patching of Mitsos's clothes was a Danaid labor, went into the house, and came out again on to the veranda with an armful of his invalid linen. There were holes to be patched in trousers, tears to be sewn in shirts, and places worn thin to be pieced.

"This is what I do when I have nought else to do," she said. "Yet if I had twenty hands, and no work for any of them, I believe I should never get to the end. The great loon seems never to sit down except as on a nail. Last month only he put his pipe, all alight, into his coat-pocket. Right through the lining went the burn, and right through his shirt, and he never knew it until the fire nipped him."

The Capsina laughed.

"How like him! Oh, how very like him!" she said. "May I help you? Yet, indeed, I think I have forgotten how to sew."

Suleima gave her a shirt to mend, off the arm of which Mitsos had torn a great piece—"as like as not to light the pipe that burned him," said his wife—and a very poor job she made of it. She held it up to Suleima in deprecating dismay when she had finished it, and Suleima laughed to choking.

"No, you shall not better it," she said, as the Capsina prepared to rip off the piece again. "Indeed, it shall stop as it is, and Mitsos shall wear it like that. He shall know who did it, and then perhaps he will think the higher of my fingers."

And she snatched it out of the Capsina's hands and ran with it into the house, where she put it among the finished linen, where he should find it, and stare in wonder at this preposterous housewifery.

The Capsina had not tried her hand at any further job when she returned, and presently after she rose.

"I must get back," she said, "for at ten we must be on the road to Nauplia. Oh, Suleima!" She paused, and the unshed tears stood in her black eyes. "I have not skill at speaking," she said, "and when the heart is full the words choke each other. But it is this: you have made me different; you have made me better."

Suleima stood a moment with that brilliant, happy smile in her eyes, her mouth serious and sweet. Then she threw her arms round the girl's neck and kissed her.

"You will be happy," she said, with her face close to hers and looking in her eyes. "Promise me you will be happy, for indeed that is among the first things

I desire."

The Capsina shook her head.

"I cannot promise that," she said, "and I do not know if it matters much. But I will be brave, or try to be, and I will try to be good. Luckily I have much to do."

"You will take Mitsos again?" asked Suleima.

"If he will come—if you will let him come."

"I let him come?" and she laughed. "I think I have not made myself plain."

They stood there a moment longer, cheek to cheek, and then the Capsina gently drew away.

"Good-bye," she said. "But I will come again before I leave Nauplia."

And she went quickly down the garden path, paused a moment at the gate, looking back, then stepped out along the white sun-stricken road.

CHAPTER XIII

Kolocotrones and his followers had had no hand in the destruction of Dramali's army—indeed, the only share he had taken in that great and bloody deed was to let the Albanian guard pass on their way unmolested; but whether on the grounds of that merciful act, or because he had been appointed generalissimo of the Greek forces, he claimed, and in fact secured, a very considerable share of what Niketas had taken. Nor had he been idle during the amnesty at Nauplia, having supplied immense amounts of grain and other supplies to the beleaguered garrison at starvation rates. Ali of Argos, who was in command of the Turks, had seen that something had miscarried in the conduct of the fleet, and was provident enough to purchase very considerable provisions, almost satisfying the greed of Kolocotrones. And now that the Turks were in no danger of being starved out, the generalissimo absented himself from the besieging force, and executed several very neat and profitable raids along the shores of the Corinthian gulf. Certainly for a month or two the town was amply provided, while the Greek fleet cruising in the mouth of the gulf of Spetzas would prevent any immediate relief being brought by the Turkish ships. When the provisions were exhausted, Kolocotrones intended to try and do a little more provision dealing, and if, as seemed possible, the temper of the army would no longer countenance this marketing, he would certainly be on the spot when the Turks surrendered, to take possession of the town in the name of the republic, and of as much treasure as he could lay hands on in his own.

During his absence, however, certain changes took place in the conduct of the siege. The other leaders, tired, perhaps, and a little ashamed of all this juggling with treaties that they never meant to abide by, and of this haggling over prices with their enemies, or else knowing that if Kolocotrones was there he would take the lion's share of the spoils, made a spirited though ineffectual attempt, since Ali had broken off negotiations, to bring the siege to a conclusion in his absence. During the spring many volunteers from England and France had offered their services to the revolutionists; there had even been formed a corps of Philhellenes, and several of these, notably Colonel Jourdain, a French artilleryman, and two Englishmen, Hastings and Hane, had put themselves at the disposal of the Greek troops in Nauplia. Jourdain, an ingenious but impractical young man, had urged the Greeks to try firing combustible shot at the town. He held out good hope that they would set the town on fire—with luck they might even demolish the enemy's powder-magazine and burn their provision houses, full of the provisions which had just been sold to them. And the captains, jingling with the gold of the payment, found this plan humorous.

The fort standing on the island in the bay had been put into the hands of the Greeks at the first pseudo-surrender of the town, and though Ali declared that the treaty which gave it them being null and void, as they had not done their part in providing transport-vessels, it should be returned to the Turks, the answer that the Greeks gave was, "Come and take it." And as the Turks were not in a position to come and take it, it was obviously misplaced Quixotism to let it stand empty. From there the ingenious Jourdain suggested that the combustible shot should be fired, but his ingenuity further served him to relieve himself of the responsibility of the attempt, and Hastings and Hane, though without much faith in the method, obtained leave of the Greek captains to do it themselves.

Accordingly, Hastings was made captain of the fort garrison, which consisted of twenty boatmen from Kranidi, who knew about as much of artillery as of astronomy, and he surveyed his men with some amusement, and spoke pithily:

"We are to make Nauplia as full of holes as a net and as hot as hell," he said. "Train the guns, if you know what that means. You do not? I will teach you."

There were half a dozen 32-pounders and three 68-pounders of seven-inch bore. The fort was an old Venetian work, tottery and unstable as Reuben, commanded by the guns of Nauplia; and Hastings, surveying it, turned to

Hane.

"From the town I could engage to knock this place into biscuits in ten minutes by a stop-watch," he said.

Hane laughed.

"We shall knock it to bits ourselves in not much longer with the concussion of our own guns if the Turks don't hit us," he said. "I would as soon sail across the Bay of Biscay in a paper boat."

Jourdain's combustible balls were made to be fired from the smaller guns, and the two spent a sulphurous morning. They made good shooting with them, and it is true that they discharged immense volumes of smoke when they struck, but there seemed no truth in the proverb that where there is smoke there is also fire. Jourdain had manufactured some twenty of them, and in an hour they had used them all up. The breeze was blowing from the town, and volumes of vile-smelling vapor were wafted on it. Hane was a man of few and pointed words.

"So here is the last of the Froggy's stink-pots," was all his comment when the last of the shells was fired.

But the Greeks were in raptures of delight. It seemed impossible that so magnificent a firework should be ineffective, and they strongly recommended a repetition of the display; but Hastings meant business, and, after some parley, was allowed to make another attempt, not with the "stink-pots," but with ordinary shot from the 68-pounders; for the 32-pounders were, so he believed, of too light a calibre to be effective at the distance.

Next day the heavier cannonade went on. The Turks returned the fire with vigor, but without much success, and, as Hastings had anticipated, the chief risk was from the concussion of their own artillery, which dangerously shook the faulty and ill-built walls. After the first day it was found impossible to fire the bigger guns, and the 32-pounders, with their light shells, were soon seen to be useless; Hastings, however, kept up the cannonade for two days more, partly to give practice to the untrained gunners, partly because he was of a nature that groans to be doing nothing.

At the end of the third day the Turkish fire ceased altogether, for the flight and destruction of Dramali's army had become known, and it was no longer possible to hope that by a show of resistance and brisk firing, they might encourage the timid Serashier to march from Argos and attempt to raise the siege. Had he known it, the town was now so well supplied with provisions that, even if they had to evacuate it, they could have joined forces with him and marched to Corinth. But now, as throughout the war, what seemed blind chance, but what was really the legitimate result of cowardly and hesitating policy, once more combined to fight against them.

So the Turkish fire ceased, and as it was proved to satiety that the smaller guns of the island fort were no more than a summer rain to the fortification of the town, Hastings ceased his fire too, and with Hane made a detailed examination of the fort, with a view to strengthening the walls, and enabling them to stand the concussion from the heavier guns. With a little pulling down, a little patching, and a rubble buttress or two, it seemed easily possible to strengthen one bastion which held two of the 68-pounders, so that they might fire without the risk of bringing down the walls on their own heads. But that afternoon a message arrived from the captain, Poniropoulos: their firing had ceased, the guns produced no impression on the fortifications. The Greeks were infinitely obliged to them, but they must not hope to share in the plunder from Nauplia, nor would rations be any longer supplied to them. For the present it was not the intention of the commanders to continue this gun practice. Dramali's army had gone; the fleet had not come; they would sit down and wait the inevitable end.

Hastings chucked this note into the sea.

"There is no answer," he said to the boatman who had brought it.

He turned to Hane.

"It is no use waiting here if we are not to use the guns," he said. "They say we need not expect plunder from Nauplia. Do they think we are all like the old man in the brass helmet?"

CHAPTER XIV

Mitsos returned home after the destruction of Dramali's army, arriving there the day after the Capsina had left. Suleima met him at the gate.

"Oh, welcome, Mitsos!" she cried, in a hurry. "And I, too, have seen her. She has been here."

"I seem of little account," said Mitsos; "but who may 'she' be?"

"When you talk of 'she,' do I not know whom you mean? You are less wise than I. And she saved my life and that of the littlest."

"The Capsina?" cried Mitsos.

"Yes, slow one."

And Suleima told him how she had fled to Tiryns, and how the Capsina had concealed her and the little one till the Turks had been routed; only she did not tell that which it was not for Mitsos to know.

"So come in now, Mitsos, and you shall eat and wash—and indeed you are as dusty as a hen—and in the evening you shall go to Nauplia, and thank her, if so be you are pleased at what she did."

Suleima went to the bedroom and laid out for him a clean fustanella and shirt, the one on which the Capsina had used her unaccustomed needle, and went out smiling to herself. In a little while came Mitsos's voice, calling her, and back she went very grave.

He held out a ragged sleeve, with stitches loose and large.

"I have a fine housewife," said he, very sarcastically.

Suleima examined the shirt.

"Indeed, it was torn much," she said; "but it does not seem to me badly mended."

Mitsos shrugged his shoulders hugely.

"It is as I have always said," he remarked; "a woman cannot even mend a shirt."

"Who mends your things when you are cruising, Mitsos?" she asked.

"I don't know. They are always well done. The Capsina is excepted; she can do everything."

Suleima could not keep the corners of her mouth from breaking down, and next moment she burst out laughing.

"It was she did who it," she said; "I swear to you it was she."

Mitsos had half slipped off the shirt, but on it went again in a twinkling.

"It is not badly mended," said Suleima, still laughing, "but I could do it better. Take another one, Mitsos. I will mend this again. Ah, it is less good than I thought. See how big and bad are those stitches. Oh, it is shocking! Off with it! I will not have for a husband one they would think was a beggar."

Mitsos looked at her darkly and sideways.

"This, no doubt, is the best way to mend a shirt, though I know nought of shirt-mending," he said. "Do not be too proud to take example, Suleima. See how fine and big are the stitches. Why, she would mend ten shirts while you mended one."

"Even so," said Suleima; "indeed, if she mended a dozen while I did one, it would not surprise me, or more than that even. And see how convenient on a hot day like this; the wind will blow coolly on your arm through the stitches."

Mitsos broke out laughing.

"She shall see me in it," he cried. "And, oh little wife, I am pleased to be home again. Dust and hot wind were the drink in the Larissa, so see that there is wine to fill even me. Oh, I love wine!" he cried.

"Ah, it is for the wine alone you would be home again," said Suleima, with the light of love returned in her eyes.

Mitsos bent down from his great height, and put his face to hers.

"Yes, for the wine alone," he said, softly, "the wine of many things. And are you not wine to my soul, my own dear one?"

Soon after they had dinner, and, dinner finished, Mitsos set off into Nauplia. The *Revenge* was fretting at her anchor in the land-breeze as a horse, eager to be off, plays with its bridle, but close under the fort where Hastings and Hane had fired the incombustible balls he saw the Capsina's boat, a light caique, in which she sailed on her hurricane errands when in port, which would go like a fish if there was wind, and could be pulled by one man. Even Mitsos, used as he was to over-canvassed boats, used to feel certain qualms when the little cockleshell, with its tower of sail, was scudding through a broken sea. But the Capsina, knowing this, used to watch his face for any sign of apprehension, till he, seeing her, would exclaim:

"It is as a bird with wings and no body, and that is not the safer sort of bird; and oh, Capsina, drowning is a cold manner of death. Oh yes, hoist more sail, by all means, and I shall pray the while."

It was the day after Poniropoulos had told Hastings that his services were no longer required, and both Poniropoulos and the gunners under Hastings were feeling a thought disconcerted. The Capsina had approved very warmly of that silent and iron man, and when, on going that morning to the fort, she had found Hastings gone she sailed across with dipping gunwale to Poniropoulos and demanded where and why he had disappeared.

Thus Poniropoulos learned her true opinion of him, and she went back to the island where Mitsos found her.

"Ignorant folk," she had been saying, "always think that no one is so wise as they. When you came here you knew nothing. You have been taught to fire off a gun without getting in front of it, and you think you know all. Why did you let Hastings go? What did he care about the plunder of Nauplia? If you had asked him to stop, he would have stopped. You know that as well as I. He saw that if you continued to fire the big guns the fort would tumble about your long ears. So what have you done since? Eaten garlic and talked about piasters! Oh, I will teach you!"

To her, shaking her fist, Mitsos appeared in the doorway. She looked up once, dropped her eyes, and looked up again. Then she turned to the gunners.

"Go away, pigs, all of you!" she cried. "He and I will talk things over, and there will soon be orders. The place must be repaired at once."

And she stood there, looking out of the window, till the men had filed out.

Then Mitsos approached.

"Capsina," he said, "I have seen Suleima. She has told me—"

He did not pause in his speech, but as he said those words, the color was already struck from the girl's face, leaving it as white as a lamp-globe when the light is extinguished, for, for the moment, she thought Suleima had told him all. She turned a little more away from him.

"She has told me what you have done for me and mine," he went on, "how you saved her; how you put yourself between her and death. And I—God made me so stupid that I cannot even find words to thank you."

It was a glorified face that turned to him one smile.

"Oh, little Mitsos!" she said. "Surely we do not need words for such things. When you saved my life at Porto Germano, did I thank you for it? I think I only said, 'How slow you are,' when you picked up my knife for me. So that is finished. We had a long talk, we washed and dressed the littlest one, and he said 'Capsina.' That pleased me in an extraordinary manner, but you remember that I like children. And Suleima is a fine woman, a woman, yet not foolish, the sort of woman that does not make one wish to be a man, and those are rare. So I approve, but I doubt whether she is severe enough to you. A wife should not be too full of care for the husband."

"Indeed, I have been speaking to her to-day," said Mitsos, "saying she is not careful enough of me. A wife should be able to sew and mend, should she not? And see what a shirt she has given me."

And Mitsos pulled his shirt-sleeve round till the patch was shown, and made a marvellously poor attempt to look grave; and, each seeing that the other knew, they burst out laughing, and the Capsina gave Mitsos a great slap on the shoulder.

"Boy and baby you will always be," she said. "And now, do you know anything of fortification work?"

"Not a thing."

"Nor do I. So we will patch up this fort, learning, as is right, by experience, and may the Virgin look to those within when we have done our mending. It is as safe as a tower of bricks that a child builds. Lad, Hastings is a brave man to stand firing the guns here with his hands in his pockets."

"The others are as brave."

"No. They did not know the danger; in fact, they knew nothing. Look at that piece of wall there! If you look hard, it will fall down like a Turk. Oh, Mitsos, if you had given the time you spend in tobacco to learning building, you might be of some use this day."

"If you wish, I will push it, and it will fall," remarked Mitsos.

The Capsina looked at his great shoulders and sighed.

"If only I had been born a man!" she said. "Oh, I should have liked it! If I pushed it now—"

"If you pushed it," said Mitsos, "you would push with all your weight. So when it fell out, you would fall with it, eight feet to the beach below; also your petticoats would fly."

The Capsina struggled with inward laughter for a moment.

"It is likely so," she said. "Therefore show me how to push it."

The fragment of wall which Mitsos was to push outward was a rotten projecting angle once joining a cross-wall, but now sticking out helplessly, in the decay of the others, into space. It was some six feet high, and the top of it on a level with Mitsos's nose. He looked at it scornfully a moment, and then at the Capsina.

"It shall be as you will," he said, "but I shall dirty my beautiful clean shirt, even tear it perhaps on the shoulder, and who shall mend it again for me?"

"Push; oh, push!" said the Capsina. "Be a little man."

Mitsos braced his shoulder to it, wedged his right foot for purchase against an uneven stone in the floor, and his left foot close to the wall, so that he could recover himself when it should fall outward. Then with a fine confidence, "You shall see," he said, and butted against it as a bull butts, sparring only half in earnest with a tree. Wall and tree remain immovable.

"That is very fine," said the Capsina. "It nearly shook."

Mitsos put a little more weight into it, and felt the muscles tighten and knot in his leg, and the Capsina sighed elaborately.

"It would have saved time to have picked it down stone by stone," said she. "But never mind now; no doubt it is trembling. What a great man is Mitsos!"

Half vexed—for, with all his gentleness, he was proud of his strength—and half laughing, he put his whole weight from neck to heel into it, doing that of which he had warned the Capsina, and felt the wall tremble. Then pausing a moment to get better purchase with his right foot, once more he threw himself at it, making a cushion of the great muscles over the shoulder. This effort was completely successful; the wall tottered, bowed, and fell; and Mitsos, unable to check himself, took a neat header after it and disappeared in a cloud of dust.

The Capsina, who had perfect faith in his power of not hurting himself, peered over the ledge with extreme amusement. Mitsos had already regained his feet, and was feeling himself carefully to see if he was anywhere hurt.

"Little Mitsos!" she cried, and he looked up. "You will want a new petticoat as well as a shirt," said she.

They spent an hour or two in the place, deciding on what should be patched up, and what pulled down, and the Capsina took Mitsos back with her to the *Revenge* to sup before he went home. The two were alone. Mitsos had much to tell of the siege of the Larissa and the destruction of Dramali's army, and to the Capsina so much still remained of that spell of soothing which Suleima, and even more the child who stammered her own name, had cast upon her, that she listened with interest, excitement, suspense, to his tale, and even half forgot that it was Mitsos who told it. But when it was over and they were on deck, half-way between silence and continuous speech, she began to think again of that which filled her thoughts. She was sitting on a coil of rope, and he half lay, half sat, at her feet, leaning against the fore-mast. The night was very hot and dark, for the moon was not yet up, and the starlight came filtered through a haze of south wind. Mitsos smoked his narghile, and as he drew the smoke in his face was illumed intermittently by the glowing charcoal, lean and brown and strong, and the jaw muscles outstanding from the cheek, and again as he stopped to talk he would go back into darkness, and the words came in the voice which she thought she knew even better than his face. Sometimes in a crowd of faces she would think she caught sight of him, but never in a company of voices did she catch note of a voice like his. And though she knew that when he had gone, for every moment he had sat close to her in the warm, muffled dusk she would sit another minute alone, helplessly, hopelessly, with his voice ringing in the inward ear, she still detained him, laughing down his laughing protests, saying that he thought of himself far higher than Suleima thought of him.

At last he rose to go in earnest, and she went with him to the boat.

"Soon the Turkish fleet will be here," she said, "and then there will be work for us, little Mitsos. Shall we work together again?"

Mitsos raised his eyebrows and spoke quickly:

"How not? Why not?" he said. "Will you not take me again?"

"I? Will you come?" she asked.

"Yes, surely. But I thought you spoke as if, as if—"

"As if what?" asked the girl.

"As if you thought we should not be together."

"Oh, little Mitsos, you are a fool," she said. "While the *Revenge* is afloat there is need for you here. Good-night. Kiss Suleima for me, as well as for yourself, and promise you will make the adorable one say 'Capsina.'"

"Indeed he shall, and many times. But when will you come yourself? I have not yet welcomed you in my home, and for how many days have I been made welcome in this swift house of yours! You will come to-morrow? Let me tell Suleima so."

The Capsina nodded and smiled.

"Till to-morrow then," she said.

But Mitsos had construed her tone aright. Even in the very act of speaking she had hesitated, wondering if she were firm enough of purpose to sail without him, and wishing, or rather wanting, that she were; and in the same act of speech she had known she was not, and the question had halted on her tongue. But it had been asked and answered now, and she was the gladder; for the pain of his presence was sweeter than the relief of his absence.

Most of the sailors were on shore, a few only on the ship, and when Mitsos had gone she went down to her cabin, meaning to go to bed. The ripple tapped restlessly against the ship's side; occasionally the footstep of the watch sounded above her head, and human sounds came through the open port-hole from the Greek camp. The night was very hot, and the girl lay tossing and turning in her bed, unable to sleep. It was at such times when she was alone, and especially at night, that the fever of her love-sickness most throbbed and burned in her veins. Now and then she would doze for a moment lightly, still conscious that she was lying in her cabin, and only knowing that she was not awake by the fact that she heard Mitsos talking or saw him standing by her. Such visions passed in a flash, and she would wake again to full consciousness. But this night she was too aware of her own body to doze even for a moment; it was a struggling, palpitating thing. Her pulse beat insistently in her temples; her heart rose to her throat and hammered there loud and quick. The port-hole showed a circle of luminous gray in the darkness, and cast a muffled light on the wall opposite; the waves lapped; the sentry walked; the ship was alive with the little noises heard only by the alert. Her bed burned her; her love-fever burned her; she was a smouldering flame.

She listened to the tread of the watch, growing fainter as he walked to the bows; he paused a moment as he turned, and the steps came back in a gradual crescendo, till he was above her head, then died away again till they were barely audible. Again he paused at the turn, again came his steps crescendo, and so backward and forward, till she could have cried aloud for the irritation of the thing. Other noises were less explicable; surely some one was moving about in the cabin next hers, the cabin Mitsos used to occupy, some one who went to and fro in stockinged or bare feet, but with heavy tread. Then Michael, who lay outside her door, stirred and sat up, and began to scratch himself; at each backward stroke his hind-leg tapped the door, and the Capsina vindictively said to herself that he should be washed to-morrow. But he would not stop; he went on scratching for ten hours, or a lifetime, or it may have been a minute, and she called out to him to be quiet. He lay down, she heard, with a thump, and, pleased with the sound of her recognized voice, banged his tail against the bare boards. Then he began to pant. At first the sound was barely audible, but it seemed as if he must be swelling to some gigantic thing, for the noise of his breathing grew louder and louder, till it became only the tread of the sentry above. No, it was not the sentry; he walked a little slower than the panting—why could the man not keep time?—and still next door the padded footstep crept about.

Flesh and blood could not stand it, and getting up, she kindled her lamp at the little oil-wick below the shrine of the Virgin at the end of her cabin, and opened the door. Michael hailed her with silent rapture and wistful, topaz eyes. She paused a moment on the threshold, and then opening the door of Mitsos's cabin, went in, knowing all the time that the tread of the stockinged feet was only a thought of her own brain made audible inwardly.

The cabin was empty, as she expected, and she sat down for a moment on the bare boards of his bunk, with the lamp in her hand, looking round the walls vaguely but intently, curiously but without purpose. Some pencil scratches above the head of the bed caught her eye, and, examining them more closely, she saw they were sprawling letters written upsidedown and written backward. She frowned over these for a moment, and then the solution drew a smile from her; and putting the lamp on the floor, she lay down on the bed, looking up. Yes, that was it. He must have written them idly one morning lying in bed. And she read thus:

"This is Mitsos's cabin.... Suleima!... Capsina!... Oh, Capsina!... Oh, Mitsos

Codones!... Suleima!..."

Again and again she read them, then continued to look at them, not reading them, but as one looks at a familiar picture, half abstractedly. The lamp, unreplenished with oil, burned low; Michael sank on to his haunches, and then lay down. Through the open cabin door filtered a silvery grayness of starlight, but before the lamp had gone quite out the girl was asleep on the bare, unblanketed bed, her face turned upward as she had turned it to read the little pencil scratches.

CHAPTER XV

During the last two months the Greek fleet had been playing a waiting game, necessary but inglorious. The Sultan, as has been seen, had sent out in the spring a great army and a great navy, which were to relieve Nauplia simultaneously. Of the army the hills of the Dervenaki knew; the navy had cruised to Patras to take on board the new capitan pasha succeeding him who was the victim of Kanaris's fire-ship, and now in September it was coming back in full force, under its new commander, in tardy execution of its aim. It had left Patras before the news of Dramali's destruction had arrived, and the Turks still knew nothing of the miscarriage of the Sultan's scheme. Round it day by day, but out of distance of its heavy guns, hovered and poised the petrel fleet of the Greeks, neither attacking nor attacked. The Greek navy had been reorganized in the spring, and the supreme command given to Admiral Miaulis, still only in his thirtieth year, brave, honest, and judicious, and distracted by the endless quarrels and pretensions of his charge. It was no part of his purpose to give battle to the Turks on the open levels of the sea, but to wait till they turned into the narrower gulf outside Nauplia, where the cumbrous Turks would be hampered for sea-room, while his own lighter vessels, born to shifting winds and at home among shoals and the perils of landlocked seas, would reap the fruits of their breeding. All the latter part of August, a month of halcyon days in the open sea, they drifted and sailed in the wake of the Turks returning with Kosreff from Patras, and each day brought them but little nearer Nauplia. Often for two days or three at a time they would be utterly becalmed, sometimes taken back by the northward-flowing current, with sails flapping idly and mirrored with scarcely a tremor on a painted ocean.

Four ships had gone hack to Hydra to guard the harbor and carry news if another detachment of Turks was sent from Constantinople. The beacon-hill, rising black and barren above the town, was a watch-tower day and night, but the days added themselves to weeks, and still no sign came from the south or north. One out of the four belonged to Tombazes, who was for a time at Hydra, and two to Father Nikola, wrinkled and sour as ever, but since the night of his encounter with the Capsina less audibly malevolent. Sometimes ships would put in from Peiraeus, or other ports, and these brought news of fresh risings against the Turks, of fresh outrages, and of fresh successes. Occasionally there would be on board men who had escaped from Turkish slavery, less often women. Then if the ship happened to come from any port near Athens, Father Nikola would hasten down to the quay with peering eyes, hoping against hope; but the faces of those who had escaped were always strange to him.

Kanaris only, who was the cousin of his wife, was in his secret, and knew why the old man pinched and hoarded with such unwavering greed, and while others cursed him for his grasping and clutching, felt a pity and sympathy in the man's devotion to one purpose. He would not have shrunk from pain, bodily or mental; he would not have shrunk from crime, if pain or crime would have enabled him to buy back his wife from the Turks in Athens; and had the devil come to Hydra, offering him her ransom for the signing away of his soul, he would have snapped his fingers in Satan's face and signed.

Sometimes Kanaris would sup with him, and while Father Nikola gave his guest hospitable fare, he would himself eat only most sparingly and drink nothing but water. He would sit long silent, playing with his string of beads, peering at the other.

Then, after a time, he might say:

"You were very like her when you were a boy, Kanaris; she had the same eyes as you. Have you finished drinking? If so, I will put the wine away."

And Kanaris, who would often have wished for more, would say he had finished.

One such evening, towards the end of July, Kanaris came up with news.

"You have heard?" he asked.

"I have heard nothing," said Nikola. "But I dropped a fifty-piaster piece to-day; I know not where or how."

"Athens has capitulated."

Father Nikola rose and brought his hands together with a palsied trembling, and then sank back in his chair again.

"Wine! Give me some wine!" he said. And he gulped down a glassful, holding it in a shaking hand and spilling much. Unused as he had been for so long to anything but water, it was strength and steadiness to him, and he got up again, renewed and firm, his own man.

"I must go, then," he said; "I must go."

"Not to Athens," said Kanaris. "A caique put in this evening. There has been a massacre of Turks, but little fighting. The Peiraeus, they say, was full of women and others who escaped from the houses of the Turks. Some have sailed to their homes; others are sailing. She was taken, was she not, at Spetzas? If she is still alive she may be there, or she may have heard you have gone to Hydra. I will help you, for she is cousin to me, and I will sail to Spetzas to-night while you wait here."

Nikola took him by the shoulder, almost pushing him from the room.

"Go then," he said. "Oh, be quick, man! Stay, do you want money? Take what you will; it is all for her."

And he walked across the room to the hearth, and wrenched up two of the stones. Below opened a space some three feet square filled with little linen bags all tied up. He took out a handful of them.

"Each is a hundred piasters," he said. "Take what you will; take three, four, all. For the time has come for me to use them."

But Kanaris, with a strange feeling of tenderness and pity, kissed the old man's hand and refused.

"I, too, will do something for my kin," he said, "She belongs to me as well as you."

"No, no!" cried Father Nikola. "She belongs to no one but me—to me only, I tell you. I will pay you as I would have paid the Turk. Oh, take the money, but go."

Kanaris shook his head.

"Very well; she is yours only. I will go. Wish me good luck, father."

But Father Nikola could not speak. He threw down the bags into their place again, and put back the stone. Then he went to his bedroom and took out his best clothes. He washed, trimmed his beard, and put on his purple cloak lined with fur, his big gold ring, and his buckled shoes.

"I am an old man," he thought to himself, "but at least I can make myself less forlorn a sight for a woman's eyes. Ah, but no woman was ever like her!"

And his old drooping mouth trembled into a smile.

Sometimes when he went out he would notice, not with pain, but with hatred, that people shrank from him, that boys called him by opprobrious miser-names, but to-night, as he went down to the quay, he noticed nothing; he walked on air, unseeing. The crucial hour was at hand, the hour that would leave him rich and alone, or a primate no more, but with another. She was his wife; that vow at least he had not broken. He would not be hissed out of his office; blithely would he go; he would have to leave Hydra; he would shake the dust of it from his feet. He would ask pardon of Economos, whom he had foully schemed to murder; he would give all but bare livelihood to the service of the war; and he would be a happier man. The little well of tenderness and humanity, which had so long been choked by the salt and bitter sands of the soul in which it rose, suddenly swelled and overflowed. Surely God was very good. He had taken him again by the hand after decades of sour and hating years; He would lead him into a green and quiet pasture.

The quay was loud and humming with the news from Athens. Tombazes was there, all red face and glory, and he clapped Nikola hard on the shoulder.

"Oh, is it not very fine!" he said. "And you, too, are fine! Oh, my silver buckles and fur cloak!"

But Nikola laid a trembling hand on his arm.

"Where are those who have escaped from Athens?" he asked. "I knew—a—a person there who had been taken by the Turks, and whom I would be glad to see again."

Tombazes giggled unprelatically.

"Some girl on a spring day," he said, "when you were a boy; oh, a very long time ago. I beg your pardon, father. But I am silly with joy to-night. Also I drank much wine because of the news. So you expect a woman from Athens, who had better not come to Hydra? Well, well, we are all miserable sinners! Go and hide, father. I will say you are not on the island, that you are dead, and that we have never heard of you. Ay, one must stand up for one's order! Did I ever tell how, ever so long ago—well, it's an old story, and tedious in the telling. The refugees from Athens? Yes, a boatful is expected. They left with those who brought the news, but they sailed less fast. Ah, is not that a caique rounding the harbor now. It will be they!"

It was nearly sundown when the first boat with the news had arrived, and by now the sun had set, but the western sky still flamed with the whole gamut of color, from crimson to saffron yellow, and the sea was its flame reflected. A breeze, steady and singing, blew from the main-land, just ruffling the water, and the caique sped on by it, came black and swift over the shining plain of water, crumpling and curling the sea beneath her bows, cutting her way

213

through the crimson and the yellow, and the shadow of deep translucent green which lay ever before her. On the quay the crowd gathered and thickened, but grew ever more silent, for none knew what friend or relative, lost for years and only a ghost to memory, the ships might bring or carry the news of. The most part of the men of Hydra were away with the fleet, and it was women chiefly, old and gray-headed folk, and children who waited there. Deep water ran close up to the quay wall, and when the ship furled all sail and swung round to come to land, it was in silence that the rope was flung from the ship and in silence that those on shore made it fast. Then the anchor plunged with a gulp and babble into the sea, and she came alongside.

Then, as those on board came ashore, tongues and tears were loosened. Among them was a girl who had been taken only two years before; in her arms was a baby, a heritage of shame. It was pitiful to see how her father started forward to meet her—then stopped, and for a moment she stood alone with down-dropped eyes, and the joy and expectation in her face struck dead. But suddenly from the women behind her mother ran out, with her love triumphing over shame, and she fell on the girl's neck with a sob and drew her tenderly away. Another was a very old man who tottered down the gangway steps; none knew his name and he knew none, but looked round puzzledly at the changed quay and the sprouted town. But there were very few to return to Hydra, for the Turks had always filled their plunderous and lustful hands from places where the men were of softer mould than these stern islanders. Tombazes, with Nikola still close to him, had pushed his way forward to the edge of the quay where the ship was disembarking; a crowd of jovial, whistling sailors poured down the plank, and still Nikola had not seen what he looked for. But at the last came a woman in Turkish dress, and at her he looked longer and more peeringly as she came down the bridge. She had removed the yashmak from her face, and her head, gray-haired, was bare. But surely to another never had the glory of woman been given in such magnificent abundance. It grew low on her forehead and was braided over her ears and done up in great coils behind her head. Her eyebrows were still black, startlingly black against that gray head and ivory-colored face, but her eyes were blacker, and like fire they smouldered, and they pierced like steel. Weary yet keen was her face; expectant and wide her eyes; and expectant her mouth, slightly open, and still young and girlish in its fine curves and tender lines. Among that crowd of merry, strong-built men she seemed of different clay; you would have said she was a china cup among crockery and earthenware. And Nikola looked, and his eyes were riveted to her, and they grew dim suddenly, and with a little, low cry he broke from Tombazes and forced his way through those who stood around, so that when the woman stepped ashore off the bridge he stood full in front of her, and his hands were out-stretched;

you would have said he held his heart in them, offering it to her. She saw and paused, her lips parted in a sudden surprise and amaze; for a moment her eyebrows contracted as if puzzled, but before they had yet frowned, cleared again, and she took both his hands in hers and kissed him on the lips.

"Nikola," she said, and no more, and for a minute's space there was silence between them, and in that silence their souls lived back for one blessed moment to the years long past. Neither of them saw that the crowd had gone back a little, to give them room, that all were waiting in a pause of astonishment and conjecture round them, but standing off with the instinct of natural effacement, a supreme delicacy, to let these two long sundered have even in the midst of them a sort of privacy. Tombazes saw and guessed, and his honest red face suddenly puckered with an unbidden welling of tears. Nikola was waiting, as he had said, for some one; this woman was she. She was the taller of the two, and laid her hand on his shoulder.

"I have come back, Nikola," she said, and her voice was sweeter and more mellow than the harbor bell. "I have come back old. But I have come back."

Anguish more lovely than joy, joy fiercer than anguish pierced him. The bitter waters were turned suddenly sweet by some divine alchemy; his withered heart budded and blossomed.

"The rest is nothing worth, little one," he said. "You have come back. I too am old."

At that she smiled.

"Little one?" she said, and with the undying love of love which is the birthright of women. "Am I still little one?" she said, and again she kissed him on the lips.

"Let us go," he whispered. "Let us go home."

The lane of faces parted right and left, and in silence they went up across the quay through the deserted streets to his house. Not till they had passed out of the sound of hearing did the silence grow into a whisper, and the whisper into speech. They crowded round Tombazes, but he could only wipe his eyes and conjecture like the rest.

"Old Nikola!" he said; "fancy old Nikola! She can only be his wife. He said he was waiting for a person. Well, you call your sister your sister, and your relations your relations; you only call your wife, when you are not imagined to have one, a person. Old Nikola! That explains a great deal. We thought him a mere old miser, and a sour one at that. I make no doubt he was saving for the ransom. No, don't anybody speak to me. I—I—" and the warm-hearted old pagan primate turned suddenly away and blew his nose violently.

No more was seen of Nikola that evening, but next morning his servant came to Tombazes, asking him if he would dine with him that day. The two met him at the door hand in hand, like children or young lovers, and Nikola, turning to his wife, said:

"Ask Father Tombazes' blessing, little one; and give me also your blessing, father."

Tombazes did so, and observed that Nikola was dressed no longer as a primate, but only as a deacon, and as they dined he told him all—how thirty years ago he broke his celibate vow and, as if in instant vengeance, before a month was passed his wife was carried off from Spetzas by the Turks; how he had moved to Hydra where the story was unknown, and how only yesterday she had come back again.

"And now, father," he said, in conclusion, "will you do me a last favor, and let the people know what has happened. I go among them as deacon, no longer as primate, and, I hope, no longer as a miser or a sour man. The little one and I have talked long together, and indeed I think I have been made different to what I was."

So Father Nikola became Nikola again, and the loss of dignity was gain in all else to him. He and Martha were seldom seen apart, and the island generally, partly because its folk were warm-hearted and ready to forgive, partly because the strange little old-age idyl pleased them, smiled on the two. Nikola's two ships still remained all August in the harbor, and it was matter for conjecture whether, when the time came for them to take the sea again, Martha would go with him, or whether Nikola would give up his part in the war. And the two talked of it together.

"It would be selfish if I tried to keep you here, Nikola," said his wife, "for since I have been in the house of the Turk it has seemed to me that all men have a duty laid on them, and that to root out the whole devil's brood."

"I care no longer, little one," he said, "for have I not got you back?"

Martha got up and began walking up and down the veranda.

"It is good to hear you speak so," she said, "and yet it is not good. There are other wives besides me; other husbands also besides you, Nikola. So do not draw back; it is for me only you draw back. Go! I would have you go!"

She looked at him with shining eyes, her heart all woman, and the noblest of woman—strong, unflinching.

He looked at her and hesitated.

"How can I leave you?" he said. "I cannot start off again."

"Leave me?" she asked. "What talk is this of leaving me?"

"But you would have me go."

"But will I not be with you? Does not your Capsina sail on her ship, and why not I on my husband's?"

"No, no!" he cried, stung out of self. "That were still worse. If I went my comfort would be that you were here safe; that, if I came back, I should still find you here.. Let it suffice then. I go, but alone."

Again she smiled.

"Let it suffice, Nikola," she said; "you go not alone."

He looked up at her with his peering eyes.

"You are greater than ever, little one," he said, "and I find you more beautiful than ever."

She bent down, kissed him lightly on the forehead, and sat by him, while he stretched his hand out to hers and stroked it.

"Would not the boys and girls laugh to see us?" he said. "For, indeed, though I am old, I think you still like to have the touch of me. I am absurd."

"God bless their laughter," said she, "for, indeed, no ill thing yet came from laughter." Then, after a pause, "And are we not enviable? Are we not content? Indeed I am content, Nikola, and content comes once or twice in a lifetime, and to the most of men never. It is the autumn of our age, and the days are warm and calm, and no storm vexes us."

"And I am content," said Nikola.

So during the hot procession of August days the Indian summer of love, coming late to an old man who had long been of peevish and withered heart, and to a woman gray-headed, but with something still of the divine immortality of youth within her, sped its span of days delayed, and lingered in the speeding; for them the wheel of time ran back to years long past, and the years were winged with love and the healing of bitterness. Indeed, a man must have been something more obstinately sour of soul than all that dwells on the earth if he should not have sweetened under so mellow and caressing a touch, for when a woman is woman to the core, there is no man whom she cannot make a man of. Late had come that tender tutelage, but to a pupil who had known the hand before, and answered to it.

Often on these sultry mornings, between the death of the breeze from the sea and the birth of the land-breeze, the two would walk up the beacon-hill above the town, where they found a straying air always abroad. Of the years of separation they spoke not at all; for them both they were a time to be buried and no thought given them, to be hidden out of sight. Thus their strange renewed idyl, born out of old age, ran its course.

August passed thus, and the most part of September, but one day, as they sat there looking rather than watching, two masts under sail climbed the rim of the horizon, and, while yet the hull of the ship was down, another two, and yet another. Before long some forty ships were in sight, heading it seemed for Spetzas or the channel between it and Hydra. They sent a lad who was sheep-feeding on the side of the hill to pass the word to Tombazes, and themselves remained to see if more would appear. It was a half-hour before Tombazes came, and in the interval the horizon was again pricked by another uprising company of masts. Then said Nikola:

"The time has come, little one. Those are the fleets. It is the Turks who are now coming into sight. Ah, here is Tombazes."

It was soon evident that Nikola was right, for before long, as the ships drew closer, the first fleet was clearly seen to be of the Greek ships, who had outsailed the Ottomans and were waiting for them at the entrance to the Gulf of Nauplia, like ushers to show them in. As soon as the Turks were once in the narrow sea, with the mouth closed behind them by the Greeks, they were as duellists shut in a room, and the fate of Nauplia this way or that was on the board and imminent. Nikola announced his intention of joining the fleet with one ship, leaving the other, if Tombazes thought good, to help in the defence of the harbor in case the Turks attacked Hydra. Martha sailed with him; and at that Tombazes glowed, and making his action fit his word, "I kiss the hand of a brave woman," he said.

She turned to her husband, flushing with a color fresh like a girl's.

"I sail with a brave man," she said. "It would ill beseem his wife to be afraid."

The other three ships, it was settled, were to stay at Hydra to guard the place, and that evening Nikola and the wife set off down the path of the land-breeze to join the fleet.

In the six weeks that had passed since the Capsina had taken in hand the repairs of the fortifications of the Burdjee, she had so strengthened the place by buttressing it with huge, rough masses of stone and rubble and demolishing dangerous walls that passed her skill to put in a state of safety, that it no longer had much to fear from the Turkish fire and, what was almost the greater testimonial, hardly more from its own. Hastings was still away, superintending the building of a steamship which he was to devote to the national cause, and Jourdain, the proud inventor of the smoky balls, had been seen once only on the island fort. On that occasion, finding there a very handsome girl and not knowing who she was, he had, with the amiable gallantry of his race, incontinently kissed her. For this ill-inspired attention he received so swinging a slap on the ear that his head sang shrilly to him for the remainder of the day, and he did not again set foot on the island while that "hurricane woman"—for so he called her after his reception—remained on it. Hane had come back a day or two before, but he suggested that the somewhat scanty ammunition in the island fort had better be reserved for the Ottoman fleet, in case they reached the harbor of Nauplia, rather than be used up against the walls of the town.

"For, indeed," he said, "we have no quarrel with those walls. As long as the fleet comes not, they pen the Turks inside, and it will be false policy to destroy them, since, if the fleet does not relieve the town, it will soon be a Greek fortress; and a fortress is ever the better for having walls."

The Capsina was on the point of setting off again on the *Revenge* to join the Greek fleet, and was in a hurry; but though she would have preferred to storm away at Nauplia off-hand, she saw the force of the reasoning.

"You have the elements of good sense," she conceded; "so good-bye, and good luck to you! The *Revenge* sails to-day, and has a very pretty plan in her little head. Oh, you shall see! If there is a scrimmage between the fleets in the harbor, don't fire unless you are sure of your aim. If you touch my ship, I will treat you as I treated the little Frenchman; at least, I will try to. But you are as big as I."

"I will take my punishment like a man from so fair a hand," said Hane, with mock courtesy. And the Capsina glanced darkly at him.

All next day a distant cannonade took place between the Greeks and Turks— the Greeks, on the one hand, preferring to stand off until their enemies were well inside the gulf, the Turks unwilling to enter the narrow sea with that pack of sea-wolves on their heels. But the approach of the Turkish fleet even at the entrance of the gulf so terrified the Kranidiot garrison on the Burdjee, who were convinced that they would be cut off on the island, that they fled by night to the Greek camp, leaving there only Hane and a young Hydriot sailor, with no means of escape, for they took the boats with them. They had made so silent a departure that neither Hane nor Manéthee knew anything of their flight till day dawned, when they woke to find themselves alone. However, as they both entertained a different opinion of the possibility of the Turks gaining the harbor, they breakfasted with extreme cheerfulness, and sudden puffs of laughter seized now one and now the other at this unexpected desertion. Afterwards they spent the morning in a somewhat unrewarded attempt to catch fish off the rocks away from the town. Manéthee, indeed, was caught by a lobster, which the two subsequently ate for dinner.

Now the Capsina and Mitsos had hatched a very pretty plan between them. Seeing that all the Greek fleet was waiting to attack the Turkish fleet in the rear, it was certain that the latter would send their transport and provision vessels on first. So, with the consent of Miaulis, they had for a whole day and night of almost dead calm edged and sidled up the gulf till they were in front of the Turkish fleet. They coaxed the *Revenge* like a child; they took advantage of every shifting current up the coast, the least breath of wind they caught in the sails, and added another and another to it, till the sails were full, and she slid one more step forward.

"And once among the transports," remarked the Capsina, "it will be strange if an orange or an egg gets into Nauplia."

Mitsos laughed.

"I have pity for hungry folk," he said. "Listen, Capsina; there are guns from Nauplia."

Again and again, and all that afternoon, the heavy buffets of the guns boomed across the water; for the Turks in Nauplia, seeing that their fleet was even now at the entrance of the gulf, had opened fire on the Burdjee, where Hane and Manéthee were catching fish. Hane had determined not to fire back, for it was better to reserve himself for the Turkish fleet, especially since there were only two of them to work the guns, and so they sat at the angle farthest away from the town, dabbled their feet in the tepid water, and watched the balls, which for the most part went very wide, dip and ricochet in the bay.

For three days the two fleets manoeuvred idly just outside the gulf; the wind was fitfully light and variable, and for the most part a dead calm prevailed, and the Turks were as unable to pursue their way up the gulf as the Greeks to attack them on the open sea. But at the end of the third inactive day the breeze freshened, and a steadier and more lively air, unusual from this quarter in the summer, blew up the gulf. Had the capitan pasha taken advantage of this, risking therein but little—for the night was clear, and moonrise only an hour or two after sunset—he could have run a straight course before the wind and been at the entrance of Nauplia harbor by morning, exposed, indeed, to the fire of the Burdjee guns, had there been any one to work them, but protected by the guns of the fort. The whole Greek fleet, so far as he knew, except for one brig that had gone sidling up the coast, was some eight miles in his rear, and, with so strangely favorable a wind, his own vessels, though clumsy in the tack or in close sailing, would have run straight before it, and the way was open. Instead, he feared travelling by night; or, perhaps, with that sea-pack in his rear, he did not mean to sail at all, and hove to till morning, sending on, however, a slow-sailing Austrian merchantman in the service of the Sultan, laden with provisions, without escort, for he knew that all the Greek fleet, except that one sailing brig, as like as not on the rocks by this time, was behind him, and he proposed—or did not propose, he only knew—to catch up the merchantman in the morning. What he had not observed was that as night fell, and the breeze got up, the floundering brig straightened herself up like a man lame made miraculously whole, and followed his transport up the gulf.

Soon after moonrise the Austrian furled sail too, and Mitsos, who was on the watch, hove to also, and when morning dawned, red and windy, it showed him the Turkish fleet some eight miles off, the Austrian about three miles from the harbor at Nauplia, and the *Revenge* not more than a mile behind the Austrian.

The Capsina was on deck early, and she surveyed the position with vivid and smiling satisfaction.

"We will not fire," she said to Mitsos, "but we will take her complete. There go her sails up, and there her flag! Why, that is not a Turkish flag."

Mitsos looked at it a moment.

"Two eagles," he said, "and scraggy fowls. It is Austrian, and in the service of the Turk. That is enough, is it not?"

"Quite enough," said the Capsina. "After her!"

It was the swallows to the raven. In a quarter of an hour the Austrian was barely a hundred yards ahead, and Mitsos rather ostentatiously walked forward and took the tarpaulin covering off the very business-like nine-inch gun on the port bow. The bright brass winked pleasantly, with a suggestion of fire, in the sun, and was clearly visible from the deck of the Austrian. He proceeded to sight the gun leisurely to amidships of the chase and just above the water-line, but before he had finished, down came her flag, and her sails followed. The two went aboard and were most cordially received by the captain, a beautiful man with long whiskers and ringleted hair, who spoke no Greek and understood as little. He pointed inquiringly to his own flag, and Mitsos, in reply, merely pointed his finger backward to the Turkish fleet on the horizon and forward to Nauplia. At that the jaw of the beautiful man dropped a little, and he again pointed to the Turkish fleet, and, in eloquent pantomime, washed his hands and tapped his breast, as if to introduce to them the honorable heart which resided there. But again Mitsos shook his head, for if a vessel detaches itself from a fleet, it is not unreasonable to suppose that it has had, or even still has, some connection with that fleet. Then the beautiful man broke into passionate expostulation in an unknown and guttural tongue, and, as further progress could not be made in this conversation, the matter was cut short, and a party of the sailors from the *Revenge* came on board armed to the teeth, while Mitsos, the Capsina, and the reluctant captain returned to the *Revenge*.

Then occurred one of those things which brand the character of a man and his ancestors eternally, and his children with an inherited shame. The capitan pasha, who had just given orders to proceed up the gulf, saw from afar the capture of his merchantman, and supposing that another Greek fleet was waiting for him in ambush ahead, without even sending on a detachment to reconnoitre, put about and beat out of the gulf. From that hour the fate of Nauplia was sealed.

CHAPTER XVI

The sum of Greek energy, like that of Turkey, had now for many weeks been entirely centred round Nauplia. The Sultan had seen months ago that to command Nauplia and hold it an open port was an iron hand on the Peloponnese, and by degrees the Greeks had learned so too. The town had now been blockaded for four months; irregular but efficient troops had guarded all the passes of communication between Nauplia and Corinth; and now, when the Turkish navy turned back out of the gulf after its abortive effort and disgraceful abandonment of the town, Miaulis did not pursue, but took his fleet up the gulf, so that, should the faint-hearted Turk return, he would find the entrance to Nauplia shut and locked by the whole Greek squadron. There Kanaris joined the Capsina again, and, as both she and Mitsos, as well as he, preferred to cruise after the retiring fleet, in the hope of doing some wayside damage to them, to remaining inactive at Nauplia, they obtained leave to follow. The rest, however, supposing that the fall of the town was inevitable, and justly desiring that they who had prevented the fleet coming to its rescue should share in the spoil, remained in the gulf out of shot of the Turkish guns in the fort, and waited for the end.

So once again the *Revenge* and the *Sophia* started on the Turkish trail in the eastern sea. The Ottoman fleet had passed outside Hydra, giving it a wide berth, for they feared another stinging nest of wasps, and the day after the two Greek ships passed close under its lee, so as to cut off a corner from the path taken by the enemy's fleet, for, having left Hydra, their course was certainly to Constantinople. To the Capsina the island seemed remote and distant from her life, external to it. A lounging lad had come between her and it, and to her he loomed gigantic and larger than life. Yet though he was all her nearer field of vision, she knew him further than all, and when she thought of it an incommunicable loneliness was the food of her heart.

The day after passing Hydra the Turkish fleet, huddled together like a flock of sheep and guarded by its great clumsy men-of-war, which sailed in a half circle, with brigs and schooners as vanguard, again came into sight, advancing slowly northward, evidently heading, as they expected, for Constantinople. Kanaris landed at his native island, Psara, and there bought a couple of rickety and hardly seaworthy caiques. They were good enough, however, for the purpose for which he wanted them, and after spending half a day there purchasing the necessary oil and fuel for a fire-ship they went northward again after the Turks, and caught them up only when they were clear of the archipelago. The two Greek brigs kept well out of range of the big Turkish guns, for their own were but light in comparison, and they would have to come perilously close to the big men-of-war to fire with effect.

Day after day the wind was so light a breath that it would have been impossible to approach with the fire-ships, except very slowly, whereas speed was almost an essential to success; moreover, in the open seas, two caiques coming up from two rakish-looking brigs might have attracted the attention even of the indolently minded. So they waited, keeping out to the west of the Turks, till they should approach the northern group of islands outside the Hellespont. There, with the shelter of the land near, and the probability of squally winds from the high ground of the Troad, a favorable opportunity might offer. Mitsos and Kanaris were to sail the one; the other was intrusted to two Psarian sailors, who professed to know their use.

That month of attendance-dancing on the Turks was strangely pleasant to the Capsina. Since her interview with Suleima her self-control had begun to be a habit with her, a sort of crust over the fire of her passion, which, so to speak, would bear the weight of daily and hourly sociability with Mitsos. For days she had fed herself on a diet of wisdom, taking the dose, like a sick man, in pills and capsules; tasteless it seemed, and useless, yet the course was operative. He, now that the Capsina was a friend of the family, spoke often of his wife to the girl, and by degrees such talk was less bitter to her in the hearing. She had faced the inevitable, and in a manner accepted it, and though the sight of the lad and the touch of him was no less keenly dear, though all that he was held an incomparable charm for her, she knew now that what was so much to her was nothing to him. He, for his part, was in his customary exuberance of boyishness, and she, with a control not less heroical, showed a lightness and naturalness which could not but deceive him, so normal was the manner of her intercourse with him.

By the 1st of November they were passing Lesbos on the east; on the 4th—for day by day went by without more than an hour or two of breeze in its circle of windless hours—the island was still a blue cloud on the southeast. Next day, however, they began to feel the backwater from the current out of the Hellespont which moves up the coast, and Kanaris knew that there was one chance more only before the ships reached the mouth of the straits and were safe under the castles which guarded it.

That day he came on board the *Revenge*, which towed the two caiques, with the Psarians who were to sail the second, and laid his plans before the Capsina.

"All hangs," he said, "on whether they take the narrow channel between Tenedos and the land or go outside the island. If they go outside, we shall have to make an attempt in the open sea, and that I do not like the littlest bit, for they cannot have failed to see the *Revenge*, so that we must seem to approach from her; and indeed by now, when a caique comes from a Greek brig, they know what that caique means."

"You mean you will have a long sail first," said the Capsina, "and a long row afterwards."

"That, and not only that," said Kanaris, "the whole fleet will see us in the open, so we must make the attempt by night, which is far less sure a job."

"It happened in the gulf of Nauplia," remarked Mitsos.

"They were not acquainted with fire-ships then," said Kanaris, "whereas now, between one thing and another, they are no longer strangers. But if they pass between the island and the main-land, first, we have better chance of a breeze; secondly, they cannot make the straits at night, for they are narrow, and there is a current; therefore they will anchor for the night, and we can approach very early in the morning, and, in addition, the *Revenge* can shelter unseen behind the headlands, so that she will be near to us. Also the fleet will be scattered; we can choose our ship, and run less risk from the rest."

Two days afterwards Tenedos rose from the north, but still no wind sprang up, and the Turkish fleet sidled and lumbered along with sails spread to catch the slightest breeze, but hanging all day idly. Next morning, however, a brisker air sprang up from the west, and making some five knots an hour, they drew rapidly closer. By three o'clock it was already clear that the Turks meant to pass inside the island, and the wind continuing, and showing signs of increasing towards nightfall, the *Revenge*, which towed the caiques, stopped to pick up Kanaris and the two Psarians, leaving the *Sophia* hove to to wait for their return. The wind had swept clear the sky, and the myriad stars made a gray shimmering of brightness on the water, sufficient to sail by. They carried no lights for an hour after sunset; the lanterns on the Turks were visible, and, as Mitsos remarked, "where you can see lights, thence can lights be seen."

Tenedos, comely in shape as a woman and tall, drew near, black against the sky on their port bow. On the starboard bow were the lights of the nearest Turkish ships, and, the wind still holding, they cast anchor under shadow of the land, some mile away from where the Turks were anchored. Like wolves they had followed the trail; here was the lair.

The night was very brisk and fresh, and the west wind sang through the cool air. Under shelter of the land the water was smooth, and in that mirror the stars shone and wheeled with scarcely less clearness than overhead. A planet, low in the east, had risen above the hills of the Troad, and traced across the water a silvery path, scarcely less luminous than a young moon. Soon after midnight Kanaris and Mitsos cast off in the one caique, the Psarians in the other, and, with the Capsina waving them farewell and good luck, rowed out of the sheltered bay till they should get the wind. But they had hardly gone a furlong from land when the wind dropped again, and they were left becalmed. The current of the backwater, however, drifted them gradually on, though diagonally to the proper path, yet diminishing the distance between them and the Turks. On the dropping of the wind a mist rose about mast high from the surface of the water, and the lights from the Turkish ships showed blurred and fogged. The ripples washed idly against the boat, rocking it gently to and fro, otherwise they were in a vast silence.

Kanaris frowned and frowned; the man was a frown.

"It is the devil's work, Mitsos," he said. "There is nothing to be done but to row in the darkness as near as we dare and wait for a wind. If there is none an hour before dawn, we shall simply row up to the nearest Turk and set light to the fire-ship. That will not please me."

"If there is no wind, where is the use?" asked Mitsos. "The flames will rise straight; they will toast their bread in our fire and then spit at it till it goes out."

"Also we cannot pick our vessel in the dark," said Kanaris. "Well, we must do the best. Come, lad, row."

They rowed on cautiously and silently till the blurred lights began to show clearer through the mist. The second caique was a little astern, and soon joined the other. Kanaris told them what to do, and giving Mitsos the first watch, he lay down, and sleep was on him as speedy and calm as if he was in his own house at home.

Mitsos sat with an oar in his hand, by which he kept the same position towards the light of the Turkish ships, whistled softly to himself, and kept an eye on the Greek sailors' "beacon star," the dipping of which was the signal for his waking Kanaris. Less phlegmatic than the other, his heart beat full and fast at the risk and adventure of the next day; he pictured to himself how they would run the ship in; he contrasted with a shudder the pleasing excitement of this adventure with the flaming horror of the other at Nauplia, and when the beacon dipped he awoke Kanaris. The latter, wide awake at once, took the oar from him and looked round.

"I dreamed there was a fine wind blowing," he said. "Good sleep to you, little Mitsos."

It was in the aqueous light of that dim hour before dawn when Kanaris awoke him. The air was tingling and cold, and the mist of the night was drifting eastward. Between them and Tenedos to the west, a mile away, the sea view was clear; in front a little mist still hung between them and the nearest Turk; a furlong off farther to the east it was still thick. Kanaris had a smile for him.

"Look," he said; "it is already clearing. Wet your finger, and you will feel it cold from the west. Oh, Mitsos, my dream is true: the wind will be here with the dawn. It and the dawn are waking together."

Mitsos sniffed with head thrown back.

"It is so," he said; "I smell it."

"There are two ships near us," said Kanaris, "both of the biggest kind. The farther one you and I take, the nearer the Psarians. Pray God, they are not utterly fools. With wind I would burn that ship with a tobacco-pipe."

Mitsos smiled sleepily but hugely.

"A fine big tobacco-pipe is this caique," he said. "Are the sails fastened?"

"I have done all while you slept," said Kanaris. "Look and see if it satisfies you. The turpentine only remains. There are the cans; we will do that now. After that no more tobacco."

"That is the drawback to fire-ships," said Mitsos.

Kanaris had nailed the sails to the mast so that they would stay there burning till all the canvas was consumed, and fastened the yards with chains so that they too would blaze until they were entirely burned, and not drop. The brushwood he had piled in the bow, half-mast high, and it only remained to pour the cans of turpentine over sails, deck, and fuel. Even as they were thus employed the stars paled, and were quenched, and with the first definite saffron light in the east a sudden shiver shook the sails, and the boat lifted and moved a little. After a moment another whisper came from the east; the sails flapped, and then began to draw. Kanaris and Mitsos went to the stern, and then Kanaris took the rudder, while Mitsos kindled an oil-lamp and soaked a little dry moss with turpentine, wherewith to fire the ship. A sudden rose flush leaped up to the zenith from the east; the boat rose to a new-born ripple and came down with a cluck into the trough of it; one star only, as if forgotten, hung unextinguished in the sky. The wind had yet scarcely reached the Turkish ships, and they still hung on their anchors, their stern swung round by the current, presenting a starboard broadside to the wind, which now blew shrill and steady, taking the caique along with hissing forefoot and strained canvas. Already Kanaris and Mitsos had passed under the bows of the first Turkish ship, and were not a hundred yards from the second when the Psarian sailors set light too soon to their fire-ship, and, jumping into the boat they towed behind, rowed away. Kanaris gave one grunt of dissatisfaction, for he saw that they had miscalculated their time, and that the fire-ship would only just catch in the bowsprit of the Turk, and also that they had fired it too soon, giving the alarm perhaps to the others. But the wind was brisk, and he had

227

hardly turned his head again, when Mitsos said quietly, "It is time."

Kanaris nodded, put the helm hard aport, and jumped into the boat behind, as Mitsos thrust into the heap of brushwood at the bottom of the mast the pile of burning moss he had kindled at the lantern. He had calculated his distance to precision. The fire-ship struck as Mitsos jumped, staggering with the shock, into the smaller boat, just abaft the forechains, and was instantly glued to the side of the Turk by the force of the wind. In a moment a pillar of flame leaped from the deck to the top of her mast; an eddy of fire shot out like a sword-stroke across the deck of the Turk. Next moment the brushwood in their bows caught, and rose, a screaming curtain of fire, over the forepart of the other. Nor was the fire-ship of the Psarians without use to them. It had caught only in the bowsprit, and was even then drifting harmlessly away to leeward; but at least it burned bravely and poured out dense volumes of smoke, which, coming down the wind, hid them from their victim. And half blinded and choked with it, yet grateful, they took up their oars and rowed away south till they were a safe distance from the anchored ships.

They did not stop till they were some half-mile from them, and then, panting and exhausted, they paused and looked back. The flames were well hold of the ship, and as they mounted and triumphed, they roared with a great hollow uproar of bellowing.

Kanaris stroked his beard complacently.

"Will that be enough for them to toast their bread by, little Mitsos?" he said. "I am thinking they will be toasting their souls in hell. Satan will see to their fuel now, I am thinking."

But Mitsos, tender-hearted, felt a certain pity through his exultation.

"Poor devils!" he said.

And that was their requiem.

But the pity passed, and the exultation remained. The stories of Greek fugitives, the monstrous sights he had himself seen at Elatina on the roads, throughout the breadth and length of his land, had become part of the lad's nature. Lust, rapacity, murder, crimes unspeakable had here their answer in the swirling flame and stream of smoke which stained the pearly beauty of that autumn morning. The wind had died down again; for scarcely an hour, with divine fitness, had it blown, and it seemed as if God had sent it just and solely for their deed. And they watched their deed, a sign of fire. From other ships boats had put off to try to rescue the doomed crew, yet as often as they got near the fierce heat of the flames drove them back. A pillar of murky flames swathed the masts, and even as they watched, one, eaten through at its base by the fire, tottered and fell flickering overboard, carrying with it a length of the charred bulwarks. Many leaped overboard, some with their clothes on fire, but few reached the boats; planks started from the deck, the bowsprit fell hissing into the sea, and before long the boards opened great hissing cracks to the air. Then the destruction reached the waterline. With a shrieking fizz the sea poured in, and in smoke and steam, midway between fire and water, she began to sink, bows first. The deck-beams jumped upward like children's jack-toys as the compressed air forced them, guns broke loose and slid down the inclined boards into the sea, and with a rending and bubbling she disappeared. Kanaris watched in silence, with the air of an artist contemplating his finished picture, and once again he fell on enthusiasm, which was rare with him.

"Thus perish the enemies of Christ!" he cried. Then, half ashamed of himself at this unwonted exhibition of feeling, "You and I did that, little Mitsos," he said. "Shall we get back to the Capsina? For it is finished."

Mitsos had been watching also in silence, with the thought that they were of the race who had taken Suleima, had dishonored Nikola's wife, burning like the ship he watched in his head, and as he took the first stroke with his oar, "God give them their portion in hell!" he cried.

Kanaris laughed.

"Do not trouble yourself," he said; "it is certain."

By the time they were close in to the promontory behind which they had left the Capsina, the stain of smoke had rolled away eastward, and now hung over the Troad. The little breeze there was was from the west, but hardly perceptible, and even if there had been any thought of pursuit from the Turks, they could not have sailed after them. But they must have been seen from the nearest ship, and while they were still about a hundred yards from the promontory, a sudden spurt of fire appeared at a port-hole of the ship which the Psarians had tried to destroy, and before the report of the gun reached them, the shot, fired horizontally, splashed like a great fish only two hundred yards from them, and with a whistle and buffet of wind, ricochetted over their heads and on to shore.

At that Kanaris laughed aloud, and Mitsos, standing up in the boat, waved his cap with a cheer of derision. Then bending to their oars again, they were soon behind the promontory.

They were received with shouts of triumph by the Capsina and the crew, and the unsuccessful Psarians joined in their welcome to the full extent of their heart and voice. Envy was dumb. Once had Mitsos, once had Kanaris destroyed a man-of-war; now the two had destroyed another together; and by the hands of the two not less than twenty-five hundred Turks had perished. Kanaris came up on the deck first, and the Capsina rushed at him with open arms, and kissed him hard on both cheeks. A moment after Mitsos followed.

She ran to him, then stopped, and for a moment her eyes dropped.

She paused perceptibly; and he, flushed with triumph, joy and the music of their welcome dancing in his eyes, stopped too. The color had been struck suddenly from her face, and burned only in two bright spots on her cheeks. But before he had time to wonder she recovered herself.

"Welcome, thrice welcome, little Mitsos!" she cried; and throwing her arms round his neck, and drawing his head down, she kissed him as she had kissed Kanaris. Her eyes were close to his; his short, crisp mustache brushed the curve below her under-lip; his breath was warm on her. And what it cost her to do that, and how cheap she held the cost, God knows.

They waited behind cover of the land till dark drew on, and then, since they were land-bound, they manned the boats and warped the *Revenge* round the promontory. The Turkish ships, all but one which now lay black and fish-haunted in the ooze of the channel, had weighed anchor again, but were moving only very slowly northward. Once free of the southern cape of Tenedos, the Greeks found a breeze in the open, and making a southwesterly course, sailed quietly all night, and in the morning found the *Sophia* waiting for them. Here Kanaris and the two Psarians left the *Revenge* to join their own ship, and once more Mitsos and the Capsina were alone.

That day it seemed that the sun and the elements joined in their audacious success. Great white clouds, light and rainless, made a splendid procession on the blue overhead, and their shadows, purple in the sea, raced over the blue below. The *Revenge* danced gayly like a prancing horse, playing and coquetting with the waves, and they in turn threw wreaths of laughing spray at her, which she dashed aside. Under the light wind their full sails were easily carried, and once again an irresistible lightness of heart, bred of success, and health, and sea, as in the first days together, possessed the Capsina. That bad moment in the morning had passed; and, with a woman's variable mood, she fell into the other extreme. Nothing mattered; she loved Mitsos, and he did not love her; here was the case stated. In any case he liked her; he gave her shadow for substance; so she would play with the shadow as a child plays.

After their midday dinner they sat on deck, and Mitsos again told over the adventure of the day before.

"And it was odd," he said, "that when I saw the ship blazing, when, in fact, I saw that that was accomplished for which I had come, I was suddenly sorry.

Now, Capsina, you are a woman, and understand things men do not. Why did I feel sorry?"

"Because you are a very queer kind of a lad."

Mitsos reflected.

"No, I don't think I am," he said; "indeed, it seems to me that I am just like others. As for Kanaris, he stroked his beard and said they had gone to hell."

"So they had."

Mitsos smiled, and looked at Michael, who had flopped himself down on deck, with his back to them.

"No doubt; but you are not telling me what I asked. Oh, great, wise Michael, come here. May I pull him by the tail, Capsina?"

"Certainly, and he *may* bite you."

"I think not. Oh, Michael, do not lick my face. You know Suleima washes my face sometimes, Capsina. That is only when she has cut my hair, and the little bits are everywhere, and the most part down my neck. But though it is kind of her, I had sooner go to the barber's for it. What can we do next when we get back to Nauplia?"

"You want another cruise?"

"Surely. Are there not more ships in the Gulf of Corinth? Indeed, I think those were of the best weeks in my life."

"That is not a bad idea, little Mitsos," she responded. "Whether there are Turkish ships in the gulf I do not know, but we might make ourselves very useful there. There is Galaxidi, for instance; we ought to have a naval station there."

"Galaxidi?" said Mitsos. "I know what is in your mind."

"What, then, is in my mind?"

"The baby Sophia you left there," said he. "Indeed, Capsina, you should have been a mother. For Suleima said you had a way with babies."

"I should have married Christos," she asked, "and been a fish-wife of Hydra? Indeed, little Mitsos, I knew not in how high esteem you held me."

And she got up from where she sat, and made him a great flouncing mock curtsey.

"Yet you are right," she continued, "I had the baby Sophia in my mind among many other things"—and she thought to herself how it was there she had learned of Suleima—"but for that reason I would not go. It is of the ship-station I am thinking. Once we have a station there, how foolish become the Turkish forts at Lepanto. Nor should it be long before we take Lepanto itself. Yet, oh, Mitsos, sometimes even in the heat and glory of it all, there is nothing I would love so well as to go quietly home and live in peace again, for of late I have had no peace; I have had no moments of my own."

"They could not be better spent," said Mitsos.

"If that is so, God will take account of them. But sometimes my heart is a child; it cries out for toys and playfellows and silly games of play, knowing that its house and its food are secure, or rather not needing to know it, and wanting only to be amused. But I doubt the toys are broken, and the playfellows are all grown up."

And she stopped abruptly.

"But that is not often," she continued after a moment. "There are other things, are there not?—and I am grown up, too—glory; red vengeance; the sharing in a great work. No, I would not sacrifice a minute of these for all the games of play. Also I think that I and the silliest boy in Greece played more in one week, that first week of our voyage, than is given to most. See, it is nearly sunset; what of the evening?"

Mitsos got up and went forward. The *Sophia* was bowling along a mile to port, running, like them, straight before the wind and keeping the pace. On the starboard bow Scyros had just risen low and dim above the sea, but the horizon was sailless. The sun was near setting; and a golden haze, curtain above curtain of thinnest gauze, stretched across the western heaven. The sea seemed molten with light. High overhead swung a slip of crescent moon, still ashy and colorless. Above the sun stretched a thin line of crimson-carded fleeces of cloud; the wind was soft and steady. He went back to the girl and sat down again.

"It will be very fair weather," he said, and she answered not, but through her head his voice went ringing on and on persistently, like an endless echo, saying the words again and again.

They stopped at Hydra a day, both to give the news and learn it. Nauplia was still blockaded; not a shot had been fired on either side. The Turkish garrison it was supposed were still not without hope that help would come; the Greeks, equally confident it would not, made no effort to storm the place, but waited till famine should do their work for them, and indeed the end could not be far off. Kolocotrones was not there; it was the earnest prayer of all the Greeks that he would be absent when the town fell, for otherwise it would be but little spoil that fell outside the brass helmet. And Christos Capsas, the once betrothed of the Capsina, who, with others like him, stopped at home at Hydra nominally to defend the place in case the Turks made a descent on it, spat on the ground.

"He is a dirty, greedy ruffian," he said.

He and his wife, slovenly and shrill-voiced, wearing the Capsina's wedding-gift, the heirloom girdle, and misbecoming it strangely, were dining with the girl on her ship, and she, looking across at Mitsos, saw his nose turned rather scornfully in the air.

"Yet he is a brave man, Christos," said she. "Do you not think so? He runs risk cheerfully, anyhow."

"For the sake of fatness and riches," grumbled Christos.

The Capsina, who loathed Kolocotrones, suddenly found herself taking his part when Christos called him to account. She laughed, not very kindly.

"Yet you are not thin, Christos," she said, "and they say you are getting rich. Ah, well, God makes some to stay at home, and others to go abroad, and thus to each is his work allotted. Now of the island what news?"

"The news of Father Nikola, Father no longer. You have heard?"

"No," said the Capsina. "He is like the lemon: the older and nearer to ripeness it gets, the sourer it grows. He must be nearly ripe in my poor thought."

"Well, then, he has become the orange," said Christos. "I love him not, yet he is sour no longer."

And he told the story of the return of his wife.

The Capsina listened in silence.

"An old man like that," she said, "and she, you say, also old. Will you love and be loved when you are gray-headed, Mitsos? And the two old folks have gone off on the brig together! How absurd it is, and how—how splendid!"

"They go hand-in-hand," said Christos, "and when the boys laugh, they laugh too."

"Nikola laughing!" said the Capsina. "I did not think he knew how."

"Yes, with the open mouth," said Christos.

The Capsina leaned forward across the table.

"He loves this old woman, you say, as others love?" she asked. "His eye glows for her? He is hot and cold?"

"That is what one does when one loves," put in the experienced Mitsos. "How did you know, Capsina?"

She laughed.

"Have I sailed with you for weeks, and not seen the thought of Suleima with you? May not I look at you now and then? And she loves him, gray-headed, sour old Nikola? That is hardly less strange."

She looked across at the fat, white face of Christos's wife, at her slovenly habit and uncleanly hands.

"Yet there are many strange things in the world," she said. "Make Michael his dinner, will you, little Mitsos?"

Christos's wife stared with interest as Mitsos put gravy, bones, bread, and, lastly, a piece of meat in Michael's wooden bowl.

"It is not right!" she cried, shrilly; "you must not feed a dog like a Christian."

"I honor his name, cousin," said the Capsina, laughing.

"His name! That is as unsuited to a dog as his food."

"Therefore I honor him," said the Capsina; and the wife, making nothing of this, thought it more prudent to be silent; and Christos, equally puzzled, hushed her.

"You do not understand," he said, which was true enough.

Next day they set sail again for Nauplia; the blockading fleet was stationed outside the harbor, and, having anchored, the Capsina, with Kanaris and Mitsos, went off to the admiral's ship to make report. As the news spread from crew to crew, the shouting rose and redoubled, and Suleima, who had come down with the littlest one, on the news of their arrival, to the quay, could scarce get at Mitsos for the press, and for the time the two had to be content with letting their eyes seek and find each other from afar, saying that it was well with them. But the Capsina had gone back to her ship, and was alone.

CHAPTER XVII

The last days of the beleaguered town had begun, and it was only from fear of treachery—not, alas! unwarranted—on the part of the Greeks that the besieged still held out. The scenes at the capitulation of Navarin, not eighteen months old, the repetition of them at Athens, scarcely six months ago, had not encouraged the Turks to hope for honorable dealings with their enemies, or rather with the half-brigand chiefs, such as Kolocotrones and Poniropoulos, who commanded the forces. Hypsilantes, they had learned from the previous negotiations which were concluded by him and taken out of his hand by Kolocotrones, was no more than a cipher put first among other figures, and while there was still the faintest hope, they had determined not to surrender.

Since the beginning of December the stress of famine had set in; already all the horses had been killed for food, their bones boiled to make a thin and acrid broth, and the man who caught a couple of rats was reckoned fortunate. Children, wasted to skeletons, with the hollow eyes of old men, were found dead in the street; their fathers thanked Allah that their suffering was over. A soldier one day fell from sheer exhaustion as he was mounting the steep steps of the fortress, the Palamede, cutting his hand badly, and a comrade, coming up a minute or two later, found him sitting down and greedily licking up the blood which dripped from the wound. At length it was impossible to hold the Palamede any longer; those who had to go down to the lower town to fetch the diminished rations were too weak to remount the long ascent, and on the 11th of December it was abandoned, the gate between it and the lower town was closed, and the whole garrison quartered in the latter.

From the ships Miaulis had seen the lines of soldiers filing out on the evening of the 11th, and gave notice of it to Poniropoulos. The latter, seeing that no treasure was possibly to be obtained from there, notified the abandonment of the fort to Hypsilantes, who with infinite difficulty was hauled up over the parapeted wall which defended the steps, and, with a voice tremulous, not with emotion, but breathlessness, took possession of it in the name of the supreme government of the Greek republic. There was still a good deal of powder in the magazines, and this somewhat barren triumph was announced to the rest of the army by volleys of artillery. The top of the fortress was quite enveloped in smoke, and the effect, if not the cause, was exceedingly magnificent.

But the sound of the guns and the smoke of the firing carried too far. Kolocotrones, still encamped on the top of the Dervenaki, in the hope that the Turkish garrison of Nauplia would attempt to cut their way through the Greeks and escape to Corinth, was waiting there for the end, seeing that the most part of the treasure of Nauplia was exhausted in purchasing provisions, and that a fine harvest might be expected from the ransom of the Turks of rank who escaped. They must pass over the hills of the Dervenaki, and he would thus gain the honor of their capture, and also, what was the dearer to him, the money of their ransom. But repeated volleys from the Palamede, while no firing came from the lower town, could mean but one thing. Were the Turks opening fire on the Greeks, they would use the guns of the lower fortress at shorter range rather than those of the Palamede. Again no answer came from either side, the Burdjee or the fleet. Also his practised ear could distinguish even at that distance the hollow buffet of blank firing from the sharper noise of the discharge of shot or shell. So on went the brass helmet, and at the head of his eight thousand irregular but strangely efficient troops, he set out for the town. Certainly none could say that he spared himself. He marched on foot with the others, all smiles and bluff encouragement, going, with all his fifty years and gray head, with a foot as light as a boy's. He roared out strange and stimulating brigand songs one after the other, the men taking up the choruses; he sat with the rest under a desolating shower for dinner, and when the repeated rain put out the fire on which he was roasting a sheep for himself and his staff, he laughed, and cut off with his sword a great hunk of flesh more than half raw, and ate it as if it had been meat for a king. They had set off in such haste that they had forgotten to bring wine with them. It mattered not; rain-water, he said, was the best of drinks, and he washed down the raw lamb with a draught from a puddle among stones. Then when at the last a flask of spirits was produced, he would none of it; he had drunk his fill, let those who had not yet drunk have the brandy. Of what good were meat and drink but to fill the stomach? His own was full, and he licked his greasy fingers.

All this endeared him in a savage way to his men. Here at least was a man who was of themselves, made generalissimo of the Peloponnesian troops by the supreme council. Indeed, had he not been without a sense of honor where treasure was concerned, they could have had no better. Petrobey had shown himself weak at Tripoli; Hypsilantes had never been otherwise; Mavrogordatos was busy with his titles.

As his custom was, Kolocotrones came laughing and shouting into the Greek army with a joke and a slap on the back for his friends, an outburst of genuine affection for his son, Panos, total indifference to the cold faces of the Mainats, and an enormous appetite.

"Tell me not a word of news, Panos," he cried, "till I have eaten. Bad news is the better supported when one has food; good news tastes sweeter after food."

Early next morning Mitsos was on the quay, having spent the night at home, but returning to the ship to ask if the Capsina would not come that day to see them. As he passed Kolocotrones's tent he came out and recognized him.

"Mitsos Codones, are you not," he said, "and connected with the clan of Maina? I have heard of that business of yours and Kanaris with the fire-ship. It was not badly done; no, it was not badly done."

Mitsos bristled like a collie dog. The manner of the man was insufferable.

"As you say, it was not badly done," he remarked, "but there was no booty to be got by it." And he turned on his heel.

Kolocotrones broke out into a great laugh. He was rather proud than otherwise at his own adeptness in matters of plunder.

"You are sulky, silent folk, you of Maina," he said.

Mitsos turned back again slowly, and let his eye rest on a level with the top of the spike of Kolocotrones's helmet.

"Little men have very fine helmets," he said.

That struck home. Kolocotrones's face flared.

"Were you of the army, I would have you whipped," he snarled.

"But I am of the navy just now," said Mitsos. "Yet if you will, come and whip me yourself. Or shall I call some three or four men to help you?"

He waited a moment, and then turned again. Kolocotrones itched to send a knife into him, but as Kanaris and Mitsos were just now the most popular pair in Greece, it was difficult to say exactly where such an action would end. For him, very likely, in the ooze of the harbor at Nauplia.

Mitsos had not gone a dozen paces when a buzzing murmur rose, which grew into a shout, and the pasty Panos rushed out and pointed to the wall above the northern gate of Nauplia. A white flag was flying there.

Kolocotrones saw it and slapped his thigh.

"It was ever so!" he cried. "I come, and they surrender."

Mitsos could not resist a parting shot.

"Not so," he cried; "you come, and the hungry are filled, and your pockets are heavy. Go, then, on the errand of mercy, and good luck to your bargains!"

Kolocotrones looked angrily round, but his popularity with his men being due to the fact that he so put himself on an equality with them, he found them laughing, as if the joke had been directed against one of them, not against their general. From all sides the men poured out of their tents to look at the flag, and Mitsos found himself in a crowd of these, to whom the news of the last fire-ship had only come when they arrived with Kolocotrones, and he was pulled this way and that and made to drink wine, and had to tell the story again, and yet again.

Presently after, Panos, also bearing the flag of truce, was sent up to conduct the Turks down to the council of chiefs. Kolocotrones was the chairman, and with him were Miaulis, admiral of the fleet, Poniropoulos, Hypsilantes, and Petrobey.

Selim and Ali, governors of Argos, represented the besieged. It was pitiful to see even two of the hated pashas so weak with lack of food. Yet, with the fine manners of their race, they bowed and smiled on their way through the crowd, and exchanged little compliments with Panos in rather halting Greek, and spoke of the freshness of the morning. Mitsos had shouldered his way back through the press, and recognizing and being recognized by his friend Selim, who had promised to put a knife into him if ever they met except in time of truce, hardly knew the man. But with a rough sort of kindness, half of pity, half of mockery from the inborn joy of seeing the foe like this, he took a loaf from a baker's cart standing near, and gave it to him.

"For to-morrow, at least," he said; and seeing the hungry gratitude which leaped to the man's eye, was ashamed at having done so little, and at the half-taunt in his words. Selim had taken one fine bite out of it before he entered the tent of Kolocotrones, and was, with watering mouth, waiting for another. He stood with it concealed under his soldier's cloak, but in sitting down it fell back from his shoulders, and before he had time to shift the loaf to new concealment Kolocotrones had seen it. He broke out into a hoarse, rude laugh, pointing at it.

"Truly it was time to come to terms," he said, "when the pashas snatch a loaf as they go by. Eat it, man; we will talk after."

Selim bowed.

"With your permission, I will," he said; "for we came in haste this morning, and without breakfast."

Kolocotrones laughed again.

"And maybe without dinner last night!" he cried.

Selim raised his eyebrows, as if in silent deprecation of the rudeness of an inferior which it was not worth the breath to answer, and breaking the loaf in half, passed the one part with quiet dignity to Ali, who took it without haste, and ate it like a man already surfeited. Kolocotrones wriggled in his chair with coarse delight.

"I warrant that tastes good," he said.

Ali looked at him a moment without speaking. Then, "We are here to discuss terms of capitulation, I understand," he said, "not the matter of our diet."

"That would be but little food for discussion there," said Kolocotrones, unabashed, and grinning at Poniropoulos, who went into wide-mouthed and toothless laughter.

Ali merely shrugged his shoulders and continued to eat his bread slowly. Indeed, it was a strange reversing of the position of Turkish pashas and Greek countrymen, and, in spite of those long years when the Turks had ground down even to starvation their oppressed province, it seemed a breach of manners to the other officers that two of them should sit cutting their blunt jokes at the men whom the wheel of destiny had brought low in its revolution, but whom it had altogether failed to rob of the dignity of high breeding in the very stress and publicity of their misfortunes. And when they had finished Ali spoke again.

"Selim Pasha and I are here," he said, "to ask what terms you will give us for our capitulation. For ourselves we offer the same as we offered before: safe transport—not such transport as was given to those at Navarin," and he looked at Poniropoulos—"to Asia Minor, and the retention of one-third of our property. It is now six months since the ships which were to transport us were spoken of. We imagine they must be ready."

"It is six months ago since those proposals were made," said Kolocotrones, becoming suddenly business-like; "for six months longer has the siege and the expense of the siege been maintained. No, no, we must find something different to that. Moreover, the treasure in Nauplia is not the same as it was then."

"But where has it gone," said Ali, "if not to the pockets of the Greeks?"

"And from where did provisions come," asked Kolocotrones, "except from whither the treasure has gone?"

Ali laughed.

"Is there not a considerable balance?" he asked.

Kolocotrones screwed up his eye in malevolent amusement.

"I have not lately examined the accounts. But what if there is? The bargain was made; we gave provisions and received money. Well, you have made your proposals; in an hour's time you shall hear ours."

Petrobey rose.

"My quarters are close, gentlemen," he said; "may I give you lodging and refreshment there while we consult?"

Ali and Selim accordingly withdrew, and Petrobey having conducted them to his quarters, where Yanni was charged with giving them food, returned to Kolocotrones's tent.

239

Already high words were passing, not on the subject of the terms of the capitulations—for that seemed to be but a secondary matter in the minds at least of Kolocotrones and Poniropoulos—but as to how the booty should subsequently be divided.

Kolocotrones was on his feet, stamping and thumping the table.

"Who was appointed commander-in-chief by the council but I?" he cried. "It is I who will take possession of Nauplia; it is I who will receive and—and distribute the booty."

Miaulis, who was seated, had hitherto taken no part in the discussion, but at this he spoke.

"The distribution of Kolocotrones!" he said, blandly. "The Lord help us all!"

This was disconcerting, for even Kolocotrones acknowledged the integrity and honesty of the young admiral, and could make no *tu-quoque* rejoinder.

"Then what do you propose?" he asked.

"That those who have besieged Nauplia for all these months have some one to represent them in the division of the booty," he said, with that wonderful, frank manner of his. "We expect fair-play from General Kolocotrones; that is no reason why we should not see that we obtain it."

Petrobey rose to his feet. That opportunity for which he had been waiting ever since Nikolas had given him the example at Tripoli was come.

"You were not at the siege of Tripoli, admiral," he said. "I was, and I do not in the least expect fair-play from Kolocotrones. Oh, hear me out; you will be the gainers; even you, Kolocotrones. I warn you, if he gets hold of the treasure of Nauplia, not a piaster will you see. What has his share in the siege been? This, that he has sold provisions to the garrison at starvation rates. Once already, at Tripoli, would he have made the name of Greece a scoffing and a by-word had it not been for the deed of a better and a wiser man than any of us, Nikolas, who stormed the place out by hand. At the Dervenaki what did he do? He let the Albanians by, as you all know. For that he claimed, out of what Niketas took, thirty thousand piasters. So be warned. And now I can only follow the example of Nikolas, and withdraw from this assembly. Hard blows are better than hard words, and, to my taste at least, better than money. The Mainats go with me, for I take it that the siege is over."

Petrobey distinctly had the last word, and the last word was a true one. All knew that he spoke facts about Kolocotrones, and none could say that he spoke from interested motives. He rose as he finished, and turned to Kolocotrones.

"I give notice," he said, "that the Mainats are withdrawn, the work of the siege being over."

Miaulis jumped to his feet.

"And all good go with you, Petrobey," he said. "I would that the fleet were as loyal to me as your Mainats are; but God knows what might happen if I went back saying that I had resigned all claim to the booty. There would, I think, be an admiral the less, and I doubt if there would be so many generals."

Petrobey shook hands warmly with him and went out, leaving silence in the tent. Many Mainats were collected outside, and his voice, as he spoke to them, was distinctly heard.

"The Mainats are withdrawn," he said; "we march in an hour."

And a clear young voice answered.

"What has the greedy old brigand been doing, uncle?" it asked.

"Be silent, Mitsos," said Petrobey. And inside Miaulis giggled audibly, and the Prince Hypsilantes visibly smiled. Even Kolocotrones took a moment to recover himself, but he recovered completely, for it was no time to think of dignity when the spoils of Nauplia were yet dangling.

"We will arrange the claims of the fleet," he said.

Again Miaulis interrupted.

"You have not yet arranged who takes possession of Nauplia, or, rather, who takes possession of the treasure," he said. "For me, I propose that it be registered in the presence of us all here assembled."

Kolocotrones could not well afford to quarrel, not only with the rest of the army, but with the whole fleet. From outside a murmur, ever rising shriller and higher as the cause, no doubt, of the withdrawal of the Mainats became known, warned him not to go too far. The whole Greek fleet was there. If he was determined to exercise his prerogative of commander-in-chief, he was not at all sure that they might not determine to resist it. And while he still hesitated Miaulis spoke again.

"I represent the entire fleet," he said, "and the fleet prevented help coming to Nauplia by sea. Also, if so I order, the fleet will storm the place. I was appointed, I may remind you, by the council which appointed Kolocotrones."

Kolocotrones lost his head and his temper.

"By the blood of all the saints," he cried, "what do you want?"

"A voice in the matter," said Miaulis.

"Do you not trust me?" he stormed.

"The fleet, who do not know you, have no reason to trust you," said Miaulis, "and I am in the interest of this fleet."

"But these others know me!" cried Kolocotrones, pointing to Hypsilantes and Poniropoulos.

"And Petrobey knew you," said Miaulis.

Kolocotrones drew back his upper lip from over his teeth and showed them in a snarl. If he had to yield, he would yield only step by step.

"Nauplia then will be taken possession of by Admiral Miaulis and myself," he said, "he representing the fleet, I the army. Is that agreed?"

"No, it is not agreed!" cried Poniropoulos. "You came here yesterday, Kolocotrones. What of me and mine, who have stood the burden of the siege? I demand that the treasure be registered and divided in just proportions. Who receives the submission of the town I care not."

"It is a fine thing," said Kolocotrones, bitterly, "when the commander-in-chief has to be watched like a school-boy lest he should steal sweets."

Again there was silence in the tent; only outside the murmur of men rose higher, almost to a roar.

"And, by the tears of the Virgin, I will not stand it!" he screamed, now red and flaming. "I refuse to accept this spying and checking."

Miaulis held up his hand.

"But it seems that many call for it," he said. "My part is done; the fleet is represented in the matter by your own promise. I will leave the generals to settle about the claim of the army."

At the end of an hour Ali and Selim again entered the tent. On the terms of the capitulation, at any rate, all were agreed. The Turks were to retain a single suit of clothes, a quilt for bedding, and a carpet for prayer, and were to be safely transported to Asia Minor, being fed on the way. All their property was to pass into the hands of the Greeks. They received the proposal in silence, and withdrew to the citadel to consult with the other officers.

Eventually, and with a very bad grace, Kolocotrones was forced to yield. Poniropoulos with two other officers, Kolocotrones with his son and another, Niketas with two officers, Miaulis with Tombazes and the Capsina, and Hypsilantes were to take joint possession of the property in Nauplia. Hypsilantes was appointed arbitrator, and was to settle the claims for the division of it in case of dispute. The town itself would be occupied jointly by

Kolocotrones and Miaulis in the name of the republic.

But no sooner were these arrangements made known than the tumult of discontent among the men rose to a head. Poniropoulos's band distrusted their commander as much as their commander distrusted Kolocotrones; Kolocotrones's men, who had taken no part in the siege, and had expected no share in the booty, hearing that their general would certainly have a finger in it and auguring ill for their own chances, fraternized with the troops of Poniropoulos, and determined to resist an arrangement which would put the whole into the hands of four or five men already fattened by the marketing with the besieged. The Mainats, discontented, yet top-heavy with pride at the action of Petrobey, and knowing that they alone were out of this disgraceful quarrel, grinned sardonically, and told the others they might as well leave too, for not a piaster would they see. Orders were issued that every man should go to his barracks. They were disobeyed. The men gathered and gathered round the gate through which the commanders would enter Nauplia, threatening to storm the place, and declaring that they would not allow the chiefs to appropriate everything. Below, in Kolocotrones's tent, sat the men who had been chosen to enter the place. They knew that their own faithlessness and avarice had raised this storm of distrust; they could not deny the justice of it; they were powerless to quell it.

Meantime in the citadel an assembly of hungry faces and hollow eyes debated the proposal of the Greeks. The terms were hard, but not preposterous, for their case was hopeless. If they refused, the Greek fleet, as they knew, could shell their walls into stone-dust; that done, they knew what to expect— pillage, massacre, and at the end a shambles. Ali and Selim alone held out. They had seen the greed in the eye of Kolocotrones, and Ali spoke.

"We may as well have the value of our money," he said. "The chiefs will again agree to sell us provisions, I doubt not, till it is exhausted. I am pretty sure our case cannot be worse. Let us surrender when the money is finished."

But the others were against him. The Greek soldiers were a mutinous crowd at the gate. It was impossible that they should allow the chiefs to sell provisions again till the treasury was empty. The troops were utterly out of hand; any moment they might storm the place. It would be another Navarin.

Then came one of those wonderful incidents which raise history to a level more romantic than the romances of a wizard. They were assembled in a room of the fort looking over the gulf, and Selim was opposite the window. He gazed out a moment vaguely, then focussed his eyes with more intentness, and rose from his seat.

"An English frigate," he said, simply.

That decided it. Selim and Ali still held out from a sort of barren pride, but in half an hour the capitulation was drawn out and signed. And Selim looked again.

"She has anchored next the admiral's ship," he said, "and a boat with officers is going ashore."

While this was going forward Kolocotrones had made another attempt to stop the riot. He was made of bravery, and had gone out alone to face the scowling and threatening riot. He slapped one on the back; he scolded and stormed at another; he gave tobacco to a third; he told a coarse story to a fourth; but the day of his gorilla blandishments was over. He pleaded the orders of the Greek government, the fear of another massacre if the soldiers were let into the place, and found only black looks and unconvinced silence. Then came the news that the English frigate had entered the harbor, and for the moment men's minds were turned to this new development in the situation. But the crowd did not leave the gate, and Kolocotrones returned.

Captain Hamilton of the *Cambrian*, frigate of war, had been for some years in charge of ships at the Ionian islands. He spoke Greek with colloquial fluency; he was known personally to Kolocotrones and other chiefs, who much respected him; and in appearance he was admirably calculated to influence the soldiers. He was tall and well made, of the Saxon type, blue eyes and fair; his voice rang true; his manner was hearty and open. And these children of the air and the mountains, who make their judgment of a man, and for the most part not erroneously, more by how he looks than by what he says, regarded him at first with friendly eyes, and, when his message to Kolocotrones was made known, with minds of admiration.

The deed of capitulation was handed out of the fortress just as Kolocotrones turned from the crowd of men he had vainly tried to pacify, to meet Hamilton, and, with it in his hands, he went back to his tent. Hamilton was already there; his words were short and greatly to the point.

"I hear there is a dispute about the division of booty, or what not," he said, "that concerns me not; but what I have seen is that now, while the capitulation is in the hands of your chief, a mob of soldiers besiege the town gate. What that may mean you know and I know. Now this I tell you: If certain disgraceful things which happened at Tripoli, at Navarin, and Athens happen also at Nauplia, to the rest of Europe Greece will appear as a country of wild beasts, of barbarous men. I care not one jot what happens to the booty, but this I will see done: I will see the Turks safely embarked, according to the capitulation, without being hurt or molested. I am here a friend to Greece, but a foe to faithlessness. There are fourteen hundred Turks still in Nauplia, I am told. I will embark five hundred on the *Cambrian*, and I will see the remaining nine hundred safely embarked on other ships, and I will escort them to Asia Minor. Do not make yourselves to stink in the nostrils of civilized countries. I have spoken. With your leave, I will go and talk to the soldiers."

He saluted and stepped out in silence, leaving the others to digest his wholesome and unsavory words, and walking with his swinging sailor's step up to the crowd around the gate, with two or three officers behind him, spoke to the men:

"What I have said to your chiefs I say to you. Let this thing be done honorably. With what follows afterwards I have no concern; but I have something to say to you which I have not said to your chiefs. You are on the eve of mutiny. Be steady till the Turks are out. Do not make brute beasts of yourselves. When the Turks are out and safe on ship I care not what happens; I will leave that to—to your chiefs and, which perhaps is the more important, you. Now do not carry tales and get me into trouble."

And with a smile and a salute to the men, he turned on his heel. There was one moment's silence, then a roar of laughter and cheering. His frankness won their hearts; his solution of their trouble amused them. By all means, the Turks out first.

His proposal was accepted by the chiefs, but with some demur. Hypsilantes, still clinging to the dream of Russian intervention, viewed with suspicion the interference of the English; others viewed with suspicion the interference of anybody. But Miaulis, Niketas, and Kolocotrones all acknowledged without reserve the honesty and reasonableness of the advice.

By the evening the ships were ready, and in perfect order the famine-stricken procession left the town. Five hundred men embarked on the *Cambrian*, the rest on the Greek ships. The quay was thronged with sailors from the Greek fleet, and with soldiers only waiting for the departure of the Turks. There they stood, eager yet patient, until the last boatload left the land; then, with a rush, they poured up into the citadel. Kolocotrones and the others reaped the well-earned fruit of their avarice. The booty was large; the inefficiency of the chiefs supreme. Poniropoulos, maddened with the thought that he would get nothing, fought and scrambled with the rest. Kolocotrones, a little more dignified, sat in his tent empty-handed. And at last Nauplia was in the hands of the Greeks.

CHAPTER XVIII

Suleima and the Capsina were sitting in the veranda of the white house a few days after this, and the adorable one was pulling Michael's tail with gurglings of glee and apparent impunity. From inside came Mitsos's voice, singing.

"So do not think thus," said Suleima, "for indeed I would have him go. What should I think of a man who loafed his days in a house with womenfolk? Such a man I should never have cared for, nor you either, so I believe."

She laughed.

"It was that I cared about first in Mitsos," she went on, "at the time I have told you of. I was pent in the perfumed house. It seemed better to live as he lived, half in the sea and all in the air; the sea-gull, Zuleika and I used to call him. So take him again. Indeed, I doubt if he would stop even if I bade it, and I do not bid it. But bring him back to me safe, Capsina; bring him yourself."

The girl sat silent, and Suleima, with a woman's tact, rose and spoke of other things.

"It is a day taken from summer," she said, "and yet in a week it will be Noël. By the New Year, or soon after, you will be back. Oh, littlest one, Michael will surely open his mouth at you and take you down at one gulp like a fig, if you are so bold with him. How would you like to have a great man, as strong as you, pull your tail?"

She picked the baby up and brought it to the Capsina.

"Was ever such a fighter seen?" she said. "He fights all the creatures of God. First he fought the frogs, and then the hens and chickens, then the cat; now it is Michael. Soon he will be fighting the boys, and come home with a blacker eye than he has already, and after that, pray God, he will fight the Turks. If there are any left to fight, oh, pray God, he will be a good fighter against the Turks."

"He will surely find none in Greece," said the Capsina. "Oh, the day is not far when not one will be left. You will see it yourself, and if I am not with you on that day, Suleima, think of me and account me happy."

Suleima looked at her out of the depths of her great eyes.

"I pray the Virgin every day," she said, "that you may be very happy, happy in all that is best, and in all that the soul and the heart desire; happy, dear friend, as you deserve. And, indeed, I think that is not a little."

The girl sat with down-dropped eyes.

"Is the Virgin as generous as you, I wonder?" she said. "You know the worst of me, Suleima; I think I have told you the worst; yet how can you think I deserve happiness?"

"You have told me the worst," said Suleima. "Yet what if I find the whole very good? Is that my fault? Not so; your own. Ah, dearest friend, I have no tongue to tell you how fully—" and she broke off. "It is best said in a word," she continued, "and that is that I love you; and thus all is said. And the blessed Mother of God is more loving than I. Let that suffice."

The child thrust out an aimless, fat-fingered hand and pawed the Capsina's face.

"Cap-sin-a! Cap-sin-a!" it crowed in a voice of staccato rapture.

The girl put out her arms suddenly and lifted the baby to herself. "Yet Capsina is a wicked girl," she whispered, bending over it, "and she hates herself. But she will grow better in time, or so we hope. In time even she may not be ashamed to look her friends in the face."

Suleima laid her hand on her knee.

"Ah, don't, don't!" she said. "Indeed you are talking nonsense."

The Capsina kissed the baby, and gave it back to its mother.

"You are right; I won't," she said, rising and giving herself a little shake. "And now I must go. I have many things to arrange in Nauplia to-night, for the *Revenge* must set off to-morrow. Tell little Mitsos we shall pass here and call for him by midday."

She held Suleima's two hands for a long moment in her own, gave her a quick, trembling little kiss, and went off down the garden-path and mounted her pony at the gate.

The Turkish fleet had gone back to Constantinople; not another ship was in Greek waters, and it was certain that until spring there would be no more work for the *Revenge*. Mitsos was too much disgusted with the conduct of the siege of Nauplia to take any part in operations by land. Indeed, the only commander he would have served under, Petrobey, had gone back with his Mainats home, vowing that he would never again co-operate with Kolocotrones. That chief was boasting far and wide of his exploits. Already he called himself the conqueror of Dramali; he had only to show himself at the walls of Nauplia, and the Turks surrendered; it was Joshua and Jericho, and not a penny of the treasure had he taken for himself. This last fact was true, and he ground his teeth at it. But Galaxidi, the port in the Corinthian gulf where the Capsina had begun to make a naval station, where also she had left the baby saved from Elatina, gave a scope to their energies, and she was going to start overland next day with Mitsos and most of the sailors from the two brigs to spend a month there fortifying and arming the place. Kanaris had gone home to Psara, and the brig *Sophia* was laid by for the winter, so, with the sailors from her and most of those on the *Revenge*, she would march four hundred men. Enough sailors were left on the *Revenge* for the working of the ship, but no more, for it was certain there were no Turkish vessels now in Greek waters. The *Revenge* meantime was to sail round, carrying on board some half-dozen guns to be mounted in a battery at Galaxidi, and join them there. The Turkish fort at Lepanto would be thinking that all the Greek fleet was still at Nauplia, and the risk of passing the guns of the fort could again be neutralized by co-operation with Germanos in Patras, to whom the Capsina sent her compliments. For themselves they were to march across the Isthmus of Corinth—a brush with the small Turkish garrison there was possible— north along the east end of the gulf, passing through Vilia, which they had defended from the raid of the Turkish ships the winter before, and so westward to Galaxidi. It was an informal, haphazard little excursion, after the heart of the Capsina, with a great goal of usefulness for its end. Nominally the march was to be on foot; any one who could do so might, however, provide a beast—the term was left vague—for himself. The keep of the beast would go to the charges of the expedition. Mitsos was in command of the men during the march, and in case of any attack; for the work of fortification at Galaxidi itself he might claim the right to be heard, and no more.

It still wanted an hour to noon when the "Capsina's Own," as Kanaris had christened them, appeared on the road from Nauplia, strangely irregular in appearance, but certainly fighting fit. A convoy of baggage-mules shambled along in front, carrying what baggage there was, and that was little, and most of the "Capsina's Own" were mule-drivers for the time being. Here a gay Turkish horse pranced along by the side of the road, the very sailor-like seat of its rider provoking howls of laughter and derision. Close beside it trotted a demure, mouse-colored donkey, the rider of which, being long in the leg, could paddle with his toes on each side of the animal. Other men, a minority, were on foot, and for these there were stirrup-leathers and tails to hold by. In the middle of the heterogeneous crowd came a great Bishareen camel, once the property of Selim, with a howdah on its back, on the curtains of which were embroidered the crescent and star; but, by way of correction, a short flagstaff, bearing the blue-and-white ensign of Greece, rose above the roof-beam and fluttered bravely in the wind. Out of the curtains of the howdah peered the face of the Capsina, rather anxious.

"Oh, lad!" she cried to Mitsos, as soon as they were within hearing, "this is like being at sea again in a heavy roll, and I feel as if I had sprung a leak somewhere. You will have to come up here and lend a hand with the tiller. The tiller is one rope, as you see, and it appears to me as if the brute's head were a long mile off. Here, furl the main-sail, one of you! I mean, take hold of its head and knock it down. I want to get off."

The camel sank down joint by joint, and the Capsina held on to the side with fixed and panic-stricken eyes.

"There are six joints in each leg!" she screamed; "and each joint is six miles long, and the joints are moved singly and in turn."

The "Capsina's Own" cheered wildly when the camel was brought to anchor and she slid down out of the howdah.

"Oh, stop laughing!" she cried to Mitsos. "Indeed, you will not laugh when you are up there. But I would have it; it looks so grand. Hark! How it groans! Am I not like some barbarous queen?"

And she gave him a great poke in the ribs, and was half-way up the garden-path to meet Suleima.

"And I have come with a light heart," she cried, "and a heavy one—heavy to go and blithe to go. Where is the child? Let him say 'Capsina,' please, so. And it is good-bye."

The two turned and walked a few paces away.

"To-day I have a light heart," said the girl, "such as I have not had for months. Indeed, I think you have laid a spell on me. I am not going to be wicked any more; indeed I am not. Where is Mitsos? Come here, lad; we will say good-bye together."

Mitsos came up the path to them, and the three stood hand-in-hand. In the middle of them the child sat on the ground, chuckling and babbling to itself.

"Pick it up, Mitsos, and lay it on your arm," said the girl. "So; it is complete."

She stood there a moment smiling, but with dimmed eyes, fresh, vivid, alert, looking first at Mitsos and the baby, then at the mother.

"So we part with a smile and with love," she said, "and there is no parting." And she kissed the baby, and clung awhile round Suleima's neck, and then, disengaging herself, stood looking at her a moment more.

"Bring him safe back, dear one," said Suleima; "bring him back yourself."

The girl nodded without speaking, and went off down the path. Mitsos handed the baby to Suleima, folded them both together in his huge arms, said only, "Suleima, Suleima!" and followed.

About four of the afternoon the cavalcade reached the hills leading up to the Dervenaki, and they encamped that night at the village of Nemea. The juvenile portion of its population were inclined to think that they were a circus, and seemed to take it as a personal matter that they were not, yet hung about, hoping that the *fantasia* might, after all, take place. Dimitri supped with the Capsina and Mitsos, and again it was like children playing. This time, at least, there was no spice of danger to make anxious any parting; they would merely advance the work at Galaxidi, returning before spring was ripe for hostile movements. The camel particularly seemed an admirable comedy. His injured, remonstrant face, his long, ungainly legs—"nigh as long as Mitsos's," quoth the Capsina—his unutterable groaning and complaints when they mounted him, were all an excellent investment in merry spirits. The men had lit their fires in a great circle in the market-place; jests, songs, and wine went freely; and after supper the chiefs visited the men of the "Capsina's Own" and made the night loud with laughter.

When the girl was alone she threw herself on to the rugs on which she was to sleep, and lay awake wondering at herself.

"What does it mean?" she asked herself. "Is it that I am cured of my suffering? Has the Virgin heard the prayer of Suleima? Yet he is no less dear." And her thoughts grew vaguer with the approach of sleep, and sleeping, she slept sound.

They passed Corinth about noon next day, openly and ostentatiously, with the hope of drawing a Turkish contingent out of the citadel; but the contingent came not, and they went by without opposition, a thing which Mitsos put down to the fierce and warlike eye of the camel.

"Let us go to Constantinople," he said to the Capsina, "you and I and the camel. Thus will the Sultan fall off his throne, and the Capsina shall sit thereon, and I shall be her very good servant."

And the howdah creaked and rocked and swayed over the broken ground, and presently after they put into port, so it seemed, for dinner. In the afternoon they crossed the isthmus, and thereafter for four days they marched an aromatic journey among the pine-woods which fringed the gulf. And if in the open the camel was a comedy, among the trees he was not less than a farce. When the older trees gave way to a garden of saplings, the howdah moved as a ship on green water above the feathery tops, and the camel grunted no more, but nipped off the young plumes with great content, but when the trees were big the progress was but slow, an endless series of collisions with and steerings round the strong boughs. Once, forcing him along, the girth snapped, and they were stranded, a preposterous bird's-nest, eight feet off the ground. Indeed, the joke seemed to be of that superlative kind in which repetition and variation of the same theme only add to the humor. Feet went silently over the carpet of needles; sea, air, and pines made an inimitable perfume; roe-deer and boar were plentiful, and it is doubtful whether, in the whole history of strategy, there was ever so cheerful an expedition.

It was still two days before the Noël when they reached Galaxidi. From the hill-side above they had seen the roofs of the Capsina's custom-houses on the quay, and descending farther, it was soon clear that the men of the place had not been idle during the year. The harbor lay looking south; on the east ran an artificial mole, continuing the line of a narrow promontory; on the west the land itself ran in a curve, making the other side of the harbor. The town itself lay to the northern end of the harbor, and on the western promontory; the eastern lay barren, for it was but narrow, and a gale from the east would raise waves which would stop traffic. On the mole itself was only the "custom-house," very business-like to the eye, and built strong enough to weather a heavy-breaking sea. And the face of the girl flushed as she looked.

"It will do," she said. "Mitsos, in a little it will do very well. Look on the west, too; they are building another custom-house, as I said. Surely the two will command the harbor so that no foreign goods shall pass."

That day, being so close to their journey's end, they had no midday halt, but pushed on, and reached the town about three. The men at once began throwing up a camp on the promontory to the west of the harbor, outside the

251

town, and close to the building custom-house. On the march they had cut numbers of poles and beams from the pine-trees, which would form the skeletons of their huts, and over these they would make thatching with pine-branches, canvas, or whatever came handy. The Capsina found lodging with her cousin, the Mayor Elias. Mitsos went with the men.

The camp was on ground sloping away to the harbor, and, like the town, below the top ridge of the promontory which rose some fifty feet above it. It lay in oblong shape; at the south end was the custom-house, and the powder-magazine adjoining it; at the north the first houses of the town began. Along the top ridge of the promontory, running down as far as the sea and up towards the town, was a stout wall, banked up with earth; when finished it would run the complete circuit behind the town and join the sea again at the neck of the eastern promontory. Thus, in case of a party landing from Turkish ships, the town was easily defensible also on the land side. As yet it was finished only from the sea on the west to about half-way between the custom-house and the town; it had also been begun at the eastern end, and was being pushed rapidly forward in both directions. Out of the three Turkish ships which the Capsina had captured at Porto Germano they had taken twelve guns, four from each. Of these, five were already mounted in the custom-house on the mole, and the custom-house on the west of the quay was to receive five more. The other two, both 32-pounders, were, according to the plan of Elias, to be mounted farther back in the harbor in case a ship got through.

Next morning the Capsina got up at the unearthly hour between day and night, and stormed at the camp till Mitsos, a sort of Jonah to save the rest, was thrown out to her, heavy with sleep. But the cold, pungent air soon shook off the cobwebs from him, and he went with the girl on a tour of inspection. The walls of the western custom-house had already risen above the gun-holes, and they could see that their position and direction was well chosen. The ports were wide, and the guns could be trained to a range of about forty-five degrees, and commanded an area some miles broad, through which ships attempting to come to Galaxidi must pass. The five guns in the other custom-house, on the contrary, commanded the immediate channel and entrance to the harbor, and could hardly fail at that close range to make good shooting. This fort was very low, and was protected outside by an earthwork and an angle of masonry.

"It looks but little like a custom-house," remarked Mitsos. "If I were a Turk I should not come near though the Sultan himself held the Turkish flag on the roof."

"I wish he did," said the Capsina, savagely; "he should not hold it long. But see, Mitsos, I have a plan in my head."

"I have sleep only."

"Well, you are awake enough to listen. There are two other guns not yet mounted, 68-pounders. Now the harbor has guns enough, or, at any rate, with the six the *Revenge* brings, will have enough. So come a little walk with me down to the water."

"The intention is kind," remarked Mitsos, guardedly, "but I will not be pushed into the sea by accident so that I may be more awake."

"You shall not be, great sleepy one; only come."

They went out, and climbing the scaffolding of the rising wall, dropped down on to the stony moorland outside. The sun was risen, and a fragrant rooty smell of herbs and damp earth rose into the morning. The Capsina sniffed it with a great contentment.

"How I know that smell," she said, "morning and the clean wind and the hills of Hydra all mixed. I have thought of Hydra much lately, and of the time when I was a toddling thing."

"A long-stepping toddler, I expect," said Mitsos, and they descended the slope to the water.

On the edge of the sea lay a ribbon of bare limestone rock, with deep fissures and ravines opening in it, and strewn about were fragments of rock as high as a man, looking as if some gigantic creature had got ready materials for his monstrous house and had stopped there. A little bay, some fifty yards across, with two jutting headlands, formed the extremest end of the promontory, and from here they got a wide sea-view left and right. Behind, the hill down which they had come rose steeply, crowned by its wall, but the custom-house, standing lower, and on the opposite slope below the ridge, lay concealed.

"And this, too, is a very convenient place," remarked the Capsina. "There is a wide sea-view; there are many large and suitable rocks. In how many shots would you wager yourself to hit a crack between two of these at a mile's distance and from a rolling ship's deck, little Mitsos?"

"In as many shots as there are hairs on my head. Why?"

She looked at him, wagging her head in reproof.

"Must I go on?" she asked. "Then in how many shots from between one of these cracks would you engage to hit a big ship at a mile's distance? Was there ever so slow a lad!"

"God forbid!" said Mitsos. "In as many noses as there are on my face. You see what I mean."

"I am not so slow as some," she said, glancing into his comely face, and in answer Mitsos smiled with eyes and mouth. He had never seen her so brilliant and good to look on. She had wound the brightly colored shawl round her head, the shawl he remembered her wearing one gray morning last year as they started from Galaxidi. But now the newly risen sun, wintry and luminously sparkling, bathed her from head to foot. She enchanted his eye, making captive of it, and he looked until the smile blossomed into a laugh.

"Oh, Capsina, may there be many long years for you!" he cried. "To-morrow is the Noël. What shall be my gift to you on the Noël?"

She paused a moment, uncertain of her answer. Then, "More of the gift you have always given me, dear Mitsos," she said, "your own help and comradeship, perhaps a little liking as well. Who knows?"

"God knows how much," said the lad.

The good moment finished. Her heart accused her of no disloyalty to Suleima, for from the heart she had spoken only of that she knew that Mitsos gave her, and flirted not with forbidden thoughts, and with that they went back to the work in hand. Yet it had been a good moment, even an excellent moment.

CHAPTER XIX

During the most of the morning the Capsina was not seen by her men, whom she had put to work on the wall which had already been begun, and on a fresh wall, which should connect her new outside battery with the other. A path also had to be made down the moor-side to the water's edge, and for this they cut away a piece of already existing wall close to the custom-house; from there was to start the new wall. Others were engaged in storing powder in the magazine on the western promontory which was built close under the custom-house, and communicated with it.

In the afternoon, however, the girl appeared again. Mitsos had passed her once in the town, walking with the foster-nurse of the little Sophia; she carried the baby herself, and she and the woman were talking eagerly together. Michael followed a few steps behind, with the air of some sedate duenna. Just before sunset they went down again to the new battery, to see how the work had progressed, and the Capsina, shading her eye against the low western sun, exclaimed suddenly:

"A ship, Mitsos! a ship!"

He followed her pointing hand.

Just visible on the horizon was a brig under full sail. After a moment she turned and looked at him.

"God forbid there should be a slower than you," she said, with a tone of calm despair. "Yet you have seen that ship before."

"The *Revenge!*"

"Certainly; the *Revenge!* She has come far quicker than I expected. It seems to me an omen of good. She will be here by the morning of the Noël. Come, lad, we will go back. To-morrow I shall be down again very early. Let us have breakfast in the custom-house, where we dined to-day, and get in good work in the morning."

Soon after sunset the wind dropped, and the wings of the *Revenge* shivered, and were still. But all night the boats were manned, and slowly in relays the tired men towed her; for in passing Lepanto they had been seen and fired at, and though the shot passed them harmlessly, they saw, emerging from the gate, a large body of armed men, some mounted, but the most on foot. All that afternoon they had watched them going eastward, and when evening fell, and they lay becalmed, the last they saw in the sunset was the glittering lines of the horse-soldiers still going on, and now ahead of them, and nearer to Galaxidi than they, the foot some miles behind, but also going. For the Turks for once had been prompt and ingenious; they had heard it rumored that fortification work was going on at Galaxidi, and connecting the passing of an armed brig with it, had set out at once to see how truly rumor spoke and get to the town before the arrival of that trim and spiteful-looking ship.

It was a little after sunrise next morning that the Capsina went down to the custom-house, as was arranged, to breakfast with Mitsos. Day had dawned with an incomparable loveliness; it was the feast of Noël, and an extraordinary blitheness of soul was hers. The day before Mitsos had asked her what gift of the season he should bring her; six months ago she would not have wagered on her answer; now she had answered him with who knows what quiet and childish memories in her mind? Her thoughts flew like a honey-bee from one pleasant thing to another, gathering sweetness from all. Now it was the vision of Suleima, busy with the child and her household cares, which fed them; now the little Sophia, still asleep under that gray house-roof; now the harbor of Hydra; and now the sunlight, falling on a patch of hoar-covered grass, was a pleasant resting-place for the mind.

And Mitsos was up and waiting for her; he had even already made coffee, and from afar off she saw him standing bareheaded in the door of the custom-house, smoking the earliest pipe. He was forever smoking. She would speak to him about it, for Tombazes had said that perpetual smoking was death to the lung-pipes, whatever lung-pipes might be. Yet death seemed very remote from the image of Mitsos. She met him smiling, and they exchanged the old greeting, "May your Noël be peaceful and full of laughter," and, as if in instant fulfilment, the childish words set them both laughing.

"Breakfast is ready," said Mitsos, "and I have been waiting, oh, ever so long. Oh, Michael, may your Noël be peaceful at least, since you know not how to laugh. Come, Capsina."

Coffee and eggs were ready, and they sat and ate. The early sunlight threw a great yellow splash through the door on to the planks of the flooring. Michael occupied the whole of it.

"The *Revenge* is yet a mile out," said the Capsina, between mouthfuls. "I could see them rowing her; I wonder they should be so hurried. Yet perhaps they would keep Noël with us all together. I love the lads, all of them, every one."

"Then I will fight them, all of them, every one," remarked Mitsos.

"For what cause?"

"Because, Capsina, you belong to Suleima and the little one and me, particularly the little one, so I think."

The Capsina laughed.

"Oh, little Mitsos, what will cure you of saying nonsense things? Hark! What is that?"

The report of a gun had come from seaward, and Mitsos, running out, saw the smoke still hanging round the *Revenge*. While he still looked another flash leaped from the side of her, and again the report followed. It seemed they were signalling. In the camp close by, the men were already astir; but they, too, had paused on the sound, not knowing what it was. One ran up to the top of the incline, where the wall ended, to look out, and in a moment, from closer at hand, the sharp firing of a musket-shot rang out, and he dropped. At that Mitsos waited no longer.

"Arm, all!" he cried; and then, turning to the Capsina, "It is the Turks," he said, "and the best of days to meet Turks on."

The girl sprang up.

"Wait here, Michael," she said, "on guard here. Little Mitsos, I am with you."

And she ran close behind him to his hut. He had not seen she was with him, but the moment after he had entered she appeared at the door.

"Quick, little Mitsos!" she cried, "Give me anything you do not want, pistol, or musket, or knife."

He turned.

"Oh, get back!" he said; "get back to the town! For the love of God, go; there is time yet. Who knows what is coming?"

"Have we not fought together before," she said, "and shall we not fight together now?"

"You will not go?"

"Not I, little Mitsos."

By this time the men had turned out under arms; and Mitsos gave the order to stand ready. The words were hardly spoken when some sixty Turkish cavalry appeared suddenly in sight over the brow of the hill. Now on such broken and uneven ground cavalry were by far less formidable than on the level, and Mitsos rapidly gave the order.

"Into cover of the huts," he cried, "and fire!"

It was so rapidly done that the enemy had hardly come a dozen strides down the hill when a scattering volley met them. They fired back, and then wheeled their horses round, and topped the hill again. The Greeks had not time to reload and fire before they disappeared, leaving some dozen, however, dead, and a riderless horse or two charging wildly right and left. On one a man still hung depended from the stirrup, and Mitsos gave a great giggle as he saw the man's head dashed to a crashed egg-shell on the corner of the unfinished wall.

But the position was still sufficiently hazardous. They had no kind of guess as to what this sudden appearance of cavalry and their withdrawal might mean. But there was no time for consideration. Next moment there appeared a quick uprising of fezzes above the ridge, and the infantry charged down on them. And Mitsos drew a little sigh of relief, for he thought he knew how the Turkish soldiers fought.

"Charge!" he cried. "Form as you can, and charge!"

On right and left out rushed the men from shelter of the huts. The line was irregular, but overpowering. The two met at about the line of the wall, and Mitsos's heart was joyful. At the corner of the wall there was a tight-huddled mass of men, the Greeks pressing upward, the Turks downward. It was more than hand to hand; it was elbow to elbow, and shoulder to shoulder. On his left was the Capsina, with the breath half crushed out of her body like the rest;

on the right, Dimitri, who, as Mitsos noticed, was whistling. For a moment there was a deadlock; then Mitsos, taking advantage of his height, shook his great shoulders free of the crowd, and down flicked his knife through cheek and jaw of a Turk who was just in front. Such was the crush that the dead thing could not even drop, but stood straight up, half the face gone, and snarling.

Again his knife was raised; but on the moment, from his left, there licked out, like a whiplash, a curved Turkish scimitar. He saw it would strike him, and, his left arm being jammed to his side, he had not means of stopping the blow. But before it fell, from his left came up an arm with a pistol in the hand; the blow fell, but it did not touch him.

He could not even look round, for in front the knives were flickering like the reflection of the sun on water; but he called out: "Thanks, Capsina," and down came his knife again.

There was no answer, not even the answer of a laugh, but next moment a sudden swirl of men bore them towards the right; those who were at the corner were swept round in front of him, and he looked for the girl. She was still at his side, but her face was pale, and a crimson stream of blood poured over her arm.

"You are wounded," he said; "lean on me. So. In a moment we shall be out of this."

From the left the Greeks poured round the angle of the wall, and before many seconds had passed Mitsos, with his arm round the girl, was left in a little backwater of men, and he forced his way out.

He tugged at the sleeve of his shirt till the stitches, those fine great stitches which the Capsina had sewn there, gave way. The wound was in the fore-arm, not very deep, and he bandaged it in two places: one over the wound, the other round the armpit to stop the flow of blood, in case an artery was severed. The girl smiled at him and nodded her thanks.

Then, without a word, he lifted her bodily up and carried her back to the custom-house. Michael was still there, and still on the floor smouldered Mitsos's pipe, only half burned out, as he had thrown it down on the alarm. The remains of the breakfast were on the log table. The girl had recovered her color.

"It is nothing, Mitsos; indeed it is nothing," she said. "Leave me here with Michael, and get you back. It was lucky, little Mitsos, that I could get my arm free."

She stood up, smiling.

"Indeed it is nothing," she said again.

"I owe you all," said Mitsos, "but I have owed you much so long. Are you safe here, think you?"

"Surely, if you get back and drive those devils away. They were already breaking. Get you gone."

With a sudden impulse, Mitsos bent and kissed her hand.

"They are already breaking," he said; "in ten minutes I shall be back. It is better, is it not, I should be with the men?"

He went out and ran across the hundred yards which separated him from the others. As the Capsina had said, they were already breaking, and in three minutes more the Greeks had gained the top of the slope and were pursuing them in all directions. Mitsos had shoved his way to the fore as well as he could, and just as he gained the top he looked round. Through the open gap which had been made for the new wall to the battery by the sea another body of Turks was pouring, taking them in the rear between them and the custom-house where the Capsina was.

"HALF A DOZEN MEN BURST INTO THE CUSTOM-HOUSE"

"Back, back!" he cried; "fight your way back. She is there."

From the door of the custom-house the Capsina had seen what had happened. In a moment she knew that her last fight was fought, and that brave spirit of hers, in the greatness and awe of what was assuredly coming to her, swept away from itself all that was unworthy of her best. For one moment the bitterness of her unrequited passion touched her, the next it was gone, and she stood sweet and clean for her last look at the dear loved earth, fit and ready for the change. Michael was with her; with her, too, was Mitsos's pipe, still alight. She put it to her lips and drew at it several times, till the core of tobacco was bright and burning. Then, "Michael," she said, "go, go, boy."

The great dog looked out, then back at her, and came to her feet with head down and furtively wagging his tail, as if in apology for his disobedience.

"Be it so, then," said the Capsina. "Here, come with me; we go together, as always, old Michael."

She went through the unfinished battery, with the pipe still in her hand, and followed by Michael, into the powder-magazine. Eight or ten sacks full lay there, and, with Mitsos's knife slitting the sides of two, she emptied them on the floor and stood just behind the pile. From outside the tramp of men came closer. She knelt down on the floor, the knife in one hand and in the other Mitsos's pipe.

"O blessed Virgin!" she said, "my whole heart thanks thee that thou hast given me the strength not to tell him; it thanks thee for the many beautiful days that have been given it. And, O most pitiful, intercede for me, for thou, too, wast a woman, and I have tried—"

Half a dozen men burst into the custom-house suspecting an ambuscade there; next moment one caught sight of her, and cried to the others:

"A woman only! Take her alive!"

The Capsina laughed, and Michael, with teeth bared and hackles raised at the intruders, yet wagged his tail in sympathy with his mistress. Four of the men rushed up the little passage from the custom-house to the magazine as another party poured in at the outer door.

"Thus!" said the Capsina, and she shook out the burning ash from Mitsos's pipe onto the heap of powder.

Mitsos from outside, for a second blinded and deafened by the explosion, saw and knew. For one moment he stood quite still; then: "Revenge her! revenge her!" he cried aloud, but with a trembling voice, and led the charge against the Turks, still pouring through the breach which led to the new battery.

There had passed scarce a quarter of an hour since the first alarm was given, and by now the townspeople had come out to aid. Step by step the Turks were driven back, and every moment a stab and a fallen heap of nerveless limbs revenged the Capsina; and by the time the church bells rang for the mass of Noël the Greeks were again in their camp, the wreckage of men lay round, and only a small body of cavalry were spurring back to Lepanto, saying these were not men, but fiends.

Mitsos was sitting with his elbows on his knees, his head in his hands, when the bell began, but the sound caused him to look up.

"Come, lads," he said, "we go to pray for the soul of the Capsina, and to give thanks to God for her"—and he clinched his teeth hard for a moment—"to give thanks to God for her great deeds and her splendid and shining life."

That afternoon the *Revenge* came into port, and two days after Mitsos was landed at Corinth. From there he went across to Nauplia, and sunset saw him at the white house, and Suleima's hands were raised in amaze at so quick a return.

"You have not brought the Capsina with you?" she asked.

Mitsos looked at her a moment, the hasp of the garden-gate in his hand, out of eyes drooping and heavy.

"No, I have not brought the Capsina," he cried, in a hard, dry tone, but at the word his voice broke suddenly, and he leaned on the gate and was shaken from head to foot with the tumult of his grief.

That night they talked long together, and their tears were mingled. At last, and not long before the dawning of the winter's day, Suleima came closer to Mitsos, and lay with her arm cast round his neck.

"She loved you, Mitsos," she said, "and I love her for it."

THE END
